Stepping Up

www.penguin.co.uk

Stepping Up

Sarah Turner

BANTAM PRESS

TRANSWORLD PUBLISHERS
Penguin Random House, One Embassy Gardens,
8 Viaduct Gardens, London SW11 7BW
www.penguin.co.uk

Transworld is part of the Penguin Random House group of companies
whose addresses can be found at global.penguinrandomhouse.com

Penguin
Random House
UK

First published in Great Britain in 2022 by Bantam Press
an imprint of Transworld Publishers

A CIP catalogue record for this book
is available from the British Library.

ISBN 9781787633070
Paperback ISBN 9781787635968

Typeset in 11.25/15.75pt Sabon MT Std by Jouve (UK), Milton Keynes.
Printed and bound in Great Britain by Clays Ltd, Elcograf S.p.A.

The authorized representative in the EEA is Penguin Random House Ireland,
Morrison Chambers, 32 Nassau Street, Dublin D02 YH68.

Penguin Random House is committed to a sustainable
future for our business, our readers and our planet. This book
is made from Forest Stewardship Council® certified paper.

For my dad, who always said I could.

And for James, who reminded me I could until I did.

*'Be comforted, dear soul! There is always
light behind the clouds.'*
Louisa May Alcott, *Little Women*

MARCH

1

The key clicks in the ignition and I groan. *Come on.* At least yesterday's clicking gave way to a more hopeful stuttering. This morning there is no such stuttering, which is just brilliant on the day I'm supposed to be having my first Personal Development Review of the new job. The *new* new job. Dad says I suffer from a ten-week itch on the job front. I haven't braved telling him that I'm already itching at the end of week four because I know he'll tell Mum, who will wheel out the reliability and commitments lecture again. *You need to stick at these things for longer, Beth. Prove yourself a bit.*

The radio springs to life with a local travel update – *a spot of slow-moving traffic on the A39 between Kilkhampton and Stratton following an earlier breakdown of a livestock container.* I roll my eyes. People in my village are always remarking how lucky we are to live in this part of the world and how dreadful the daily commute in a big city would be but at least in a big city I wouldn't have to stop for farm animals. I get it, the underground on a hot day smells like armpits and socks, but muck-spreading season in north Cornwall isn't exactly a treat for the senses either.

I try the key again. *Click, click, click,* nothing.

There's a bottle of water in my bag and I unscrew the cap and glug all of it, cursing myself for not rehydrating before I got into bed. My sister swears by drinking a pint of water as soon as she gets in from a night out (though, as I have to keep reminding her, a meal with her husband and another couple talking about sleep training and primary-school applications does not a 'night out' make). She's big on mantras, our Emmy, and *Do your future self a favour* is her latest. I have mocked her relentlessly for this, of course, but secretly I think she's on to something. I can only imagine that Future Emmy is permanently delighted with Past Emmy's forward planning. Future Beth, on the other hand, feels perpetually let down by Past Beth, who brings nothing but a world of good-idea-at-the-time regret to the table. I imagine that's what's going to end up on my headstone: *Here lies Beth. Beloved daughter, sister, aunty and friend. Full of good ideas at the time.*

The fifth glass of wine was a mistake. I think about messaging Jory to tell him about my car woes and find out if he has a hangover, but he'll already have started his day of teaching by now. He's not a fun best friend during the work day and rarely engages with my bored-in-the-office WhatsApp advances. I raised this with him as a grievance once, but he just laughed and said, 'But I'm *working*. You'll understand one day, when you grow up.'

I rest my forehead on the steering wheel and weigh up what to do. Mum and Dad aren't home, so I can't ask them for a lift, or plead to borrow their car again until I get mine sorted (or until Dad gets it sorted; I'm trying not to think about how much I still owe him for the last garage bill). They left for grandchildren-babysitting duties before I was even awake, which means my sister isn't around to rescue me either. Emmy would obviously have done her future self a favour and *not* bought a rusty, decade-old Vauxhall Astra with patchy service history to start with. 'You know what they say, Beth. You buy cheap, you buy twice.' As I keep telling her, I buy cheap because I am skint.

She's right though, as usual. I *should* invest in a more reliable car but I'm supposed to be saving up to move out, or move away, or just do something that isn't living with my parents which, since turning thirty last year, has become a rather tragic state of affairs. It never seemed quite so bad when I was still in my twenties but waking up in the room I grew up in on my thirtieth birthday was not a proud moment. I went out and bought a Swiss cheese plant and a mustard velvet armchair to try to make my childhood bedroom feel more sophisticated, but when Jory helped me redecorate, we forgot to freshen up the ceiling and now when I'm lying in bed I can still see the old Blu Tack marks where I stuck a picture of J from Five. J nearly gave me a heart attack a couple of times when he fell down from the ceiling on to my face in the night but I always stuck him back up and he stayed there for years, looking down at me with his edgy eyebrow piercing. A quick google tells me Jason Paul 'J' Brown is now forty-two. Even Bradley from S Club 7 is nearly forty. I need to move out.

The cheery local radio presenter announces the time between songs, reminding me that I am now running very late. The only feasible option I have left is to walk. It would show willing, perhaps even impress my new boss. *Beth's car broke down but she still made it in. Way to go, Beth!* The trouble is, I've been sitting here for almost half an hour now and another idea has been percolating. I could just *not* go. Bend the truth a little. Replace 'car problems' with 'under the weather'. It's not an ideal solution, I know, but if I go with honesty, my boss might drive over to get me and I can't face Malcolm on a hangover. It's bad enough sitting opposite him all day doing the donkey work for his finance deals.

I think that settles it. Given that I already lied and took a day off for fictitious 'women's problems' less than a fortnight ago, I can't use that as an excuse even though I am genuinely now due on. There must be a lesson there somewhere. *The Woman Who Cried Period.* I'll tell Emmy that one later.

I press send on my apologetic email to Malcolm and skip back indoors, the glorious promise of a whole day doing nothing stretching out in front of me. I wonder if there are any pizzas in the freezer. Mum sometimes picks up the takeaway-style ones I like when they're on offer ('daylight robbery' at full price, apparently). I ought to switch my phone off in case work try to call but first I'm going to delete the Instagram Stories of me and Jory in the pub last night. I don't think anyone from the office follows me on social media – I haven't really been there long enough to make friends – but my profile isn't private and it would be embarrassing if they hear about my migraine then stumble across a clip of me dancing suggestively with a pool cue. I cringe as I watch it. Why do I always *gyrate* like that when I've been drinking? I must have thought I looked good in the moment and, what's worse, I must have asked a not-quite-as-drunk-as-me Jory to film it. I smile when I hear his laughter at the end of the clip then I delete it, hoping the 237 views it's clocked up haven't included anyone at Hexworthy Finance.

The second I turn my phone off, I remember that I was supposed to text Emmy to wish her and Doug luck with their mortgage appointment. Bugger. That's why Mum and Dad aren't here. They are at hers, looking after Ted and making sure Polly gets on the bus OK (even though, at fourteen, Polly is plenty old enough to get on the bus OK). I really need to show an interest in their quest to own their home after fifteen years of renting it. I *am* interested, it's a huge moment for them, I've just heard rather a lot about it from Mum already this week. *They've worked hard and done so well. Hasn't your sister done well, Beth?*

The house is silent. I make a cup of tea and take it through to the lounge, picking up my laptop from the coffee table. The home phone rings but I ignore it, settling myself on the sofa with my legs tucked underneath Dad's tartan blanket. '*Cornish* tartan', as he likes to remind me, forever baffled when this clarification doesn't immediately increase my affection for said blanket. Dad is very proud of his Cornish roots.

Purely out of habit I look at jobs for a bit, which is always a tricky exercise, noting I can neither decide what I want to do nor where I want to live (other than not what I'm doing now, and not here in St Newth, where the annual highlight is maypole dancing). By the time *This Morning* starts, I have run out of things to look at so resort to a Facebook scroll on the laptop, which always feels a bit 2006. My niece's generation, those at secondary school now, will never understand the hours of dedication it took to upload entire albums of night-out photos on a laptop, sometimes multiple albums from the same night (*why?*), nor will they appreciate the race we had to de-tag ourselves from the unflattering ones.

To my great surprise, Jory has sent me a message on Messenger. I click on it and am disappointed to find not a single hangover GIF or meme. His tone is very direct and a bit bossy, if I'm honest.

Beth, where are you? Please turn on your phone.

He's a fine one to talk. It's dicey but I decide to risk a call from the boss. Within moments of my phone screen illuminating to life, the vibrating pings of dread start. Oh god. Malcolm must have left a voicemail. I check the messages. Voicemail, unknown number (probably work). Voicemail, Dad. Voicemail, Jory. *Jory?* He never leaves voicemails – why is he phoning from school?

I'm just about to listen to the voicemails when I get a flurry of text messages. Dad has attempted to phone me seven times in the last half an hour. He's also texted twice, once to ask me where I am and the second to tell me to phone him back as soon as possible. No 'How are you?' or kisses. Maybe he phoned the office for some reason and got told I had a migraine. It's good of him to check in on me but seven missed calls seems like slight overkill on the worry front. It also wouldn't be very helpful to someone who genuinely did have a migraine, I don't expect. I hit return call and walk into the hallway to reach the best of the signal. He picks up after two rings.

'Is that you, Beth?' His voice sounds smaller than normal. I feel bad now that he's worrying.

'Yes, Dad, it is I. Did you phone my office? Sorry, *bit* of a misunderstanding on the headache front—'

He cuts me off by saying my name. He says it three times. There's something about his tone that makes the hairs on the back of my neck stand up.

My heart is beating faster now. 'Dad, what is it? Where's Mum?'

He pauses. The dread in my chest tightens as he begins to speak very slowly. 'Your mum's here with me. Are you with someone? You're not driving, are you?'

'No, I'm not driving. I'm at home. God, Dad – what is it?' I am trembling.

He's talking away from the phone. I can hear a muffled conversation with Mum, who sounds upset. *Peppa Pig* is on in the background, so I know they're still at Emmy's but there's another voice talking, too. A man. I don't recognize it. It's not Doug, my brother-in-law.

'Stay there, love, just hold tight and I'll be over as soon as I can.' Dad is crying.

Now I am crying, too, without knowing why we're crying. 'No. Whatever it is, just tell me now, Dad. Please.'

He isn't phoning about my headache. He has tried to phone seven times about something else, something he feels it would be best to tell me in person, something that is making him cry. It has to be something really fucking bad.

And then he says it.

'I'm so sorry, love. It's your sister and Doug. There's been an accident.'

2

I don't remember Jory arriving or picking me up off the floor, but he must have done because I am sitting in the front of his van, his hands on either side of my face. He is speaking to me but there is no sound. I watch his mouth moving slowly, the same exaggerated miming he used to do when we were kids attempting to talk underwater in the swimming pool. We would laugh as we surfaced for air, treading water as we reported back what we each thought the other had said. In over twenty years of friendship, I have never seen him look so worried.

'Beth?' Sound returns to my ears and I remember with a jolt why I was curled in a ball on the hallway floor. My entire body begins to shake.

'Doug is dead.' I state this as fact but look pleadingly at Jory, willing him to correct me or at least provide an updated, less devastating scenario, but he does neither. 'Emmy is going to die, too, isn't she?' I want so desperately for there to have been a mistake, a mix-up. Improbable, I know, but not impossible. I begin bargaining. With God or anyone who can hear me. *Make this not true and I will do anything. Bring back my brother-in-law, don't let my sister die, undo the accident and I will never complain about my life again.* My teeth chatter.

'We don't know that. Emmy's made of strong stuff.' Jory's hands leave my face and he takes his suit jacket off, draping it around my shoulders. I remember him doing the same the night my first boy-friend finished with me following a drunken row. Jory arrived to find me shivering from shock, or adrenaline, or perhaps both. We sat on the kerb outside the nightclub with burgers from the burger van and he told me that everything was going to be all right. I want him to tell me that everything is going to be all right now but he isn't going to. He starts the engine. 'We really need to get to the hospital. I just wanted to make sure you weren't having a panic attack first.'

'Please just drive. I need to get there. How long—'

'One hour twenty-five,' he says, handing me a bag. 'There's a fresh bottle of water and a plastic bag in there in case you need to be sick. You said you felt like you might. I picked up your glasses, too. I thought your contact lenses might get sore. I didn't know what to pack and you were just screaming . . .' His voice trails off. It looks as though he has been crying. I have only ever seen Jory cry once, when I was at his house in Year 9 and Bramble the springer spaniel had just died.

I hold the things he has passed over in my lap, swallowing the lump that keeps burning the back of my throat. 'I can't lose her, Jor. Polly and Ted need her. I need her.'

He glances sideways at me but doesn't answer.

I gnaw at my nails. *Doug is dead.* This keeps repeating on a loop in my head. I saw Doug two days ago. I went to their house, gate-crashing dinner after I heard they were having lasagne. My sister makes the best lasagne. She lets the top go a bit crispy, which is how I like it. I had spent the evening taking the piss out of Doug's dad jeans and Emmy's garden shoes. Now, there are police in their kitchen, saying things we don't want to hear. How can he be *gone*, just like that?

Jory turns the radio on but swiftly turns it off again when the news reports a fatal accident on the M5. We sit in silence for the rest of the journey, the lump still burning in my throat.

*

The hospital is a maze of corridors and waiting areas. We walk as fast as we can without running. At one stage, a jog creeps in but Jory slows me down when I almost collide with a patient who is being wheeled out of the lift on a trolley.

'Level 2, Area K.' He repeats the directions we were given at reception for the Intensive Care Unit. 'We're nearly there.'

Mum and Dad are half an hour behind us. They've had to collect Polly from school and break the news before setting off. Ted doesn't know about his dad yet but is coming with them to see his mum. We don't yet know what the situation is with Emmy, other than it being serious, and it's a long way to go back if it turns out he needs to be here. I can't think about the kids right now because doing so makes my heart feel quite literally broken. I am stunned at just how physical the pain of this news has been, as though my chest is in a vice.

We buzz on the door to the unit and a nurse comes out to meet us, asking which patient we are here to see. I glance past his shoulder. I have visited people in hospital several times before, but this ward doesn't look like any of those. There are no patients sitting up in beds, watching pull-out tellies with grapes and Percy Pigs to hand. Instead, there are several private rooms with closed doors and a general quiet permeated only by the beeping of machines.

'Emmy. Emily Lander. I'm her sister, Beth,' I say.

He nods hello then looks at Jory.

'And this is Jory. He's my friend.' It doesn't sound enough. 'More like family, really,' I add.

We are ushered in, past the quiet cubicles to a long corridor with a row of chairs outside what looks like an office. The nurse points Jory in the direction of the nearest coffee machine. I don't want a coffee. I sit down but immediately stand up again and begin pacing. We're not waiting long before a doctor comes out to chat to us.

'Beth? I'm Dr Hargreaves. I understand your mum and dad are on their way.'

I nod. 'Can I see my sister?'

She gestures for me to sit down and I do so reluctantly, clenching my hands into tight fists, nails digging into my palms. Has something happened since they last spoke to Dad?

'Your sister is really very poorly.' Her voice is low, measured. *Really very poorly*. Really very poorly means she is alive. The relief of this thought alone floods my veins, despite the concern on her face. Poorly has always been Mum's go-to word when we have colds or sore throats. It definitely sounds worse now a medical professional is saying it about my sister.

She sits down next to me. There's a pen behind her ear. I try very hard to concentrate on what she is saying.

'Emmy sustained a significant head trauma during the crash and when the paramedics arrived on the scene, she wasn't responsive and her breathing was slow.' A sob escapes my throat, my brain now forming images of the crash. Jory puts a hand on my shoulder and squeezes it.

'Is she talking? Does she know where she is? Or what's happened?' *Does she know her husband has died?*

She shakes her head. 'Your sister is currently experiencing severely impaired consciousness and is on a ventilator to assist with breathing. In simple terms, she is in a coma, though really there is nothing simple about brain trauma.'

'Is she going to die?' I meet her eye, not wanting to know but needing to know at the same time. I wonder if she knows how important it is that she fixes Emmy. I suspect that she does, that she has had hundreds of families sitting where I am now, relying on her to save a special someone within this bleak bubble of the hospital where all the patients are really very poorly. But all those other patients aren't my sister.

'It's too early for me to be able to answer that question with any certainty. Emmy's condition is what we call critical but stable. What this means is that it is life threatening but her vital signs are within normal limits, at the moment.' Dr Hargreaves puts her hand on my arm. 'I will do everything I can for your sister. Shall we go and see her now?'

Jory holds out his hand and I cling to it. I am still wearing his jacket, the one he should be teaching a history lesson in right now. It's as though we've hopped across to a parallel universe and I want nothing more than to go back to the other one, the one where Jory is too busy teaching to answer my texts and I am shirking work under Dad's Cornish tartan blanket, pondering what hangover carbs to cook for my lunch. How wonderful that other life was. How stupid I was to take it for granted.

We head back to the corridor of cubicles. *Lander, Emily* is written on a whiteboard outside the one at the far end. We step gingerly inside and I swipe at my eyes, trying to clear the tears so I can see her properly. My hand goes to my mouth the moment I do. There are bandages around her face, stretching from underneath her chin all the way over the top of her head where her usually blonde hair is dark and matted with what I guess must be dried blood. There is a tube in her mouth and various dressings and wires in both her arms. I reach out to touch her, looking at Dr Hargreaves to check I can. She nods yes and I sink into the chair beside the bed, gently placing one of her hands in both of mine. I think of Doug, Emmy's first and only love, a brilliant father to Polly and Ted, lying somewhere – I don't even know where – on his own. I rest my head gently on the edge of her pillow.

'I'm here, Em. Jory's here too,' I say.

Jory shifts his weight from one foot to the other before clearing his throat. 'Er, hey, Emmy. What have you been up to, eh?'

She doesn't move. The machine beside her beeps. 'Can she hear me?' I ask.

Dr Hargreaves holds out both her palms. 'We don't know. We're not sure how locked in to the coma Emmy is at this stage but there is a chance she can hear you, yes, and she is much more likely to respond to a familiar voice than to one of ours.'

I nod, unsure of quite what to say next. There are voices further down the corridor. Jory pokes his head out. 'Your folks are here,' he says. 'And the kids, too, I think.'

'OK,' I say. It's very much not OK. I wish more than anything that the kids didn't have to see their mum like this.

Dr Hargreaves leads us to a private room with comfy chairs where Mum and Dad have already been taken. There are cushions on the chairs and a vase of dried flowers on a coffee table in the middle. This is a room where lives fall apart, I am sure of that. They don't provide scatter cushions and vases for happy news.

There are a lot of us in such a small space. The man's voice I didn't recognize in the background of the phone call earlier belonged to our newly assigned Family Liaison Officer, who is talking to Dad. He nods hello to me as he squeezes out, telling my parents that he will be back later with an update on the investigation. Dad opens his arms out wide and I fall into them. His shoulders begin to shake and I stretch my arms around his middle, squeezing him tight. His woolly jumper smells like him. For thirty-one years, he has been the one squeezing me, usually when I've screwed up, always the best at reminding me things will look brighter in the morning.

'Have you seen her? Is she saying anything yet?' Dad breaks away from me and clears his throat. I tell him that we only had a couple of minutes with her before he arrived but that she is unresponsive. He nods and nods some more until the nodding becomes a little manic.

Mum steps forward with Ted in her arms and kisses me on the head before she signals for Jory, who is hovering outside the door, to come in. He looks uncomfortable and she reaches up to touch his cheek. My mum loves Jory, she always has. 'Thank you, for bringing Beth here,' she says.

He meets her eye. 'Moira, I am so sorry about what's happened.'

She smiles sadly. 'I'm glad you're here, love.'

Polly is standing in the corner of the room by the window, looking pale and shaken, her long hair still pulled high into a ponytail from the PE lesson she was pulled out of. She has been told the news about her dad, I can see it on her face. I look at Ted and then at Mum, who understands what I am asking without the need for me to say it. She shakes her head. *He doesn't know yet.*

Dr Hargreaves encourages us all to sit down, though Polly resists, and begins to go over what she has told Jory and me already, though I hear it more clearly second time around. We are all eager to get to Emmy but Dr Hargreaves explains that ICU policy is to have only two bedside visitors at any one time and we therefore agree that Mum and Dad will go in together before coming back and taking Polly and Ted in shifts.

Mum is talking softly to Polly. 'Is that all right with you, sweetheart? If your grandad and I go and see your mum first, then come back for you?'

Polly shrugs, turning her face away from everybody.

Ted, who has managed to wedge Postman Pat's van under the coffee table, looks up and says, 'My mummy and daddy are here.'

We all freeze, except Jory, who crouches down to retrieve the van. 'Hey, buddy, do you want to see some ambulances? There are loads out the front, if you want to have a look?' He looks at my mum and dad. 'I mean, only if that's helpful? I could take him outside for a bit, give you guys some space?'

There are nods of agreement. Ted rotates one hand above his head like a siren and shouts, 'NEE-NAW NEE-NAW WOO WOO WOO!' as Jory steers him out of the room. Mum and Dad follow Dr Hargreaves out, leaving Polly and me alone in the bad-news room.

I fiddle with one of the cushions, wondering what I can say to my niece to appropriately fill the silence. Our relationship is founded on a regular teasing of each other and a collaborative teasing of her mum and dad. My sister is always there when I see Polly. I have never been one of those aunties who takes my niece shopping, or to the park, or out for a hot chocolate, and I've only ever been tasked with babysitting her and Ted a handful of times. Emmy stopped considering me a viable childcare option the night she and Doug returned early from a dinner date and walked in on me in a compromising position with my then-boyfriend. They were livid. Worse than livid, they were disappointed. People are disappointed with me a lot, I find.

I move closer to Polly at the window, opening my mouth then closing it again, settling on gently rubbing her back instead. We stand like that for a while. When she speaks, her voice is small and broken. 'I can't bear this, Aunty Beth.'

'I know.' I search for comforting words that will lift how she is feeling but she's just found out that her dad has died and her mum is in a coma at the end of the corridor. There is nothing in the whole world I can say to make this better.

Her eyes are wide. 'Dad should have gone to work this morning. They never go anywhere on a weekday, not ever, and on the one day they do, this happens.'

'You can't think like that,' I tell her. 'I wish more than anything that they hadn't been on that particular bit of road at that particular time – but they were and there is nothing any of us can do to change that now.'

Polly shakes her head. 'I should have made them stay at home. She's going to die, isn't she?'

'No.' I say this with greater conviction than I feel.

'Does she look really bad?'

I am tempted to play down the shock I felt when seeing Emmy for the first time, but Polly will see for herself before long and it might be helpful to prepare her. I tread carefully. 'No, not bad, it's just a bit alarming, seeing her with bandages and wires and machines. Ignore all of that and just look at her face. Your mum needs you, Pol. The doctor said she might even be able to hear us.'

'Does she know? About Dad?' She starts crying and I feel my heart break all over again.

'I don't think so, no.'

'Have they said where they were driving to? The police, I mean. Do they know why they were on the M5?'

I shake my head. 'No, but we know that, don't we? They had their mortgage appointment. And your nan thinks that maybe they headed to Ikea after, which is why they were on the motorway. It's not a million miles from where they would have been, for the meeting. Nan feels bad because she told them to make a day of it. It's *not* her fault, just as it's not yours for not stopping them leaving. You could never have known.'

Polly is torturing herself by going over the accident in her head, I can see it. I was doing the same on the way here.

'Do you want a hot drink? I'll go and get us a tea or something.' She shakes her head. 'Are you sure? I need to find the loo anyway. Do you want to come with me?' I don't want to leave her on her own. She shakes her head again and I tell her I'll quickly find the toilet then come straight back.

The moment I step out of ICU, I burst into tears. Huge, fat tears roll down both my cheeks. I don't swipe them away this time. Instead, I let them fall and allow my shoulders to shake with such force that people are staring.

In the toilets, I am startled by my own reflection. My face is wet with tears and I grab a paper towel to dab at my cheeks, tucking the frizzy strands of hair that have fallen loose from my bun behind my ears. The sheer horror of what has happened keeps

17

coming at me in waves and with it comes a crippling fear of more bad news. I am petrified of what is going to happen next and panicked about having zero control over any of it. My instinct in a crisis has always been to get out. I am a runner, a bolter, reliably Team Flight in a fight or flight scenario. But there is no flight option here, no way of making myself disappear until it's safe to come out. This isn't the time to hide. I give myself a shake then I walk as fast as I can back to ICU, towards my family and our very worst nightmare.

3

'You've added a McChicken Sandwich twice. Did you want two?'

Mum frowns as she peers closer at the screen. 'No, I wanted one. And I didn't want large chips, it's put those in my basket without asking!' She is getting frustrated, as she always does whenever technology is involved. I put my arm across the screen and gently move her back.

'I'll do the order. Is Dad having his usual? What's Polly having?' I look over at the table. Dad is sitting with his shoulders slumped, staring vacantly into the crowd of diners. Ted is watching cartoons on Jory's phone while holding tight to his favourite soft toy, Mr Trunky the elephant. Jory catches my eye and smiles. It's a small smile, a sad one. I smile sadly back. Polly has squeezed herself into the corner of the table and has her head in her phone. She doesn't want anything, Mum says.

I order her a hamburger anyway and take the receipt with our order number, grabbing straws and napkins then pumping some ketchup into two of the tiny white pots. I don't know a lot about what Ted eats or drinks in a normal day, but I do know that he won't entertain the idea of chips without ketchup. I send Mum back to the table with the condiments and hover to one side of the tills until our order is ready. The smell of fast food is turning my stomach. It feels nothing short of preposterous to be standing in the middle of McDonald's at this moment in time. Had it just been us adults, or us adults plus Polly, there is no way a pit-stop for food would even have entered our minds, but with toddlers it seems the show must go on. Bellies need filling.

It's Friday night, which means the world and his dog are in here. I was just about holding it together while I was busy rescuing Mum from the confusion of touch-screen ordering, but now that I am standing still, the crowd feels as though it is closing in. I don't want to be here, surrounded by people spilling in and out of the door as they laugh loudly and slurp on milkshakes without a care in the world. I am insulted by their cheer and want to scream, 'Why are you laughing? Don't you know what has happened today?' Of course, they don't know what has happened today and, even if they did know, it wouldn't take long after saying 'I'm so sorry, that's dreadful' for the laughing and milkshake slurping to return. It's not their tragedy, is it? Not their problem.

We pick at our food in silence, occasionally responding to Ted, who has already inhaled the tiny pots of ketchup and asks his nan to get him some more. Mum gets him three more and he looks up at her in amazement before getting stuck back in. I wonder if he knows he could ask us for anything today.

Polly hasn't even unwrapped her burger and has barely touched her drink. Where Mum and Dad look withdrawn and exhausted, Polly seems nervous, on edge. I don't know if this is a normal reaction to shock and grief or not. Maybe it is. Maybe she's the only one reacting appropriately. The rest of us, meanwhile, are reluctantly eating meals we weren't hungry for in order to keep things as normal as possible for Ted, who still doesn't know his dad has died and thinks his mum is having a really big nap. He was the only one of us who didn't gasp in shock when he saw the head bandages and wires. 'Mummy's got an ouchie!' he told the doctor. 'And she's a bit tired.'

'What are we going to do?' I ask quietly. 'Tonight, I mean.' I don't know what any of us are going to do in the wider, longer-term sense of the question either but that's probably not a chat for McDonald's.

'Polly and Ted ought to stay at ours, I think,' Mum says.

'No.' The force of Polly's response makes me jump.

'No?' Mum asks her.

'I don't want to stay at yours, Nan. I want to go home.'

I fiddle with the paper wrapper my straw came out of. 'I can stay with them at Emmy's. I'll sleep on the sofa.' I had wanted to stay at the hospital, but Dr Hargreaves took Dad to one side and told him we all ought to go home. She's aware we live over an hour away so has promised to call if there are any notable changes in how Emmy is doing. Dad nods his approval. Mum isn't sold on the idea. I can tell by the way she is clenching her jaw. 'Mum?'

She wobbles her head in a gesture that is neither yes nor no. 'It won't hurt for one night, I suppose,' she says. 'I would stay myself, but I won't be able to sleep on the sofa – not with my dodgy joints – and it wouldn't feel right, sleeping in, well . . .' *Their bed* hangs between us and we concentrate very hard on Ted as he finishes off the last of his chips and licks his fingers.

Mum begins reeling off a list of instructions, as though I am taking the kids on a faraway expedition, not overseeing them sleeping in their own beds for one night. She doesn't think I am up to it. In fairness, I have never once looked after them overnight on my own and, as much as I could sit here and pretend that I know what their routines are, she's already thrown me by mentioning a nappy when I thought Ted was potty-trained.

'I didn't think he wore nappies any more?'

'At bedtime he does, love. Not *during the day*.'

'Oh right, fine. Well, I'll work it out.'

'We'll come round first thing in the morning to help sort things out,' Mum says. *To take over*, is what she means. I'll be grateful for it, I'm sure.

As we file out into the car park, Ted asks if he can have a ride home in Jory's van, and when Mum tells him no, he drops to the floor and starts shrieking. It's a surprisingly loud noise from such a small person.

'He's gone past the point of tiredness now,' Mum says as she lifts him off the floor, ducking out of the way of flailing limbs. 'Could he ride back with you, Jory love?'

Jory nods and goes with Dad to fetch the car-seat. I call over to Polly to tell her I'll see her at home. She stares back at me but doesn't answer.

By the time we get back to Emmy's, Mum and Dad have let themselves and Polly in. Ted has fallen asleep and after a fiddly struggle to unclasp the straps of his seat, I lift him out. I can't remember the last time I picked him up and he is a lot heavier than I expected.

Jory swings the van around then stops beside us, his window open. 'Are you sure I can't stay? I don't think you should be on your own.'

I want nothing more than for him to stay but I want Polly to feel as though she can talk to me, if she wants to. She probably doesn't want to but I'm in charge of her and Ted tonight and she might feel weird if Jory is there. It's a scary thought, that I am to be left in charge of anything, let alone children. I shake my head.

'OK,' Jory says, but he doesn't move. 'I hate the thought of you being upset when you're on your own, that's all.'

'I'll be fine, I promise. Besides, if you stay you know we'd be breaking our Golden Rule enforced after the Winter of 2015?'

He laughs. 'I'm pretty sure these are extenuating circumstances but yes, it would be a violation. I'll message you later.'

As I carry Ted up the path, there is movement in the living room next door and I catch a brief glimpse of Emmy's neighbour, Albert, before he disappears back behind the curtain. Emmy talks about Albert a lot. *He's in his eighties, you know, but still sharp as a pin.* I've found myself wishing recently that she wouldn't talk about him at all, preferring not to be reminded of the unfortunate incident a few months ago when I had too much to drink and was sick in his plant pot. Emmy and Doug were mortified. I was supposed to apologize to Albert the next day, after Doug had cleared up my mess, but I didn't because I felt so rough and, after that, the moment had gone. I am certain he now dislikes me because I feel him staring intently at me whenever I'm working my hardest to avoid meeting his eye. I realize, as I wait for Mum to open the door, that awkwardness with my sister's elderly neighbour has been, up to now, the sort of thing I've considered to be an issue in my life.

Mum lets us in and immediately takes Ted from me, his bedtime nappy, pyjamas and toothbrush in hand so she can get him straight to bed. The Family Liaison Officer we met earlier at the hospital is here, talking to Dad in the living room. We have already been told that the lorry driver is in hospital recovering from a stroke and that the stroke is almost certainly what caused the crash. I don't want to hear any more about the investigation, so I sit at the bottom of the stairs and stare at the family photos on the wall instead.

Emmy spent ages deciding between photos then arranging the frames, trying to imitate a 'gallery wall' she'd seen on Instagram. I mocked her relentlessly for this, as I always do when she obsesses over something she's seen an *influencer* do, but they look great. The frames she has chosen are a mix of bright colours and I find myself drawn to the orange one housing a black and white picture of the four of them on the beach. I don't think I've ever seen it before, and I stand up to peer closer. Doing so immediately brings tears to my eyes. Ted is on Emmy's hip and Polly is standing in front of her dad, his arms draped loosely over her shoulders. Something must have made Ted laugh just before the photo was taken because he has thrown his head back in the biggest cackle and his mum, dad and big sister have turned to look at him. None of them are looking at the camera – Polly has her hand to her mouth in a giggle, Doug appears to be in the middle of saying something and Emmy's curly hair has been caught by the wind so is partially covering her face. Just by looking at the photo, I can hear them. The four of them laughing and Emmy saying with mock annoyance, 'Mummy just wants *one* nice family photo. Is that too much to ask?'

'I took that.' Dad appears beside me from the living room.

I lean my head on his shoulder. 'Widemouth?' I am trying to make out the dunes behind them.

'It is,' he says sadly. 'That was Mother's Day, last year. We went for a walk in the morning then came back here for a roast, do you remember?'

I remember the roast. I didn't make it to the beach because I'd been to the pub with Jory the night before so stayed in bed watching reruns of *The Hills*. The memory of a message my brother-in-law sent that day makes me laugh and Dad looks at me, puzzled. I gesture at the photo. 'I wasn't there, for the walk, but Doug sent me a WhatsApp picture from the beach. It was of him doing a star jump, with the caption, "This is what a hangover *doesn't* look like." I sent back the middle-finger emoji as my reply.'

Dad tuts but it has made him smile. Our smiles drop when Polly storms out of the living room, her face twisted with rage. 'How can you be out here *laughing* like this?'

Dad and I look at each other, mouths open. It was a memory of Doug, a happy memory. We just wanted to share it, to have a moment amidst this madness. I feel immediately guilty for not looking more upset. Mum hisses down the stairs, telling us to keep the noise down as Ted has just dozed off.

'Polly, love . . .' Dad struggles to find a reply. He tries to encourage her back through to the living room but she stands firm at the bottom of the stairs.

I don't know what to say either. I point at the photo, wanting to explain, hoping she might come and look at it with us. 'I was just telling your grandad about a funny message your dad sent me on the day this picture was taken. He was teasing me because—'

'*No.*'

I stop. Polly is shaking her head so vigorously I am worried she is going to injure herself. The teenager in front of me now with her wild eyes and tense shoulders is so far removed from the carefree teenager in the beach photo that I barely recognize her. She is wearing enough anguish for us all. It hits me that though we are, all of us, grieving, it is Polly and Ted's world that has been turned upside down the most.

'I'm sorry for laughing, Pol. We didn't mean to upset you. Can we do anything? Do you want to talk?' I look at Dad for help.

'He was so proud of you, love,' Dad tells her. I reach out for Polly, hoping she might let me hug her or at least give her hand a squeeze. She is still shaking her head. What her grandad has said only seems to have made her more agitated. 'No, he wasn't.' She pushes past us and runs upstairs. I step forward to go after her but Dad tells me to give her some space. We both flinch as her bedroom door slams. The Family Liaison Officer appears with a cup of tea that he passes to me. He smiles apologetically at Dad.

'I didn't make you one, Jim, as Moira said you'll be heading back to your house shortly.'

Dad tells him it's fine and that they'll soon be on their way. I don't want them to be on their way. I feel a rising sense of panic and wonder if I ought to tell Mum that we all need to go back to theirs after all. I can't hold the fort. I've never held any fort.

'Grief doesn't always come out in the way we expect it to,' the Family Liaison Officer says, nodding his head upstairs.

'She's just so *angry*. I don't know what to say.' I take a sip of my tea. 'When we tell Ted tomorrow, about his dad, will he . . . you know, understand?'

Dad puts a hand on my shoulder and gives it a squeeze. 'We're all exhausted, Beth. It's been ever such a long day. Shall we worry about tomorrow, tomorrow?'

'OK,' I say, even though I am worrying about it now.

When he and Mum are on their way out, I find myself clinging to the pair of them, my fingers gripping the fabric of their coats. I want to tell them that I don't know how to deal with Polly, or what to do if Ted wakes up in the night, but I don't. When I release my grip, Mum is giving Dad a look I can't read.

'I can stay instead, love,' she says. 'You go home with your dad?'

'No, I'll be fine. You'll be back in the morning anyway.' The Family Liaison Officer leaves, too, to let us all get some rest.

When I close the door, I can hear the faint sound of crying coming from upstairs. I follow it and find Polly in her mum and dad's bedroom, her back resting against their bed, a jumper of Doug's in her lap. I join her on the floor.

'Is he really gone?' She turns her head towards me, searching my face.

I nod. 'I'm so sorry, Pol.' I put my arm around her shoulder, holding on to her as she collapses against me, her face in the jumper.

We stay sitting on the floor for a while, until we are cried out and empty. As Polly heads off to bed, I offer to sleep in her room with her, but she says she'll be fine and that she'll see me in the morning. Before going back downstairs, I check on Ted, who is snoring lightly, his tractor duvet kicked to the bottom of his bed. I can feel my chest tightening at the thought of us breaking the news, a new wave of dread sweeping over me. As I pull the covers gently over his legs and tuck him in, I try to concentrate on his peaceful snores instead.

'Sleep tight, buddy,' I whisper. 'I'm so sorry.'

4

It was worse than I ever could have imagined it would be, in the end. Ted was confused by what we were saying and the more confused he became, the more direct we had to be with our messaging. It was eventually down to Mum, who seemed stronger than the rest of us in that moment, to kneel down to his level, take his hands in hers and explain in the clearest of terms that his daddy wasn't at work, or getting better in the hospital. *He won't be coming home, my darling, but he didn't choose to leave you and your sister. He loved you very much.* Ted had sat very still for a moment before asking for his mum, prompting another difficult conversation. 'Will she be back in a minute?' he kept repeating. 'When she's not tired?' I have never had to work so hard to hold back tears.

We have returned to the hospital, this time without Ted, who is being looked after by Emmy's friend Kate. Mum said it was better for him to have a 'play date' with Kate's daughter, who is the same age, rather than being carted back and forth to the hospital. I thought about asking whether it might be good for him to see his mum again, and for her to see or at least hear him, but Mum had already made the arrangements. She arrived just after seven this morning, slightly manic having not been able to sleep, ready to give us our orders. My first instruction was to get some clothes out of the drawer for Ted, but as we left, I noticed the clothes I'd picked out for his play date weren't the ones she had put him in, so I'm not sure why she bothers delegating. Every job only gets redone anyway. It's the way it's always been.

Polly has barely said a word and is tired and jumpy. I seem to be the only person who managed any sleep last night and I think that was down to the hangover I'd forgotten I had catching up with me the moment I stretched out on the sofa and turned off the lamp. I woke with a stiff neck and only remembered where I was, and why, when Ted shouted for his mum and dad from upstairs.

Dr Hargreaves has assembled us all in the bad-news room again. She is flustered today, busy, but still takes time to carefully explain what's going on with Emmy. There is no good news to share, she says, but there is no immediate cause for alarm (beyond the alarm we already have) either. None of us are quite sure how to process this update. *It could be worse* is what I keep thinking, which is possibly ludicrous when in all honesty it couldn't be much worse. However, Emmy is alive when the odds were very much stacked against her. She shouldn't be here, but she is. We cling to this while at the same time feeling a great sense of disappointment that she has not woken up and started talking.

'Do you have any questions?' Dr Hargreaves addresses us all.

'She's not going to get better, is she?' We all turn to look at Polly, surprised to hear her voice after such a lengthy silence, and then back at Dr Hargreaves, who seems to be carefully considering what to say. At fourteen, Polly's not an adult but she's too old to be spoken to as though she's a child.

'The honest answer is that we just don't know. We have done lots of scans and tests over the last twenty-four hours and there are many more to come. Your mum will be scored against the Glasgow Coma Scale, which assesses a patient's level of consciousness. It's a scale we'll use consistently, so it will offer us a good indication of improvements and also show us if things unfortunately go the other way and there is a deterioration. Brain injuries are unpredictable and, because of that, there is a long and uncertain road ahead. I can't promise you that your mum will recover, either fully or at all, as there is a chance she may not. However, I am hopeful that she might.'

I feel myself nodding, encouraged by the fact she has used the word 'hopeful'. We are all of us hopeful, of course, but the rest of us don't have a clue what we're talking about. The hope in a doctor's hopeful holds more weight than ours, surely?

As we can only visit Emmy in twos, Mum decides that she and Polly will go in first then we'll swap after an hour. Dad and I do as we're told. Neither of us fancies sitting still and when we're politely asked to vacate the bad-news room to make way for another family on the bad-news conveyor belt, we decide to take a wander.

Dad is talking a lot, and quickly. There are dark circles under his eyes and grey stubble across his neck and chin. He never misses a shave and I haven't seen him looking this dishevelled since the summers we used to go camping. Those weeks in the school holidays were some of the happiest of my life, and yet when Emmy and Doug tried to get me to join them and the kids under canvas in Polzeath for a week last summer, I made my excuses. I should have gone with them. I took it for granted that there would be plenty more trips to come.

We take the lift down to the main reception and head outside for fresh air. There's a free bench which looks damp, but we sit on it anyway. Dad is talking about probate and wills.

'Do you need to worry about all that immediately?' I can feel the chill of the bench through my jeans and readjust my coat so it's pulled down over my bum.

Dad sighs. 'Unfortunately, I do have to worry about it all pretty soon. Your sister and Doug, they appointed me as executor to their wills. And with Emmy being so poorly, I am duty bound to start overseeing Doug's affairs. He didn't really have anyone else, did he?'

'No.' I say. 'I hadn't even thought of that.' Doug never knew his dad and had a difficult relationship with his mum, who he's barely been in contact with since she moved to Ireland. I remember an awkward family gathering many years ago where she and Mum were fighting over who got to hold a toddler Polly but I don't remember her ever even meeting Ted. Mum and Dad were the closest thing Doug ever had to a family really. And me, I suppose. He told me many times that it was like having an annoying little sister of his own.

'I still can't believe he's gone.' I pick at the fraying edges of a hole in the knee of my jeans.

Dad shakes his head. 'Me neither. I keep thinking about the day they gave me copies of their wills for safekeeping. I filed them in a drawer in your mum's old bureau and I remember saying to your sister, "Let's hope I never need them!" We laughed because it just seemed so *unlikely* then. It was a just-in-case thing. "Belt and braces," she said. Having it all written down meant she could sleep better at night. I never thought . . .' His voice trails off. We are quiet for a moment. I rest my head on his shoulder and he places his hand on my arm. 'They chose you, love. In their wills. To be Polly and Ted's guardian in the event of their joint death. You know that, don't you?'

I nod. I did know about the wills, but it is still a shock to be reminded of them. *In the event of our joint death* is what they said. Emmy is not dead.

'Your mother, she's got herself in a bit of a state about it already.'

'What do you mean? We're all in a state.' I know exactly what he means though. Mum doesn't think I'm a suitable choice of guardian. She wasn't happy about it when Emmy brought it up over dinner at the time. After a short period of silent sulking,

Mum had raised her concerns as she served up pudding. 'And you're sure you want *Beth* to take care of the kids? What do you make of this, Beth love? You're not the best at looking after yourself, you'd admit that, wouldn't you? How on earth would you look after *children*?' I had shrugged and tucked into my cheesecake, not managing to find the energy to be bothered by her disapproval over my selection for something that was clearly never going to happen. She'd then managed to bring up my 'job-hopping' habit, my personal debt, my disastrous dating record and the six speeding points on my licence, all before it was time for coffee, concluding with, 'I just thought you might have chosen someone a little more responsible, Em. More of a *grown-up*, that's all,' to which Emmy had reminded her that I was already older than she had been when Polly was born.

'Your mum just worries about how you'd cope. She thinks it would be too much for you.' Dad is treading carefully. 'You *know* I think you can do anything you put your mind to. But reliability and responsibility are not your strongest points. They're just not.'

'I worry about how I would cope too,' I tell him. 'But maybe Emmy and Doug had more faith in me.'

'Yeah. Maybe.'

'Bloody hell, Dad. You could at least pretend to be a bit more convinced.' It's rare for us to have cross words but I feel like he's taking Mum's side.

'I'm sorry, love.' I don't ask whether he's sorry because that wasn't what he meant or sorry that he couldn't disguise it. I imagine it's the latter. The truth is, I am just as surprised as anyone that Emmy and Doug settled on me as the most suitable guardian for their children. Doug in particular, who once told me I reminded him of the teenager trapped in an adult's body in *13 Going On 30*. I can't help but wonder whether he ever fully endorsed the guardianship decision or whether he was simply appeasing my sister, who, in a flurry of love and hormones, found herself having a panic about death in the months after Ted was born. They were talking hypothetically about something he never imagined would come to pass. Maybe Doug didn't put much thought into it at all. Only he and Emmy know what they agreed, and why, and neither of them is able to tell us.

We watch as people get in and out of taxis at the front of the hospital. A lady in a wheelchair who looks to be around the same age as Mum pulls down an oxygen mask to smoke a cigarette underneath a sign that reads *No smoking*.

'Your mum thinks Polly and Ted should stay at ours while all this is going on. She wants to look after them herself.' Despite not having jumped to my immediate defence about Emmy and Doug's will decision, Dad's tone suggests he doesn't think Mum having them is a particularly good idea, either.

'But Polly doesn't *want* to stay at yours, she wants to be in her own home. We don't know how long an arrangement it's going to be, and Mum, well, she isn't getting any younger, is she? I know her arthritis is getting worse, Dad. I've seen her struggling with her hands.' Mum never complains of any pain but I can tell by the way she's always clenching and unclenching her fingers.

Dad turns to look at me. 'You mustn't talk like that in front of her.'

'Why?'

'Because you know what she's like. Proud to a fault. Hates a fuss. She doesn't want people to feel sorry for her.'

He's right. She has always underplayed how much she's struggling and she would be horrified if she knew any of us have noticed that her hands have been getting worse. I promise him that I won't say anything but suggest he gently reminds her that looking after the kids full time would be too much of a strain physically. She is still much better qualified to look after them than I am, I think, but I don't say it. There is no winning solution, whatever we do. They need their mum and dad.

We watch the world go by for a while longer until Dad slaps his thighs and says, 'Right then,' which is code for let's get going. I don't move from the bench. 'Beth, love? Are you all right?'

'No,' I say. 'I don't want to be here.'

'I know, sweetheart, but you need to be here. Your big sister needs you. Polly and Ted do, too.'

'What if I'm not up to it, Dad?' *What if Mum's right?*

He puts his hand over mine and squeezes it. 'Whose opinion do you value most in the world, above anyone else's?' When I look confused, he adds, 'It's possibly a joint first-place tie with Jory.'

'Emmy's.'

'Same as it ever was,' Dad says. 'And who, when making such an important decision, thought you *were* up to it?'

I wipe my nose on the cuff of my coat. 'Emmy.'

Dad gives me a familiar look, his classic 'Well, there you are then' nod, before he gets to his feet, holds out his hand and pulls me up. My sister had faith that I was up to the job. I just hope I can prove her right.

Next-door's curtain is twitching again. After an emotional day and roadworks holding up our drive home from the hospital, I feel like pressing my face against the glass and shouting, 'Do you want to take a picture?' but I remind myself that Albert is in his eighties and I'm only paranoid about him staring at me because I never said sorry for being sick in his lavender.

We stopped at Kate's to get Ted on the way back and Mum has carried him to the door. 'Do you want us to come in, Beth? Help you with tea and bedtime?'

'Oh – I don't mind, it's up to you.' I was banking on them coming in to help with tea and bedtime. The idea of them not coming in hadn't even entered my mind.

Mum looks exhausted. I am about to tell her as much when I remember what Dad said at the hospital. I'm a little surprised that she's asking me if I *want* her to come in. Dad must have had a word with her.

He puts his hand on Mum's shoulder. 'We'll head home, shall we, love? Beth knows we're only up the road if she needs anything and we'll be back again in the morning.'

Mum hesitates, just for a moment, before nodding and handing me Ted. 'He's already had his tea at Kate's, but there's a pizza and some salad in the fridge for you and Polly that I put in there this morning – I didn't think you'd want to worry yourself with having to cook something. I'll phone you later, make sure you're all right.'

'Oh. OK,' I say. Polly has already gone straight upstairs to her bedroom.

As Mum and Dad walk down the path, Ted shouts, 'Do the beep, Grandad!' Dad puts his thumb up. I lift Ted higher on my hip and we watch them get in the car. Ted waves frantically and I feel myself on the verge of tears. Dad beeps the horn and Ted giggles.

'BEEP! You do it, Aunty Beth.'

I muster a beep and Ted's immediate scowl tells me it was lack-lustre at best. I repeat my beeping with a bit more vigour and he cheers before peering closer at my face. 'Are you sad?' he asks. I hadn't realized I was crying but now he's pointed it out I can't stop the tears. He puts his arms around my neck and says, 'Do you want some juice?' which makes me laugh then cry some more.

I put the telly on for Ted and shout up to Polly to see if she needs anything. A muffled reply comes back, it sounds like no. I shout up again, this time to tell her I'll get Ted ready for bed then sort out our pizza, if that's OK. No answer. I run upstairs to get Ted some pyjamas but have to run straight back down again when there is a knock at the door. Perhaps Mum didn't think I could be left unattended after all.

'Oh. Hi.' It's Albert, from next door. He is wearing a chunky

34

beige cardigan and fiddling with a hearing aid that's letting off a high-pitched bleep. There's a small bunch of white flowers in his other hand.

'I'm sorry to intrude, Beth – it is Beth, isn't it? I don't think we've met,' he says.

'Yes, I mean, no. Yes I'm Beth, no we haven't met.' I can feel myself going red. 'Nice to meet you.' *Very sorry for puking in your lavender.*

There is an awkward silence where I smile politely, waiting for him to tell me why he has knocked on the door.

'Sorry, you must be ever so busy. I just wanted to give you these.' He hands over the flowers.

'Right. Um, thanks.'

'They're snowdrops,' he says, as though this explains everything.

'Lovely,' I say. *Is this really the time?*

He studies my face. 'Your sister, she said they're her favourites . . .'

'Oh, yes of course.' I think it rings a bell somewhere. Possibly. I never pay much attention to garden chat. He looks embarrassed and I feel guilty. Emmy would appreciate this kindness. 'Thank you, Albert. That's really lovely of you. Emmy talks about you a lot.'

He smiles. 'They're the first bulbs of the year to flower, heralding the end of winter. I usually pass a bunch or two over the fence February time, but they were a bit later coming up this year and then . . .' He pauses. 'I'm really sorry about Douglas, he was one of life's good guys. Terrible shock for you all. I hope Emmy gets better soon.'

As he is already moving away from the door, I don't have the heart to tell him that she might not get better at all so instead tell him that I will take the snowdrops to her at the hospital tomorrow. His face lights up at that and I decide against ruining an otherwise pleasant exchange by apologizing for the vomit in the plant pot. Next time.

Back in the living room Ted, who has been happily watching telly, gets annoyed when I interrupt CBeebies to start getting him ready for bed. It doesn't help that I've put his bedtime nappy on the wrong way round, as pointed out by Polly, who has come down to get a drink. Her face is blotchy. I ask if she's OK and she says she is, even though she isn't.

I wrestle Ted's nappy back on, the right way this time, then put him in some pyjamas that are so big I have to roll the waistband over at the top.

'Not Ted's,' he tells me, with a very serious face.

'They must be yours,' I say. 'They were in your drawer.'

'If they're massive they're from the next-size-up drawer,' Polly says, as she retreats back upstairs. 'Mum buys the next-size-up clothes in the sale, ready for when he grows out of the current ones.'

I stare after her. Of course Emmy does. I can't say I'm surprised to discover my sister has implemented a next-size-up drawer system when she also vacuum-packs her summer wardrobe and watches 'clothes folding hacks' on YouTube.

I check the instructions on the back of the pizza and spend an embarrassingly long time trying to work out which setting on the oven is the right one. I consider getting Polly back down to ask her but it feels a bit pathetic. It seems to be heating up so I just have to hope it's the right one.

Aside from the CBeebies bedtime story, the house is now quiet. I need to get Ted to bed but I stand still for a moment, taking in the signs of Emmy and Doug that are everywhere. Handwritten reminders about the dentist and Polly's upcoming swimming gala stuck to the fridge. A recently watered houseplant on the draining board. One of Doug's fleeces draped over the back of a dining chair. My eyes wander over the spice rack on the wall and I realize for the first time that the tiny jars have been arranged alphabetically. How have I never noticed this before? I laugh and want so badly to talk to Doug about it; for us to tease Emmy about her habit of sorting and sticking labels on everything, the way we always do. The last time we mocked her labels she stormed off in a huff, coming back with her label maker then printing two labels saying 'Bellend' that she stuck on our cups of tea. I long so desperately to be sitting on the sofa having a cup of tea in a mug with a Bellend label on while she fusses over making dinner and sorting Ted's bedtime. I shouldn't be the one doing those things, it's all wrong.

I ask Ted if he wants some warm milk and he looks at me, puzzled, but says yes. I don't know if he has warm milk before bed any more. He definitely did, at one stage. It shouldn't feel this alien, stepping in to look after my niece and nephew. It's what aunties do, isn't it? But it's not what I do. I am a hands-off type of aunty. Or at least I was.

When Ted's beaker of milk is finished, we head upstairs. I close the blind in his bedroom then turn off the light, which makes him shout until I turn it back on again. He points at a night light in the shape of a star and I switch it on before turning the big light off again. He is looking at me strangely now, as though he is unsure why I am there. I tuck the covers in around him.

'I want Mummy,' he says. I was expecting this but it's a punch in the stomach all the same.

'Mummy's not here, Ted. She's in the hospital, do you remember? We went to see her yesterday.'

'I want Daddy.' His bottom lip wobbles then tears begin sliding down his cheeks and on to the farm animals on his pillow.

'Shall we read a story?' I try.

He nods and sniffs at the same time. 'Ted at the zoo with the snake story.'

He means one of his dad's made-up stories. This is so far outside of my comfort zone I find myself looking for a way out of it but he has tucked Mr Trunky in beside him ready to listen, so I smile and hope he believes I do this sort of thing all the time.

'Once upon a time there was a boy called Ted and he went to the zoo.' His thumb is in his mouth, which can only be a good sign. I make it up as I go along and it seems to be going all right, not as hard as I thought, until I get to the end.

'Fireman Sam didn't come!' He starts crying again and punches his duvet with his fist. When his daddy tells the story, Ted always calls Fireman Sam. This is how the story *always* ends. I have got it wrong. It's ruined. He has worn himself out crying and not long after his thumb returns to his mouth, he starts drifting. I sit very still beside him on his bed, certain my being there is not helping in any way with getting him to sleep but at the same time not wanting to leave him on his own. His breathing steadies and I think about lying down next to him until the moment of peace is interrupted by Polly shouting from her bedroom.

'Aunty Beth, what's that smell?' She appears on the landing.

I run to Ted's door with my finger to my lips. '*Ssssh*. He's just gone off.'

'Is something on fire?' she whispers.

'*Oh, fuck*.' I run downstairs to a smoke-filled kitchen and turn off the oven. More smoke billows out when I open the door and at the centre of it lies our pizza, burnt to a crisp. I look sheepishly at Polly who has followed me down. 'I think the pizza's done.'

'No shit,' she replies and though I'm sure I should be telling her to watch her language, I remember I've just said *fuck*.

'I forgot it was in there,' I tell her. 'Sorry. I'll make us something else.'

'I'm not really hungry anyway.'

'Yeah but you have to eat something.' I begin rummaging through the cupboards. I don't want her to disappear to her room again and food is the only way I can make her stay. 'Beans on toast? I'll try not to burn it.'

She shrugs and sits down at the dining table while I make our new dinner.

'Your nan is going to be livid that I cremated the pizza.'

'Yeah,' Polly says. She is staring at her hands. I continue to waffle about the pizza disaster, getting only grunts in reply.

We eat our tea in silence and it's properly awkward, every clink of cutlery against plates sounding deafening. I don't want it to be awkward, but it is. Polly barely touches hers, moving the beans around on the toast with her fork.

'Crikey it's quiet, isn't it,' I say. A statement rather than a question.

She pushes her plate away. 'Thanks for tea.'

'Pol . . .' I hesitate and she looks at me, waiting for me to say whatever I'm going to say so she can head back to her bedroom. 'I know you're *not* OK, so I'm not even going to ask if you are, but I'm really worried about you. Do you want to talk about anything? Or everything? Or just something?'

She looks away from me and when she speaks her voice is quiet. 'I can't bear this.'

I push my plate away to join hers in the middle of the table. 'I know.'

'I wish it had just been a normal Friday,' she says.

'What do you mean?' It's the same thing she said at the hospital.

'Yesterday. I wish Dad had gone to work and Mum had been at home with Ted all day, like *every* other Friday. Then this wouldn't have happened.' The horror of it all is etched on her face.

I reach out and put my hand on her arm, half expecting her to shake it off, but she doesn't. 'Trust me, I have had those same thoughts since I heard the news,' I say. 'What if they had cancelled their mortgage appointment? What if it had been on a different day? What if they had stopped at the services or had to slow down for roadworks, knocking their journey a few minutes – seconds even – off the course it was when the accident happened. But you can't think like that, you just can't.'

She is trembling, I can feel the tremor in her arm. 'They shouldn't have been there,' she says.

'But they *were* there, Pol. And there is absolutely nothing any of us can do about it.'

She swipes at tears on her cheeks. 'Can I leave the table now please?'

I nod. 'I'm here, if you want to chat. I know I can't make it better but I'm here, whenever you're ready to talk—'

She is already halfway up the stairs.

APRIL

5

Ted has been jumping all over me for what feels like hours. He is using my thighs as a trampoline and holding on to my neck for balance, little hands occasionally tugging at loose strands of hair that have dropped from my ponytail. The more I say 'ow' the more he seems to think it's hilarious. I duck my head out of the way of his elbow.

'Ted, I think that's enough,' I say.

'Five more minutes!' he says with a grin. *Five more minutes* is, I'm learning, Ted's answer to everything. After five more minutes, he will ask for five *more* minutes, and so on.

I slap at my cheeks in an effort to re-energize my face, immediately regretting doing so when Ted looks up and copies me, slapping his own cheeks then laughing.

'Your aunty Beth's just a bit tired, Ted. I need to wake up a bit.'

'*Wake up!*' he shouts in my ear. 'Is that better?'

'Hmmm, much better.' I pat his leg. Until recently, being shattered or knackered or exhausted stemmed from what Mum said was me burning the candle at both ends. Too much drinking, not enough sleeping, a failure to eat my five-a-day and a terrible habit of slobbing about watching entire box sets without coming up for air. People on social media bang on and on about the importance of self-care but it only actually seems trendy to have a rest day if you're used to going to the gym or smashing out a quick 10k or being a 'mumpreneur' (shudder) or getting out of your duvet to chant an affirmation stuck to a mirror. Emmy had started getting quite into affirmations before the accident. She had ordered a pack of motivational cards after being influenced by her favourite mum blogger and stuck them around the house. They were – luckily for me and unfortunately for Emmy – plain white cards with black writing, which meant I was able to use a black pen and some Tippex to subtly change the message. Doug had laughed to the point of tears the day she had stomped downstairs to tell him I had changed 'I am a magnet for success in everything I do' to 'I am a maggot for success in everything I do,' and that it had taken her reading it aloud to notice.

Ted and I aren't going to see Emmy today. Mum is taking Polly with her this afternoon and then tomorrow I'll go with Dad, and maybe Ted. Ted's been finding hour upon hour sitting next to 'sleeping Mummy' boring, which means he plays up (which isn't at all his fault, but he is louder and more boisterous than is appropriate for such a serious setting). The woman next-door to Emmy in ICU died last week. Her parents had to give their permission to turn off the machine. We'd seen them most days, nods of empathy exchanged as we passed them on our way in or out, so seeing the empty bed had been sobering. Dad and I couldn't seem to find anything to talk about on our drive home after that.

There's a crash in the kitchen and I twist round to see the back of Polly's head as she looks for something in the cupboard.

'Are you all right, Pol?' I ask.

'Yep,' she says. We perform this conversation multiple times every day. She's not all right, I know she's not all right and she knows *I* know she's not all right, but we keep dancing around each other anyway.

'Shall I make us a cup of tea?'

'No thanks.'

'A hot chocolate then?'

'We haven't got any,' she says.

'Oh. OK. A bacon sandwich?' My tone is getting a little bit desperate.

'There's no bacon.' She pulls open the doors and gestures at the almost empty shelves. 'Or bread.'

'There's bread in the freezer,' I say defensively.

'No, there isn't. I got that out yesterday. A new loaf doesn't just appear.'

'Right, well, clearly I need to do a shop. I've been putting it off, if I'm honest. I tried to get a click-and-collect slot but there were none left.' I feel attacked.

She narrows her eyes. 'Why can't you just *go* to the shop?'

I'm starting to wish I hadn't engaged in a conversation at all. Now there's a bad atmosphere about bread. 'I can. I will. Your nan and grandad will be here soon. I'll see if I can nip out on my own to do the shop while Dad has Ted and you guys are at the hospital.'

Polly mutters something I can't hear.

'What was that?'

She slams the cupboard door and the noise makes me jump. 'I *said*, just take Ted with you. That's what Mum has to do.'

'Right,' I say. 'You're right.' I've been nipping to the little shop in the village most days, or relying on Mum to do a shop and bring it over. I've never really had to do a weekly groceries shop, with or without a toddler, having spent three decades living with my parents. I am grossly underqualified for all of this, not just the shopping and childcare but the pretending to be a fully function-ing adult who has her shit together. Precisely none of my shit is together.

I grab the notepad and pen that's stuck to the side of the fridge and write down: *ketchup, bread, hot chocolate*.

'I didn't mean you had to go right now.' Polly pulls out a squashed bag of crisps.

'Well, there's no time like the present.' I add *crisps*. 'What else do we need?'

'Just the usual, I suppose,' she says.

'Right,' I say, despite having no idea what 'the usual' constitutes. 'Do you want to come with us? Get out of the house for a bit? You can point out the snacks you want?'

'I'm not five,' she says.

'No, of course not. I just thought if the three of us went we could tackle it together.' As conversations go, this is proving hard work.

'No thanks. You can leave me here on my own. Mum and Dad do.'

I raise an eyebrow. It's true she has been left on her own before but only occasionally when they've popped out. I look at the clock. Her nan and grandad will be over any moment and she's only going to be hiding in her room again, so it doesn't seem like the riskiest plan.

I root around in the kitchen for some shopping bags. The only drawer I haven't checked seems to be stuck and I yank it with force until it opens, smiling when it does. Just a week before the accident, Emmy forced me to watch a YouTube video where a woman folded her stash of supermarket Bags for Life into tiny triangles that she then stored neatly inside another Bag for Life. The video was titled something like 'shopping hacks for busy mums' and I told Emmy it was the most tragic thing I'd ever seen.

Polly is staring at the open drawer. It's little things that get me the most, too. The signs around the house that remind us she is in hospital, and not here. At least with the Emmy signs, we are holding on tight to the hope that she will be coming back. The Doug signs are unbearable. I've had to nudge his slippers under the armchair until someone gives me direction on what I'm supposed to do with it all. I think Emmy should be the one to sort through his stuff but Emmy is not here. And if she were here, she would want him wearing the slippers. She wouldn't want to be deciding whether they should go in the Dump or the Donate pile.

I pull out five folded bag triangles and put them on the work-top. I have no idea if this is the correct number of bags for a weekly shop but that's what we're going with. As I close the drawer, it jams again and I can't close or reopen it. I reach for the utensils drawer.

'What are you doing?' Polly takes a step towards me.

'I think something's fallen down the back of the drawer. It was a bit jammed when I opened it. I thought I could use some tongs or something long to unstick it,' I say, rummaging through the wooden spoons and spatulas.

'I'll do it.' Polly grabs a palette knife and slides it as far in as she can before giving it a wiggle. The drawer still refuses to budge.

'Here, let me have a go,' I say. I hold out my hand but she doesn't release it. 'Pol? Can you let me have a try?'

She hands it over grudgingly. I slide the knife in as far as I can reach, switching from a wiggle to a lever motion, which manages to unstick the jam, though in the process I knock the drawer off its runners and it collapses into the one below. Polly lurches forward and sticks her hand in, knocking me sideways.

'Jesus, Pol, what has got into you?!'

'Nothing.'

'Then why are you so bothered about these drawers?'

'I was just trying to help you.' Her voice has gone weird. She is holding something she must have pulled out behind her back. It looks like an envelope. She nods towards the drawer. 'You can put it back now.'

'I will,' I say. 'What's that?'

'It's nothing.'

'Let me see?' I step towards her, catching a glimpse of hand-writing. I would recognize my sister's handwriting anywhere. I grab it, ignoring Polly's protests. It looks like an official sort of letter and has been opened. There is a small typed return address on the back and a 'Dear Mr and Mrs Lander' at the top of the letter. I unfold it. It's a letter from the bank, confirming their appointment to discuss their mortgage application and detailing a list of documents they needed to take with them. There is nothing strange or interesting about this letter yet all the colour has drained from Polly's face.

'Why were you so keen to grab this?' I ask her. 'Or is there something else hiding in the back of the drawer that I need to fish out?'

Polly shakes her head, her eyes still on the mortgage appointment reminder. I look at it again, this time my eyes drawn to Emmy's scrawl on the envelope. A date and time have been written in biro and circled with pink highlighter. *Saturday 23 March, 11 a.m.* I read the date she's written then read it again, cross-checking it with the date on the letter itself to make sure she scribbled it down right. She has, but it doesn't make sense. Saturday 23 March was eight days after the mortgage appointment they were on their way back from on the day of the accident. *Friday 15 March*, the true date of that meeting, will be etched in my brain for ever. There could be all manner of explanations for this date discrepancy. An admin error, a change of plan. But if that is the case, why is it hidden in a drawer?

'Polly, what's going on?'

'Nothing. I was just helping you with the drawer, that's all.' She is shaking her head, her eyes wide.

'I'm confused.' I read it again. I check the envelope again. 'The date is wrong, isn't it?'

'I don't know anything about their mortgage,' she says.

'You knew there was a letter about it in the drawer though?'

'Oh what does it matter what date it says on a bloody letter? There isn't going to be a mortgage, is there?' Her raised voice has caught Ted's attention. I give him my widest smile to show him everything is all right and he goes back to playing with his toys. Polly storms upstairs, the conversation unfinished. Or maybe it is finished. I'm learning that our limited conversations are finished when Polly decides they're finished.

I am racking my brains to think of a logical explanation, both for the wrong appointment date on the letter and for Polly's reaction. It's just a letter, it's no big deal. And yet. I replace the drawer on its runners as best I can, though it doesn't close smoothly. Emmy *definitely* said they were going to a mortgage appointment on the day of the accident. That was why Doug had taken a Friday off work and why Mum and Dad were babysitting here when my car wouldn't start. If that *was* where they were going, why would Polly be acting so strangely about a letter with a different date on? And if it wasn't where they were going, why would they have lied?

After picking up the shopping bags from the counter, I tell Ted he needs to try for a wee and find his shoes before we brave the supermarket. He frowns at me and I tell him I'll buy him a treat, some chocolate buttons or whatever he wants, which is enough to get him racing to the door.

Polly is lying about something. This realization hits me as I look for my own shoes. The way she has been on edge these past few weeks, how her mind is constantly preoccupied and elsewhere. I have put it down to grief about her dad and worry about her mum but the expression on her face just now didn't look like either of those things. It looked like she had been caught out.

6

There are more people than there are seats and Doug's friends line the edges of the room, their bright shirts and jazzy ties at odds with their sombre faces. Mum leans down to retrieve Mr Trunky from the floor, passing him to a wriggling Ted, who is on Dad's lap. Polly is staring straight ahead, her expression blank. She looks so much like Emmy did at the same age, it's staggering. I never used to see it but now it's all I see, as though it's 1999 and I'm staring straight at my sister who is cross with me for borrowing one of her tops without asking.

Jory is nodding at me as though trying to communicate something. Clearly the length of my dramatic pause and the wiping of my eyes and runny nose on the sleeve of my dress has led him to believe that it has all become too much. I give him the nod to say *I'm OK, I can do it.* I owe it to Doug, for the generosity he's shown me over the years and for rarely complaining about his annoying sister-in-law inviting herself over for yet another family dinner, or tagging along with weekend plans because she still hadn't made a decent dent in sorting her own life out.

All eyes are on me and I'm trying to recall the breathing count Emmy is always banging on about, the one she practised when in labour with Ted that has also, she says, proved helpful whenever she's feeling overwhelmed with life more generally. *In for 4, out for 8*, I think. Or was it in for 8, out for 4? I had laughed until I'd almost wet myself the day I discovered she'd paid good money to go on a course to learn how to breathe. 'Those hippie-birthing people saw you coming,' I'd scoffed and she'd rolled her eyes and said, 'It's called *hypnobirthing*, you tosspot, and it works.' And of course here I now am, despite years of ridiculing, about to rely on my sister's advice as I stand in front of a roomful of mourners to say lovely things about her late husband, because she can't.

I've never been tasked with something this important and the responsibility of it, alongside all the other responsibilities I seem to have collected over the last few weeks, is weighing heavily on my chest. I managed to get through reading all the anecdotes from Doug's school years but now the time has come to talk about him meeting my sister and the life they've shared since, I can feel my composure dissolving.

After a deep breath, I read aloud everything on the now tatty piece of paper in my hands about the inimitable Douglas Lander and my sister, from their romance in the sixth form of Budehaven school to the last few years as a family of four. I talk about their joy at finding out they were expecting Polly when they were only twenty, a happy surprise, and how they spent the next eleven years thinking she would never have a sibling, until the miracle of IVF blessed them with Ted. I talk about how content Doug was with life, how the only dreams he had were of owning a house with Emmy and one day throwing a party big enough to properly celebrate the tiny wedding they'd had when Polly was a baby. I talk about the speech he'd made in front of us that day, how proud he had been to call Emmy his wife and how they had slow-danced to a Bob Dylan song played by a busker on the steps outside the registry office. After stopping to blow my nose, I read the final paragraph. The ink has smudged but it doesn't matter. I think I know this bit.

'Doug would have had you believe there was nothing extraordinary about his life. However, I do believe that on that front he was mistaken. His talent for finding the joy in the everyday, for loving and appreciating his family, for relishing those nothing-really-happening days at home in his slippers – *always* in his slippers – is precisely what made him extraordinary. He never seemed to get bored, or fed up, or restless. *But life is good, Beth. Life is good,* he used to say, whenever I turned up moaning about all the ways my life wasn't good. That was the basis of our relationship, really. Me with my half-empty glass and Doug showing me, always with kindness, that there were plenty of ways to fill it up. I've spent most of the seventeen years I've known him teasing him for being old before his time. And now, in the cruellest twist of fate . . .' I swallow the lump in my throat. *In for 4, out for 8.* 'In the cruellest twist of fate, Doug didn't get to grow old at all, and we find ourselves saying goodbye to him very much before his time. I know some of you are hoping to raise money for a memorial bench overlooking one of the beaches he loved, and I think that's a lovely idea, I really do . . . but I also think the greatest tribute we could pay Doug would be to keep searching for the joy in the nothing-really-happening days, to try to keep our glasses half full in the same way he did and to *always* appreciate a good pair of slippers. If we don't, we risk only realizing how remarkable the unremarkable days were when it's already too late.'

When I sit back down, Dad gives my hand a squeeze. I lean forward to look at Polly, but she doesn't meet my eye.

'Give her time,' Jory whispers, and I nod *I know* while continuing to stare at her. I don't know what I was expecting. It's silly – selfish probably – but I can't help but feel wounded by the complete lack of acknowledgement. I am cross with myself for feeling like this – she doesn't owe me, or anyone else, anything – but something about the way she has behaved over the past few weeks has been troubling me and I think maybe I just hoped today we would see a breakthrough.

I have zoned out from what the celebrant is saying and a

sudden blast of electric guitar makes me jump. My instinct is to rush to turn it off, the first few bars of 'Rock 'n' Roll Star' by Oasis jarring with the occasion. I grimace as I look behind me at the rows of people, convinced this will prove Mum right when she said, *It's a funeral, Beth, not a disco*. But the smiles spreading across Doug's oldest and dearest friends' faces tell me that we haven't got it wrong at all. Even Mum has conceded defeat and is tapping her foot. I think of Doug jumping around the living room as he tidied up, picking up objects to be dusted while warbling that tonight, he was a rock and roll star. The same Doug who himself admitted that the most rock 'n' roll thing he'd ever done was having a double espresso at the end of a meal out which made his heart race when he got into bed. *I couldn't seem to come down from it, Beth. Like an adrenaline rush it was.*

Ted is clapping along to the music, his face lit up as though to say, *Now we're talking, thank god the boring grown-up bit is over.* When Mum arrived and got him changed this morning, he proudly puffed out his chest and told me he was wearing his party shirt. Indeed he is – it's a checked shirt-and-tie set Emmy bought him 'for special occasions' and, as far as Ted is concerned, today *is* a special occasion. He has been told that his dad has died and he has been told that today is a funeral but I don't believe for one second that he understands the link between the two, or has any idea what today really means. Even as the hearse carrying his dad's coffin pulled up and a hush fell over the crowd gathered outside, Ted could be heard chatting happily to his nan.

The song finishes and as the coffin slowly disappears behind the curtain, Polly crumples into her nan's arms and I hear Dad say, 'Goodbye, son,' the finality of which feels unbearable.

After the service, I go through the motions, nodding *Thanks for coming* and *Good to see you* at the rows of people leaving their chairs and piling out into the crisp April sunshine. In the absence of Emmy – and with only Doug's mum here from his side of the family, and keeping her distance at that – it is predominantly Mum, Dad, Polly and I who are receiving the words of condolence. Sympathetic head tilts are being directed at Ted, in Mum's arms, who has just asked loudly whether there will be cake at the special buffet. There is something of a bottleneck as we approach the double doors and while we are stationary waiting for the crowd to thin, I find myself feeling hot and claustrophobic. I don't feel right at all. I need to get out.

Ted comes to my rescue by telling Mum that he needs the toilet. I reach out my arms and take him from her, much to her surprise.

'Excuse me, sorry. I need to get this one to the loo. Sorry, thanks.' I push my way through the crowd and into the disabled toilet just inside the entrance.

'Is it just a wee?' Ted nods and I put him on the toilet before gripping the sink. My heart is beating quickly and the back of my neck feels hot and prickly, as though it has only this second hit me that we are saying a final goodbye to Doug and I am looking after his children while my sister makes a recovery, or maybe doesn't, from her coma. After helping Ted pull his trousers up, my legs wobble and I pull the toilet seat down and sit on it myself, trying to regain some composure. Ted turns the hand drier on, then off, then back on again, the hot air blowing his hair back. I think I might be on the verge of a panic attack. I want so badly to transport myself *home*. To Mum and Dad's, where I can go back to my childhood bedroom with the Blu Tack marks on the ceiling and worry about things that aren't even worries. Not home to Emmy and Doug's, where they should be.

I'm so absorbed in mentally talking myself down from my escalating panic that I don't notice Ted getting bored with the hand drier and unlocking the door, revealing me on the toilet to the last few stragglers of the funeral congregation who are making their way outside. They peer in at me, as of course they would.

'Aunty Beth is doing a wee-wee with her clothes on,' Ted tells them, as though this explains everything.

'Ted!' I hiss, leaping up to push the door closed, my legs still shaking. I splash my face with water to cool down, embarrassment now adding to the flush of my cheeks. I run my fingers underneath my eyes where my mascara has smudged before opening the door, hoping the small crowd didn't pay any attention to my toilet flash that wasn't even a toilet flash, just a flash of me having a breakdown while using my nephew's bladder as an excuse to have a timeout. They probably didn't even hear him.

Jory's smirk tells me otherwise. 'A wee-wee with your clothes on,' he says quietly, his hand to his mouth. He stops smiling when he studies my face. 'Hey, are you all right?'

'Not really,' I say, taking hold of his arm, though I feel better now we have made it outside. 'Do you think anyone will notice if I don't go to the wake?' I'm joking but I'm genuinely not sure I can face it. Ted runs ahead of us, joining Mum and Dad, where there is more hugging and crying and nowhere to escape.

'Hmmm, I think they probably will. It'll be over before you know it, though,' he says. 'And I'll be there to hold your hand. Give me the ear-scratch signal if you need rescuing.'

I begin manically scratching at both ears. 'May Day, May Day.'

'It'll be *fine*,' he says. 'Come on. You've already done the hard bit.'

'OK,' I say, though I have a feeling the hardest bit is yet to come.

'Aunty Beth!' Ted is crying out again. I have been back up and down the stairs four times since putting him to bed and nothing I do seems to settle him. He was so exhausted when we got back here after the wake I honestly thought he would be out for the count, but every time he drifts off, it's only minutes before he cries out again, as though he is having the same nightmare every time. I suppose he is.

I rush back up the stairs and perch beside him. 'I'm here.'

'I couldn't see you,' he says. He eyes me suspiciously.

'I just nipped to the bathroom,' I lie. It's unlike him to be concerned about whether I am close by or not at bedtime. I wonder if I ought to set up a makeshift bed on his floor for the night and keep him company after such an intense day.

'Mummy night-night,' he says, sitting himself up.

'Oh, Ted, your mummy's still—'

'Daddy night-night.'

I chew my lip. 'Your Mummy and Daddy aren't here to do your night-night.'

He shakes his head, frustrated with me. We've had this same conversation so many times since the day of the accident but tonight he seems to be asking something different of me. I try again. 'We said goodbye to Daddy today, didn't we?'

'Nunight, Mummy. Nunight, Daddy,' he says, as though Emmy and Doug are in front of him or he's speaking to them on the phone. 'You say it.'

'Nunight, Mummy and Nunight, Daddy,' I say, and as I do, I have an idea. 'Hold on two seconds, champ. I'll be right back.'

There is a photo in a yellow frame on the multicoloured gallery wall downstairs of Emmy and Doug in Rome. I run down to get it, silently apologizing to my sister as the picture strips it has been stuck up with rip off the Farrow and Ball Elephant's Breath painted lovingly underneath. Emmy took *ages* deciding on the colour she wanted for the hallway and I was there when she picked up the tin, irritating her all the way back to the car by insisting on calling it Rhino's Burp instead. I miss her being irritated with me.

With the frame in my hands, I jog back up to Ted's room, stopping momentarily at his threshold, suddenly doubting whether this is the good idea I thought it was on the way down. After peeling off the paint-covered sticky strips from the back of the frame, I hand it to him.

'That's Mummy and Daddy!' He points at their faces, his smile so wide I immediately relax.

'I know! It's a lovely photo, isn't it? That was when your mummy and daddy went to visit the Colosseum.'

'The see-um?' Ted peers closer at the picture. He picks up Mr Trunky and presses his trunk against the photo so he can see too.

'Yes, that ginormous thing you can see behind them, that's the Colosseum. It's very famous.'

'Wow.' His eyes are wide, he's impressed.

'Would you like to keep this photo in your room? Then you can say nunight to Mummy and Daddy when you go to bed.'

He is nodding. 'And nunight, see-um.'

'Yes and nunight to the Colosseum too, if you like.'

He begins kissing the photo and I concentrate hard on the teddies lined up along his windowsill, fighting back the tears I know are coming, wanting to halt them just for a minute more so I don't alarm Ted, who finally seems to have settled. He says 'nunight' to them in turn: nunight, Mummy, nunight, Daddy, nunight, see-um, then he hands me back the photo. I place it carefully next to his Peter Rabbit alarm clock on his bedside table, angled towards his pillow so Emmy and Doug's tanned and smiling faces can look over their boy as he snuggles back under the duvet and closes his eyes.

7

When Jory phones to see if I fancy getting out of the house for a few hours, I tell him I can't. A proper catch-up is long overdue, I know, but there is always so much to *do* now. Between firefighting chores and kids and the three-hour round trips to the hospital, I can't seem to find any spare time at all and I've not even gone back to work yet, though that's on the horizon. I am running on empty.

Mum and Dad are here ahead of our Emmy visit later. We're going to the hospital en masse this afternoon for Dr Hargreaves' fortnightly 'update chat', which none of us want to miss, even though we know there has been little change since the last update chat or the one before that. We are hoping for glimmers of recovery and praying for a miracle. God knows our family is owed one. I know it doesn't work like that, that no greater odds are stacked in our favour just because we've been dealt such a shitty hand already, but sometimes that is the only thought that keeps me going. Emmy is going to live because Doug didn't.

'Was that Jory, love?' Dad must have overheard the tail end of my phone call as he comes over to have a word, tea towel over his shoulder. 'Why don't you phone him back? You could do with some fresh air.'

A cup tumbles from the dirty-dishes Jenga that has piled up beside the sink and Mum mumbles something I can't quite hear but get the gist of. What I could do with is a long hot shower and a decent night's sleep, but I text Jory to say he can pick me up after all. I want to see him and a trip out of the house will at least give me some respite from Mum's incessant nagging. I don't think she realizes she's doing it half the time but it's like being appraised 24/7. Jory once described how it felt having his History lessons observed by an Ofsted inspector and that's the same vibe I get from Mum whenever she's here. She doesn't even have to say anything, I can just sense her beside me, silently making notes. My crimes this week include messing up the recycling and killing a fiddle-leaf fig. 'Years Emmy's had that one, Beth. *Years.*' I hardly think it's surprising that houseplant-watering has fallen through the cracks and I also don't think it's surprising that I know nothing about recycling when Mum has always *insisted* on sorting ours at home. How was I to know that I had to separate the recycling into the different-coloured sacks Emmy kept under the sink? Refuse and recycling appears to be a full-time job and I've half a mind to stick two fingers up to the bureaucracy of waste collection and put the next lot of recycling straight in the bin, though I'd never get away with it. Mum will probably do a bin audit, recycling proficiency no doubt forming part of the probation she seems to have put me on, despite this being a 'job' I didn't apply for in the first place.

The doorbell rings and when Jory leans in for a hug, I whisper, 'Save me from the Moira regime.'

He laughs. 'I've packed two wetsuits, just in case. Can you grab a towel though?'

I pull away from him and gesture at the sky, the clouds dark and dense.

He rolls his eyes. 'Just get a towel and get in.'

We park to one side of the lifeboat station and Jory goes to get a ticket. I get out and immediately regret not tying my hair back as it blows in front of my face. My hair is thin and flat compared to my sister's thick curls. I've always said I wanted more volume, just not like this.

'There's one in the van,' Jory says, tucking the ticket on the dashboard.

'One what?' I pull a strand out of my mouth.

'A hairband.'

'Oh good. Yes please. Wait – why do you have a hairband in your van? Whose is it?'

'Is that a genuine question?' He zips up his jacket and passes me my coat, along with a hairband. It is one of mine.

I shrug. 'I don't know who you've had in your van, do I? I hope they got out alive though. I've always said it's a bit shady, you having a van rather than a car, like normal people. You're not a tradesman.'

'We're in Bude, Beth. It's for my surfboard. Look around you.' He gestures at the mostly vans in the car park.

'*Right*, but these people go surfing all the time. You just kit yourself out in head-to-toe Zuma Jay then go paddling.' He hates it when I mock his local surf-shop wardrobe. I give him a nudge with my elbow to show I'm only joking. 'Do you have duct tape and cable ties in the back as well?'

He laughs. 'If you must know, the hairband is from this annoying girl I sometimes give lifts to, though I haven't seen quite so much of her recently. She wears them around her wrist but pings them off when she's inebriated. I keep them in the glove box for windy days when her hair makes her look like a yeti.'

'Still sounds a bit Ted Bundy.'

We walk out and over the dunes at the side of the lifeboat station and head down towards the sea. The tide is a long way out and the sky is even darker than when we set off. Jory is looking animated, which usually means I'm about to get treated to an interesting fact. I shiver and pull up my coat collar over my mouth, a smile forming underneath it when he begins.

'Bundy drove a VW Beetle during his murder spree, *not* a van. His Beetle was tan in colour, but he later stole a second Beetle that was orange. They knew he was a wrong'un by then, of course.'

'I think *wrong'un* is putting it mildly,' I say. ' "Extremely wicked, shockingly evil" was what the judge said.' Jory looks surprised at this knowledge but laughs when I reveal my source. 'It's the title of the new Zac Efron film that's out soon. You fancy it?'

He makes a face. 'Not really, but if you're asking whether I would watch it with you, then yes, I would. It's probably the least I can do. How is everything, anyway? Your folks still coming over every day?'

'Yeah.' I dig my hands deep into my coat pockets. 'When I left just now, Mum was busy adding a new set of instructions to a notebook I think she must have bought specifically for the occasion. She's written *Beth's Book of Jobs* on the front. Beth's fucking book of jobs.'

'She has not,' Jory says, though he doesn't look at all shocked by this. He has known my mother for almost as long as I have. I fill him in on the last few weeks.

I tell him that Polly is a shell of herself and now wants to quit the swimming team, something she has loved being a part of for years. I tell him I've not got to the bottom of the mortgage-appointment letter and nobody seems to think there's anything at all odd about the date discrepancy, or the way the letter was wedged in a drawer that wouldn't open, except me. I tell him that I watch my nephew say goodnight to his mum and dad in a photo every evening and when I finally make it downstairs, I'm so tired I fall straight to sleep on the sofa, which luckily is big and comfy enough to sleep on because I still can't even entertain the idea of sleeping in Emmy and Doug's bed. I tell him that last week I went five days between hair washes and he laughs and says, 'Oh, Beth.' Sometimes I get annoyed when people laugh and say 'Oh, Beth' as though I am one instead of thirty-one, but I don't mind when Jory says it because he is my best friend and is on my side.

I report on life since the accident in quite a matter-of-fact way but when he says, 'And how are you feeling, *really* feeling, I mean?' I can't find the words. I want to tell him that I am overloaded both with tasks and emotions. That I am completely out of my depth and when I pause to think about life now compared to before the accident, I truly cannot believe it is the same life at all. This new one feels pretend.

We stop a few metres from the sea and I take my shoes off, tucking my socks inside them. I nod towards Jory's trainers.

'You must be joking? It's far too cold and wet for paddling.' He points at the sky.

I shrug. 'We're cold and wet anyway.'

He mutters something about me being a madwoman but begins, reluctantly, to untie his laces. We stand quietly for a moment, burying our toes in the sand. The month-old varnish on my toenails has all but chipped off. When I was living at Mum's, I'd got into the habit of having a little pamper session on a Sunday night, doing a face mask in the bath then applying fake tan and painting my nails while I waited for the fake tan to dry. Having an hour or two just *spare* like that seems nothing short of crazy now, which is probably the reason I'm back to my natural Casper-the-friendly-ghost shade. I don't care about the lack of tan or tatty nails now though.

'That's heart-breaking about Ted and the photo. Poor kid.' Jory is trying to roll up his jeans but gives up when he finds they are too skinny at the ankle to budge beyond his calves.

'It is, but weirdly he seems to relax after saying goodnight to them, so I'm rolling with it. He seems to appreciate the routine. We have to do the same bedtime story every day, too. Doug used to tell him this story about a snake and Fireman Sam. It took me a good week to get the plot right and even now he doesn't seem impressed by my voices, despite me giving it a really good go.'

Jory is laughing. 'I would pay *a lot* of money to hear your best Fireman Sam voice. Go on, just give me one or two lines.'

'Piss off,' I say, but I follow with, 'A good fireman is never off duty' in my best Welsh accent, which Jory says is a lot better than he was expecting.

'You should show your mum that, a positive new skill you've learned. It might counterbalance your questionable recycling and cooking skills.' He shoots me a sideways glance and I sigh.

'Honestly, Jor. It's intense. It feels like Mum's waiting for me to mess up so she can say I Told You So then whisk Polly and Ted back to hers where she'll feed them a diet more varied than my pesto pasta with sausage.'

Jory clutches his chest in mock surprise. 'You're putting *sausage* in your pesto pasta now? You've changed.'

'I can do omelettes now. *And* I'm becoming an expert at making Ted's favourite, cheesy sauce soldiers. I've been rather enjoying the cheese on toast strips with a little ketchup dip myself.'

We take a few steps forward and let the waves wash over our feet. It's a release, talking about Mum to someone other than Dad (who is understandably caught in the middle). Before now, I've saved the worst of my mum-rants for Emmy, who says things like, 'You two just clash, you know she loves you,' then rolls her eyes when I respond with, 'Yeah, but she loves you more.'

The rain is getting heavier and I look up, letting the drops rest on my face, enjoying feeling so awake. 'Do you know yesterday she started firing random questions at me, like a test?'

'What sort of questions?' Jory is trying but failing to hide his amusement.

'Stuff like, tell me where the stopcock is, and what would you do if Ted had a seizure?, when he has never before had a seizure. Honestly, it's putting me on edge.'

'Bloody hell. It was always going to be impossible to live up to the Moira Pascoe standards of excellence though, wasn't it? And Emmy, well, she does take after your mum, at least a bit, in the "everything being just so" respect,' he says.

He's right. Emmy, though considerably more laidback than our mother, is still worlds apart from me on the tidy and organized scale and, though I wish it wasn't true, I can't deny that Mum has grounds to be a bit concerned by how low I have set the bar on some of the basics.

'I don't know how to cook, Jor,' I say. 'I don't know how to look after a toddler. I don't know how to guess what's going on in Polly's head, or why she hid a letter about Emmy and Doug's mortgage appointment, if indeed she did. I don't know how to read an electricity meter, or what any of the bills mean. Luckily Dad is overseeing that side of things or we'd be up an even shittier creek without a paddle.'

A wave crashes in that's higher than the others, taking us by surprise. It reaches my knees, touching the bottom of my rolled-up jeans. Jory's very much still rolled-down jeans are soaked through, which I know he will hate. He flinches but is otherwise doing an impressive job of acting casually about it. 'I can always help if you need. You are terrible at asking for help, you always have been. I think now is probably the time to put your big girl pants on.'

I swat him on the arm. 'I always wear my big girl pants, there's nothing worse than a too-small knicker.' He raises his eyebrows. 'Anyway, Emmy was my help. That's why I need her to be out of hospital, badgering me to apply myself at work, sort out my credit score and invest in a face serum with retinol in it.'

'I'm just saying, there are other people who care about you.' He looks down at his jeans, the wetness now spreading towards his thighs.

'I know. Though I'm not sure I'd come to you for face serum advice. I'm sorry, by the way, that I haven't been a good friend lately. We've not even made it to the pub. Is this our longest dry spell since school? Mum says I need to think about getting Ted dry at night soon but that's a different sort of dry.'

Jory is giving me a stern look. I think it must be his teacher face. 'Beth, you've just said goodbye to your brother-in-law. Your sister is in hospital. You have been thrown in at the deepest of deep ends. It's no great surprise that you're not up to a night at the Black Horse getting thrashed at pool and flirting with Tony the "fit farmer", who is very married, by the way.'

'Oh, is he *very* married? That's annoying, I thought he was only a bit married. I don't flirt with him, anyway. Not when I'm sober.'

'You are never sober.'

'Well I am now.' We stand quietly for a while longer. After several weeks of navigating awkward silences with Polly, it's nice to exist inside a silence that isn't awkward at all. It's raining but I have acclimatized to the cold and wind – either that or my legs have gone numb – and suddenly I have an impulse that is not very like me at all. I run back towards my shoes and pull my jeans off.

Jory looks at me, mouth agape. 'What are you doing? It's freezing!'

'Let's go in!' I say, pointing at the choppy water.

'But I left our wetsuits in the van because you didn't seem keen. Shall I go and get them?' He looks up the beach, now cloaked in a sea mist.

I have already taken off my coat and I smile as I lift my jumper and vest over my head, shrieking as the rain hits my back. 'Well, I wasn't keen earlier but I am keen now. Come on, Mr Clarke, live a little.'

He shakes his head but strips down to his boxers, placing his hands over himself at the front. 'It's a cold day, all right?' he says and I laugh. I am losing my nerve now I'm faced with the sight of the really rather grey and choppy water. Jory is right, it is *freezing*. I am grateful for the warmth radiating from him when he moves beside me. We shiver, each of us with our arms wrapped around ourselves.

I think of all the times Emmy and I have run into the sea here. When we were kids, body boards secured around our wrists, Mum hovering nearby to check we weren't drowning. When we were teenagers, trying to impress the lifeguards with our brand-new bikinis and highlights. All of our recent trips before the accident were with Ted, who squealed with delight while clinging to his mum's hand as they jumped the waves together. I usually offered to sit with the bags, grateful for the peace so I could spend time looking at my phone. All those wasted hours of being there but never really joining in.

'On three then?' I say. Jory's posture is a picture, his head bowed and his shoulders hunched. He mutters something I can't hear and I remind him once again that this whole outing was his idea.

He holds out a hand for us to go together but I am already running and he swears as he follows behind, shouting that going on the count of two is cheating. He is still banging on about wetsuits when I splash water in his direction making him shriek, before I submerge myself, the cold shock of it taking the wind out of my lungs. My eyes are stinging and I am crying and laughing all at the same time.

This is exactly what I needed. To let something out, to admit to someone that I'm terrified, to release today's build-up of worry and tears before going back to Emmy's and telling my mother that no, I don't know where the stopcock is and no, I haven't researched what to do if Ted has a seizure, but I am willing to learn all those things if only she'll let me try. Tonight, when we all return from seeing Emmy, I am going to cook something for Polly and Ted that *isn't* pesto pasta and sausage. Prove her wrong.

As Jory and I wade through the shallows back to the beach, I think about what's in the cupboard. It might still have to be pesto pasta and sausage after all. One step at a time.

MAY

8

'Do you usually iron your uniform, or does your mum or dad do it?' I suspect I can guess the answer.

Polly responds from the sofa, without looking up from her phone. 'Dad did it.'

'Right. Well, I'll do it for you tonight then.' I'll probably have to iron something for my first day back in the office anyway. 'And you're sure you're ready to go back? I can speak to your head of year if you need more time?'

'I'm going back tomorrow,' Polly says.

'OK. You're the boss.' I chew at an already gnawed thumbnail as I take in the state of Emmy and Doug's once orderly living space. There is mess on every imaginable surface as well as on surfaces I never imagined could get messy. Washing is hanging clumsily over chairs and radiators, half-dry towels somehow smelling worse than before they were washed. There is jam and peanut butter (I hope it's peanut butter) smeared on one end of the dining table and an untidy stack of letters and magazines balancing precariously at the other end. Rubbish spills out of a bag that I have taken out of the bin but not yet tied up. I don't know where I'm going to put it as I forgot once again that it was bin day earlier in the week so the big bin outside has three weeks' instead of two weeks' worth of rubbish in it already.

In the living room, a trail of toys spreads outwards from the epicentre of chaos where two wicker baskets have been turned upside down. Ted is wearing the smaller of the two baskets on his head and when he gets up he walks straight into the fireplace. I lurch forward, anticipating a two-second pain delay before the inevitable screaming kicks in, but to my surprise he doesn't cry at all, instead laughing to himself inside his little basket helmet. As he sits back down on the carpet, he uses his hands as shovels to part the sea of toys. I watch as some of them spread under the sofa where there's already a half-eaten banana just out of reach. Mum is going to have an absolute field day when she gets here. I'm tempted to just shove *all* of it out of sight under the sofa and worry about it later, but I don't want to get mushed banana on everything.

I decide to do what I always do when I'm overwhelmed by the number of things that need doing: nothing. Mum is just going to have to take us as she finds us today. I can't imagine she'll be very happy with how she finds us but I also can't imagine she'll be particularly surprised. There has been a lot of tutting and exchanging of glances with Dad recently. On Wednesday, after I texted her to ask if she knew whether Emmy had any tin foil or cling film so I could plate up some of the chilli she'd made us, she phoned in a panic to tell me that reheating rice more than once could kill us. 'I think you're being a tad dramatic,' I told her before googling 'death by rice poisoning' and discovering that she wasn't being entirely bonkers with her cautionary tale on this occasion. I honestly don't understand how I'm expected to just *know* all this stuff. How can it be right that I left school having been taught how to spot onomatopoeias in the Anthology and knowing the piano notes for 'Frère Jacques', yet at the same time having absolutely no idea that double reheating rice could lead to death. Where were the *life skills*? A broader and more practical education would have gone some way to solving many of my current failings, I'm sure of it. As would have moving out of my parents' house and doing my own washing before the age of thirty-one, but we are where we are.

At least Ted and I are dressed this morning, which is more than can be said for Polly, who is still in her pyjamas with her face glued to her phone, as seems to be her resting state. I'm not one to talk about smartphone dependency, I know. Until recently, I was regularly falling asleep with a claw-hand and strained eyes after one social-media-app refresh led to another, but I've had considerably less mindless-scrolling time since the accident. I'm starting to miss it, which is stupid really when all my notifications ever tell me is that someone I went to school with is having a 'cheeky brunch' of poached egg and smashed avocado on toast that for reasons unknown they have to photograph and upload immediately with the hashtag #brunchgoals. I can't stand 'cheeky' things that are in no way cheeky. *A cheeky pint, a cheeky biscuit, a cheeky little number.* Jory once said my fury over the inappropriate use of 'cheeky' was an overreaction and now uses it all the time just to wind me up. I feel a pang as I think about all the hours Jory and I used to spend talking about nothing much at all. Perhaps it's not the mindless scrolling I miss, as such. Just having time to waste.

'Do you want a cup of tea, Pol?'

She says no without looking at me. I get the same responses on repeat. *She's not hungry, she doesn't want to talk, there's nothing I can get her.* If I'm being honest with myself, I knew we weren't exactly close before, but we always got along and enjoyed each other's company and now, in the absence of her mum and dad, I feel like a gulf has opened up between us. Every time I open my mouth to talk to her about anything deeper than what she wants to eat or drink I hesitate for too long and close it again, worried that whatever I say will only widen the gulf.

Ted has been playing nicely on the floor, but I can sense him getting cross. He is trying to stuff an army of little figures through one door of his fire engine and becoming increasingly frustrated when they pop out the other door. As he slams the whole engine on the floor, both doors fall off and I watch as a cloud of rage spreads across his face. 'I can't do it,' he says, the last syllable long and drawn out the way it always is when he's whingeing. He comes over, fire engine in one hand and two little red doors in the other. 'Aunty Beth fix it,' he says, knocking my hand, which splashes tea over my T-shirt. I put the cup down and take the vehicle from him, making a mental note to wipe the tea that has pooled on the coffee table. After reattaching the doors, I hand it back to him. He yanks the driver door and it falls straight back off. 'It broken *again*.'

'That's why you need to be *gentle*. Look, I'll show you,' I say. I crouch down to reattach the door once again, then I demonstrate how to open and shut it with less force. He lurches forward and smacks the toy out of my hand before dropping to his knees in despair. I'm not sure I have ever seen anything so ridiculous.

I take a deep breath. 'Ted, don't be silly. I was just showing you how to open the doors without knocking them off. I was trying to help you. Why are you getting cross?'

'*Mine!*' He is screaming in my face suddenly, a high-pitched scream that feels as though it is vibrating through my skull. His ability to go from nought to sixty on the anger scale in a matter of seconds is something I'm still not used to. How can such a small person be so livid, and so loud? His screaming ignites my already shortened fuse.

'Well, you can sort the bloody doors out yourself then!' I regret the way it comes out the moment it does.

'Wow, there's no need to swear at him.' Polly is scowling at me from the sofa. It's good of her to wait until the shouty moment to get involved.

'I didn't swear at him.' I'm not convinced 'bloody' is even a swear word these days and I was directing my rage at the toy and its stupid doors, not Ted. Maybe it was a bit at Ted.

He is crying, clutching the fire engine and its doors to his chest. This is what toddlers do. They shout and scream and make you cross, then within seconds do a sad pouty face, sometimes with a thumb in the mouth for extra effect, which makes you feel like a complete monster for losing your cool.

I hold my hands up. 'You're right, there is no need for it. I am sorry. Both of you. Maybe there's a way of attaching the doors more permanently. I'll get Grandad Jim on the case. For now, shall we find you something else to play with?' I gesture at the toys all over the floor. Ted trundles over and picks up another toy with unreliable doors. 'Polly, do you think you could go and get dressed please? Your nan and grandad will be here any minute.'

'So . . . ?' she says. Her tone is one of pure teenage annoyance, with a face to match. She scrunches up her nose as though I've just walked shit through the living room.

'So it's nearly lunchtime and you're still in your pyjamas. Please, just freshen up a bit.' The last bit is definitely pleading and she knows it. I feel pathetic.

'You're only worried about me "freshening up" because if I don't, it looks bad on you. Why you care about me being in pyjamas I have no idea – look at the state of the place, and look at the state of *you*.' She leans backwards to look out of the window. 'It's too late now, anyway.' It's only then that I process what she's said about the state of me and I look down at my tea-splashed top and joggers, trying not to take it personally, even though it was clearly intended to be personal.

Mum's usual rat-a-tat-tat on the door is closely followed by her key in the lock. Her rat-a-tat-tats are always more an announcement of her arrival than a request to come in. She would come in anyway. Ted runs out to greet her. I hope he doesn't tell her that his aunty Beth said 'bloody'.

'Good morning, darlings.' Mum greets Polly and Ted with cuddles. I get a frown instead of a cuddle. 'What's that dreadful smell?'

73

'It's the bin. Don't worry, I was just about to sort it.'

Dad follows Mum in, carrying a bag of what I'm assuming is our lunch. He kisses me on the cheek. 'How are you, love?' I can see him scanning the chaos over my shoulder. Mum has tied the top of the bin bag and is chucking it out the back door. She has been here thirty seconds.

'I'll do that in a minute, Mum. Tea? Coffee?' I force a smile.

'A tea would be lovely,' she says, her head under the sink where she pulls out a roll of bin bags. 'It could do with a little bleach or an anti-bac wipe, that bin.'

'I said I'll do it in a minute.' I'm talking to myself, clearly, as she puts on a pair of rubber gloves.

'I know you will. I'm just mentioning that bins get a bit stinky if you don't give them a wipe down every now and again.'

'Stinky bins, got it,' I say. 'Polly was just off to get changed, weren't you, Pol?' Polly glares at me but finally removes herself from the sofa.

There are no clean mugs in the cupboard and I haven't put the dishwasher on yet so I grab two dirty mugs from the worktop and dunk them in the sink. Mum has stopped anti-bac-ing the bin for a moment and is looking at me with concern.

'I was going to sort the dishes and everything in a minute,' I say, without meeting her eye. 'We've had a bit of a lazy morning.'

'I can see that,' she says. There's an awkward silence as I strain two teabags with a spoon then Mum claps her hands together and says, 'Right. I'll put the lunch on. I've cooked most of it already so it should be ready for two-ish, which gives us a chance to spruce the place up a bit after our cuppa.'

'Brillo,' I say, putting their teas on the dining table next to mine before giving her a sarcastic double thumbs up.

Dad puts what looks like a crumble in the fridge before putting an arm around me. He is deliberately ignoring the state of the house, which makes me feel as though he is in my corner. 'How are you, love? All set for work tomorrow?'

I lean my head on his shoulder. 'Yeah. I'm fine.'

'Is that fine or fine fine? When your mother says she's fine I know things are far from fine.' He looks over at Mum, but she can't hear him because she's got the hoover on and is grumbling about the tiny pieces of toys she can see in the cylinder. She stares closer at the mass of hair and fluff. 'It looks like tiny shards of *glass* in there. Glass! Please tell me you didn't use this to clear up something you broke?' *Something I broke.* Because it's always my fault.

With Dad's eyes on me, I feel suddenly as though I might cry. I'm *not* fine but I don't want to tell him I'm not fine because it might tip me over the crying edge. Crying always leaves me feeling drained, as though I could sleep for a week, and I definitely can't sleep for a week. I can barely sleep for a night. Just after midnight last night Ted had a nightmare. *Keep the giraffe out!* he kept repeating, over and over as I wiped the sweat from his brow, with absolutely no idea what he was going on about. It was only after an hour of him whimpering about closing all the doors that I realized he had misunderstood me when I had mentioned keeping the *draught* out. If I'm this tired today, I have no idea how I'm going to function tomorrow.

Polly returns downstairs wearing what is essentially a cleaner version of what she's just changed out of. Emmy sent me a video not long before the accident of Polly and two friends doing a Tik-Tok dance in crop tops and tracksuit bottoms, all of them looking like Sporty Spice just with bigger eyebrows. Polly didn't even know who Mel C was when I mentioned it, making me feel about ninety-seven.

She is hovering in front of me and her grandad. 'Aunty Beth, can I have a sleepover at Rosie's next Friday?'

I narrow my eyes. Though it's possible she's received this invite from Rosie in the five minutes she's been upstairs, I suspect she was deliberately waiting until her nan and grandad got here before asking. Maybe this is part of my probation, another test. What is the protocol for teenagers and sleepovers? At fourteen, I imagine it's fine, but in the absence of a taking-on-two-kids induction pack, I can't check that my answer is right.

'Oh. I don't know.'

'Michaela's going. And Sam. Sam*antha*, obviously,' she laughs. Her face is lit up, which immediately makes me want to say yes to whatever she's asking. I wonder if she knows the happy face is so much more effective than the angry silence.

'Right, well, if you let me have a number for Rosie's mum or dad, I'll have a quick word. I can't see why it would be a problem though.'

She punches the air in triumph. 'Can you text rather than phone her mum though? Like, don't make it a big deal? It's just a sleepover.'

'I know,' I say. 'I'm just, *like*, trying to be responsible by checking in with another adult.' I am saying all this for Mum's benefit. The responsible tone does not come naturally to me and I wonder if it's something you have to stand in front of a mirror to practise.

Polly is still querying my mode of contact. 'Can you be responsible by text though? I've just WhatsApp-ed you Rosie's mum's mobile number. She's called Suzy. Can you do it today?'

'Yep,' I say.

'In a minute?'

'Oh my god, OK. I'll do it *right now*.' I grab my phone and compose a quick message checking it isn't going to be too much of an inconvenience for Polly to stay over. I've not even put my phone down before the reply comes back.

Of course it's not a problem, I'll make sure they get some sleep!
Suzy x.

I show Polly the message. Mum, who has stopped vacuuming to make the gravy, comes over and strokes two strands of hair away from Polly's eyes. 'I don't know how you cope with hair in front of your face like that, it would drive me potty. A sleepover sounds fun, love? It'll be good for you to get out and do something different with your friends.'

'Sleepover!' Ted runs over, his eyes wide.

I pick him up. He smells of hula hoops and orange squash. 'Well, your sister is going for a sleepover next weekend, at her friend's house. Maybe we could do something fun, just us two?' Exactly what, I have no idea.

He shakes his head. 'Ted have a sleepover.' Great. Something else he will be disappointed about that I won't know how to make better.

Mum hands me a sponge and nods towards the sink. I follow with my feet. It's quite remarkable how she does that, turns up and immediately takes charge. She has paused and restacked the dishwasher – clearly however I loaded it was wrong – and filled the bowl to wash everything else, the first few glasses with soapy suds now upside down on the draining board. I want to be cross at the bossiness of it, but I am relieved more than anything. I don't often feel fussed about mess, but the state of things here has been starting to put me on edge.

'Ted can come to ours for the night next Friday,' Mum says. It's more statement than question.

'Oh right. Yeah, I suppose.' I can't imagine what a night to myself would look like now. Dad says something I can't hear. 'What was that, Dad?'

He's perched on the edge of Doug's armchair with Ted at his feet, about to experience the fire engine with dodgy doors trauma for himself. 'I said you should do something with Jory. Your mum and I, we were just saying on the way over that it's a shame you've not seen so much of each other lately.'

'Unsurprisingly I've had less time to go to the pub recently. Major life events and all.' I gesture towards Ted.

It's hard to believe I used to crash into Sunday lunch just as food was being served, Emmy's roast dinner plus a can of coke providing the best hangover cure in the world, bar none, as Doug quizzed me on my shambles of a love-life and teased me over whatever Instagram posts I'd been tagged in the night before. The Glory Days, for more reasons than I could have known.

Mum tuts as she sticks her head out the back door. 'I agree with your dad that you should make more time to see Jory but it's no bad thing that you've stopped going to the pub all the time. I can see you've been making up for it here. Did you miss the glass recycling as well as the bins?'

'No,' I say.

'That's *all* from this week then?'

There's no point in lying. 'Yes, Mother. Christ, if I'd known I was having an inspection, I would have had a tidy-up.' It's three wine bottles, tops, and I haven't even been opening a bottle until Ted is in bed. Well, except on the night he wanted the Fireman Sam and snake story twice. I won't tell Mum about taking a glass of red wine upstairs. She'll only worry about the carpet.

'A little tidy-up wouldn't go amiss, love,' Mum continues. 'And your dad's just reminding you not to let your friendship go.' She puts a weird emphasis on *friendship*. 'There aren't many boys like Jory, you know.' She still talks about him like he's a sixth-former, not a history teacher who has his own class of sixth-formers.

'Yes, yes, OK. You've made your point. I'll see if he's free on Friday when Ted's at yours, if that gets you pair off my back.'

Dad smiles. 'That's good, love. I've got a lot of time for Jory. He's always made sure you've got home safely whenever you've been paraplegic.'

'Paralytic,' I say.

'Don't be clever. I must say, I'm surprised he hasn't been snapped up by a nice young lady by now. Or a man. Whichever is his preference. Perhaps it's both. That's very trendy these days, isn't it?'

I don't answer, unwilling to get into another conversation about whether Jory is gay, or has a secret girlfriend, or – as they suggest periodically – is waiting for me. Which is rubbish, as I've told them time and again for the past twenty-something years. I'm never going to tell them that we almost went there once because it would only add fuel to a fire that isn't even a fire. Besides, Jory and I made a pact to never let it (almost) happen again, to avoid things getting weird between us. We combated the initial awkwardness with humour and now the 'Winter of 2015' only ever gets mentioned sporadically, usually when one of us (me) has been drinking. I do think about it sometimes. A single scene in an otherwise hazy night, so vivid I'm beginning to wonder whether I dreamed it.

'Do you want me to lay the table?' I ask, hoping Mum says no.

She shakes her head. 'I think I'll warm the plates first, but you could sort some of this washing out. Has that load in the machine been done?'

'Yep.' I don't mention that it was done two days ago and has been sitting there since.

'Shall we get it on the line then? It's good drying weather.'

'OK.' I open the machine and bundle the damp clothes into my arms.

'Where's the basket?' Mum asks.

'No idea.'

'Well, how are you going to put the washing out and get it back in again without a basket?' She says this as though it is the craziest thing she's ever heard.

'Like this,' I say, as I cling to the bundle and walk gingerly to the back door, willing the little socks that are poking out to stay bundled so I can prove a pointless point.

I can hear Mum scoffing behind me. 'Honestly, you do make things hard for yourself. Doesn't she, Jim? She's putting the washing out *without a basket* now. Whatever next!'

'I'm sure it will still dry, love,' Dad says. 'Leave her be.'

9

I make it a metre down the garden path before I drop a pair of Ted's pants, losing a further pair as I stoop to retrieve the first pair. I curse out loud, really hoping Mum isn't watching.

'Oh dear, one of those days, is it?'

I jump at the volume of the voice coming over the fence. It's Albert from next door. 'Jesus Christ, Albert, you frightened me.'

'Sorry, was I loud? My hearing aid's turned down.' He fiddles with it and it beeps. 'It's most peculiar. I don't seem to have trouble hearing certain things, like the television, but voices are harder. I never know if I'm shouting.'

I can't say I'm surprised to learn he has no trouble hearing his television when I have no trouble hearing his television either. I pick the stray pants back up and place the whole bundle on the garden bench before expanding the rotary line on the lawn. More socks and pants fall through the gap in the bench and I concede that Mum has won this one. I do need a basket.

I can feel eyes on me. Albert hasn't made small talk with me before and I desperately want to say something friendly but I'm not sure what to go in with. He beats me to it, studying me over the top of his glasses. 'How are you getting on then?'

'Oh we're doing all right, thanks,' I say. 'How are you?' A peg snaps in my hand, a little plastic shard pinging across the lawn.

He shrugs. 'I'm fine. To tell you the truth, I've had problems with my bowels this week but a young lady like you doesn't want to hear about the workings – or not – of a geriatric bowel.'

I laugh and wave my hand to show it's fine. It's quite nice to be called a young lady. Besides, chat about a geriatric bowel is still favourable to being nagged about my domestic shortcomings by Mum. 'Well, I'm very sorry to hear that. Is there not something you can take to, erm, help?'

'Oh, I'm sure there is,' he says. 'But they're saying it's my diet, you see. All these freezer meals I get delivered on a Wednesday, not good for my digestion. My knee's been giving me gyp, too. Last year it was the other knee. It's high time they sent me to the knacker's yard.'

'Nonsense. I must say, your freezer meals sound marvellous. I could use some of those for Polly and Ted.'

'They're tasty enough. I did have to phone to ask them to stop trying to poison me after they started doing Meat-free Mondays but aside from that I can't complain. At least they're quick and easy. I imagine it's hard work thinking of things to make for dinner every day.'

I nod, though I've only really 'made' a handful of dinners. Another peg snaps between my fingers. Albert looks at the broken peg but doesn't mention it. 'How are the children doing? All still a terrible shock, I'm sure. Is there any update on Emmy? Sorry, you don't have to answer, you've probably not got time to be interrogated by an old codger like me.'

I fiddle with the snapped peg, the tiny spring digging into the palm of my hand where it has come away from the bright pink plastic. Mum and I were so excited during a recent hospital visit after we spotted Emmy's eye twitching, only to be told by Dr Hargreaves that it was more than likely involuntary and not a deliberate attempt by her to communicate with us. She is still sitting at the lowest possible score on the coma scale. I shake my head. 'There's not really any change, with Emmy. Ted's doing as

OK as can be expected, I think. Obviously he's missing his mum and his dad but young kids are extraordinarily resilient. It's not quite as easy to tell with his big sister. Teenagers, you know,' I say.

Albert looks away for a moment, his eyes focused towards the rose bushes at the bottom of his garden. 'I'm afraid I don't know very much about teenagers. My wife Mavis and I, we never had children.'

'Oh.' I pause, trying to find the appropriate response. 'I don't know if I should say I'm sorry to hear that or not, Albert. Did you want to have children?'

He nods. 'We did, dear. We lost our baby in the summer of 1956. A little boy. We were going to call him Thomas. Mavis wasn't able to fall pregnant after that.'

'Well, I'm definitely sorry then. That's so sad,' I say.

'It is but we had a long and very happy life together. I have been a grumpy old git since she died, of course, but that's nothing when I think of poor Douglas and your sister. I'm not a religious man but I have been praying for Emmy.'

Now that he's mentioned Mavis, I have a vague memory of Emmy telling me that the lady next door had died and that Albert was all on his own. Had she told me about them losing a baby? Possibly. I'm ashamed to admit that my sister warbling on about an elderly lady I didn't know having died and how she was worried about the widower left behind hadn't meant an awful lot to me then. Albert was just the curtain-twitcher next door, one I assumed was judging me, following my drunken misadventures on his doorstep. I'd never even spoken to him until he brought the snowdrops round. It's time to bite the bullet.

'Albert, I'm very sorry about the time I was sick in your plant pot.'

He laughs then, a deep laugh from the belly that lights his face up and crinkles his eyes in the corners underneath his glasses. It's so loud that Mum pops her head out of the door to see what the fuss is about. She waves hello to Albert, who waves back before wiping a tear from his cheek. Mum hovers on the patio.

'How are you getting on with that washing, Beth? Lunch is nearly ready.'

'OK, I'm nearly done,' I say, grabbing a pair of jeans from the bench to peg up. I turn back towards the fence. 'It's *not* funny, Albert. I'm mortified,' I say, but a smile has spread across my face, too.

'There's no need to apologize, dear. I'm only laughing because you have avoided looking at me since then. I was beginning to wonder if you would ever mention it.'

'Oh god. I wanted to but I didn't know what to say. Emmy and Doug were *furious* with me. Said I was a disgrace. In my defence, I had been on a *very* bad date, which set in motion a much higher than normal number of wines in a dangerously short window of time. I didn't mean to fall on top of your plant pot and when I landed, the sick, well, it just sort of fell out.'

'I'm not sure my lavender ever recovered,' he says. His eyes are twinkling and he looks mischievous, a different man entirely to the one I've been picturing behind the curtain.

I groan. 'Honestly, I really did intend to knock on your door to apologize the morning after but I was so hungover and ashamed, I just couldn't do it, and after that, I thought the moment had gone. I was planning on just avoiding you for ever, to be honest.'

He is studying me intently, a bemused expression on his face.

'What?' I say.

'You're very different to your sister but also a lot like her, at the same time. It's rather fascinating.'

I nod. 'People tell us this a lot. Chalk and cheese. She's the better half of our cheesy chalk, obviously.'

'Well, she speaks very highly of you too, you know.'

'You have to say that. I bet she's always moaning about me.'

He shakes his head. 'Not at all. I do remember that she wasn't exactly complimentary about you after you vomited on my door-step, but she says ever such nice things about you, usually. She thinks settling down with a nice young man would be the making of you.'

'Oh well, never mind. There's not much chance of that now.' I peg up the last of the washing, silently cursing as a third peg snaps. 'I'd better go in for my dinner before I get told off by my mum.'

He smiles. 'Yes, I mustn't keep you any longer. It's been very nice to chat to you at last.'

'You too. I really am sorry about the lavender incident.'

'A peg bag is what you need,' he says.

'Sorry?'

'A peg bag. If you get a weatherproof one you can keep the pegs in it, outside on the line. Stops them going brittle and snap-ping. Mavis taught me that.' He is proud of this tip, I can tell.

'Oh, right. A peg bag. Thanks. Do you get a frozen roast din-ner on Sundays?' I am joking but he nods.

'Beef today. It's not bad, grey roast potatoes aside. And it's ready after five minutes in the microwave.'

'Well, um – enjoy. See you later.' I head back inside, where I find Mum, Dad, Polly and Ted already seated at the table. I sit next to Ted, who has taken all the vegetables off his plate and stuffed them under the tablecloth. Where has a tablecloth come from? Mum must have searched for it. I reach across for the carrots. I don't see the point in tablecloths. It's much easier to wipe a table after eating than it is to wash a huge piece of fabric that inevita-bly ends up stained with gravy. Then again, as someone who thinks eating a bowl of Coco Pops on the sofa is a decent evening meal arrangement, perhaps I'm not the target tablecloth market.

Mum has persuaded Polly to put her phone down for lunch. Polly doesn't seem to complain when her nan asks her to do something.

'This looks lovely, Mum,' I say. Dad and Polly murmur their agreement.

Mum performs her usual modest brush-off. 'I've made far too much again. It's hard – adjusting the portions for . . . well, you know.'

I do know. She has got used to cooking for seven. Emmy bought an extending dining table that seated eight compared to the usual six once you put the middle panel in. Doug always joked that they only ever extended it for Hungover Aunty Beth, as me turning up on a Sunday, alongside Mum and Dad, made us a seven. Now there is no need for the middle panel at all. We are a five. Even with Emmy back, something we are keeping focused on, we will be a family member short for the middle table panel.

Mum is piling seconds on to plates that are still half full with firsts. I put my hand up to tell her I don't need any more, but a large serving of cauliflower cheese comes my way anyway.

'It's good to see Ted eating a proper meal, full of goodness,' she says.

I can't help but think this logic is flawed, noting he is eating nothing but Yorkshire puddings. However, the fact his plate at least started out with peas and carrots on (before he squashed them into a pile of mush beneath the tablecloth) seems to make Mum happy.

'Did you get round to phoning the bank, Dad?' I ask. The mood around the table is suddenly tenser and I regret changing the subject from Ted's vitamin intake.

Mum shakes her head at me as if to signal *Not the time*. 'He doesn't need to phone the bank, love. We've sorted all that. More gravy?' She waves the jug around.

'But what about that appointment letter?'

Dad shrugs; he doesn't know. 'I didn't phone them again, no. I didn't see the point. I'd already phoned once asking for the mortgage application to be paused. Whether that letter was an old one or there was just a mistake with the date it doesn't really matter now, does it?'

'Well, no, but the letter—'

Mum cuts me off. 'We know where they were going because they told us.' She looks at Polly. 'Your dad had even taken a day off work, hadn't he? So it must have been important.'

Polly nods but is silent, pushing food around her plate.

'I know that's what they said but it still doesn't answer why an old or incorrectly typed appointment letter was hidden in a drawer,' I say.

'It wasn't *hidden*, love. Don't be so dramatic. It probably just found its way in there with the shopping bags when Emmy put them away. Honestly, you're creating a mystery when there isn't one.'

'Am I?'

Polly has got up from the table. 'I think I'll have my pudding later, Nan. I'm a bit tired.'

Mum looks up, concerned. 'You do look a bit peaky, actually. You go have a lie-down and I'll save you a nice big bit.'

'Ted have big bit too!' Ted's not braved anything other than Yorkshires but will still get a large helping of crumble I'm sure. I keep my eyes on Polly as she picks up her phone and heads back upstairs. How can it only be me who thinks she's acting strangely? Every time I mention the letter she finds a reason to leave.

Dad is watching me, watching her. He puts a hand on my shoulder as he reaches over to help Mum clear the dishes, making space for the crumble. 'Perhaps the letter is a reminder of why her mum and dad were where they were and she doesn't want to think about it. Which would make sense, don't you think?'

'Of course, but why was it – oh, forget it,' I say.

'Exactly, let's forget it. I've been making my way through sorting as much of Doug's admin as I can, and I have to say, it's not been a pleasant task. Let's not find additional things to fret about. It's pudding time, anyway.'

Ted bangs his spoon on the table. 'My dad's called Doug.' He says this as though it's a coincidence we're talking about another Doug. 'And he's deaded.'

Mum freezes as she makes her way over, holding the first two bowls of crumble. Ted has been coming out with a lot of strange things as he tries to make sense of his dad being gone but he usually just says that he misses him, or that he has gone to the sky. *Deaded* is the bluntest we've heard to date.

'Do you want custard or cream, sweetheart?' Mum asks him.

Ted frowns.

'That's a silly question, isn't it?' she says.

'Silly Nanny!' he says and we all laugh, relieved by the lightness of it. It is indeed a silly question. Ted will have both custard and cream because that's what his dad used to have and he wants to be just like his dad.

Mum is telling me how she's plated up a decent portion for Polly but there is still plenty left and that maybe we could have it tomorrow for our pudding, or I could take some into work for my first day back. I'm about to ask whether double-heated crumble could kill us the same way that rice can when I have an idea.

'Were there potatoes left, too?' I ask.

'Well, yes, but what on earth are you going to have them with tomorrow?'

I abandon my crumble and hover my hand over the bowl with the potatoes in. Still hot. Lovely. 'I'm not going to have them tomorrow.'

Mum looks at me, puzzled, but doesn't object. I dish up a bowl of crumble and cover both that and the potato bowl with foil before carrying them to the front door. Nobody should have to make do with grey potatoes.

10

'How's the first day back going?' Jory asks.

'Fantastic. It's everything I dreamed it would be and more.'

He laughs. I'm taking my lunch break early so I can talk to him on his. As I leave my desk I lower my voice, which denies Malcolm, who is suddenly concentrating very hard on his computer screen, his eavesdropping fix. Malcolm is perplexed by the idea of a platonic relationship between members of the opposite sex, so much so that when I mentioned going to the pub with Jory, he remarked that it was 'a wonder anyone knows where they stand these days'. I don't tell Malcolm that I've seen him parking a hundred yards down the road, waiting for Bev, the receptionist from the office next door, to get in, nor that I can't help but wonder whether his wife of thirty years *knows where she stands*. It's none of my business.

It's a lot warmer than it was when I arrived this morning and I cradle the phone to my ear with one shoulder so I can wriggle out of my cardigan. It's quite common for Jory not to return my calls until after the school day but I prepped him with a message as soon as I woke up, threatening to withdraw our best-friendship if he didn't support my return to work following a family bereavement, particularly as my only other pillar of support is in a coma. There wasn't a lot he could say to that.

'I'm very glad to hear you're loving life at work once more,' he says. 'Did you have to give Malcolm a welcome-back cuddle?'

I crinkle my nose. 'Ew, absolutely not. Honestly, I don't think he likes me very much. His latest gripe is how women are trying to take over the world, starting with Sky Sports News presenters. If he says "PC Brigade" one more time I might put his PC up his—' I cough as I pass a colleague on their way into the building. 'How's your day going, anyway? Any school scandal?'

'Nothing juicy, I'm afraid,' Jory sounds distracted, as though he's walking somewhere. 'I'll be ten minutes. Sorry, Beth. You were saying?'

I raise an eyebrow. 'Oh, don't let me keep you. It's only the first proper chat we've had this week.'

It's shady on the bench at the front of the office so I head to the back of the building and perch on a drystone wall separating the 'rural business park' (a grand total of three offices) from a working farm. Jory is grovelling and I smile as I open a packet of beef and onion Monster Munch, enjoying hearing him sweat it out a little while longer.

'I know, sorry, I am *all* ears – I just wish we could chat in the evenings or at the weekend, work days are not ideal. It would be nice to see you properly. I'm not going sea-swimming in my pants again, though. It took me three days to warm up.'

'I must say I'm surprised to hear that, coming from a seasoned surfer dude such as yourself. I enjoyed it too, you know I did. We'll do another beach walk or something again soon, I promise. I really miss you. There's just been a lot going on at home.'

'I know. How was Polly this morning?'

'Why?' I feel my chest tightening.

He lowers his voice. 'Because her dad has died, her mum's in hospital, she's just gone back to school and on top of all that, her slightly batty aunty is in charge of dinners . . .'

I exhale, puffing my cheeks out. 'Sorry. It's just with you working at the school I worry "How's Polly?" questions are loaded. You would tell me if you heard something about her, wouldn't you?'

'No,' he says. 'But that's only because it wouldn't be my place to, as I've told you. Her form tutor, Mrs Sandford, or her head of year would raise any concerns with you if they had them. You have to trust the system.'

I pout even though he can't see it. 'I don't see why you can't do a bit of incognito investigating in the staffroom and report back to me. I won't grass you up.' I am being deadly serious. I don't trust any systems.

'Beth, if ever you are worried about Polly's behaviour, phone the school. Make an appointment. I don't teach her and I'm certainly not going on a spy mission for you – it would be unethical and unprofessional.'

'Damn your professionalism,' I mutter.

'There is nothing wrong with taking pride in your job. You should try it some time.'

'Good one. I'm back here at work, aren't I?' I say.

'That's true. I must admit I was surprised when you said you were going back so soon. Nobody would have blamed you, you know, if you needed a longer break.' He is starting to sound like my dad.

'Yeah, well, it felt like the right thing to do. It's *intense*, being at Emmy and Doug's 24/7. Besides, it's only part-time. For the moment, anyway.' I explain how Malcolm has agreed I can work three days a week to start with, while Ted gets used to being back at nursery, and we're following a rota for keeping Emmy company. Every day starts with Mum confirming who is visiting the hospital and ends with whoever has visited giving an update on how Emmy is doing, the rest of us getting our hopes up in between. We have been keeping each other going with 'no news is good news' reassurances but I've been feeling increasingly worried that no news means no recovery.

'How did you get on this morning, getting Ted to nursery? Were you on time?' Jory knows I am never on time.

'Of course not. Honestly, Jor, getting us both out of the door this morning was such a mission. I think I'm going to have to start washing my hair the night before. *How* I used to struggle to get just myself up and out of the house, I'll never know. I had bugger all to do in the mornings but still ran out of time. What was wrong with me?'

'I suspect it had something to do with you being one of those weird alarm-snoozers.'

We are going over old ground with this debate. '*Normal* people don't wake up and hop out of bed like Grandpa Joe on his way to the chocolate factory. We put a pillow over our heads and wish it was the weekend.' I realize I'm now talking about a past version of myself, having not snoozed an alarm in weeks.

'Which bit took so long this morning then?'

All of it, I think, but I can't expect him to understand what it's like getting a toddler ready for nursery while also shouting at a teenager who seems permanently aggrieved to be sharing the same air as me. None of it sounds plausible from the outside. I never appreciated how the morning could go downhill in an instant because jam has been spread the wrong way on Ted's toast, or he doesn't want to put his trousers on, or the sun is too sunny.

I tell Jory he wouldn't understand and he says, 'Try me,' but I don't have the energy. Instead, I ask him what he's going to have for lunch as I pick at the sorry excuse for mine. At least Ted's lunch is sorted by nursery, which affords me a mini-break from what feels like a hundred days of making cheesy sauce soldiers. It's something of a shift, coming to work for a break, when I used to do my best to get out of coming to work at all. It's been almost meditative working my way through checklists paperclipped to the front of finance proposals, making sure all the necessary accounts are attached. This morning has allowed me a few hours to do something other than fret about my sister and panic about whether Polly's recent behaviour is to be expected or whether I am staring red flags in the face. I tell Jory that she spends all day on her phone.

'Well, that's definitely not an alarm bell in itself. One of our Year 12s walked straight into a glass door last week because she was watching something on YouTube. Did you ever get to the bottom of that letter about the appointment?'

'No!' I say. 'And nobody's listening to me. When I pleaded with Dad to phone up, just to double check, Mum intervened, as is her top skill, to say I was talking nonsense and creating problems where there aren't any. Emmy told Mum and Dad, just as she told me, that she and Doug were off for a mortgage appointment on the day of the accident, which is why they needed a babysitter. Therefore, there is no mystery.'

'Well then, maybe there isn't?'

I think Jory must be in the staffroom as I can hear another voice.

'Hmm, maybe. I dunno.' Jory must have covered the phone or moved it away from his ear as his talking has become muffled. I can just about make out him telling someone that he'll be there in a sec.

'It sounds busy there. Do you need to go?'

'I do have to go now, sorry, Beth. I've not eaten yet. But I'm really glad your first day back is going OK.'

'OK. Can I hear someone badgering you to be their sandwich buddy? Who is it?'

'Yep. OK then.'

'OK then what? Who is it?' I repeat. His voice has changed, which can only mean that someone is listening to his side of the conversation, which is why he's gone all weird. The penny drops. The last time we went to the pub, he told me – before my memory of the evening gets cloudy – that he thought another teacher might be interested in him, a suspicion corroborated by Polly,

who made a throwaway comment about Miss Greenaway fancy-
ing Mr Clarke and 'everyone knowing it'.

'It's Sadie Greenaway, isn't it? Are you eating your sandwiches
together? That's cute.' I know I ought not to tease him because
he'll be going red, blotches creeping from his neck up to his
cheeks, but I can't help it. 'Don't let me keep you, we'll catch up
later. Make sure you haven't got any rocket in your teeth and that
you've got a Tic Tac for after.'

'Goodbye, Beth.' He hangs up and I feel a bit flat. *Miss Greenaway fancies Mr Clarke.* At least he has someone to eat his lunch
with. I could go and mingle in the work kitchen upstairs. Make
the effort. The problem is, I don't want to. Particularly not today,
on my first day back, when people don't know what to say so
either opt for a quick 'Sorry to hear the news' (with no eye contact) or say absolutely nothing, despite my being certain that
they've been talking about nothing else the whole time I've not
been here. The crash was big news locally and people seem to
thrive off the drama of it. I can't blame them. If it had been someone else from the office's family, I would have been swept up in the
buzz of it, too.

I put my half-eaten Wagon Wheel back in its wrapper and
twist to look in the field behind me. We used to come lambing
somewhere near here as kids. Mum's got a photo in an album at
home of Emmy around nine or ten wearing dungarees, holding a
tiny and still slippery lamb against her chest, beaming. I am
standing behind her in the photo, scowling with my arms folded,
having decided age six or seven that lambing was rubbish. I
wanted to do an urban and street dance class so I could learn
some moves to TLC songs but urban and street dance groups
hadn't reached St Newth then (or now, probably) so I had to
stand in a shed watching lambs being born instead.

I check my phone, wondering if Jory is enjoying his flirty lunch
break with Sadie in the staffroom. I type a message to that effect

but when I read it back it sounds like I'm jealous so I delete it (because I'm not jealous). I'll ask him later. Or I might not. I'm not bothered either way.

The afternoon flies by in a blur of phone calls, spreadsheets and coffees. On my way out, I get held up by Malcolm, who decides that 5 p.m. is an appropriate time to start mansplaining the strong residual values of tractors. 'There's less risk, you see, Beth. If it all goes tits up, we still have an asset that's worth something.' I don't tell him that I learned all of this on the e-induction I was made to do, complete with a test at the end, because I wager I'll escape quicker if I let him think he's teaching me something new, even though he isn't. His fascinating insight still makes me late.

By the time I arrive at nursery, the car park is packed and I have to do what feels like a fifty-point turn to squeeze Emmy's car into the only remaining space between a people carrier and a shed with a sign reading: *Caution! Free range children!*

I ring the bell, flustered and sweaty. A note on the door tells me it's Fancy Dress Friday this week. Luckily Ted doesn't go to nursery on a Friday. I struggle to work out which normal clothes to put him in, let alone costumes. I haven't helped myself by getting his normal clothes mixed up with clothes from the next-size-up drawer. Every morning is now a lucky dip, size wise, and Mum says she's going to have to come over and reorganize things.

A nursery worker in a yellow Happy Chicks T-shirt opens the door.

'Hello. Who are you here to collect?'

'Ted Lander.' I'm trying my best not to pant from all the rushing.

'And the password?'

Balls. 'I can't remember.' I move myself to one side to let a snake of parents and toddlers out.

She looks behind her, panicked. 'I'm not allowed to let you in without a password. I'm so sorry. It's my first week and I'm just getting to know everyone.'

I smile to show I understand. When it comes to kids and security, it's better to be safe than sorry, so I can't be annoyed with her for following the correct procedure. I rack my brains for a password. I don't remember being given one. 'I totally understand. Don't worry. Do you want to go and ask someone? They'll know to expect me as I dropped him off this morning.'

Just as she turns to find someone else, a nursery worker I chatted to at drop-off appears. She looks between the two of us. 'Everything all right, Lauren?'

Lauren nods her head in my direction. 'Ted's mum is here but she can't remember the password.'

There is an awkward exchange of glances. Red faces. Lauren realizes at once that she must have misunderstood the situation and proceeds by digging a deeper hole. 'Sorry, I just assumed – are you his step-mum?'

I consider telling her that yes, I am his step-mum, just to bring this painful exchange to an end. However, I might see her again in the weeks to come so I decide to treat it like ripping off a plaster. 'No, I'm Ted's aunty, but I've been taking care of him since March, since his dad died. His mum is very poorly in hospital.' I step gingerly inside the building now that I've got through security.

'Oh my god, I am *so* sorry.' Her eyes are wide and I can see the creeping embarrassment on her face, the wish for the ground to swallow her up whole. I am eager to make her feel better. There is nothing worse than the abject horror of putting your foot in it. I remember the torture of having to sit through an eye test after I'd asked the optometrist whether she knew what she was having. It was a boy, she said, and she knew this because she'd had him thirteen months before. It still brings me out in an all-over cringe.

I wave my hand to dismiss her concerns. 'Honestly, it's fine – you weren't to know. Besides, Ted looks a lot like his mum and I look a bit like her too so it's an easy assumption to make. Please don't worry.'

She smiles weakly, evidently still mortified. The uncomfortable pause that follows is interrupted by a flash of blond curls as Ted runs out of the rainbow room downstairs, his key worker Natalie hot on his heels. Natalie is the one who helped us work out a return-to-nursery plan.

'Good to see you, Beth. Ted shot up and ran to the door, kicking over the train track we've been building. It caught me by surprise.' She laughs. She stops laughing when she catches wind of the atmosphere.

Ted is looking behind me at the door, his smile wide. 'Mummy's here!' He looks up at Natalie, excitement on his face.

'Oh, Ted. I . . .' Natalie closes her mouth, waiting for my response.

I crouch beside him. 'Hey, Ted. Aunty Beth's come to take you home.' I reach out my hand, but he doesn't take it. He is still looking at the door.

'My mummy's here,' he says, his brow furrowed. Excitement has shifted to confusion.

'Your mummy isn't here, Ted,' I say.

He is quiet, his bottom lip wobbling. 'Ted's mummy is here,' he whispers.

That's what he heard, when he was playing trains in the rainbow room. Even worse than seeing the misunderstanding unfold between a group of adults out here in the hallway, he heard *Ted's mum is here* and believed, for the briefest but loveliest of moments, that she was. He had dropped what he was doing and run to his mummy, only to discover me instead. He is cross with me, I can tell. I am not who he wants.

I put my hands on his shoulders and move him gently to one side so the next wave of parents and children on their way in and out can get past. Natalie, Lauren and the other one, the three of them standing as a trio of yellow Happy Chicks T-shirts, are all visibly upset by what's happened. All eyes seem to be on me to fix it, to make it better, which of course I can't. Ted is crying. Even more dreadful than the loud tantrum sort of crying I've been getting used to, these tears are small and silent.

'Could somebody grab his bag and coat for me please?' Natalie rushes off to get them. 'And maybe a tissue?' I call after her.

Ted's nose is running and he wipes it on the sleeve of his Thomas the Tank Engine jumper. I open my arms out wide and he steps into them, his head bowed and shoulders shaking. When Natalie returns, I stand and take Ted's bag and coat from her before picking him up. It's the best way of getting us out of here, pronto.

'Are you going to say bye, buddy?' He doesn't answer, his face still buried in my shoulder. I steer us out of the door then turn back to the trio in the hallway, all of them looking towards us but none of them meeting my eye. 'We'll see you Thursday. Could somebody message me the password or let me know how to set a new one? I'll need to let his nan know, too . . .'

There are murmurs of agreement and a lot of nodding, everyone keen to avoid the same upset in future.

I carry Ted out to the car and strap him into his seat. He has stopped crying and is staring straight ahead now, his thumb in his mouth and his index finger stroking his nose.

'Do you want Mr Trunky, Ted? I think he's missed you.' I pick up the cuddly elephant from the front seat and poke his trunk over the headrest, putting on a silly deep voice: 'I've missed you, Ted.' He reaches out his hands and takes Mr Trunky without even a hint of a smile.

It has started to rain and I sit watching the drops collect on the windscreen for a moment before I flick the wipers on and start the engine. I take out one of the tissues Natalie fetched for Ted and blow my nose before looking in the mirror and dabbing at my mascara, which is running. Ted's favourite CBeebies CD comes on and I leave it playing, even though I know there's little chance of him singing along.

'Come on then, champ. Let's get you home.'

Home, I think, as I pull out of the car park. Except it's not my home, and it's not Ted's home either, not without his mum and dad in it.

11

It's late Friday afternoon when Mum calls in a fluster to report that Dr Hargreaves has been on the phone with some news. Two nurses, on two separate rounds, have observed movement in the little finger of Emmy's right hand. 'Movement, Beth! "Less like a twitch and more like a wiggle," the nurse said. *A wiggle*!' Dr Hargreaves also told Mum that it's very important for us not to get carried away, but we are, of course, all getting completely carried away and have decided we must visit the hospital immediately to witness this miracle for ourselves.

Dad's car is outside in minutes, just as Polly arrives home from school. She flies through the door in a hurry, eager to get changed so she can head over to Rosie's for the sleepover, but as soon as we fill her in on the finger movement update she texts Rosie to say she'll be over once she's seen her mum. I send a quick message to Jory to let him know I might be slightly later getting to the pub than originally planned but I'll keep him posted.

There is an energy in the car as we drive out of the village, a livelier level of chat than I can remember in a long time.

'It doesn't mean she's going to get better,' Dad says. 'We all know that, don't we?'

'Yes, but it's a good sign, isn't it, Jim?' Mum turns to face him.

'It's a bloody good sign.' Dad holds his hand out and Mum squeezes it. 'Who wants to choose a song?'

'Meeeeeee!' Ted throws an elbow in my face as he begins reeling off every song he knows. I'm wedged between him and Polly in the back seat and even Polly voices a request, though I have to ask her to choose another when I realize it's one about gun crime, drugs and prostitution.

Mum is staring blankly at the car stereo. 'How do I get the songs on, Jim?'

Dad points at the glove box. 'You need to put Spotty-fy on. There's a lead in there.'

Mum looks at him, agog. 'How do you know about leads and Spotty-fies?'

'Because Beth sometimes puts songs on for me when we're doing this journey. All through her phone. Like magic, it is.' He looks at me in his rear-view mirror. 'Can you do that thing with the set list, love?'

'It's a *playlist*, as I tell you every week, but OK.' I take the lead from Mum and press play on the first of Ted's picks. Justin Fletcher, who Ted likes watching on telly, starts singing about hamburgers and cheeseburgers to the tune of 'Macarena' and, despite it being the single worst thing I've ever heard, I join in.

Dad instructs us to get out so we can head straight upstairs to Emmy while he fights for a parking space. We race up to the ward and as we approach the nurses' station, a bounce in our step and grins on our faces, it becomes apparent that the nurses' level of excitement is significantly lower than our own. Sofie, one of the two nurses who observed Emmy's finger movement, comes to speak to us on her way out of the unit, hurrying to take a break she is no doubt already supposed to be on.

'What sort of movement was it, love? Can you show us?' Mum stares intently at her finger.

'Uh, sure. Like this.' She holds out one hand and keeps it still apart from her little finger, which she lifts and puts back down again, as though it's gently tapping a single key on a laptop.

'And someone else saw it, too?'

'Yes, Janine did, a short while after me.'

'Incredible,' Mum says. '*Such* good news. We can't believe it!'

Sofie smiles but it's a small smile and she is looking at Mum with concern. It's not hard to read what she is thinking. *You're jumping the gun. It's just a finger wiggle. Please don't get your hopes up.*

Mum goes in to see Emmy with Ted first, while me and Polly wait on chairs in the corridor outside the bad-news room. Polly's mood has dipped since the car singalong and, though she doesn't say as much, I sense that she has picked up on the nurses' caution over our overexcitement, too. I'm grateful when Dad joins us, though I can feel myself wincing as I hear him say, 'Fantastic news about the finger wiggling, eh?' to someone on his way through.

When Ted comes back, he announces with a sigh that his mummy is 'fast asleep again' and that she has 'stopped wriggling'.

'It was just Mummy's *finger* that moved,' his nan reminds him. 'And two nurses saw it so we know it happened. It's good news.'

'Wiggle wiggle.' Ted moves his finger like a worm then laughs. 'Aunty Beth do it.'

'Wiggle wiggle,' I mirror his worm with my index finger, which he then touches with his. As Polly and I head to Emmy's room, I can hear him getting cross with Mum because his worm now has no one to play with. Mum isn't concentrating on his worm worries because she is busy talking to Dad in a serious voice.

Though we weren't told to expect otherwise, I can't help but feel disappointed that Emmy looks exactly the same as she did when I saw her two days ago, which was just the same as every visit before that. It's remarkable just how much of how a person looks, ordinarily, is based on their movements and mannerisms. My sister sticks out her tongue when she's concentrating on something, like using scissors or sewing up a rip in Mr Trunky. She constantly tucks her hair behind her ears and when she feels awkward she laughs a little too loudly. The Emmy in front of me does none of those things.

Polly and I sit on chairs either side of the bed. When I lift Emmy's hand and place it in mine, I hold my breath, daring to hope just for a moment that I will feel a wiggle for myself. Polly kisses her mum on the cheek then we sit back, each pretending not to be staring intently at her for any sign of movement. Dr Hargreaves has stressed the importance of talking to coma patients but Polly doesn't look as though she has much to say just yet so it looks like it's down to me to break the silence. I've recently started sharing some headline good news for the visit followed by some headline not-so-good news, then filling in all the other stuff around the edges. It gives me a sense of purpose.

'Today's good news – other than you wiggling your finger, which we would very much love you to do again, by the way, but no pressure – is that your "magnolia tree is looking resplendent". That's a direct quote from Albert, who was admiring it when we were chatting over the back fence yesterday. Obviously, I didn't even know it *was* a magnolia, but I thought you'd be pleased to hear about its resplendence and, if nothing else, it has given me an excuse to say the word "resplendent". Have you got any good news to share with your mum, Pol?'

She shrugs but when I nod my head towards Emmy she says, 'I went back to school.'

I wait for something more. 'And . . . how's it been?'

'Fine.'

Right. 'Well, today's headline *bad* news has to be Mary from the WI bringing over a second ginormous batch of liver and onions, so soon after the first batch went in the bin. I was hoping it was a one-off food donation but when I saw her in the Post Office, she asked if we'd all enjoyed it and, under pressure, I told her it was really tasty. The only way round it is for us all to become vegetarians with immediate effect.' I chuckle at my own joke, stopping when I see that Polly's eyes have filled with tears. 'Hey, what is it? I promise I won't make you eat it, though it's still probably nicer than any of my cooking.'

'Can I have a minute with Mum?' Polly sniffs and looks down at her hands. 'On my own?'

'Oh. Yes. Of course you can. Er, right – I'll just be outside then.' I give Emmy a kiss on the head then reverse out of the room and close the door, leaving the two of them alone. Dr Hargreaves is now with Mum, Dad and Ted outside the bad-news room. Nobody looks excited any more.

'Hey.' I nod hello to Dr Hargreaves. I catch Mum looking behind me. 'Polly's just having a minute on her own with her mum. What's the latest? We've got carried away, haven't we?'

Dr Hargreaves smiles sympathetically. 'Yes and no. I was just telling your mum and dad that the whole team here are delighted about the movements observed earlier today. It's a small but significant development, which is why we were keen to share it with you, too.'

'There's a but, isn't there?'

She opens her hands. 'We don't want to give you the wrong impression. Recovery from this sort of trauma is rarely like you see in the movies, where hands twitch before eyes open and the patient instantly recognizes the loved one sitting beside them. It's possible that this morning's wiggles are the first of many wiggles to come, each one bigger than the last on an upwards recovery trajectory.' She angles her arm into a slope. 'But in many cases, there are more dips than there are climbs. And in this case, Emmy still isn't showing signs of responding. We've talked about the Glasgow Coma Scale, and really for an improved score we'd be looking for clear signs of voluntary movements in response to a command.'

'You were so positive on the phone, Doctor. I think I just clung to it.' Mum's disappointment is evident by the slump of her shoulders.

'I understand. Believe me, it's those glimmers of hope that keep us going, too, and we are very much encouraged by what we've seen today. We just need to make sure we are being honest with you about the complexity of the recovery that may – or may not – lie ahead.'

When Dr Hargreaves has gone, Ted complains he's thirsty and I reach for my bag before realizing I've left his drink in the car.

'I'll go.' Mum gets up from her chair, but I put my arm out to stop her when I notice she is wincing.

'Mum, what is it? What's wrong?'

'Nothing's *wrong*, love. Just my dodgy joints, the usual story.' She is holding her wrist awkwardly and I look at Dad, whose shake of the head tells me *Don't make a fuss.*

'Right, well, you rest it,' I say. 'I'll take Ted downstairs to get a drink. Come on, champ.' Ted doesn't need telling twice and skips ahead of me, out of the ward and all the way down to the shop by the main entrance where I buy a carton of Ribena for him and a can of Coke for me. We take them outside and, as none of the benches are free, we sit on the grass.

'Is Polly bigger than me?' Ted is waiting for me to pierce his carton with a straw.

'Yes, Polly is bigger than you. Here, two hands, don't squeeze it.'

'Why is she bigger?'

'Because she's older than you are.'

'Why?' He sticks out his bottom lip.

'Why's she older? Well, because she was born first. *Two hands,* Ted.'

'That's not fair!' He squeezes his carton in fury and Ribena squirts all over his top. He begins to cry, saying his top's wet and that it's not fair that Polly is older. By the time Mum, Dad and Polly join us, I have just about managed to calm him down.

'What's the matter?' Mum looks between the two of us.

'Ted's just a bit cross that he wasn't born first.' I pick up the now empty carton and my Coke can. 'The usual injustice.'

As we stroll back to the car, Polly falls into step beside Dad. 'Can you drop me at the leisure centre, Grandad? I'm meeting Rosie and Michaela there, before the sleepover.'

'No problem.' Dad puts his arm around her shoulder. 'I can give you all a lift to Rosie's, if you want?'

'No, it's OK. Rosie's mum is going to get us, we've already planned it. But thanks.' She gets her phone out of her pocket and puts her headphones in.

Dad starts the engine. 'It was worth coming this afternoon anyway, wasn't it? Never a wasted visit. Onwards and upwards for our girl.'

Mum and I don't say anything. Ted starts whingeing that he wants his songs on again and I replay the playlist we had on the way here. When he falls asleep, Mum turns the stereo off altogether and I stare out of the window, thinking the whole vibe of this return journey could have been transformed if only we'd witnessed a finger wiggle for ourselves.

12

The pub is busy and the lively chatter I thought might be jarring is actually proving a welcome change from the constant drone of worry in my head. Jory is fiddling with a beer mat, frowning thoughtfully as he turns it over in his hand. 'She said they were encouraged, though? Doctors don't throw words like "encouraged" around for fun, do they?'

'No. I dunno. I suppose not.' A group of thirty-somethings passes our table and Jory nods hello to one of them. I cock my head to one side and he laughs. 'George Barratt. Chemistry teacher. You're *so* nosy, do you know that?'

'I just like to know who you're saying hello to, that's all. If that makes me nosy then I don't ever want to be unnosy. Unnosy isn't a word, is it?'

'No, I think that's probably just called minding your own business. The girl behind George is Danni Parsons. Do you remember her? She was in our year.'

'That's never her?' I crane my neck to get a closer look as they settle round a table. 'God, it is her. I got off with her brother at a rugby club party once.'

'Of course you did.'

I roll my eyes. 'There was nothing else to do. They were such shit parties but we absolutely lived for them, didn't we? I used to agonize over what to wear, how to do my hair, who could get served so we could get pissed.'

Jory nods. 'I think that's probably why we lived for them. Your sister used to buy us two Bacardi Breezers each then tell us to piss off, do you remember?'

'I do.' The memory of my big sister in a pink leather jacket (that was definitely not real leather) pretending she didn't know me makes me laugh. 'We never did piss off far though.' I trace my finger round the edge of my wine glass. 'We breezed on to the ward like idiots this afternoon, Jor. We were so excited.'

'You're not idiots. Anyone would be excited – it *is* exciting. Don't beat yourself up for being hopeful.' He drains the last of his pint of Tribute then points at my glass. 'Same again?'

'Yeah, why not.'

As he waits for our drinks at the bar, he checks his phone. He checked it when I was getting the last round, too, I noticed. I could see him smiling to himself as he typed something. I must be looking at him quizzically when he puts my wine down because he furrows his brow and says, 'What?'

'Nothing.' I take a large sip, enjoying the fuzzy feeling that's just starting to take hold, as though the pub and all the people around us have been smudged. 'Who are you texting?'

He pushes his phone to one side. 'Oh, that was Sadie. She was just asking me something.'

He hasn't said much about Sadie since I overheard the staff-room sandwich date but I know they've seen each other a couple of times. 'How's it going with you two, anyway?'

'Yeah, it's good. She's amazing, you'd really like her.'

Amazing. I nod. 'I'm sure I would.'

Jory raises an eyebrow.

'What?'

'I just know girly friendships aren't always your comfort zone.'

'Well, it's not like I haven't tried, you know that, so you can lower that eyebrow right now.' I really have tried, too, but it always comes back to the same thing. Me feeling awkward, saying the wrong thing and never quite managing to fit in. I have all the friends I need in my sister and Jory, anyway, but for his sake I'm not going to be a dick about making an effort with Sadie. 'If you like her, I'm sure I will, too. So, are you going to make it official, you and her? Love's young teaching dream?'

He looks at me sheepishly. 'We sort of already have.'

'Oh. Wow!' The pitch of my voice has gone funny, as though I'm super excited, even though I'm not. 'That's good then. Congrats.'

Jory's neck has flushed pink. 'Thanks. I wanted to tell you in person, rather than sending a message. I only asked her if she wanted to – well, you know – be my girlfriend, on Wednesday.'

Be his girlfriend. Jory has a girlfriend. Has that happened quickly? It feels like it has happened quickly. It's such good news for him, though. I smile then take another large sip of wine. More of a glug this time. 'Well, I'm made up for you. It's about time someone snapped you up. That's what my mum's been saying for years.'

He smiles. 'I do love your mum.'

'She loves you, too.'

He clears his throat. 'It would mean a lot to me if you guys got on. I'm always talking about you so she probably feels like she knows you already.' I do a double thumbs up and he laughs. 'She's really fun, I promise.'

'OK.' I definitely can't say no now I know she's *really fun* as well as *amazing*.

'Good.' Jory leans back in his chair and lets out a long breath, as though he's been building up to telling me this news and feels lighter having parted with it. I feel lighter too but it's a different sort of lightness, as though I have become estranged from my body and am listening to my best friend chat about his new girl-friend without really being *there* at all. I guess that's what three large glasses of Sauvignon will do to you.

Jory walks me home, despite me telling him there is no need because I can almost see Emmy and Doug's house from the pub. It's pitch black and he puts his phone torch on. As we walk down the grassy verge beside the park, I lose my footing and he grabs me before I fall over. 'Steady.'

'The grass is really slippery tonight, isn't it?'

'Hmmm.'

I can't see him but I can hear him smiling. I reach for his hand, the same way I have done on many a night-out walk home, but this time he moves it out of the way and links his arm through mine instead.

'Oh, I see. Like that, is it?' I try to keep my voice light, but it comes out a bit wounded.

'Beth—'

'I'm just messing. Of course you don't want to hold hands with me now you've had an upgrade on the hand-holding-partner front.' It's the drink talking. Luckily, we're now only metres from Emmy's front door.

'It's just, if someone saw us . . .' Jory sighs. 'Other people don't always understand you and me, do they? You know what people say. And if Sadie or someone she knows saw us holding hands it might look like we're more than friends, which wouldn't be fair on her.'

'But we're not more than friends,' I say, struggling to fish my key out of my bag. 'Do you want one for the road? There's some whiskey in the drinks cabinet. Lord knows why. I never once saw Doug drink whiskey.'

'No. I should probably get going.'

'Oh. Okey-dokey. You're not being weird because I tried to hold your hand, are you?' I turn the key in the lock. 'Don't be weird, Jor. Sadie has nothing to worry about. I'm more like a sister, remember?'

'You're certainly annoying like a sister. Are you going to be all right here tonight on your own? I do feel a bit guilty leaving you.'

'I'll be fine. Now bugger off.'

'OK.' He pecks me on the cheek. 'Night then.'

'You could always stay and we could re-create the Winter of—'

He cuts me off, the porch light illuminating the shake of his head. 'Goodnight, Beth.'

'I was joking,' I call after him. 'Remember jokes?'

'Go to bed,' he calls back, and that's what I do.

By ten o'clock the following morning, I'm not quite sure what to do with myself. Polly is still at Rosie's and I was expecting Ted home this morning but Mum has texted to say they're going for a walk along the canal before bringing him home. She adds a PS to inform me she's put some new bathroom cleaner in the cupboard under the sink, Mum code for 'You need to clean the bathroom.' Through sheer boredom, I'm going to do as I'm told. I take a picture of the bathroom and throw in some cleaning emojis before typing a quick message to Jory.

> Glad we didn't move on to whiskey, this is what my morning looks like! (Mum's orders!) Congrats again re your news, I'm dead happy for you ~~both~~.

I delete 'both' because I don't know Sadie so it's a bit weird to say I'm happy for her, too. Or maybe it isn't. It's too late now, I've sent it.

When the bathroom is clean – to my eye anyway, undoubtedly below Mum's exacting standards – I give Ted's room a quick tidy. There is a light knock on the front door and I lean out of his window to see Polly and her overnight bag on the front step. She looks up at me, her hand shielding her eyes from the sun above the house, but doesn't say anything when I shout, 'Give me two seconds!'

Her chattiness level doesn't increase when I let her in. As she drops her bag at the bottom of the stairs, I peer closer at her face.

Washed-out would be an understatement. 'Oh, Pol, you look shattered. At the risk of sounding like your nan, did you get *any* sleep last night?'

'Not a lot.' There are shadows under her eyes and her skin looks almost grey. Maybe a sleepless night at the end of her first week back at school, on top of everything else, has been a bit much. I follow her into the living room.

'Can I get you anything?'

'Have we got any chicken nuggets?'

'Chicken nuggets?' I laugh as I check my watch. 'It's eleven o'clock.'

'I haven't had any breakfast yet.'

'Oh. Didn't Rosie's mum or dad make you something?' I am certain Emmy would have made a fuss of Polly's friends if they'd slept here.

'I wasn't hungry then.'

'But now you want chicken nuggets.'

'Now I'm starving.'

'Fair enough. Do you want chips or beans or anything, or just chicken nuggets?' I don't think she's ever told me she's starving so I'm rolling with it.

'Just chicken nuggets. And ketchup.' She collapses on the sofa and begins looking through her phone.

'Was it a good night then?'

'Not bad.'

As that's all I'm going to get, I put the radio on and empty the dishwasher while the nuggets are cooking. I put some in for me, too, and when they're ready we eat them in bowls on our laps in front of the telly, the bottle of ketchup between us. Polly devours hers as though she's finally found food after fasting for days, inhaling each mouthful without pause. She may be quiet and in need of sleep, but if she's got her appetite back, perhaps a sleepover with friends was just what she needed after all.

JUNE

13

'Morning, Albert!' I say, a little louder this time as he didn't hear me the first time.

He gets up slowly from his kneeling position and waves at Ted and me over the front hedge, a pair of secateurs in his hand.

'Hello, dear. Lovely day,' he shouts. 'You heading anywhere nice?'

I wince at the volume. 'Just the park. Then I've promised Ted some chocolate buttons.' Ted is pulling on my hand, eager to get moving.

'Excellent. Don't forget it's recycling tomorrow.'

'I won't,' I say. I had forgotten, obviously.

'They do come early this time of year so get it out tonight if you can,' he says. 'And I hope you don't think I'm meddling, but I put the black bag you'd left on the pavement last week in my bin.'

I shake my head. 'You don't need to give me your bin space, Albert. It's poor bin management on my part. I just keep forgetting. Thank you, though.' I feel ashamed at the thought of him heaving a full-to-bursting refuse sack into his bin, after dark.

'Well, there's a cat at number five who's always ripping open bags given the chance, and I don't know if you know but . . .' He hesitates, as though he's said too much already.

'Know what?' I ask, before whispering at Ted that I'll be just a minute more.

'Well, the last time your outside bin was full, the bag on the pavement was ripped – probably by number five's moggy, though I have no proof – and a chicken carcass plus other waste was dragged across the road. Pictures ended up on the village Facebook group.'

Oh, brilliant. Now I feel even more ashamed, both for the bin saga and the fact that Emmy's eighty-year-old neighbour is more on top of the village social-media dramas than I am. I am flabbergasted that my mother hasn't mentioned this and the shame it has brought on the family. Any time shame is brought on the family, it's my fault.

'I told them it was mine,' he says.

'Wait, what? Why?'

'On Facebook. When I was at the Age Concern cafe and they showed us how to find the village page. I put a message – you know, where you can leave a message underneath a picture?'

'A comment?' I offer.

'Yes, one of those. I put a comment to say that it was my bin bag and that I was very sorry but I hadn't been able to lift it due to a problem with my shoulder. I didn't want you getting in trouble. I thought you had enough on your plate. Village folk put their pitchforks down when they realized it was a senile old man.'

'Albert, that is so kind of you.' I know it's only a bin bag but I'm genuinely touched that he would publicly take the rap for my mistake and save me another Mum lecture. 'You are definitely not a senile old man.'

'Are you a hundred?' Ted asks. It comes out of nowhere.

'Ted!' I say, but it makes me laugh.

'Not quite, no. I'm eighty-three,' Albert says.

'And after that will you be deaded?' Ted says.

I cover my face with my hands. 'I'm so sorry,' I say, but Albert is laughing now.

'I don't know, but perhaps,' he says.

'Shall we get to the park then? Leave poor Albert alone.' I begin to steer Ted down the path.

'We're going on the roundybout.' 'We' being him, Mr Trunky the elephant and Mousey the mouse he's made me pack in the bag.

'Well, have fun,' Albert says.

We cross over at the end of the road by the bus stop and climb up on to the green. Ted lets go of my hand and runs as fast as his legs will carry him to the play area in the middle surrounded by a wooden picket fence. The roundabout and swings have been replaced over the years, but the slide is the same one that's been here since Emmy and I were kids. It's the sort of shiny metal slide that burns the backs of your legs in the summer and fires you off the end of it when it's been raining. I'm surprised it's passed the relevant modern safety tests and been allowed to stay.

'You can't catch me!' He opens the gate and races in. I probably can't catch him, given my current state of fitness, so I don't even have to pretend to fail. I jog to him, puffing out my cheeks when I get there.

'You win,' I concede. 'You're just too fast!'

He giggles and I lift him into the swing.

'Do the rocket!' he says, squirming in the seat with excitement. The rocket is another of Doug's specials. It involves holding the swing, with Ted in it, high in the air and then counting down before releasing it. A bit like the bedtime story, and my cheesy sauce soldiers, my rocket was below par when I first gave it a go but I'm getting the hang of it.

He is looking at me expectantly. I grab the swing and pull it towards me, holding all of his weight up in the air. 'Are you ready? OK. Three, two, one – *blast off!*' I release my grip and the joy on his face as the swing drops backwards brings a smile to mine. 'Do you want your teddies in with you?'

He nods and I retrieve Mr Trunky and Mousey from the bag, tucking them in beside him in the swing. There's a missed call on my phone from an unknown mobile. I used to pride myself on my ability to ignore missed calls, investing in the 'If it's important they'll call back' motto, but since the day of the accident, anything missed on my phone makes me feel sick until I can work out who it is and why they're calling. There's no voicemail or text message. I return the call, moving to stand behind Ted so I can give him a push and talk at the same time.

A woman answers. 'Is that Beth? It's Suzy here.' She pauses. 'Rosie's mum.'

'Oh hi. How are you?' I breathe out, relieved it's not the hospital, while at the same time wondering who these people are who phone rather than texting.

'Yeah I'm OK. I'm a bit stressed out about Rosie, to tell you the truth, and I thought I'd phone as I'm guessing you're going through the same with Polly.'

'The same?' I say. I have no idea what she's talking about, unless she means the hiding in bedrooms and scowling at everyone.

'After we got that message from school about the house party, it's been playing on my mind. I just wanted to know what you've found out. Compare notes a bit, I guess.'

Message from school. House party. I'm so lost, it's like she's got the right name but the wrong number. Ted is whingeing that he's not going high enough and I push him harder.

'Sorry, I'm a little confused here. A lot confused actually. Whose house party was it? Are you saying the girls were there? When?'

'God, I'm sorry, Beth, I thought you knew. It was last Friday,' Suzy says.

'But they were having a sleepover at yours last Friday.' I have a bad feeling in the pit of my stomach.

'They weren't. They both slept over at Michaela's.'

'OK, now I'm *really* confused – Polly said she was staying at yours last weekend.'

'I know, and Rosie told me she was staying at Michaela's – which she was – but Michaela's parents weren't home. Michaela told them she was staying at yours. So, each of us was lied to.' Suzy sighs.

Ted has put his arms up to get out and I lift him down then follow him over to the roundabout, putting the phone back to my ear. 'I can't believe this.' I think back to the chat with Polly about the sleepover, which only makes me more confused. 'But I texted you about the sleepover and you texted back. I've got the message.' I take the phone away from my ear, looking through my contacts until I find *Rosie's Mum*. 'The number ends in 265?'

'That's Rosie's number.'

'Wow. So, this party –' I swallow, not sure I even want to know – 'what happened? How did the school find out?'

'There were a lot of sixth-form kids there. The police were called due to the noise disturbance.' Suzy sounds worried. 'They were drinking.'

'Christ.' I think back to Saturday when Polly came home. I'd put her pale face down to tiredness, not an excess of vodka or whatever it is that fourteen-year-olds neck these days. That's if it was just drink. When I was fourteen it was only ever booze but teens these days seem to do everything sooner, larger, faster. I dread to think. 'What are you going to do? With Rosie, I mean?'

'I immediately confiscated her phone because it was just about the worst punishment I could think of. She reacted as though I had taken away her oxygen.'

I laugh, despite the situation. 'I have no doubt it will be the same here, but I guess we have to do something that makes them think before doing it again?'

'Yeah. I'm sorry, Beth. You've already got such a lot going on, perhaps I shouldn't have troubled you with this on top.'

'No, I would rather know. Thank you for phoning.' After saying goodbye, I put my phone in my back pocket. Ted has got down from the roundabout and has both arms in the air, pointing at the sky. I touch him lightly on the head. 'Don't grow up, Ted. It's a trap.'

'Look, Aunty Beth, plane puffs!'

I tip my head back and watch as a small plane passes overhead. 'Contrails, they're called. Short for condensation trails. It's basically just water but it leaves a cloud-shaped line because—' I stop myself when I see the way Ted is looking at me. 'Plane puffs sounds much better though, doesn't it?'

He is jumping up and down and waving at the plane. 'Are they waving back?'

The plane is so high we can barely see it, let alone make out anyone in it. 'Erm . . . I'm not sure.'

'They are!' he says. 'And my daddy is in the sky but he's not in a plane.' He looks up at me as though waiting for clarification.

'No, not in a plane, as such,' I say.

'But maybe in the clouds!' Ted says, hope lighting up his face. 'You're not waving, Aunty Beth. At my dad.'

I do as I'm told and we stand there long after the plane has disappeared, waving at the sky. It seems to make Ted happy, this connection to his dad. I want to feel happy, too, but instead I feel guilty. As I'm waving, I send a silent apology to Doug for letting his daughter get drunk at a house party I didn't know she'd gone to, before she slept in a house with no adults. Unless of course there *were* adults (but if there were, I doubt they were there to supervise). I think of all the lies I told my mum and dad when I was Polly's age, all the sneaking out and sticky situations Emmy had to get me out of. I almost talk myself out of punishing Polly for this very reason – surely it's hypocritical of me to pretend I was any different? – but the truth is that I did a whole heap of stupid stuff and I only *didn't* get punished when I didn't get caught. Polly has been caught and I can't just ignore it. The phone confiscation is going to go down like a lead balloon.

'Can we watch *Hey Duggee* now?' Ted has stopped waving. 'I need a wee-wee.'

'OK.' I follow him out of the gate, past the pub and back down the grassy verge towards the bus stop. The ladies in the bus stop smile and nod hello but I can hear their chit-chat lower to a gossipy murmur as we cross over the road. They are not as quiet as they think they are.

'Poor little mite,' I hear one of them saying. 'He's so young,' says another. *Too young to remember any of this*, is what they mean. The idea that Ted might be too young to remember his dad is so dreadful I immediately want to do something to fix it, but I'm not sure where to start. As we walk back up the road to Emmy's house, I think about phoning Mum and telling her about the sleepover but I don't think I can face a lecture just yet. I decide to call Jory instead. It goes straight through to his voicemail, which I should have known it would because it's mid-morning on a Wednesday (and he's not working a three-day week like I am).

Hey, you've reached Jory – or rather, you haven't! As you can probably tell I'm not available right now but please leave a message after the beep and I'll get back to you. Have a good day.

His greeting is warm and cheery, if a little awkward, which is classic Jory.

I wasn't planning on leaving a message at all but the beep sounds before I've had a chance to hang up. 'Hey, it's Beth. Er – I don't know why I'm calling, you're at work – of course you are – but I didn't want to call my mum so that's why I'm leaving you a voicemail even though I know you can't phone back yet. Maybe at lunch? If you get a minute and you're not cheese-sandwiching with Sadie. Have you got to the stage in the relationship where you've confessed that you only eat mild cheddar yet? Because I feel like this is the sort of thing you ought to disclose, in case it's a deal breaker. Only maniacs and babies eat mild cheddar. Even Ted will eat medium.' Ted wants to unlock the door so I pass him the key and lift him up awkwardly, while still cradling the phone. 'Anyway, I'll catch you later. Maybe. Hopefully. Just call me back. If you can. No rush.' I'm waffling, and contemplate going through the voicemail options to rerecord, but Ted tells me he's 'desprit' for a wee, so I hang up and lead him indoors. By the time I kick my shoes off, we're too late on the wee front.

14

Polly senses something is up the moment she gets back from school to find Ted set up with *Wreck-It Ralph* and Pom-bears, and me waiting at the dining table. I gesture to the chair in front of me.

'What's going on?' She hovers in the doorway.

'You tell me.' I point again to the chair and I'm surprised when she sits down without protest. I'm calling on all the serious chats Mum has given me over the years to inform how this one should go, which so far means crossing my arms and raising my eyebrows accusingly.

She shrugs. 'I dunno. That's why I'm asking you.' *Well played.* It's exactly what my response would have been at fourteen, too.

'I had a call from Rosie's mum this afternoon.'

I can see the horror washing over her. 'What did she want?'

'Oh, *come on*, Pol. I know about the sleepover that wasn't a sleepover, and the house party, and the booze. Was it just booze? Or was it booze and drugs? Or booze and drugs and sex?'

'What? No! God, I wouldn't—'

'Well, you'll have to forgive me if I don't know what to believe.' A classic line of Mum's. If nothing else, I'm starting to understand what I put my mother through at the same age.

'I'm sorry, Aunty Beth. I know you won't believe me but, for what it's worth, I wish we never went to the stupid party.' She looks tearful and I have a sudden stab of panic that this situation is more serious than I imagined.

'Nothing happened, did it? Did someone make you do something you didn't want to do?'

'No. Nothing like that. The party was shit, that's all. Are you going to tell Nan?'

'Why, what's your nan got to do with it?'

'I don't want her getting stressed about it. She's not been looking well.'

Polly's right, though it's a surprise to me that she has noticed, too. Mum hasn't said anything, but Dad admitted, after I pressed him, that the new injections Mum's been having for her arthritis have made her feel 'a bit off'.

'I haven't decided whether or not to tell your nan and grandad,' I tell her. I have, though. I'm not going to admit that it was the risk of proving her grandparents right – that I'm *not* capable of being responsible – that was already putting me off telling them, and that this extra layer of worry over Mum's health has only further cemented that decision. I reach out my hand. 'I'm going to need your phone.'

'What? Why? If you're going to put the content-control thing on it there's no need. Mum already did it.'

'Just pass it over please.'

She pushes it slowly towards me but keeps her hand over it. 'Don't take it away from me, please, Aunty Beth.' The shift from angry to pleading almost makes me reconsider.

'I know it's hard, Pol, but Rosie's mum took her phone away for a few days so it's not an unfair punishment. You must understand that?'

'Rosie's *mum*.' The anger has returned, I can tell by the curl of her lip. 'You're not a mum though, are you? You're no one.'

'Right.' I take hold of her phone.

Polly is crying. 'It's shit that you're looking after us. *Shit*. And

I hate you, do you know that? I hope you know that because it's true.'

Ted looks up from his film and I angle my face away from him, so he can't see the tears filling my eyes. My voice is low and wobbly. 'Say what you like about me but please don't shout at me in front of your brother.'

'Oh, don't pretend you care about him either.' She is standing now, heading towards the stairs.

'What's that supposed to mean?' I ask, though I'm not sure I want to know.

'You heard. You're only looking after us because you didn't have a choice. You never had any interest in us before the accident.' She runs out and I stare after her with my mouth open, flinching when her bedroom door slams shut and the whole house shakes. Her phone is still in my hand and I stare at the lock screen, a photo of her mum and dad with goofy grins, their sunglasses on upside down. Holding the button down and turning it off is all I can do to keep it together.

You're no one. I'm the first to admit I haven't got everything right since stepping up to look after Polly and Ted but, my god, I have been trying. And still, after all this time, *don't pretend you care* is what she thinks of me. If her intention was to wound me, her attack has landed bang on target. I take myself over to the sofa and pull Ted on to my lap, inhaling the biscuity scent of him. 'Aunty Beth loves you, buddy. You know that, don't you?'

He fiddles with the fabric of my shirt. 'Can I watch *Paw Patrol*?'

'You don't like the film?'

'I chained my mind.'

'You've *changed* your mind? All right.'

While he's absorbed in more telly than his mum or nan would ever allow, Jory phones and I take the call into the garden.

'Hey.' I slide my feet into Emmy's Crocs and tread the stepping stones down to the pergola at the bottom of the garden.

'I got your message. Is everything OK?' He is outside some-where. The wind is buffeting and I can hear seagulls.

'Not really. I've just had to confiscate Polly's phone after finding out she went to a house party last weekend when she was sup-posed to be at a sleepover.' I'm pacing, walking back up towards the house again. 'Honestly, Jor, when she returned looking like she'd been on a massive bender, I didn't for one moment think it was because she *had* been on a massive bender. I thought they'd stayed up all night watching films. I have been – what is it the kids say? – mugged off.'

'Oh dear.'

'They stayed at Michaela's when her parents weren't even there.' A conversation I had with Polly about school friends in different tutor groups comes back to me. 'Hang on, isn't Michaela in your tutor group? Michaela Brown?'

'She is, but—'

'So you knew, about the party?' When he doesn't immediately deny having known, I make a low whistling sound. 'Wow. Thanks for the heads up. If you'd known Polly had been there, you'd have told me though, right?'

'Beth . . .' Jory sighs. 'It wasn't my place to tell you. I spoke to Michaela's parents about the party because that's part of my job, as her tutor. It wasn't my place to interfere where Polly was con-cerned. That was up to Mrs Sandford.'

'Who didn't even contact me—'

'She must have done. In fact, I know she did because there was a wider conversation about the party in the staffroom. Have you checked the—'

I cut him off. '*You* could have told me. Just given me a little FYI. It was hardly a secret, was it? Other people knew there had been a party. *Everyone else* by the sounds of it. Just stupid old Beth who was still in the dark.'

'If I'd told you there was a party, it would have put me in a tricky situation, professionally. You would have grilled me on who was there, what I knew, what all the other teachers had said.'

'No I wouldn't. And even if I had, what's so wrong with that? If the shoe had been on the other foot, I would have told you.'

'Yeah well . . .' His voice trails off.

'Yeah well what?'

'Nothing. Forget it.'

'No, go on.' I kick at a clump of moss on the wall beside the back door.

'*Yeah well* you never much concern yourself with being professional, do you? But it's important to me. Which is why I trusted the system and left it to Polly's tutor to contact you.'

'Well, the system failed, so thanks a lot.' I kick the wall harder, pain shooting through my toes. When I step back, I knock over a rake that was propped against the wall and it hits the patio with a clatter.

'What was that? Are you all right?'

'Fine.'

'Look, Beth, I'm sorry I didn't tell you about the party but I'm a rule-follower at work, it's how I'm built. You know that.'

I've upset him, I can hear it. And now I feel bad because though it's true I would have told him if I had been the teacher, I am not a teacher. The very idea of me being a teacher is ridiculous. 'I know.'

'I've got to go now, Beth.'

'OK.' I bite my lip and before I can tell him that I'm the one who's sorry, that I'm just having a really hard day and I'm sad about what Polly said, he has gone.

When he sends a message just moments later, I read it three times, thinking at first I must have read it wrong, or at least misunderstood what he meant. I haven't read it wrong though, and I've understood it perfectly well. The problem is, it wasn't meant for me at all.

Just spoken to her. All the drama. She's angry with me but you were right about not telling her. It could have caused me all sorts of problems. I'll be leaving here just before 5. See you later. Love xx

My heart sinks lower than I knew it could sink. Sadie was *right about not telling me*. What has any of this got to do with her? I consider phoning him back, or sending a furiously typed reply saying I thought he had my back. But I don't send anything because, really, there is no point.

'Oh, it's you!' Albert is peering at me over the fence, his hand to his chest as though he's had a scare. 'I heard a crash and thought maybe there was a cat in your garden. I was going to hiss at it to stop it doing its business in that pile of earth.'

'Right. Sorry, it was this.' I point at the rake but don't bother picking it up.

'You remember the cat from number five – our prime suspect in the bin bag and chicken carcass episode, the one that ended up on the St Newth Facebook interweb page? Well, he loves a pile of earth. Your sister, I've seen her get quite angry about cat poo so I promised her I would keep an eye out. Like Neighbourhood Watch but for cat mess. Beth, are you all right?'

I shake my head. 'I'm not having a very good day.'

He studies me for a moment and then raises his finger as though he's just been struck by an idea. 'I've got something that might cheer you up.'

I force a smile. 'Sounds intriguing.'

'Stay there.' He shuffles over to his shed and pops his head inside it, leaving me staring at the back of his cable-knit jumper. 'Ah ha!' When he reappears, I can't quite make out what he's holding. Something green and flat, wrapped in plastic. He passes it over the fence. 'It's a peg bag.' He clasps his hands together. 'No more brittle pegs for you.'

Without warning, I am crying. The sort of ugly crying where your whole face collapses.

'Oh dear.' He looks at me, his mouth open. 'I've still got the receipt if you don't like it.'

'No – it's – great.' I manage between sobs. 'Thank you.' I clutch it to my chest and tell him I need to check on Ted, before turning on my heel and hurrying indoors.

Much later, when Polly and Ted are in bed, I perform the nightly ritual of pulling the double guest duvet out from behind the sofa and folding it in half lengthways to create something resembling a sleeping bag, without the zip. On cold nights, I have been putting one of Emmy's crocheted sofa blankets over the top but tonight is mild and I'm grateful for the open duvet edge so I can poke one foot out and rest it on the cool side. I turn the lamp off and fidget until I find the right position. I should have been asleep an hour ago, but I spent that hour looking at Jory and Sadie's Instagram and Facebook pages. The deeper I delved, the harder it was to stop. There wasn't much of a trace of them as a couple and no close-ups of her but in her latest profile picture she is wearing his coat. I wonder if that was taken before or after she told him not to tell me about the house party. It's no use trying to kid myself that I'm angry with Jory when the truth is that, more than anything else, the message he sent – that wasn't meant for me but is about me – has made me feel lonely. As though there is nobody left in my corner, or at least nobody who wants to be there. How could I have failed to notice that I'd become such a burden? *Causing him all sorts of problems. All the drama.* That's me, though, isn't it? Silly old dramatic Beth. Jory's just taken longer than anyone else to reach the same conclusion.

I roll over and switch the leg that's on top of the duvet. What I want, more than anything, is to talk to my sister. For her to open her eyes and say, 'What's up, Bethmeister?' when she sees the familiar sight of me agonizing over the shambles that is my life. I'm not sure she would be her usual level of amused if she knew I had extended the shambles of my life to her life, and her house, and her children. But I also don't understand how she could ever have expected anything else. As my eyelids start to close, I think of Polly at a party she shouldn't have been at; and Ted waving to his dad in the sky; and Albert with his peg bag; and Sadie wearing Jory's coat.

15

Oh, come on. I tilt my head down to one shoulder and back up again before repeating on the other side, hoping this brief pause for a neck stretch might stop me setting fire to my laptop. Polly is right, the broadband speed here is dire, which is probably why Doug was never tempted to work from home.

I've been trying to watch a YouTube video about combine harvesters for the past hour but it keeps buffering and now I'm losing the will to live. I think I've probably seen enough, anyway. I close the video and click on the credit application for Mr and Mrs Penhale of Trelinney Farm. The combine they are financing is so expensive because – I check the notes I've scribbled on my notepad – it's significantly more powerful than other models and can cover the ground quicker. Admittedly this is *not* the direction I ever dreamed my career would go in but these facts might give me something else to wow Dad with. He seemed genuinely impressed when I told him Malcolm was sending me out to a farm to do the information gathering today. I didn't mention that this was only because Malcolm cocked up his Outlook calendar and double-booked himself because it felt nice that Dad was impressed. I've seen how hard Dad searches for impressive things I've done so he can big me up. Thirty-one years of, 'Well, at least you gave it a good go, love,' even when we both know I haven't given it, whatever *it* is at the time, a good go at all. At least he still looks for things to praise me about, and doesn't wear the disappointment he feels about my lack of career/relationship/life choices on his face. I think back to Mum's resigned expression when I quit the job I had before this one. She seemed to think it was unreasonable for me to have concluded I didn't like it after four days. '*Quit while you're ahead?* You quit before you've even started, Beth.' My employment track record backs her up, I know.

The email – complete with attachments Malcolm is waiting for – is hovering in my outbox. *Unable to send.* I drum my fingers on the dining table and let out a long sigh. I should have gone back to the office after my farm visit but with only an hour of the work day left, and as Mum has offered to get Ted from nursery *and* pick Polly up from swimming, I had my eye on a very small window of peace at 5 p.m. I was thinking about having a nap. I could just nap now . . . but then what about Malcolm, and the email? I think this might be a new feeling. Ordinarily, I would rush to inform Jory that I forwent a nap in favour of *responsibilities*, certain he would be proud of my personal development, but he still hasn't noticed he sent me that message in error and I'm not going to be the one to tell him. He left a voicemail yesterday asking if I was OK (because I was 'acting weird') and I sent a WhatsApp back saying it was just the *usual drama* here.

I'm midway through composing a message to Malcolm to say I'm having wi-fi issues when a miracle occurs and the email sends. I am jubilant, elated, and I realize with a grimace that what Polly was saying about relying on her phone's 3G because *the broadband is shit* was probably not a lie. I thought she was just coming up with another angle from which to object when faced with the temporary confiscation of her phone. I held firm for two days and eleven hours before caving under the pressure of a 14-year-old girl with no phone, which was quite unlike any other pressure I've ever experienced. Teenagers are relentless. She was in my face with her big, sad, blue eyes and 'I'm sorry, Aunty Beth, it won't happen again' on repeat and I kept thinking of her mum in the hospital, and her dad's coffin at the funeral, and wondering if normal punishments should even apply when someone who's really just a kid has been through all of that.

I check the time: *4:45*. I could squeeze a little nap in now. If I get my head down quick, I might even get forty-five minutes. I shove the laptop back in its case and am just about to dive on to the sofa when I spot the parcel I've taken in for Albert. It'll keep for another hour, I'm sure. I close my eyes.

But what if he's sitting there, waiting for it?

I open my eyes again. For god's sake.

I'll just nip it round, quickly.

'On Wednesday afternoon I did,' Albert says. He is shouting at me from his kitchen. 'I think it was Wednesday. Yes, it was definitely Wednesday because I was heating up my ready-meal fish supper at the time. I always eat my tea early, you see. Other than that, not a peep.'

I perch on the edge of the larger of two brown sofas. Everything in Albert's living room is brown or beige, as though someone has sepia-toned the whole house. It smells of soap and charity shops. It is odd sitting inside the mirror image of Emmy and Doug's house, with everything positioned in the same layout but the 'wrong' way round.

Albert carries over a teapot, two china cups and saucers, a matching milk jug and a plate of Hobnobs on a silver tray. The tray wobbles as he lowers it on to the coffee table. It never even occurred to me that you could get tiled coffee tables. Brown tiles, too. So much brown.

I had no intention of staying but by the time I'd carried his parcel through to the kitchen, he'd put the kettle on and instructed me to take the weight off my feet. There was no way I could turn him down. I glance at the clock on the mantelpiece. It's 5:20 now, which means my nap window has been and gone. I might as well have a biscuit.

'Still, I'm sorry for any shouting you may have heard. Polly, she was pretty angry about the prospect of not having a phone and things got a bit . . . tense,' I say. I suspect Albert is downplaying the amount of arguing he heard through the living-room wall but he *is* hard of hearing so I suppose it's not impossible that he only caught a snippet of our row. Hopefully it wasn't the bit where Polly shouted *It's shit that you're looking after us* before slamming the door.

'Is that not par for the course with teenagers, the mood swings?'

'It is, but Polly's got more on her plate than the average teenager so her moods are even worse than they might have been. She lied to me about something that could have put her in danger, which was why I took her phone away. I think I might have been too harsh but there's nowhere to check the protocol on this sort of thing.' I give him a brief rundown of sleepovergate.

'What do your mum and dad say about it?' Albert asks.

'Oh, erm, not a lot really.' I take a sip of my tea. I can count on one hand the number of times I've had tea in a proper cup and saucer like this. I'm not convinced I'm even holding the cup right, it seems fiddly.

'Did you not give your mum and dad the run-around at Polly's age?'

I grimace. 'You could say that.'

'Well then, they must have some advice for you,' he says.

'Hmmm.' I look down at my lap, suddenly feeling a bit awkward. Albert peers over the top of his glasses at me. 'I haven't told them, about Polly's lie.'

'Oh?' He snaps a Hobnob in two and dunks half in his tea.

'It's just easier, if they don't know.'

'Why's that then?'

'Because Polly begged me not to and Mum's been feeling a bit off recently and I don't want her worrying. And also . . .' I

hesitate. 'Because I could really do without an "I told you so."
Mum in particular doesn't think I'm up to all of this.'

'All of what?'

'Looking after Polly and Ted. She is already disapproving of
my cooking and cleaning and all the other household-running
jobs I've not yet mastered. If she knew I'd messed up on something bigger, it would only prove her right. That I'm not up to it.'

'And do you think you're up to it?'

'Crikey, Albert, this feels like an interview.' I put my cup down
on the coffee table and he tops it up with fresh tea from the pot.

'Sorry, dear. I didn't mean to pry.'

I smile to show I'm not offended. 'I'm not confident I am up to
it, to be honest. But my sister and Doug chose me to take care of
the kids. So for now at least, I have to.' A black and white photo
on the mantelpiece catches my eye. 'Is that you and Mavis?' A
young couple on deckchairs are holding hands, their eyes bright
and smiles wide.

Albert nods. 'It is indeed. She always was a knockout.'

'I can see that. She looks lovely. You don't look too shabby
yourself, it has to be said.' It's a relief to step away from chat
about Mum and Dad and the lie I'm telling them about Polly's lie.
It's a web of lies.

'Well, that's very kind of you to say so.'

Is he blushing? I think he is blushing.

I look again at the photo. 'You remind me so much of Emmy
and Doug. How they looked together. Just sort of radiating
contentedness.'

'Do you know, Mavis said the same, about your sister and
Douglas, when they first moved in. She took them over a tin of
her famous Bakewell tarts. Mavis made the best Bakewell tarts,
they always had a generous slab of icing on top. When she came
back from dropping them off, she told me that Emmy and Douglas reminded her of a young us. A very happy couple.'

'Yeah, they are. Were.' *Were.* I hate how it no longer makes sense to speak of them as a couple in the present tense. I think of the framed picture of them on the beach, in a similar spot on the mantelpiece next door. There had been another photo beside it, of the four of them on bikes at Center Parcs, a rosy-faced Ted poking out from behind his dad in one of those little plastic baby seats. I took the photo with me to the hospital and placed it on the shelf beside Emmy's bed. I know she hasn't opened her eyes yet, but when she does, I want her to have familiar faces nearby. I try not to think for too long about what we'll have to say when she comes round. The coma that is keeping her from coming back to us is also protecting her from the pain of finding out that her husband has died.

'And you've found your happy couple, too?' Albert says.

'Have I?' It's news to me.

'That lovely young man with the van. Georgie, is it?' Albert points towards his window. 'Ever so polite he was, when his wheels had churned up my lawn a bit. Offered to come and make it good with grass seed.'

'Oh – no, we're not – that's Jory, he's just a friend.' *And he thinks I'm a burden anyway.*

'Oh.' Albert sounds surprised and, I think, possibly a little disappointed. 'Apologies, I assumed you were courting. Still, you young ladies these days, you're all independent and "feminist" and everything, aren't you?' He has put his cup down and makes quotation marks with his fingers.

'And what do you think about feminists, Albert?' I ask.

He leans forwards. 'I'm terrified of them, truth be told.'

I laugh. 'Well, *I'm* a feminist and I'm not terrifying, am I?'

'No. You're not so bad,' he says. 'I probably have the wrong end of the stick about what it all means these days. I'm a bit behind on the times, you see. Do you still have to go on marches?'

'Well, there are marches to go on but it's not a requirement.

There are some good podcasts you could listen to, if you did want to be brought up to date. Emmy also has a book—'

He cuts me off. 'A what cast? A pop cast?'

'A podcast,' I say. He looks at me, blankly. 'Uh, it's sort of like a radio show but it's released as different episodes, as part of a series. There are some brilliant ones. You could probably find a nice gardening one.'

Albert doesn't look convinced. 'And I listen on the wireless, do I?'

'Do you have a mobile phone?'

He shoots up from his spot on the sofa, taking me by surprise. 'Yes! I do. I don't have a clue what to do with it.' He makes his way over to the sideboard, reaching into one of the drawers and pulling out a phone. 'It's far too fancy for me,' he says, bringing it back to the sofa.

Fancy is not the first word that springs to mind when looking at Albert's phone. It's even older than Mum and Dad's mobiles. In fact, I think Jory had this exact phone about fifteen years ago. We were awestruck by its ability to take a picture, even though the quality was so bad it was hard at times to make out who or what was in it.

Albert is smiling at me expectantly. I think he is waiting for me to compliment the phone. I genuinely can't think of anything good to say. 'I don't think you'll get podcasts on this but it seems a shame to keep it locked away in the drawer?'

'I don't have any need for it, Beth. If I'm making a call I much prefer the landline, you see. And I don't really have anyone to call, in any case . . .' His voice tails off and then he laughs. 'Mavis, she bought us both the same one – god knows why – and hers was the only "text message" I have ever received.' He does the finger quotation marks again, as though text message is something new. He shows me the one and only message in his inbox.

HELLO ALBERT. LOVE M XXX

I smile at the shouty capitals. There are no other numbers in his address book.

'Albert, who would you call if there was an emergency?'

He thinks for a moment. 'I don't know.'

'There must be someone. A relative perhaps?'

'Not nearby, no.'

'Do you mind?' I ask. He shakes his head, a bemused expression on his face, and I take the phone from him, typing my number in.

'Obviously in most cases it would be easier to just bang on the wall, but I have saved my number just in case you need help. *Or* you need to tell us to stop shouting because you're trying to get to sleep.' I hand the phone back, still not quite able to fathom how he only has two numbers in his phone, one of those being his late wife.

'I wouldn't worry. I never sleep well, regardless of noise,' he says.

'Why's that?'

'I struggle to drift off. I think it's because I don't do anything to make me tired. My body is always tired but my brain is wide awake the moment I get into bed.'

'You should read a book,' I say. 'That's a good way to unwind. Unless it's a particularly jumpy thriller. Or something racy.' I don't tell him I never read books before bed because I am too busy looking at my phone, or that sometimes that turns a bit racy. Or at least it did before I took over caring for Polly and Ted and now any private phone-time I manage to find is spent googling 'brain injury recovery' and 'How often should a three-year-old poo?'

Albert sighs, his eyes returning to the photo of him and Mavis in deckchairs. 'I used to enjoy reading before bed, but –' He clears the frog in his throat. 'Well, I liked having someone to discuss the book with. It probably sounds pathetic. I know you young people have lots of conversations, on phones and so on, with lots of different people. But not us. We had each other. And that was just how it was. We started reading the same books, at the same time.'

'Albert, that doesn't sound pathetic,' I say. I have visions of him and Mavis sitting up in bed (in a bedroom I can only imagine to be brown with more dark wooden furniture), identical book covers in front of their faces. Their two-person book club is possibly the cutest thing I have ever heard. 'It is a bit of a shame to give up reading altogether, though?'

'The fun just isn't there any more, without someone to chat with. Shall I top up the pot with some more fresh water?'

'Oh not for me, thanks. I need to get going.'

'Of course, dear, don't let me keep you. I've wasted enough of your afternoon already. I bet you were hoping just to drop the parcel off.'

'No, not at all!' The pitch of my voice no doubt gives away that that was exactly what I was hoping to do. It didn't prove to be a chore to stay for two cups of tea though, in the end. Quite the opposite. I tell Albert he doesn't need to get back up from the sofa again but he insists on escorting me to the door, his slippers shuffling through the thick carpet that slightly pushes the brown-colour-scheme boundaries by having swirls of mustard in it. I think about his phone with no contacts and of him spending all day in his chair before putting an uninspiring freezer meal in the microwave and finally heading off to bed where he can't sleep. I understand now why my sister was always finding excuses to pop next door. She wanted to check in on him. I speak before I've really thought it through. 'Albert, would you like to do a book club?'

'A book club?'

'Yeah, you know, reading a book and then reporting back on what you thought of it . . . at least, I think that's what you do at a book club. I've never actually been to one,' I admit.

'I don't think so, dear. The one at the Age Concern cafe will be full of people who look half dead already and it'll only remind me that I'm not far off a visit from the Grim Reaper myself. I have no desire to sit in a roomful of people with no teeth, all of us shouting because we're a bit mutton.'

'Mutton?'

'Mutt and Jeff,' he says, as though this provides clarity.

I shake my head.

'You'll have to speak up, I'm a bit mutton!' he says, in an accent that is somewhere between Phil Mitchell and Dick Van Dyke. The whole exchange is so ridiculous, and I'm so confused, that it sets me off into uncontrollable laughter.

Albert continues doing his silly accent and saying 'Mutt and Jeff' as though he cannot understand my confusion, which only makes me laugh harder. Finally, he points towards his hearing aid and says, '*Deaf.* It's Cockney rhyming slang.'

I wipe my eye with my jumper sleeve. 'Well, I've never heard of it. There aren't many Cockneys in St Newth.'

'True. My Mavis, she was born within the sound of Bow Bells before coming to Cornwall.'

I shake my head, lost again.

'Never mind. We talked in Cockney rhyming slang all the time. It was one of our things. I forget it's unfamiliar to other people, particularly down here.'

He opens the front door and I step out on to the doorstep. Mum's car pulls up beside us and I give her a wave. Polly flies indoors without acknowledging anyone.

I turn back to Albert. 'Well, I wasn't actually talking about the "mutton" people from the Age Concern cafe for your book club. I meant me. Though I have no doubt theirs would be a bit more professional.'

'Me and you?' he says.

'Yeah,' I say. 'But it was a silly idea.'

Mum carries Ted over to join us. His jumper is covered in paint and what looks like pasta sauce. 'What are you two up to?' she says.

I give Ted a tickle under his arm and he giggles, thumb still in mouth.

'We were just talking about starting a book club,' Albert says.

Mum laughs, putting her hand to her mouth when she realizes he's not joking. Albert looks from her to me and back again.

I wish I hadn't mentioned it. 'As I said, a silly idea. We better get you some tea, Teddles.'

'I could never get Beth to read, Albert,' Mum says. 'We got called in to school once because she'd downloaded someone else's summary of a book rather than reading it herself. Paganism.'

'*Plagiarism*, Mum. And it was at least fifteen years ago. Thanks again for the tea, Albert.'

He is still looking strangely at my mother, but nods and tells me the pleasure was all his before closing the door with a click. Ted is whingeing that he's starving.

'Did you manage to get something in for their tea?' Mum asks me. There is no sign of Polly downstairs. She must have gone straight up to her room.

I have been working all day, I hadn't even thought about tea. I open the freezer. 'I thought they could have fish finger sand-wiches,' I lie, relieved to find that there are fish fingers left.

Mum makes a face and puts Ted in his booster seat. '*Luckily*, Nanny made a casserole this morning,' she says, pushing aside the mess on the dining table to make space for a plate. She tilts her head towards the fridge. 'There's enough for all of you. Prob-ably best to microwave his now though as it'll soon be bath time.'

I close the freezer door and open the fridge, feeling my face flush. It's not even leftovers from her and Dad's casserole, it's one she's made just for us. 'What if I had got something in for their tea?' I say.

'I knew you wouldn't have, love.'

And yet you still asked. I dish up enough for Ted and put it in the microwave. 'How did Polly get on at swimming?'

'Fine,' Mum says. 'I was chatting to Geraldine – you know, Pilates Geraldine – for most of the session but I did look in through the viewing gallery a couple of times. Polly makes it look effortless, doesn't she? No splashing whatsoever.'

'Yeah, she's always been a natural. Is the gala next week?'

Polly continuing with swimming club formed part of the bargain of me not telling her nan and grandad about the sleepover and letting her have her phone back sooner.

Mum pulls a letter out of her handbag that's hung over the back of Ted's chair. 'Yes, they have to be there earlier than normal and she needs to wear the club tracksuit for a team photo. I'll stick this on the fridge to remind you, shall I?' We both know she will phone me to remind me anyway, so the sticky notes all over the fridge are essentially just decorative.

The microwave dings and I take the plate out, sticking Ted's little bamboo fork in to test a bit before blowing on the rest of it.

His face is a picture when I present it to him. 'Wassat?' His eyes are wide.

'It's your nanny's famous casserole.'

'I wanted fishy finger sandwiches,' he says, craning his neck to look behind me as though another course might be on its way.

'Full of goodness for a growing boy, that is,' Mum tells him. 'You've eaten it before. Give it a try, sweetheart.'

He curls his top lip in a sneer and though I work hard to suppress a smile, I think Mum spots it by the half tut she gives on her way out. 'Can you get to ours at nine, tomorrow?' she says.

'OK. Shall Dad and I take Ted with us?'

'I shouldn't think so, no.'

'It might be nice? For him to see his mum. And for Emmy to hear him.' It's been over a week since he came to the hospital with us.

'We don't know if she can hear him, love,' Mum says quietly.

'No, but we don't know she can't, do we?'

'Let's see how he is in the morning,' she says. 'It's not fun for him, sitting in that stuffy room for hours at a time. No place for a child, really.'

It's *no place for anyone, really,* but I don't argue. Mum has given me the grown-up version of 'We'll see,' which only ever means no. After she leaves, I shout up to Polly to see if she wants some casserole and she appears at the top of the stairs, her hair still wet from swimming.

'Casserole?' she says. 'Seriously?'

'Afraid so, although' – I check behind me that Mum hasn't snuck back in – 'I have got fish fingers and triple-cooked oven chips in the freezer, if you don't mind waiting and promise not to tell your nan.'

'Deal,' she says, padding downstairs in her hoodie and jogging bottoms. 'Nan's the word.'

'Good one,' I say. 'Swimming was all right then?'

She shrugs. 'Boring.'

'Right, well, stick at it.'

'Like you did,' she says, and it takes me by surprise. I take Ted's untouched plate of casserole away and tell him that the main course of fish fingers is on its way and that he can watch a bit of CBeebies while he's waiting. He is very pleased with this turn of events.

'That's different. I was never as good as you are,' I say.

'That's not what Coach Draper said.'

'*Greg* Draper? Christ, has he not grown up and left the poolside yet?' I think back to the Friday evenings of my teenage years spent at the leisure centre. Greg Draper was on my 400-metre mixed relay team. He took it all very seriously.

'He said you were really good but gave up before you ever had a chance to win anything. He's coaching us ahead of the gala.'

'Is he now? Good for him.' I don't quite know where to steer this chat now Polly knows I'm trying to talk her out of doing exactly what I did, at pretty much the same age as she is now. *Do as I say and not as I do*, isn't that what parents say? I don't know if the same applies to aunties. Unluckily for Polly, she has agreed to keep up with swimming in exchange for my silence over her recent misadventures so I can ignore this assassination of my teenage character.

I throw a generous helping of oven chips on a baking tray and put aside fish fingers to go in after ten minutes or so. I learned the hard way last week, as the fish fingers became crispy while the chips lay there looking like Ron Weasley's legs in winter, that the suggested cooking time on an oven chip packet is the greatest lie ever told. Not today, though. Today I have adjusted the cooking time accordingly and that, coupled with my work effort this afternoon and the half an hour I spent keeping Albert company, has left me feeling something close to virtuous.

I scrape the casserole Ted hasn't eaten into the bin and contemplate asking Alexa to play 'My Way' before I tackle bedtime. Too far, I decide, but I can't stop myself from humming it as I get the ketchup and tartare sauce out.

JULY

16

'We're going to be late.' Polly gestures out her window at the traffic.

'We're not,' I say, even though we are. I flash my lights at the car waiting to pull out of the petrol station so he can edge out and join the snake of traffic. There is no acknowledgement from the driver. 'Oh you're welcome, dickhead,' I mutter. 'It's not like we're in a rush.'

'Welcome dickhead,' Ted repeats from the back seat.

Polly and I exchange glances. 'I said, "You're welcome, *stickhead.*"'

'Stickhead, stickhead,' Ted chants, bouncing Mr Trunky on his knee.

'What's one of those then, Aunty Beth?' Polly asks.

'Don't start,' I tell her. 'I could really do without your brother swearing in front of your nan.'

We crawl through the rest of the Friday-evening traffic in silence. When the leisure centre is in sight but the lights have changed back to red for a third time without us getting past them, I instruct Polly to jump out. 'You need to get yourself changed. We'll see you in there.' I shove her swimming kit out the door behind her. 'Good luck!'

I'm about to give myself a pat on the back for parking Emmy's tank of a family car under pressure, when I hear a crunch and realize I've shot too far forwards in the space, grinding the bumper on the kerb in front. 'Oh for—' I glance in the rear-view mirror, stopping myself short of another swear – 'funky monkey.'

Ted laughs at me from the back. I open my door and do my best Flat Stanley impression to slide my body out without hitting the car to our right. There's even less space on Ted's side, which means I have to stretch awkwardly across the seats to unclasp his straps before dragging him out. By the time we make it through the double doors, I'm out of breath, sweating and I think I've pulled a muscle in my neck. Taking care of a small child is so much more physical than I've ever given my sister credit for.

The smell of chlorine and the excited hum of chatter coming from the viewing gallery immediately transports me back to my own swimming-club days. It was by far my longest-lasting hobby, but by the time I was Polly's age I was working up to telling Mum and Dad that I wanted out.

A small crowd has gathered already, noses pressed to the glass. I scan the row of backs until I spot Dad's coat. They're at the far end, in what is arguably the best spot. Mum probably put a towel down to reserve it days ago.

'Beth Pascoe, well I'll be damned.' A voice booms behind me from the direction of the changing rooms and I spin round. Greg Draper smiles down at me. It's the same smile he's always had, as though something's funny but I'm not yet in on the joke.

'Draper.' I nod, surprised the old habit of a surname-only address has resurfaced automatically. '*Coach* Draper now, I hear?'

He nods. 'They never let me out. I live in the changing rooms now.'

'Little bit creepy,' I say, and he laughs. He looks less uptight than teenage Greg and, judging by the shape of him, it seems more likely he lives in the gym. It's quite disconcerting that his voice is so deep and his shoulders are so broad, even though it shouldn't really come as a shock that he looks and sounds like an adult, noting we are both now in our thirties.

I ask him how Polly is doing and he tells me she is their star swimmer, or at least she would be if she committed to training. 'She reminds me of someone I used to swim with a lifetime ago.'

'Is that right?' I move my eyes away from his shoulders, nodding towards Mum and Dad. 'I'm going to head over to my folks now. Nice to see you though. Good luck. I hope you win.'

'Thanks. Good to see you, too.' He moves his hand and I think for a moment he's going to touch my arm but he puts it back in the pocket of his shorts instead. 'And I'm really sorry, about your sister and Doug. I hope she gets better soon.'

'Me too,' I say. Ted is getting heavy on my hip and I put him down, keeping a hold of his hand as I weave us both through the tables between reception and the gym towards the viewing gallery.

'Talk about cutting it fine.'

'"Hi, Beth, how are you?" Oh I'm fine, thanks for asking, Mum,' I say.

She lifts Ted up so he can look out to the pool. I shimmy myself in beside Dad, smiling apologetically at the woman behind who got here on time but will still be looking at the back of my head. She smiles back, her eyes on Ted as he points and shouts that he can see Polly. Toddlers are good for that. They give you a free pass for stuff.

I follow his gaze. Swimming-capped heads are huddled together in team talks, their bodies slender, athletic. Polly is on the edge of her team's huddle, a bright flash of green down the sides of a navy-blue swimsuit. I try to catch her eye, but she is staring at the water. She looks as though she would rather be anywhere else.

'Nerves, I expect,' Dad says.

'Yeah,' I say.

'Or she's sulking because Rosie's not here,' Mum whispers, though it's something of a stage whisper so I imagine anyone within ten metres of us will have heard.

'Why isn't Rosie here?'

'I think they might have had a bit of a falling out,' Dad says.

'You know what girls are like. Always up to no good at this age. Heaven knows you were.' He laughs.

My stomach churns. He doesn't know the half of it. Not for me, then, and not for Polly, now. I wonder if their falling out has anything to do with the sleepover.

Polly isn't in the first few races, but we clap and cheer for her teammates. Greg is standing poolside and I somehow manage to catch his eye at the exact moment he unzips his hoodie, which is great, as now he'll think I was checking him out. He is wearing a vest. Jory and I have always mocked vests, but I can't say this one looks too bad on Greg. It's not bad at all.

'He's single, you know. Greg.' Mum's face pops up extremely close to mine.

'That's nice,' I say. 'Are you planning on asking him out?' I can feel Dad chuckling beside me.

'He looked quite taken with you, when you were chatting earlier,' she continues. 'And you do go back a long way.'

I roll my eyes. 'Hardly. We swam together yonks ago and I haven't spoken to him since.'

'Well, you have now. And I know it's not the most exciting career, but he looks happy enough, and he's in great shape,' she says, counting on her fingers as though she's been weighing up the dating-Greg pros and cons. 'You can't be too choosy at your age.'

'Unbelievable.'

'Your dad won't encourage it because he's still hoping you'll marry Jory but I've told him that ship has sailed. Or rather it won't sail now. Such a shame.'

'Any other males I've spoken to that you want to marry me off to? What about Albert?' I am grateful when Polly gets in the pool, the first to swim from her mixed medley relay team. *Come on, Pol.*

'Backstroke first,' Dad says. 'Tough gig.'

She is in one of the middle two lanes and the swimmers on either side of her are adjusting their goggles and moving their heads from side to side by way of a stretch. They look animated, alive, looking up and listening to last-minute instructions from their coaches and teammates. Polly's stillness sticks out among them. Her goggles are still on her forehead.

'What's she doing – is she OK?'

'I think she's just getting in the zone,' Mum says, but her tone suggests she's not so sure. The other swimmers have assumed their start positions, hands gripping the edge of the pool ready to launch themselves backwards when the start-gun fires. Polly only puts her goggles on when Greg shouts at her.

'She's not OK,' I say. 'Something's wrong.' Mum and Dad don't say anything. I can feel my heart pounding as her competitors curl up like springs. Finally, the gun is fired. The cheering goes mad and it takes me a few seconds of looking at the figures gliding backwards in their lanes to realize that Polly isn't one of them. The families of her teammates around us begin talking at once.

'What the—'

'What's she doing?'

'Why isn't she moving?'

I watch as she climbs out, saying sorry to Greg, who has both hands on his head. He asks if she is all right as she rushes past and I am grateful to him for showing some compassion, which is more than can be said for one of the spectating dads, who is banging his hand furiously against the glass. 'Who is our number one? The Lander girl? Well, she's fucked that.' There are whispers as people point out with embarrassment where we are standing. He doesn't care. 'Well, she has, she's royally fucked it.'

Polly flies past us on the other side of the glass, heading for the changing room.

'I'll go,' I say, glaring at Angry Dad as I squeeze out. 'Her dad has just died, you arsehole.'

'Beth.' Mum is clearly mortified at the prospect of a scene.

'No, she's right, love,' Dad says, and I shoot a nod in his direction, a thank-you for the back-up.

The girls' changing room is full of clothes, bags and shampoo bottles but is empty of people, save for us two. Polly is hunched on the bench underneath her peg, water dripping on to her lap. I prise the towel from her hands and wrap it around her shoulders. There is a dent across her forehead where the swimming cap has been. Beyond the showers, we hear a crescendo of cheering followed by an eruption of clapping as the winning relay team is crowned. Polly flinches at the noise but says nothing.

'Pol? What happened?' I sit beside her on the bench. She sniffs and shakes her head. 'I know your heart hasn't been in all this recently' – I nod towards the pool – 'and I do understand what that feels like.'

'No, you don't,' she says. Her voice is small.

'Try me, then. What's going on?'

'I've ruined everything.' It's hard to know what she is referring to. Is she talking about the race? A falling out with Rosie? Or is she talking about life in general because of everything that has been going on? Maybe it's all of it.

A swimmer from one of the other teams comes into the changing room to use the toilet, trying very hard not to look at us as she tiptoes past. I lower my voice. 'I know things are bleak at the moment. And I know you probably feel like it's never going to get better, but it won't always be like this.'

'I've let everyone down.' Her nose is running and I reach up and grab a paper towel from the dispenser next to the sinks.

'No, you haven't. OK, you didn't start *one* race, but your mind was elsewhere. People will understand.'

'*I don't care about the stupid gala!*' Her sudden increase in volume makes me jump. The toilet flushes and the other swimmer slips out behind us, heading back to the event.

'Well, what *do* you care about?' I hold the paper towel out towards her. 'I can't help, if you don't let me in.'

She takes it and wipes her nose. 'You can't help anyway.'

'I know I can't bring your dad back, or make your mum better, but—'

She cuts me off. She is crying again. 'I just want to undo it.'

She's right, I can't do that. We sit in silence for a moment until Polly starts to shiver. I reach into her bag and take out her pile of clothes, placing them next to her on the bench. 'Put these on, then I'll take you home.'

She stands up and yanks her costume down, stepping out of it and kicking it to one side alongside the towel. I don't know why it is a surprise to see her naked – we are in a changing room, after all – but she seems out of sorts, frantic. I nudge the clothes pile a bit closer towards her. She doesn't pick any of it up. 'You don't have to keep up the swimming,' I say, 'if you don't want to do it any more.'

She looks at me, confused. 'You said I did.'

'Because I think you should. But you're right, *I* didn't stick at it. I gave it all up. I regret that, to be honest. I wish I'd had more staying power but, as your nan will tell you, I have a habit of quitting, so I have no right to tell you not to do the same.' Polly has moved away from the bench and is walking up and down the length of the lockers. 'Come on, Pol, you need to get dressed.' It's a struggle to maintain a conversation with someone who is angrily pacing without any clothes on.

'Why?' she says, her tone contrary.

'Well, because . . .' My eyes dart towards the showers, beyond them the entrance to the pool. There can't be many races left to swim, which means it won't be long before the changing room fills back up.

'I don't care if people see me naked.' Polly flings her arms outwards. 'I don't care if *everyone* sees me naked. I don't care about any of it.'

'OK.' I put my hands up. 'I'll wait for you outside then.'

'I keep going over it, in my head,' she says. 'When I close my eyes, I can see Mum and Dad driving away from our house that morning.'

'Oh, Pol.' I put my hands on her shoulders. Her face is pale.

'It's all my fault, Aunty Beth,' she whispers.

'No, *none* of this is your fault.'

'What if it is?'

I shake my head. 'But it's not. How can it be?'

She puts her bra and knickers back on. I think for a moment she is going to say something more but the sound of voices approaching seems to flick a switch and she mumbles at me to forget it. The intensity of whatever moment we were just having, the conversation we were sharing, has gone, and the guarded Polly I've been living with for the last few months is back. She pulls her T-shirt over her head. 'I'll be out in five.'

'Well?' Mum and Dad are hovering next to the reception desk. Ted is beside them, eating a bag of crisps from the vending machine.

'She's just feeling a bit overwhelmed.' It's an understatement of epic proportions.

'Oh dear. Maybe we've been expecting her to be more OK than she is. Do you think that's it?' Dad asks.

I roll my lips inside my mouth. I should have told them about the sleepover. I am more convinced than ever that Polly is hiding something, but telling them about the sleepover and house-party business now feels worse than if I'd filled them in when I found out. *I forgot to say, she did lie about something but I bribed her by promising not to tell you guys what's been going on if she kept up the swimming. We didn't want to worry you, Mum. Everything's under control though.* It would only serve to further confirm how irresponsible I am. Besides, Polly *almost* opened up to me just then. If I betray her trust now, she might never open up again and we'll never get to the bottom of what it is she's not telling us.

I look over Dad's shoulder at the crowd of spectators who are dispersing from their huddle as they wait for their own teenagers to get changed. 'Was anything else said? About the race?'

Mum and Dad look at each other. Mum looks momentarily horrified and I worry for a second that something terrible has unfolded out here until I notice Dad attempting to conceal a smirk.

'What?'

Dad laughs and Mum hits him on the arm. 'It's not funny, Jim.'

'It is a bit funny, love,' he says.

'Can one of you just tell me?'

'Your dad will have to tell you. I'm so embarrassed.' Mum shakes her head.

I look at Dad, who gives a very unsubtle nod in the direction of the angry swimming dad who was shouting his mouth off about Polly messing up the race. 'He came over to apologize, in fairness to him. Said he'd heard what Polly had been through and that he'd got caught up in the moment.'

'Because his son is the "finisher" in the relay team,' Mum adds. 'He's been building up to tonight for ages, terrible shame for him.' She always does this. Instructs Dad to tell the story then takes over anyway.

'So he apologized. That's good, isn't it? Quite right too,' I say.

'He did apologize,' Mum says, glancing behind her to check he's not listening, 'and then when we said that we understood why he'd got cross, no hard feelings and what have you, he said thank you . . .' She puts her face in her hands and waits for Dad to fill in the ending.

'And then Ted here, who was in his nan's arms at the time, said . . .' Dad pauses for dramatic effect. '"You're welcome, stickhead."'

Despite the drama of the evening, I laugh.

Mum is shaking her head. '*Stickhead*, though, Beth. Where on earth has he got that from?'

17

The sun is out, and we stop to admire the bank of wildflowers on the walk to the main entrance. I have acclimatized to the smell of the hospital over the last few months, barely noticing the anti-bacterial spray mixed with school dinners aroma that used to hit me the moment we arrived. Our route through the maze of corridors has changed slightly since Emmy was moved to Bracken ward a few weeks ago. When Dr Hargreaves told us about the change of ward, we dared to hope it was because she was showing signs of getting better. The true motivation behind the move, we've discovered, is that she simply isn't showing signs of getting any worse, and her ICU bed was needed for new patients needing a greater level of care. Most of those who have come in after Emmy have either gone home by now, because they are better, or won't be going home at all. All the while my sister is baffling a team of professionals by lying peacefully in her bed, like Sleeping Beauty, unable to communicate with any of us but not showing obvious signs of severe or permanent brain damage either.

We are greeted by Keisha, one of the nurses on Bracken ward. Keisha is fast becoming my favourite because she always makes the most effort with Ted. 'He's sitting it out again today,' I tell her, 'but will hopefully be in to see his mum tomorrow.' It is getting increasingly difficult to keep Ted's spirits up about his visits here.

This ward is busier than ICU, but Emmy is still tucked in one corner and the bed next to hers is empty at the moment, which means I will at least feel less of an idiot when I'm talking to myself. I'm carrying a bundle of lavender tied with a ribbon that Albert gave me to bring in. At first I thought he was making a joke about the plant-pot sick but it turns out he was thinking more about its scent after I told him that strong smells can be an important tool in both testing the responsiveness of coma patients and helping to stimulate their senses. I rub the flowers gently between my fingers, taking a deep sniff and imagining for a moment what it would be like if Emmy did the same. She doesn't respond but I place them on her chest, just in case.

Dad has gone to get us both coffees. I suspect he'll go back to the cafe on the ground floor and buy a newspaper while he's down there so he can come back and read the crossword clues aloud. He's not very good at crosswords and neither am I, which means it takes us ages to complete one. I drape my coat over the back of the chair and move it closer to the bed, gently placing Emmy's hand in my own. Her lips look different today. They're slightly turned up in the corners as though she's smiling, or perhaps in the middle of a really good dream. I wonder if that's what it's like in her head right now. A really long, deep dream. Or perhaps there is nothing at all. Every chat we have with her doctors ends on the same note: they just don't know. Emmy might be in a very deep sleep, she might be awake and 'locked in', or she might be neither of those things. I try very hard while I'm here not to think about any of the possibilities that don't result in her coming home, but those are the thoughts that continue to flood my brain when I'm drifting off to sleep. Alongside worry over Polly and what it is she's hiding.

I rub my thumb over the top of Emmy's hand. 'Today's good news is that I forgot to put a bedtime nappy on Ted last night and he was still dry this morning, hurrah. I know there was a bit of luck at play because most mornings his nappies are bulging with wee so he's probably not ready to go nappy cold-turkey yet, but I thought you'd like to know anyway. I haven't mentioned it to Mum because the last time I told her he had a dry nappy she said I wasn't giving him enough to drink. Classic Mum. I am, by the way, giving him enough to drink. He actually has loads to drink. Unfortunately, he seems to have developed a real taste for apple and blackcurrant squash, but we all have our vices.'

I study my sister's face for a movement, anything to signal that she knows I am beside her talking about her son's drinking habits, with a strong waft of lavender under her nostrils, but there is nothing. Assume she can hear everything, Dr Hargreaves said, so that is what I shall continue to do.

'The apple and blackcurrant squash habit isn't the bad news, I'm afraid. Today's headline bad news is that I have broken your hoover.' I pause and grimace, even though I know I'm not about to get told off. 'I didn't realize how stupidly delicate they are and it appears I was a bit gung-ho with yours. I know this will be difficult to hear because it's the posh cordless upright one Doug bought you, but you should know I tried to do the right thing after Mum flagged that there was an issue. Dad dug out the warranty from your paperwork – which was easy to find after we discovered you keep a whole folder dedicated to "receipts and warranties" *and* that they're all in alphabetical order. (I'm impressed and depressed for you about that in equal measure, by the way.) Anyway, I phoned the manufacturer, who was extremely unreasonable and told me that my use of the vacuum cleaner had not been in line with the manual and that the breakdown was due to "misuse, neglect or careless operation of the machine". If you're wondering what I did, I hoovered up a smashed glass because I couldn't find the dustpan and brush, then, when it started making a funny noise I ignored it, hoping it would go away. And, well, apparently a shard of glass got lodged in the motor, which is why eventually it started smelling of burning. It's completely had it. Sorry about that.'

If anything was going to prompt a glimmer of reaction from my sister, it would be this. I can imagine the exact expression she would give me under normal circumstances. The one that says she is shocked we came from the same womb when I do shit like this and she has a catalogued folder for receipts.

Dad returns with our drinks before I've had time to confess to scuffing her car. I crane my neck to look in his back pocket. 'No paper?'

'Oh, do you know, I completely forgot about the paper. I bumped into the Doctor . . .' A mischievous smile spreads across his face.

I wag my finger at him. 'Don't you dare.'

Too late. He puts the coffees down and pretends to get inside a telephone box, spinning around and around in a circle. When he stops spinning, he stumbles and I laugh.

'You're so embarrassing, do you know that?' I say. 'What did Dr Hargreaves say? Or did you make up seeing her just so you could play charades?'

He takes the second visitor chair and carries it round to the other side of Emmy's bed. 'No, I really did see her. I think she was taking a very rare five minutes for coffee so I didn't want to bother her but she did say there's not been any big change.'

'Right.' We sit in silence for a while, blowing on our hot drinks and staring at Emmy.

'Work all right?' Dad asks.

'Yeah, fine.' I think back to the last conversation I had with Malcolm. 'Actually . . .'

'Uh-oh.' Dad gives me a look. I know exactly what he is expecting me to say and I can't blame him for that, really. Chats about work, in the past, have mostly led to me declaring that I'm thinking of quitting whatever role I have been doing and asking him to help me break the news to Mum.

'It's nothing bad,' I say. 'Possibly the opposite. I don't know.' I give him a summary of my last meeting with Malcolm, who has asked me to step up a bit on the finance deals front. He wants me to change my title from portfolio assistant to senior portfolio assistant. There's a little bit more money in it for me.

'A promotion then? That's fantastic!' Dad says, and I can't help but beam under his praise.

'It's not really a promotion. Well, I suppose it is, a slight one. I'm still Malcolm's dogsbody, I just have more responsibility.'

'And you want to do it, do you? You've said yes?'

'Yep.' I don't tell him that it came completely out of the blue and I didn't have a chance to consider it properly as an offer. It was more a statement. 'You will now be doing' rather than 'Would you like to?' I also don't tell Dad that I already feel like I am doing too much at work and that it's starting to make things unravel with Polly, Ted and running a house even more than it was already. Mum and Dad seem to think I'm coping, dubious domestic skills aside.

'That's brilliant, love. It really is. Your mum will be delighted.' I give him the double thumbs up and he laughs. 'She's proud of you, you know.'

'Hmmm,' I say. My mum hasn't told me she's proud of me since I won the 100 metres breaststroke in 2001. She finds my inability to commit to things 'really rather baffling'. She said exactly this herself on New Year's Eve last year after she'd had a couple of port and lemons and her mouth delivered what I can only assume her brain had been thinking for years. We had been discussing the year ahead, our resolutions and what not. Emmy and Doug had come over with the kids and I'd stayed with them for a meal before Jory came round and we went to the pub. 'Perhaps this will be the year you finally sort yourself out, love,' Mum had said, her cheeks flushed from the port, though she blamed it on the heat of the Aga. 'Get your life on track.'

'Bloody hell, Mum – say what you think next time, eh?' I had laughed along with my family while they did what they always do and chuckled at the improbability of me getting anything on track. I have no doubt that chat about my lack of direction in work, love and generally being an adult amused them all long after Jory and I had left.

'Beth?' Dad has been asking me questions about the new step-up at work. I missed the start of it.

'Sorry, miles away.'

'I was just saying, we should do something to celebrate.'

'It's really not a big deal. The monthly pay rise is barely enough to fill an extra tank of fuel.' *Or pay to fix the bumper paintwork.*

'Well, we don't have a lot to celebrate at the moment, do we, but this is something good. What is it your sister is always saying? Celebrate the small wins?'

I stroke Emmy's hair, tucking a dark blonde wave behind her ear. I move my head towards hers. 'Dad's started repeating your mantras now. I think it's time for you to come back to us.' I glance sideways at Dad and put on a stage whisper, '*And* he did the Doctor joke. Please come back.'

I thought this would make Dad smile but he shakes his head at me sadly. 'I don't know how you do that.'

'What do you mean?'

'Talk to Emmy as though she can hear you. You talk to her like it's just a normal chat, but it's not normal.' I follow his gaze, the stark strip lighting overhead illuminating the patterned curtains and the two generic and impersonal paintings on the wall. Flowers in a vase. A fleet of ships on a stormy sea. I know what the hospital is trying to do but in all honesty this space would be improved without the paintings.

I look back at my sister. She looks thin. I don't know if she's lost weight because she's only eating via a gastronomy tube in her tummy or because her muscles are wasting away. Either way, it's a shock every time the nurses come in to bathe her and I glimpse the body that lies below the neck. It's Emmy but not Emmy. I look back at Dad. 'When I talk to her, I just imagine she can hear every word. If I stop to think about it, *really* think about it, I'm not convinced she can. But I need to go on believing she can or else – well, you know.'

He nods. 'I'll try harder.' He moves closer to Emmy, so we are huddled as a trio. 'I hope you can hear us, Emmy Lou. Your sister's telling porkies, by the way. It was a brilliant Doctor Who impression.'

In the car on the way home, I switch Absolute Radio 80s to Absolute Radio 90s when Dad's not looking, though I'm sure it won't be long before he notices. He's always saying proper music died in the 1980s. We talk about Emmy and Doug, as we always do on our hospital journeys, then Dad starts asking me about Jory.

'Did your mum tell you she saw him with his girlfriend? Sadie, is it?'

A funny feeling appears in my chest, like something heavy has just been poured inside it. 'No. When was that?'

'At the weekend, I think. In Morrison's. They were ever so couply, she said.'

'Oh right. That's nice.' I hit the radio button, silencing Cerys Matthews and her case for Mulder and Scully.

'What's up?' Dad is eyeing me nervously.

'I just hate that song, that's all. Always have.'

'I must admit I didn't realize they were around in the eighties. Nothing's happened with you and Jory, has it? You're still friends?'

'Yes. No.' I sigh. 'I dunno. There was this message he sent. It wasn't meant for me but it was about me.'

'Oh. What did it say?'

'Just . . .' I can't mention Jory not telling me about the house party Mum and Dad have no knowledge of. 'It just made it sound like I was a nuisance, that's all. Like all I bring is drama.'

'Really? Well, I'm surprised at that. He's always been a crack-
ing friend to you. Have you told him you're upset?'

'No.' Every time he calls I make excuses not to chat, and when
Ted and I bumped into him in the village shop he said again I was
'acting weird'. It's funny, the harder you focus on not acting
weird, the weirder you act.

'Hmmm.' Dad taps the steering wheel gently. 'We all say things
we don't mean every now and again, love. And if he doesn't know
you're upset, he can't make amends, can he? Why don't you see if
he's free to meet for a drink? Celebrate that promotion. Your
mum and I can have Ted and Polly for a night.'

'Yeah, I might do.'

'Good.' Dad turns the radio back on, satisfied he has helped
solve my problem. When 'Love Me For A Reason' comes on, he
wags his finger. 'Now they're just being silly. Boys 2 Life weren't
around in the eighties! I'm going to write in and complain.'

'*Boyzone.*'

'Is it? Who were Boys 2 Life then?'

'There was never a Boys 2 Life. You're mixing up Boyzone,
Boys II Men and Westlife.'

'So I am.' Dad laughs. 'And Boyzlife were Irish and when I said
"So I am" I sounded Irish, didn't I? Your sister fancied the blond
one, Keegan, was it?'

I mime hitting my forehead with the palm of my hand and
when the song finishes, I switch it back to his 80s station to keep
him happy for the rest of the journey.

There's a big part of me that wants to say yes to Mum and Dad
babysitting so I can ask Jory out for a drink, but an even bigger
part of me knows I'm not going to. The more we haven't been
seeing each other, the more I've started to realize that it's not just
hurt pride over the message he sent by mistake that's behind me
acting weird. I've been acting weird because I feel weird, and I feel
weird because Jory has a girlfriend. If I sit down with him in the

pub again, I don't trust myself not to do or say something that will reveal the truth of it. I am jealous. Jealous of her. Jealous of them.

When we get back, Mum and Ted are out and Dad says he's going to stretch his legs and find them. 'Your mother's probably gossiping somewhere between here and the green. Do you want to come?'

'No thanks. You go. I'll see you in a bit.' When I get indoors, there is a small brown-paper parcel on the doormat that has come through the letterbox, my name scribbled on the front of it in curly writing. I carry it through to the kitchen before peeling off the paper.

Inside is a copy of *Jane Eyre*. It's a library copy with a clear plastic jacket slipped over the cover. I turn it over in my hands. I haven't been to the library since failing to return three Point Horrors in Year 7. Mum gave me the option of earning back the fine I'd incurred by doing chores around the house or never being allowed to borrow from the library again and, in the heat of the moment, I chose the latter, which is why I'm even more baffled that there is a library book inside a parcel with my name on it. Among the paper I've discarded on the worktop is a handwritten note on a William Morris postcard.

Dear Beth,

I think you had a great idea and I wondered if perhaps this could be our first read? I have a copy already, so I borrowed a second copy from the library when the Age Concern bus took us into town. I suggest we convene one evening next week and that I come to you. Perhaps you could send a text message with a convenient time? It would do me good to practise replying on my mobile phone. That said, if you are now too busy or have had second thoughts please just post

the book back through my door and I will say no more about
it. I realize I have more time on my hands than you do.
  Best,
  Albert

I don't know why, but Albert's note and the library book have made me feel a bit teary. Emmy would have an absolute *field day* if she saw me welling up over a book from her next-door neighbour so soon after crying about his gift of a peg bag. I reach for my phone and open my contacts to find him: Albert Next Door. I don't know any other Alberts but I like to add a descriptor with every name, one of only a few things I have inherited from Mum, whose contacts include Trevor Gutter Cleaning and Carol Pete's Wife. I flick the switch on the kettle and type my message.

How about Wednesday?

A reply comes back a few minutes later.

HELLO BETH ITS ALBERT I JUMPED FEET WHEN THE PHONE BEEPED NEXT WEDNESDAY IS GREAT SEE YOU THEN

18

It becomes apparent almost immediately that Albert is taking the book club a lot more seriously than I am. I had my suspicions this might be the case when he turned up with a folder containing a notebook and some things he'd printed off the internet during this week's library trip, and now that he's requested we sit at the dining table rather than on the sofas I know for sure I should have read more of the book. I open a bottle of red wine and pour us both a glass.

'Are those *worksheets?*' I lean over the table to see what he's taken out.

'Not worksheets as such, more of a guide. I was talking to Patricia at the library – she supervises computer time for old-timers like me, you see – and she directed me to an interweb site with some prompts for these book clubs. They're all free! I just had to pay five pence per sheet to print them. Isn't that marvellous?' He passes two sheets over to me and the way his face lights up when he's talking is so infectious I can't help but smile. 'Now, I know you said you haven't finished the book yet, so we'll just chat about where we have got to. Have you got it there?'

'Oh, yep. Two seconds.' I grab it from the kitchen counter, unfolding the corner of page five so Albert won't realize I've not yet made it past the first chapter. I thumb through my copy, trying my best to look forgetful. I've regressed to feeling like I'm at school. 'Hmm, I can't remember exactly where I've got to but it was just after Jane arrives at Thornfield.'

Albert is beaming. I have never seen him look this happy, not even when he is pruning in the garden. My quick glance at SparkNotes while I was sitting on the floor waiting for Ted to go to sleep has come up trumps. I do vaguely know the Jane Eyre story but only because I've seen the film.

'I see, well, we could start with this question.' Albert looks at his sheet. 'Mr Rochester tells Jane, "If you are cast in a different mould to the majority, it is no merit of yours." What do you think about this statement?'

'I think he's talking in riddles,' I say. Albert waits for me give a serious answer. I wish I had read it, though I don't expect I would understand it any better even if I had.

Albert is stroking his chin thoughtfully. 'It's complex, isn't it. I think he finds her strength of character rather fascinating. We must remember these were different times, old-fashioned. I imagine my idea of what would be acceptable in courtship is very different to yours, and Mr Rochester is even more of an ancient codger than me.'

'Are we supposed, as the reader, to think Rochester is a bit of a dick?' I say. 'Is that part of his appeal? Sorry. Dick was probably not an acceptable term when you and Mavis were courting. My generation swears all the time.'

Albert laughs. 'I think we are supposed to find Rochester mysterious and a little bitter, which leads us to wonder what his story is. And I wouldn't worry too much about your language. Mavis was delicate and graceful but if another driver cut her up on a roundabout, the air would turn blue.'

'Would it really?'

'Yes. I have never loved her more than when she was getting angry in the car. She was witty and strong like Jane Eyre, my Mavis.'

'I often get angry with other drivers, too. I'm sad I never got to meet Mavis,' I say, topping up Albert's glass. He puts his hand up to indicate that's enough.

We talk about Mr Rochester and Jane for the next forty minutes. I sink three glasses of red in that time and when I pop upstairs to check on Ted, I find myself stumbling on the first step. It is the most tipsy I have felt in months and I'm not sure if getting smashed at a two-person book club with an octogenarian on a Wednesday is an all-time low or a new high. Ted is asleep, starfishing on top of his duvet in his Captain America pyjamas. I don't want to risk waking him by pulling the duvet out from underneath him so I grab a blanket from underneath his chest of drawers and drape that over him instead. I knock on Polly's door to see if I can get her anything and it is no great surprise when she says no, then looks straight back at her phone.

'Are we doing more *Jane Eyre* next time, Albert?' I'm hoping I'm not swaying too much as I slip back into my seat.

'That's up to you, dear. We can do, or I can deliver you a new book after next week's library visit?'

'Let's do a new one,' I say, handing back *Jane Eyre*.

'Do you not want to finish this one? You can have it until Thursday,' he says.

'Oh, OK. Shall we leave it two weeks? I won't be able to read one and a half books in one week,' I say. *As it took me eight days to read five pages.* 'What day is best for you?'

'I don't ever have any plans, Beth.'

'Oh right. What did you used to do, when you did have plans? Other than your two-person book club. What do you miss doing?'

He thinks for a moment. 'Going out for dinner,' he says.

'That's settled then. Our next book club will be over dinner. Though I haven't been out for dinner in a while either so I'm not sure where to book. If we do a Tuesday evening next time, Mum can have Ted and pick Polly up from swimming. That's if we can persuade Polly to get back in the pool.'

Albert is looking at me strangely. 'You don't have to take me out for dinner. You have enough on your plate without old-man-sitting, too.'

'What if I want to take you out for dinner? I mean this in the nicest possible way but it will give me an excuse to get out of the house. I don't have much in my diary, either, outside of work and the hospital. Certainly nothing fun.'

'Wouldn't that lovely lad want to take you out for dinner instead? Drury?'

'*Jory*,' I say. 'And no, he's got a girlfriend now so we probably won't be seeing so much of each other, even as friends. It's complicated, to tell you the truth. Story for another day.'

'Oh. I really thought—' He stops himself. 'Never mind.'

I put the book-club printouts and notepad back in the folder and help Albert with his coat and flat cap. I love the fact he has dressed for a full outdoor adventure when he has in fact only ventured five metres next door.

He is studying my face. 'I'm sorry to hear about the other woman,' he says, which makes it sound as though Jory snuck off for an illicit affair.

'Don't be sorry! We weren't – well, you know. It doesn't matter,' I say.

He nods but is still looking perplexed. As he steps out into the night I promise to book us a table at a restaurant for our second book-club session. I might even get us a taxi, I tell him. Go wild. It is, after all, the closest thing to a night out I will see in a while. We say our goodbyes and I have a pang of sadness when I think of him heading back to an empty house. 'Albert, can I ask you something?'

'Of course.'

'You said Jane Eyre reminds you of Mavis. Is that why you picked it, as our first read?'

He smiles, his big smile that reaches from his mouth to the outside corners of his twinkly eyes. 'Something like that, dear.'

While I'm cleaning my teeth, a Facebook notification flashes up on my phone.

Greg Draper liked your profile picture.

I spit my toothpaste out in the sink. Greg Draper liked my profile picture, did he? What does that mean? Nothing at all. Just that he 'liked' it. (Because he *liked* it?) I run a flannel under the hot tap then wring it out before swiping it across my face, watching as my make-up begins to slide. After dabbing my face dry with a towel and slapping on some moisturizer, I pop my head in on Ted, who is fast asleep, and Polly, who has her headphones in and grunts when I tell her it's time to get some sleep. Then I pad downstairs to set up my sleeping spot on the sofa, phone still in hand.

Why is Greg Draper looking at my profile picture at 9:42 on a Wednesday evening? It's not even a new profile picture, and I haven't posted anything that would put me on his timeline, which means he must have gone looking for me. I'd forgotten we even were 'friends', a hangover from the days when Facebook was new and exciting and we added everyone we had ever been to school with, writing on each other's 'walls'. I click on his profile. His picture is one of those silhouette-against-the-sunset jobs, where it's hard to see anything, though the broader than average shoulder span is unmistakably my old swimming teammate. I hover my finger over the message icon underneath his picture.

I think of my sister. How she would tell me to sleep on it, to make sure there is no risk of message regret in the clear light of day. Her head would be shaking. *Don't do it, Beth. Drunk-messaging is always a terrible idea.* I put my phone down then pick it straight back up again. I'm not *drunk*. I've had a few glasses of wine but those have all but worn off. It is late, though, and everyone knows you don't send messages at night, after drinking wine, unless . . . well, unless I don't know what. I don't know a lot, right now. Except that I usually message Jory when I've been drinking. Before the accident, I used to be *with* Jory whenever I was drinking. In the pub, when life was easy and I had no idea how much I took it all for granted. But Jory is busy. And Greg has liked my picture.

I open a new message and begin typing.

19

'Two secs, Pol.' I'm replying to an email while walking. I left the office midway through submitting one of Malcolm's deals and now he can't find the accounts to go with it. 'Actually, I might just phone him.' Polly sighs as she checks the time on her phone. 'I'll be *really* quick, I promise.'

When I've finished telling Malcolm for the third time where to find the file, I drop my phone in my bag and we head towards the main entrance. Polly hasn't said more than two words since I picked her up. I do what I always do when she's mute and keep talking anyway, hoping it might spark some conversation. 'They've certainly upped my duties at work. I can't keep up with it all.'

Polly grunts.

'I don't know if I even want this step-up, to be honest.'

Nothing.

I try a change of topic. 'Blimey, it's changed loads. You see where those granite boulders are?' Polly moves her head in a nod so slight it would be easy to miss. 'Well, that's where your mum used to hang round, when she was at school. I used to hang round behind the science block. Are those huts still there? They were *freezing* in winter. Always a good place to hide when we were smoking though. Don't tell your nan I said that.'

We file through the doors, past reception and down the corridor towards the hall. I feel simultaneously young, as I remember walking this exact route as a teenager, and really old, as I realize it has been seventeen years since I was the same age as Polly is now. Back then I wanted to move to London and be a journalist, or run my own business. Instead, I became a serial job-quitter who still lived with my parents until I took on guardianship of two children following an accident. Not something any careers advisor could have predicted, I don't expect.

A very cheerful deputy head, who herself looks about twelve, comes out to tell us that parents' evening slots are running around ten minutes behind but that we should make our way to the right table zone and wait there.

'Have you got the time I gave you?' Polly gestures towards my bag.

'Oh, yes, it should be in here somewhere.' I'm lying. I know for a fact I haven't got the time she gave me. I wrote it on my hand this morning, which I thought was organized enough. I rummage through my bag anyway. 'I must have left it on my desk at work. I think it was five thirty-five though, with Mrs Sandford.' I squint at my hand. 'Actually, it could be five forty-five.'

Polly mutters 'For god's sake' under her breath. The deputy head takes pity on us, probably familiar with Polly's story. She checks a list on her clipboard. 'Five thirty-five for you, Polly. If you make your way to the history tables at the far end of the hall, Mrs Sandford is near the window.'

It would be the history tables. Polly's tutor could have taught anything but of course she teaches the same subject as Jory. I spot him immediately, the jacket he gave me to wear on the day of the accident hung over the back of his chair. He is deep in conversation with a parent.

After loitering while we wait for our turn, Mrs Sandford asks us both to take a seat in the blue plastic chairs that are usually stacked to one side of the hall. She pushes her glasses up her nose then looks at Polly before turning her attention to me. 'I'm glad you've been able to make it for this chat, Miss Pascoe.'

I smile. 'Of course.'

'I know things have been extremely difficult for your family these past few months and I appreciate how much you've had on your plate.'

'OK.' It's a little more of an intense start to our chat than I was expecting.

'I thought perhaps we ought to first run through where Polly's grades are sitting.' She rotates a piece of paper and pushes it towards us, pointing at two columns with her red pen. 'This column shows the grades we expected Polly to achieve this year, based on her performance in previous years. And *this* column is where her grades are now, at the end of the school year, after the last set of tests we did.'

'Right.' My smile slides as I take in the drop between columns one and two. 'Well, we were always expecting a dip, weren't we? With everything that's been going on.'

Mrs Sandford smiles thinly. 'Indeed. And if it was just a drop in grades, I don't think we would be too worried at this stage. There is plenty of time for an upturn in the right direction. However, it's Polly's behaviour that I have been wanting to talk to you about.'

'Oh.' I look sideways at Polly, who is not even attempting to engage in the conversation with her tutor, instead staring out of the window overlooking the tennis courts. 'What sort of behaviour?'

Mrs Sandford takes a sip of her coffee then leans forward. 'Polly, what sort of behaviour do you think we are most concerned about?'

Polly shrugs. 'Dunno.'

'She hasn't been herself,' I say. 'For obvious reasons.'

Her tutor nods. 'Of course. We have certainly made allowances for this – and will continue to do so. However, her behaviour has been *so* out of character that it's become hard to manage at times. She has been disruptive, loud, rude to her teachers. When we have followed the usual processes in terms of discipline, she has become emotionally volatile. She has been skipping lessons. That's why we have been attempting to get a meeting with you sooner.'

'But this is the first parents' evening since March?'

'It is, but we emailed you about coming in a few weeks ago. And there have been several messages on the portal.'

'I don't . . .' I look at Polly, who tenses beside me. 'I never got any messages? Why didn't someone phone me?'

'The messages are showing as read . . . It's all there on the hub, when you click through to Polly's profile. If you're having any trouble at all accessing the messages, please speak to reception as it's really important that we keep the lines of communication open.' Mrs Sandford is measured, sympathetic, but it still feels as though we are being told off and I am more than a bit confused at the mention of portals and hubs.

She moves on to talking about counselling available through the school and I am midway through telling her we don't need it (because Polly and Ted have a grief counsellor already assigned to them, should they want to start having sessions) when a phone rings, Trigger Happy TV loud. I mirror the parents either side of me and look around, catching Jory's eye as I scan the desks between where we are sitting and the stage at the front. We used to have our assemblies in this hall.

Jory is trying to communicate something, nodding at my feet. I shake my head. *I don't know what you're saying.* He points at the floor. My bag is ringing. *Shit*, it's my phone. Of course it would be my phone. In my haste to reach it and cancel the noise, I bash my shoulder into the table, knocking over Mrs Sandford's coffee. 'Christ, I am so sorry. I'll get a wipe.'

She picks up Polly's report papers that are swimming in warm, brown liquid, the columns with the should-have-been and actual grades now illegible. I begin grabbing wipes out of a packet in my bag, throwing them on the table.

She puts her hand up. 'It's fine, honestly. We've reached the end of our slot anyway.' She glances behind me to where a queue of parents are waiting. 'But I am going to set up another meeting for us, to make a plan for next term. I'll put it on the app.' Another teacher with glossy dark hair is rushing over with a large roll of blue paper towel. Mrs Sandford mouths 'Thank you' at her. Glossy hair teacher smiles widely at me and I tell her I am sorry for being so clumsy, thanking her for the paper towel. I know her, I realize. Where do I know her from? I grab my bag and promise Mrs Sandford I will make sure I work on a plan of action for Polly at home before the next meeting. 'They're going to see a big improvement in your attitude by September, aren't they, Pol?' I pick up my coat and look over my shoulder. Polly has already gone.

'*Apps, portals, emails.* You didn't brief me on any of this. How come I never got an email about a meeting?' I take the car keys out of my bag but don't unlock it. Polly is standing next to the car, kicking one of the tyres.

She shrugs. 'Maybe you missed it.'

'I haven't been getting anything from school. Which is most peculiar as I just double-checked with reception and they've got the right email address.'

'Maybe they're going into your spam.' She looks at her feet.

'It seems I was also supposed to be logging into an online portal. For notices etc. You never told me that.'

'I forgot.'

'You told me you were doing OK, with your grades and everything. How am I supposed to know what's going on if you're making it difficult for me to get notifications about things like parents' evenings?' I blip the lock and we get in.

'Is it any wonder that I don't want you coming to my parents' evenings? The clue is in the name, by the way.'

It takes me longer than it ought to to process what she means. 'Wow. Doing my best over here.'

'What, by leaving your phone on loud and throwing coffee at my teachers? You are *so* embarrassing.'

My cheeks burn and I open the window to let in some fresh air. 'I appreciate that wasn't ideal but there was no harm done, was there? Typical that Jory was there to witness me causing a scene.'

Polly pulls her knees up to her chest and stares out the window. 'And his girlfriend. *Cringe.*' Glossy dark hair. Sadie. Excellent.

Mum has done the nursery pick-up and taken Ted back to Emmy's. When we get there, after a silent journey, I send Polly in ahead and tell her I'll follow in a moment. She slams the car door and leaves me sitting outside.

I scroll down through my call history to find the number for Suzy – the real one – and call it. When she answers, I ask if I can pick her brain about portals and hubs and parents' evenings.

There's an app I can download to access the portal, she says. Once I'm logged in, it's like an interactive noticeboard. When I tell her I've never even seen the portal, she can't seem to get her head round it. 'But how did you book your parents' evening slot?'

'Polly gave me a piece of paper with the time on. Did you get one of those?'

'No. Nobody gets paper these days. It's all done online. She must have printed it out, though I don't know how. Students don't even have access to that bit of the app. They have a different login.'

'Well, Polly seems to have access to that bit of the app. And I don't seem to have any access whatsoever.'

'Oh dear.' I can hear Suzy grimace. 'I hope you get it sorted.'

After thanking her and hanging up, I check my email inbox, searching by the school name and the name of the portal, to no avail. After several more minutes and a scan over my settings, my suspicion that Polly has somehow intercepted my account is confirmed. An email rule was created months ago blocking all communication from the school. *Gotcha.* After unblocking, I download the app and reset the password for my portal account. When I log in, I discover a series of messages and notifications that 'I' have been replying to since March. It's the first time I've seen any of it. I'm biting on the inside of my cheek and wondering how the hell to deal with this level of deceit when my phone beeps with a text message.

ARE YOU OK IF YOU SIT THERE ANY LONGER ILL HAVE TO
BRING YOU OUT A CUP OF TEA PS HOW DO YOU DO AN
APOSTROPHE FROM ALBERT

I look over at Albert's window and sure enough, there he is, holding his phone in one hand and giving me a thumbs up with the other. He looks at me expectantly and I type a quick reply.

I'm fine. I'll give you an apostrophe lesson at our next book
club.

I add book and wine emojis and can see his eyes widen from here.

YES PLEASE AND THE LITTLE PICTURES TOO FROM
ALBERT

As I get out of the car, I return his thumbs up and he beams.

Inside, Mum and Dad are chatting to Polly, who shakes her head at me. *Don't tell them.* I want to tell *her* that quite frankly I'm done with not telling people things but when Dad asks how it went and Polly says it was fine, I don't correct her. It's the end of term, isn't it? Maybe we should draw a line under the last few months. By September, I'll be on top of messages and apps and portals. It'll be a fresh start.

Jory has messaged to check I'm all right following the parents' evening fiasco and ask if I am free to meet up one day next week when he'll have broken up for the holidays. I have held firm on not doing another pub date, certain that wine-fuelled truths will lead to me ruining our friendship once and for all, but a daytime meet-up is harmless and I text back to say as much before I change my mind.

> Hey, I'm fine, if a little mortified. Yes please to a meet-up next week. Can you do Weds and if so, do you fancy a walk somewhere? I'll have Ted (sorry) x
> PS do you think anyone noticed my phone going off?

He replies within seconds.

> Great, a walk sounds fun and don't apologize, it'll be great to see Ted too. A cheeky Wednesday walk it is, just let me know where x
> PS I'm sure no one noticed the phone.
> PPS 'PS' was a lie.

Mum is watching me, her head cocked to one side. 'Who's that you're messaging then? Coach Draper?'

'No.' I narrow my eyes. 'Why would it be Coach Draper?'

'No reason.' She stares a little too hard at her cup of tea. 'Polly mentioned she saw a message flash up on your phone from him, that's all.'

'Oh brilliant. Shall I just give you all my passcode, knock yourselves out.'

Mum laughs. 'Don't be so dramatic. Though Ted did tell Albert you had a boyfriend, when we saw him in the garden yesterday. Poor Albert seemed a bit confused.'

'What are you *talking* about? Why would Ted think I had a boyfriend?'

'He overheard us talking, I think. Albert thought Ted was talking about Jory at first. It all got a bit muddled when Ted mentioned Greg.'

'Right, well, there is no boyfriend, no romance, so you can pass that on next time you're gossiping about me with the neighbour. And you can stop giving me that look.'

'You are funny, love.' Mum holds both hands around her mug. 'I'm not giving you any look. I'm just saying you could do a lot worse than Greg. Couldn't she, Jim?'

'What's that, love?' Dad looks up from watching the news.

'Coach Draper.' She nods her head pointedly at me. 'And Beth.'

'Oh, yes. Nice lad.' He looks back at the telly. 'Built like a brick shithouse.'

AUGUST

20

Ted is wearing so much outerwear, including a hooded puddle suit and wellies, both of them bright yellow, that he looks as though he has arrived to sort out a spill of hazardous waste rather than stomp around a forest. I told him it was far too hot for his wet weather gear, but he insisted, meaning I've had to take off pretty much everything he was wearing underneath it except his pants. Luckily, it's cold for this time of year and we have at least had a bit of rain, making the wellies seem slightly less insane. I still noticed some strange looks when we got out of the car though, from parents rounding up their kids in shorts and hoodies.

'Where's your one of those?' Jory nods at Ted.

I laugh. 'They didn't do it in my size.'

'Shame. You couldn't convince Polly to come then?'

I shake my head. 'She thinks going for a walk with you would be "cringe".'

'Wow, brutal. How has she been?'

'Not good,' I say. 'I thought we might have made a break-through after the swimming thing but after parents' evening we're back to hardly speaking and looking sad all the time. And that's just me.' We stop to wait for Ted, who is squealing as he jumps in puddles.

'What age do we lose that, do you think?' Jory is staring,

fascinated, at Ted. He is well versed in high-school kids from his day job, but toddlers are unfamiliar territory, even though he's always seemed more at ease with babies and small children than I have.

'Lose what?' I steer Ted in the direction of the shortest and easiest forest walking trail.

'That carefree abandon. I know he's seen more turmoil in his life to date than most people will ever see in their whole lives but look at how happy he is, in that puddle. So *in the moment*. When does that leave us?'

'It left me on Friday the fifteenth of March this year,' I say. Jory looks at me as though he's not quite sure whether I want him to laugh. 'There are much bigger puddles round the corner, Ted.' He bolts past me in a flash of yellow.

'How often do you come here, to know the biggest puddle locations?' Jory says.

'I don't,' I admit. 'I've no idea if there are *any* puddles round the corner but it's an incentive to keep him moving.'

'Crafty.'

We plod on with our walk, stopping to look every time Ted brings us a stick that looks just like the last one. At one stage Ted's legs get tired and Jory offers to give him a shoulder ride but his knees lock while he's crouched down and I have to give him a hand standing back up, instructing Ted to hold on tight so he doesn't fall off. This sort of thing would usually be the source of great banter between Jory and me, with me squeezing his arms while questioning whether his gym membership was a waste of money, but now I'm second-guessing whether touching his muscles is appropriate. Maybe it crosses a line, like hand holding. Things *look* the same between us, two friends catching up on a walk, but they're not the same. I refuse to break first and mention the elephant in the room, or rather the elephant in the woodland. Not that I'm saying Sadie's an elephant. Judging by her Facebook photos and elegant parents' evening glossiness, she's more like a gazelle. I wonder what animal I would be in the wild. Something that's tired.

As we near the end of the trail, Ted now in my arms, Jory does a small cough and I bite down on my lip to stop myself filling the awkward silence. He caves, in the end. 'Beth, are you cross with me about something?'

Clever. Putting the slight atmosphere between us on me. 'Why would I be cross with you?'

'I don't know. I just know I don't want us to fall out. I hate it.' He looks down at his boots. They're proper walking boots, something else I would usually rib him for.

'We haven't *fallen out*. You generally have to have an argument to fall out.'

'So what is this, then? This weirdness,' he says, gesturing between us.

We keep walking for a minute before I answer. 'You texted me, after I phoned you about the party,' I say. 'But it wasn't meant for me.' It's a can of worms, I know, but I'm getting fed up with keeping lids on all my worm cans.

'Wait. What?'

I find the message on my phone and read it aloud. '*Just spoken to her. All the drama. She's angry with me but you were right about not telling her. It could have caused me all sorts of problems. I'll be leaving here just before 5. See you later. Love kiss kiss.*'

'Oh god.'

'Yep.'

'When you read it like that it sounds bad. But I swear that wasn't how I wrote it.'

'Wasn't it? It made me sound like a nuisance. And I know I have a tendency to overreact, but it really upset me that you were talking about me like that. With her.'

'With who?'

I roll my eyes. 'With Sadie. Who do you think?'

'But that message wasn't for Sadie, it was for my mum.'

'What?' I read it again. 'But —'

'After I found out that Polly had been at that house party, I was genuinely conflicted about whether or not to say something to you. So I spoke to Mum about it. She asked me what my gut feeling was and I told her my gut feeling was to let the school sort it out so there was no chance of me saying the wrong thing, or saying too much. That's why she said I shouldn't tell you. I was going to hers, the evening after I spoke to you.' He looks embarrassed. 'She still does some of my washing, on a Wednesday.'

I laugh, not minding the thought of him talking about me to his mum half as much as him talking about me to his girlfriend. 'I really thought . . . I'm sorry, for being an idiot.' Ted gives me a pine cone and I tell him it's wonderful before suggesting he finds another one. 'So, how's it going anyway, with you and Sadie?'

Jory gives me a sideways glance as if assessing whether this is a trick question. 'Uh, yeah, it's really good, thanks. We've been seeing each other quite a lot now it's the school holidays and we're both off.'

Not just good then. *Really good*. 'Cool.' *Cool?*

'It's still early days though.'

'I'm made up for you,' I say, not because I am but because it's what I think I should say.

Ted is getting whingy, so I unzip the rucksack for a snack. We're almost back at the car park but I plonk him on a bench and hand over a yoghurt pouch before sitting beside him.

Jory remains standing. 'I find it a bit awkward, talking about Sadie with you. I don't want it to be awkward. I guess partly I just feel guilty telling you that things are going well when you've got so much stuff to deal with.' He fiddles with his watch.

'Well, that's just ridiculous. I'm not so wrapped up in my own misery that I can't be pleased for happier news. I'm glad you're happy. You should know that.'

'OK. Good. That's good. It was thanks to you, anyway.'

'What was?'

'Me and Sade.' *Sade.*

'How so?' I reach for a packet of wipes and mop up the yoghurt Ted has managed to get all over his face from overzealous yoghurt-pouch squeezing. I fail to see how Jory sliding into Sadie's DMs is my fault.

'You told me to go for it,' he says.

Oh. 'Did I?'

'Remember the night in the pub, the night before . . .'

The accident. I nod, though that night, other than a memory of trying to pole-dance around a pool cue, remains a bit hazy.

'Well, you were quite pushy about it. Kept bringing Sadie up. So we messaged her.'

'What do you mean, "we"?' I have certainly never messaged her.

'Well, *I* messaged her, but we wrote it together. You told me to, Beth. Do you really not remember any of this? You were drunk but I didn't think you were wasted.' He shakes his head. 'That's why when we went out for that drink and I told you I'd asked her to be my girlfriend, I didn't think it would be quite so much of a surprise.'

'Was it my input into the wording of the message that sealed the deal?' I can't believe him taking the plunge where Sadie was concerned was my idea. Well done, me.

'I imagine so. I was hoping maybe the two of you might get on but, well, I dunno.' Jory frowns.

'But, well, you dunno what?'

'Sadie, she gets a bit funny when I talk about you. Sometimes people find it weird, don't they? A boy/girl best-friendship. It's probably just that.'

'I'm sure it's that.'

'Sometimes it's almost as though she thinks—'

'I need a poo,' Ted interrupts us. Excellent timing.

'There aren't toilets here but we're only ten minutes from home. Can you hold it?'

He is jumping from foot to foot. 'I'm desprit.'

'OK.' I lift him up, take his wellies off and start pulling his puddle suit down.

'What – where –' Jory looks around us.

'It's called a nature poo,' I tell him, and I laugh as his eyebrows shoot skywards.

'*Here?*'

'Not right here, no. It would feel improper to leave a toddler turd underneath a bench where people have picnics. Here, hold this.' I pass the puddle suit over and pick up the wipes, carrying Ted behind one of the largest trees to do the necessary. He really was 'desprit' because we don't manage to catch all of it in time. I shout to Jory from behind the tree. 'Can you get me a spare pair of pants and one of those little nappy sacks, from the bag?'

Jory carries the bag closer to us, catching sight of the scene behind the tree. 'Jesus, what's he been eating?'

Ted laughs, his bottom exposed to the elements as we await clean pants. Jory passes them over along with a nappy sack, his other hand over his mouth. When I've finished freshening up Ted, we rejoin the path. Jory is looking at the nappy sack in my hand, which contains Ted's soiled pants. I tie it to the strap of our rucksack.

'*Surely* that just goes straight in the bin?'

'No. It depends on how bad they are. If I threw away every pair of pants when he hasn't quite made it to the toilet in time, he would have no pants. I just put them on a hotter wash. The only trouble is, I'm still not that good at knowing what all the symbols mean on the washing machine and the other day I set it to what must have been inferno temperature as everything shrunk. Polly hasn't dis-covered her tracksuit bottoms yet. They'll probably fit Ted.'

Ted is running ahead, doing impressions of Jory. '*Jee-is, what's he eating?*'

'I don't sound like that!' Jory laughs.

'He sounds just like you, to be honest. Wait there, Ted.' Ted doesn't wait so I do a little jog to catch up with him, taking hold of his hand as we approach the car park.

It seems daft now that we came here in two cars. Well, a car and a van. I was still wounded by the text message he'd sent by mistake when I told him we'd meet him here, not realizing I'd got the wrong end of the stick. Even with the right end of the stick, I can't say I've entirely shaken the bad-mood cloud that descends when I think about him and Sadie spending the summer holidays together. We reach the van first and Jory gets his keys out of his coat pocket. 'I forgot to ask how your book-club date was with Albert.'

I frown. 'Did I tell you about that?'

'Yeah.'

'Oh.' I don't remember telling him about it. 'It was wonderful,' I say, without any hint of irony, because it was.

'That's good. I'm glad.'

'Right, well. See you soon then?' I say. 'Will you come to his p-a-r-t-y in a couple of weeks?' I spell it out and nod my head towards Ted, who doesn't yet know there will be a party. His birthday isn't until September but Emmy always does his party in the holidays. I'm yet to arrange anything or invite anyone else. 'You're welcome to bring a plus one . . .'

'Send me the date and I'll check, but I'd like to. Thanks, for today.'

'I bet you don't have to help clear up a toddler poo explosion on your Sadie dates,' I say. 'Not that this was a date. You know what I mean.'

'Beth dates are always an adventure,' he says, before giving me a peck on the cheek and ruffling Ted's hair. 'See you soon, mate.'

'Bye. Can I have lunch?' Ted says.

We walk back to the car and I strap Ted in. 'Yep. When we get back I'll do you some lunch,' I say. 'And then we might go to see Mummy this afternoon at the hospital, with Nanny, if you like?'

Ted thinks for a moment. 'Can I have cheesy sauce soldiers?'

'Yes, you can have cheesy sauce soldiers.' As I walk back to my door, Jory's van approaches and I wave. I think for a moment he is trying to mouth something to me but realize as he drives past that he is speaking on his hands-free. Already on the phone and he's not even left the car park.

'And some Pom-bears?' Ted continues his lunch order from the back seat.

'Whatever you want,' I say, watching the van disappear out of sight.

21

I used to think hell would look and sound like a nightclub playing drum and bass music when you're sober, but I was wrong. Hell itself has turned up in my sister's living room under the ruse of a fourth birthday party. The sounds are worse than the sights at this stage. Three toddlers are running in a circle around the coffee table, screaming in a pitch that is making my ears bleed, and out of nowhere Mum appears with little foam pads to stick on the corners of the table.

'That's a clever idea, Moira.' A mum of one of the toddlers, I have no idea which one, gestures at the foam pads in Mum's hand.

Mum smiles. 'Emmy has a whole drawer full of useful things like these. So organized.' I don't know if I imagine it but I sense her glancing in my direction when she says *so organized*. I stifle a yawn.

Ted has taken his T-shirt off and is jumping around with it on his head. Other children seem to be in various states of undress and I lean forward to grab a carton of orange juice that is about to tumble off the sideboard. Mum heads back to the kitchen to 'check on the sausage rolls' and I wish she would just let them burn because now I am stuck next to Other Toddler's Mum, which makes my underarms feel sweaty. I have absolutely zero mum-chat. I don't think I would have mum-chat even if Ted was my child.

'The sugar rush has kicked in, I see,' I say.

She smiles weakly. 'That's a myth, actually. Eating lots of sugar is actually more likely to cause energy levels to dip within an hour than it is to cause a spike.'

'Oh right,' I say, ducking as a cushion flies past my head. 'Doesn't explain this lot being off their tits though, does it?' I chuckle to myself before realizing Other Toddler's Mum has moved and joined another huddle of toddler mums, all of them in dungarees. They also all seem to have scarves in their hair, like that *We Can Do It* wartime poster, only instead of rolling up their sleeves and clutching their biceps, they're clutching drinks beakers and little packets of yoghurt raisins. She says something and they all turn to look at me. It seems this isn't a safe space to describe toddlers as being 'off their tits', even though they are guests in *my* space. Sort of.

'I wouldn't worry. It's all a bit *on Wednesdays we wear pink* with that lot. Or denim.' Kate appears beside me, Leila on her hip. 'How are you doing?'

'I'm all right,' I say.

She raises an eyebrow. I know Kate at least a little better than the dungaree gang. She is one of Emmy's newer friends but has been a good one, so I feel as though I can answer the question in her raised eyebrow a little more safely.

'Honestly? I feel like I've arrived at the seventh circle of hell. Other than that, not too bad.' The screaming seems to have gone from the having-fun kind to the horror-movie kind and we look behind us to see two toddlers having a physical fight, broken up by an older sibling who is eating more than her fair share of crisps from what's left of the party buffet.

'Coincidentally, the seventh circle in Dante's inferno is violence,' Kate says.

'Is it really? Well, I'll be damned. What's the eighth?'

'Fraud,' she says, and the serious delivery makes me laugh.

'Is this what it's like for you mums? Is this a social event? Like, do you *look forward* to this?'

'God no. I mean some are worse than others –' she looks around the room and catches herself – 'sorry, Beth, I didn't mean this one. I'll shut up.'

'I just want it to be over. What time can I do the pass-the-parcel then tell everyone to fuck off?'

'Soon I reckon. Are you doing party bags?' My face tells her I was not planning on doing party bags. I'm only doing a pass-the-parcel because Mum made one and brought it round. 'Well, do you have any balloons? All people really need is a bit of birthday cake in a napkin, or a balloon. Personally, I like party bags because they're a good way of giving people a more subtle fuck-off. Here's some plastic tat and a sliver of cake, party's over, bye.'

I like Kate's thinking. 'I'll put something together,' I tell her.

'I'll give you a hand,' she says. 'Leila, why don't you go and find Ted?' Leila does as she's told and potters off, straight over to a group of three- and four-year-olds. How wonderful it must be to be able to join in, just like that. I've only ever approached groups I barely know when I've been fuelled by gin and tonic.

Dad is in the kitchen, fussing over a portable CD player. He looks stressed.

'You all right, Dad? Had enough of the "Hokey Cokey" and switching to The Jam?'

He smiles gravely. 'It's not funny, love. It keeps sticking and I need it running smoothly for pass-the-parcel.'

'You don't need a CD player. We can just use my phone,' I tell him. 'I'll find a kids party playlist on Spotify.'

This only seems to make him more worried. 'But you know I don't know how to use Spotty-fy.'

'I'll do it then,' I say.

'Will you?' He looks unsure.

'Yes, say no more about it. Oh, wait a second . . .' I lift my phone to my ear. '1995 called and wants its CD player back.'

He concedes defeat and carries it back out to the car. Polly is hovering at the bottom of the stairs and looks as though she's planning on retreating back up them when she's spotted by Kate.

'Ah, there she is! Come and give us a hand with some balloons, Polly,' Kate says.

To my surprise, Polly does just that. I don't suppose she can ignore party guests in the same way she can her nagging aunty. The three of us stand away from the thick of the party action, blowing up balloons and folding slices of cake into Peppa Pig novelty napkins (another gift from Mum). Kate directs a lot of questions at Polly and though she doesn't get a lot back, she keeps asking more, which I think means she's deserving of a bigger piece of cake.

'Did you ever get to the bottom of that phone drama?' Kate passes over some napkins.

Polly lets go of the balloon she has almost finished blowing up and it flies in a loop-the-loop beside my head, whistling as it deflates.

'What phone drama?' I ask, licking a stray bit of Colin the Caterpillar icing from my thumb. Mum said that when I told her I was 'sorting the cake' she actually thought I was going to make one. Instead, I bought two. Two Colins.

'It was nothing,' Polly says. 'Just a Facebook thing.'

Kate frowns. 'Oh right. Your mum was getting all in a tizzy about it the last time I saw her. The last time I saw her not in the hospital, I mean.' Kate has been helping out visiting Emmy on the days none of us can get there.

'About what?' I repeat. I don't remember Emmy getting in a tizzy about a phone.

'Oh, you know what Mum's like,' Polly says. Her tone is casual, light, but I've clocked the expression she's wearing and she knows

I've clocked it because she's refusing to look at me, busying herself counting heads of toddlers then checking the numbers of cake parcels. It's the same face of panic she wore when I found the mortgage appointment letter in the jammed bag-for-life drawer.

Kate doesn't seem to have noticed and continues chatting. 'Wasn't it something about a phone you were selling? Something about Facebook? I can't remember, I just know Emmy was worrying about it on our last Leila and Ted playdate. I'd better go and check on Leila, actually. She's not had a wee in a while and sometimes when she's excited she forgets. You know what they're like. The other day . . .'

I smile and nod along to her story about a wee mishap at soft play but have zoned out, my eyes following Polly, who is using the change of subject as an opportunity to sneak back upstairs. She hasn't said one word to me about a phone drama and neither did my sister, I am sure of it. I do remember Emmy mentioning that Polly had sold her old phone but that was weeks before the accident. Why would they be fretting about an old phone so long after selling it? Unless Kate got muddled . . . but if it was nonsense, why did Polly look as though she'd seen a ghost again?

Mum has come to get me. It's pass-the-parcel time. I thank Kate for her help and follow Mum to the living room where the coffee table has been pushed against the radiator and the toddlers are sitting on the carpet in a circle.

'And you're sure you know what you're doing?' Mum says, as though I am about to wire a plug, not press play on the Kids Party Mega Mix I've just downloaded.

'Yes, Mum. Right, is everybody ready?' I ask.

The kids scream yes, they are ready. Some are banging their hands and stomping their feet in the middle of the circle. I start the music and the kids start passing the parcel around in a circle, though what they're really doing is lobbing it at each other. One little girl with pigtails and a sparkly unicorn top moves the parcel as though in slow motion across her lap and I am tempted to stop the music and let her win the little bag of Haribo between the layers for clearly being brighter than the rest of them. I stop it on Ted first, because he is my favourite and it's his party. The dungaree crew are visibly incensed by this favouritism and I flash my widest smile in their direction. One of them didn't let her daughter have any party rings or chocolate fingers from the buffet so the Haribo are probably considered contraband anyway.

I start the music again. Pigtail toddler's mum has had a word in her ear and told her she can't hog the parcel and must move it at normal speed. I'm fairly sure I spot an eye roll, which is quite sassy for a three-year-old, so I let her win the next packet. As the game goes on, the parcel passing gets more frantic. One kid seems frightened of the music stopping on him so treats the parcel like a ticking bomb. Another kid is crying because the parcel hit him in the face. I can't stop thinking about Polly and what she isn't telling me. I haven't been able to shake the feeling that something is amiss ever since she behaved so strangely over that letter, and now there's some sort of phone drama I had no knowledge of thrown into the mix. I wish she would just talk to me. I haven't got the energy to get all Poirot over it. I just need her to be honest. Emmy would have told me if Polly had done something bad, and she didn't tell me anything. So what is going on?

'For goodness' sake, Beth, you had one job.' Mum appears beside me.

'What? What's the matter?' I look down at my phone to find I have stopped the music unintentionally. The children are – oh god, everyone appears to be crying, including one of the mums. I worry for a moment that I might have sworn out loud without realizing. Mum has taken my phone from me and restarts the music after hastily rewrapping the last layer. Everyone is looking at me. I have no idea what is going on.

'You gave Matilda two prizes,' she hisses, before plastering a very big and very fake smile on her face. I stare at her blankly. 'There are exactly the right number of layers and prizes, including the one in the middle, for every child to win. If one child has two, another child will win nothing. It's birthday party basics.'

'Is that it?' I say. 'Is that the crime? Someone got two packets of Tangfastics and you're reacting like I've given them dog food.'

She tuts at me then lowers her voice. 'Of all the kids it had to be *Matilda,* Beth. Matilda isn't very good at sharing.'

The parcel continues to be passed but I have never seen a more miserable group of children. Matilda has left the circle and is sitting on the lap of her mum, who is stroking her hair to calm her down.

'Right, well, I'm sorry then. I didn't think.' I'm still shocked at the level of commotion a badly timed music pause has caused. I'm tempted to say something about lessons in life, about how we can't always win every game we play and that sometimes other people will have more Haribo than us, that's just the way it goes, but Mum responds before I launch my rant.

'That's the trouble with you, Beth. You never do.'

Fine. I leave my phone with her and walk back through the kitchen. It's hot outside and I plonk myself down on the bench. It would have been so much nicer to have the party out here, as I suggested, but apparently it's not good for toddlers to be out in the midday sun because they're vampires or something.

The back door opens and I pray to god it's not Mum, coming out to continue her lecture about birthday party 101.

'It's five o'clock somewhere in the world, right? Isn't that what they say?' Kate appears with a bottle of Prosecco and two mugs. I can see why my sister likes her.

'I think if you've been fired from pass-the-parcel it's acceptable to drink at any time of day,' I say.

She fills up one of the mugs with a generous glug of fizz and hands it over. 'Well, the mugs offer us protection from judging

197

eyes anyway. If we get rumbled out here, I'll stick the bottle behind the compost bin and it'll look like we're drinking coffee.'

'Sneaky. I like it,' I say. 'How come nobody gave me the memo about Matilda being an arsehole? Like, am I supposed to just know?'

Kate coughs and a bit of Prosecco flies out, making us both laugh. 'You can't really say *arsehole* about kids. But if you could' – she lowers her voice – 'Matilda would definitely be one.'

'Well, now I know. Not that I'll ever be trusted to host a child's birthday party again.'

We are on our second mug of fizz before Dad comes to find us, Ted in tow. He hands me my phone, which is still playing 'Cha Cha Slide'.

'Can I leave Ted with you, love? Your mum wants to blitz the place now everyone's left.' He is wearing Marigolds and carrying a bin bag.

I give him a thumbs up. I would much rather be on Ted watch out here than under the Moira regime in there. She will be a woman possessed.

'My friends gone home,' Ted says, climbing up on to the bench beside me.

'Oh, have they?' *Thank god for that.* 'Did you have a nice time?'

He nods. 'I made *two* wishes on my cake.' He is pleased with himself and evidently not scarred for life by the lack of home-made birthday cake.

'Don't tell us your wishes or they won't—' Kate starts but Ted begins telling us anyway.

'For my mummy to wake up,' he says, counting the first wish on his finger. 'And Daddy to come down from the sky.'

'We all wish for those, Ted,' I say.

'But you didn't make a *birthday* wish,' he says. He swings his little legs back and forth under the bench. Kate and I look at each other, a shared and understood pain, without saying anything. I want so badly to be able to tell Ted that I'm sure his wishes will come true but I know one of them never will and, despite a rollercoaster of hope and lots of 'good signs', there is nothing concrete to suggest the other one is going to either.

'Can I do another candle later?' He looks up at me hopefully. I dread to think what the third wish is going to be.

'We don't have much cake left, I don't think. Maybe half of Colin the Second's head. But sure, we can do another candle.'

'I'm going to wish for Rubble.'

'Some rubble? Like bricks?'

'Aunty Beth, you're so silly,' he giggles.

Kate laughs. 'I think he means Rubble from *Paw Patrol*. His language is exceptional for an almost four-year-old, isn't it? Like he's really smart.'

'Is he? I don't know what three- or four-year-olds are supposed to sound like.'

'Yeah, he's very advanced.'

'Oh right. Lovely,' I say. There's a message on my phone from Jory saying he's sorry again he couldn't make the party and that he'll come over with Ted's present tomorrow.

I sigh and lean on Kate. 'Is there any of that coffee left?'

22

Sunlight floods through a gap in the living-room curtains and hits me square in the face. I roll over, squeezing my eyelids shut, desperate to get back to sleep. I haven't even lifted my head off the sofa yet, but I can feel the hangover oozing out of my face, as though I am sweating Chardonnay. I *knew* this would happen. Despite having twice cleaned my teeth and drinking a pint of water before turning the lamp off last night, there is no mistaking the wine fuzz coating my tongue. I didn't even drink that much – not *really*, not compared to Old Beth standards – but Old Beth never had to make breakfasts and supervise children. Old Beth would have stayed in bed for an entire day. I could try to blame Kate for setting me off with the daytime drinking, but I can't blame her for the bottle I opened on my own and drank while sobbing through *Notting Hill*. It's Emmy's favourite film and I just felt like a bit of Hugh was what my evening needed.

All is quiet upstairs. Ted and Polly must still be asleep. I reach for my phone to check the time, but it's turned off. Either that or it's out of battery. I sit up and squint at the little carriage clock on Emmy's mantelpiece: 7:30. Blimey, a lie-in. I plug my phone in to charge and turn it on, remembering as I do so, with the hugest pang of hangover regret, why I turned it off before going to sleep. I put my glasses on but wonder if it's safer to keep them off.

I can't look. I have to look. I open my messages.

Oh *god*. There is a long conversation chain with Jory. Very long. And by 'conversation' I mean multiple messages I've fired at him with little response. I hover over delete before reading them but I can't delete them at his end so really what is the point?

I decide what I need more than anything is to have a bath. I *will* read the messages, I just need to be lying somewhere comfortable first. I tiptoe upstairs, wincing as the floorboard on the landing creaks. There is faint snoring coming from Ted's room. I'm not feeling too bad, now I'm up and about. I just need to shift the headache that has formed over my eyes.

I click the door shut quietly and turn the taps on before opening the picnic basket Emmy uses to store all her toiletries, picking out a bottle of fancy bubble bath I bought for her last year that she's barely touched. I wonder if that's because she doesn't get much time for baths or because she can't bring herself to use something that costs around £1.50 a wash. I suspect it's the latter. She has never been good at spoiling herself with expensive things, my sister. I, on the other hand, have always been more than comfortable spoiling myself with expensive things, despite never having the funds to support such luxury. I pour the liquid under the tap and take my pyjamas off.

I consider going to get the new book-club read that Albert has given me but it's downstairs and I can't be bothered to run down there in a towel. We didn't get around to going out for dinner for session two but it's on the cards for our third meeting next Tuesday. I need to read, or at least skim-read, *Little Women* before then.

The spa-day scent of the bubble bath fills my nostrils, and though the water is still shallow, I get in and let the mixer tap continue to run at my feet. It's hot, almost scalding. Perhaps if I sit sweating in the bath for long enough it will cleanse my body of the wine. I give the cold tap a blast and fill up a plastic cup from the side, drinking it then refilling for a second cup. Drinking cold water while sitting in hot water is one of life's underrated pleasures, I've always thought. Admittedly, I prefer to drink from a glass than a plastic Lego cup that came free with a Happy Meal (and is ordinarily used to rinse a toddler's hair) but in my state of hot dehydration it tastes just as refreshing. I keep running the water until it's deep enough to submerge myself before wiping my hands on the towel and picking up my phone to assess the damage. There were eight messages from me, before a response came. Eight. It's a level of desperation I'd like to say I haven't stooped to before but I know I have. Drinking and texting too often results in me sending things I would never, ever send if I were sober, leading to mammoth regret the next day.

8:05 PM

Alright Jor, hows it going, alright?

8:06 PM

*How's even. Before you get your red teacher pen out! And that was supposed to be Gavin and Stacey's Nessa. Accents get lost in messages.

8:35 PM

I'm glad you're popping over tomorrow as I was getting a bit worried that our woodland trip has put you off the toddler life altogether. It's not for the faint hearted. Are you at Sadie's? Nudge.

8:37 PM

(Nudge was what we used to send on MSN messenger when the other person hadn't replied. In case you've forgotten and thought I was being weird about you being at Sadie's.) Nudge. Haha.

9:17 PM

Are you ignoring me? Have I done something? I was giving you the benefit of the doubt but WhatsApp actually tells me you're online RIGHT NOW yet there are still no blue ticks under my messages so you're choosing not to read them, which is nice . . .

9:28 PM

That's a yes then.

10:04 PM

Jory, I really miss you. I'm sorry if I've handled you having a new girlfriend badly but you must understand why that is. It's the same reason it's weird when we talk about it. Or at least I think it is. Please can we talk.

The last one, clearly the one after *Notting Hill* and the bottle of Chardonnay, is full of typos but unfortunately still makes enough sense for Jory to get the gist.

11:25 PM

Im so sad thi sis happened to us. I thoght orr firnedhsip was difefegetnmt. I dont know if there's any pint in us even being friends if it's groin to be weird. Have a good evening with Spadie. Or should I say SADE.

Jory. 11:40 PM

Evening Beth. I can tell you're drunk, both from your horrendous spelling and the fact you are saying stuff you never

say sober. I'm sorry it took me a little while to reply but I have
been out with SADE this evening and she was understandably
a bit annoyed that my phone vibrated every five seconds with
messages from you. It caused a bit of a row actually, so thanks
for that. Have some water and go to bed. I'll see you tomorrow.

I groan and put the phone on the floor before lowering my
shoulders beneath the water and letting the steam circle my face.
Why did I have to send so many messages? Jory didn't reply to the
first one and that should have been the end of it. To keep bom-
barding him with more was unnecessary. Not to mention desperate.
I sound bitter. And the spelling, oh god the spelling. If it's *groin* to
be weird. I don't know if there's any *pint* in us being friends. Have
a good evening with *Spadie*. They are the sort of typos Jory and I
would usually howl with laughter at, but this time I don't think all
will be forgotten simply by me sending a monkey-hiding-behind-
his-hands emoji. The SADE in capitals was actually a bit
aggressive. I am just weighing up whether to cry or scream about
the horror that is my life when Ted bursts in, rubbing his eyes.

'Hey, Ted. Did you sleep OK?'

He blinks. 'I need the toilet.' *Good morning, Aunty Beth.*

'OK. If you pull your bedtime nappy down, you can do your
wee-wee yourself, can't you? Take your bottoms off and then you
can sit up on the seat like a big boy.'

He looks cute in his half-asleep state. 'You got boobies,' he
says, staring at my chest. 'My mummy got boobies too.'

'I have,' I say. 'Make sure your willy is tucked in.'

'Where's your willy?' he says, peering over the side of the bath
and searching for it.

I cross my legs. 'I don't have a willy. Remember when we had
this chat at swimming?'

'Oh no,' he says, as though the lack of penis is a great shame
for me.

'Have you finished your wee?'

'No.'

'OK.' As I continue to lather up my arms and legs I realize, with a creeping horror, that Ted – whose bum on the toilet is only around 50cm from my head – is also doing a poo, which is not at all conducive to the relaxing hangover environment I was trying to achieve. It suddenly smells a lot less like a spa day.

'Finished!' he says, unravelling the toilet roll.

'Right, well, I just need to wash my hair, but I'll be quick. Do you want to have a try wiping your own bum?' I ask.

'No. Aunty Beth do it,' he says, unravelling more toilet roll.

'Seriously? Hang on.' I clamber out and wrap a towel around me so I can do the necessary. 'All done. You need to wash your hands now, buddy.'

He is looking at the bath. 'I want a bath in the morning.' He emphasizes *in the morning* as though bathing at this time of day is an exotic treat. I suppose he doesn't normally wake up and have a bath straight away, unless he's been ill.

I flush the toilet and wash my hands before opening the window as wide as it will go.

'Another day you can. I've just got to wash my shampoo out quickly then I'll do us some breakfast? Ted—'

Already naked from the waist down, Ted has got his arms in the air and is taking his top off, too. I sigh. I don't have the energy to say no today. 'Hold on, I'll have to put some cold water in as it's too hot for you as it is.' I top up the cold and add some more posh bubbles, silently apologizing to my sister for now being at least £4 down. I did buy it though, so.

'Come on then.' I lift him in before climbing back in myself. 'If you turn around, I can wash your hair, too.'

Ted shifts to sit with his back to me, so that my legs are either side of him. I gently tilt his head back and, using the Lego cup, I lather and rinse his hair.

'That's nice,' he says, with such a strong appreciation it makes me laugh. Pouring warm water on his head has given him goose bumps and, as I wash his back, he hums a little tune.

'Does my daddy do his wee in a rhino, in the sky?'

'In a rhino?'

'Yeah, for his wee?'

'Oh, I don't know.' I have no idea why he's talking about rhinos. My fuzzy wine head hasn't completely lifted and I'm not convinced I've managed to wash myself properly but, even so, this has been quite a nice way to wake up. 'We can do this again another day if you like, champ?' I stroke his damp curls.

'Can I bring my boats in?'

'Of course.'

'And my fire engine?'

'If it hasn't got batteries, yes.'

'And my train track?'

'Not sure about the train track. Urinal!' I say, my brain catching up. 'That's what you meant. Not a rhino. A rhino is an animal and we don't wee on animals, do we?'

Ted shakes his head.

'I don't know if there are urinals in the sky, to be honest. I guess so. Shall we go and sort your breakfast out now?'

'Five more minutes,' he says. Five more minutes it is.

The doorbell rings as I'm helping Ted build a den in the living room. I lean across the window to see who it is, quickly leaning back again when I see Greg on the doorstep. What is *Greg* doing here?

Polly pads downstairs. 'I'll get it,' she says. 'It's my new club tracksuit.'

I move to the kitchen where I grab a lipstick from the counter and apply some while I'm hovering out of sight, unsure whether I should say hi or not. He's not here to see me but we've been messaging quite a bit so maybe it would be weirder not to say hi? The red lipstick suddenly feels OTT and I grab a tissue to tone it down a little before moving into the hallway to stand beside Polly, who is clutching the new club tracksuit. I smile at Greg.

'Hey. Tracksuit drop-off, is it?' *Good one, Beth. State the obvious.*

'That's the one.' He smiles back at me. 'How are you doing?'

'Yeah, I'm all right.' Polly turns and squeezes past me, a rare but unmistakable smirk on her face. 'I'm a tiny bit hungover to tell you the truth but, as always, I only have myself to blame.'

'Oh dear. Was it worth it at least?'

'Not really. It was fourth-birthday-party induced. If someone ever invites you to a kids' birthday party, say no. Run. Save yourself.'

Greg laughs. 'Got it.'

'Do you want to come in for a coffee or something?'

He looks back at his car, a flashy BMW. A van has pulled up behind it and I squint at the number plate. Jory's van. Excellent.

'I would love to come in, but I've got to deliver the rest of these then I'm booked to do some private swim coaching,' Greg says. 'Sorry.'

'No, it's fine.' Jory has got out and is walking towards us, a gift bag in his hand. Ted's present. I'd forgotten all about it and it's a surprise that he's turned up after my barrage of text abuse last night.

Greg is still talking. 'I'd love to come in for a coffee another time. I'd better get going now though.' He spins and almost collides with Jory. 'Oh. All right, mate.'

Jory returns the 'All right' with a nod. Greg is several inches taller and Jory takes a step back, so he's not looking directly at Greg's jaw. I look between the two of them, feeling increasingly self-conscious about my lipstick.

'See you later, Beth. I'll speak to you soon.' Greg gives me a knowing look as he leaves, a reference to our messages. I wonder if he would have made the look quite so obvious if Jory hadn't been here. There's a throaty roar when he starts his engine and Jory mutters something I can't hear.

I nod my head inside. 'Are you coming in?'

'No. I'm just dropping off the present.' He hands over the bag and I put it on the doorstep.

'OK. I'll get Ted. *Ted!*' I fiddle with the drawstring on my hoodie. 'Look, about last night—'

'It's a bit rich, don't you think?' Jory is talking quietly but I can hear he is angry. 'Ruining my evening with Sadie, messaging me things I *know* you don't mean, when all the while you've got your-self a new boyfriend anyway.'

'He's not my boyfriend.'

'Well, he obviously wants to be.'

I open my mouth and close it again. 'I'm sorry, OK? I had too much to drink, I was upset you weren't replying.'

Ted appears beside me with a Power Ranger mask on, pointing at the gift bag. 'Is that for me?'

Jory shakes his head gravely. 'No, I'm afraid this present is for Ted Lander, who is four very soon. It's not for Red Ranger.'

'RAH!' Ted pulls the mask off. 'It's me, Jor-eeee! It was just pretend.'

Jory mimes being shocked. 'Well, you had me fooled. In that case, it *is* for you.'

Ted looks up at me and I nod. 'Go ahead, open it.'

While Ted is busy tearing off the wrapping paper, I touch Jory lightly on the arm. He doesn't move my hand but won't meet my eye either. I lower my voice. 'I shouldn't have kept messaging you, I'm sorry.'

'I don't understand you, Beth. You've been making excuses whenever I try to arrange a catch-up. I know you have because your mum told me she'd offered to babysit again, yet you told me it would be impossible to get to the pub. And then you messaged all that stuff about missing me and needing to talk . . .' He looks down at Ted who has wrestled most of the paper off.

'Well, I do miss you. A lot. But I won't send a million messages in a row when you're having dinner with your girlfriend ever again. Brownie's promise.'

His mouth twitches in the corners. 'You quit the Brownies.'

'Yeah but that wasn't my fault. Brown Owl was a bitch.'

Jory laughs. Ted waves a little *Paw Patrol* vehicle under our noses. 'It's Rubble! Thank you, Jor-eeee.'

'Is it OK? It was a bit of a lucky dip at the toy shop.'

'Yes, it's the best one. Polly, *look*.' Ted runs back inside to show his sister.

'Thank you for his present. Are you sure I can't persuade you to come in? We're getting the Lego out in a minute.'

Jory shakes his head. 'I can't. Sadie wants to go to one of those antique fairs. She likes all that vintage stuff. I said I wouldn't be long.'

'Oh. OK.' I do a little pout. 'Well, have fun. And I'm sorry again about last night.'

'Maybe just rein in the drinking and texting. Mind you, Greg with his vest and big engine probably likes it. You always said you hated vests.' Jory's face is suddenly mischievous and when he opens his arms for a quick goodbye hug, I grip a little tighter and for a little longer than I normally would, pressing myself against him. His hair smells fruity. Like Body Shop shampoo, which isn't his as he's been using Head and Shoulders for ever. 'Yeah well, people change, don't they?'

'I guess they do.' Jory pulls away slowly and clears his throat. 'I'll see you later, then.' He has got his van keys in his hand but is lingering on the path.

'OK.' I meet his eye and a flash of something passes between us. It's a subtle something – a nobody-else-would-notice something – but to me, it feels electric. As he nears his van, he turns and looks back at me again. We have shared more than twenty years of goodbye hugs but this one hasn't been like any of those. When I close the front door, there is a fluttering in my tummy, similar to nerves, only fizzier. I can hear my sister, in my head. *Butterflies, Beth. That's when you know.* I can't help but feel my butterflies have terrible timing.

23

'So here's the thing. I *really* need you to wake up and tell me what to do.' I rest my head on the edge of Emmy's pillow. 'I'm thinking of doing something . . . but I'm not sure if I've lost the plot. This is where you step in, to tell me one way or the other. There's nobody else I can ask for advice, except Jory, and unfortunately, in this instance, Jory is involved.' I stare up at the strip lights. 'You can go straight back to sleep afterwards, if you like. I just need a quick nod or a head shake. Yay or nay. Please, Em.' I sigh. 'I miss you making grown-up decisions for me.'

In my bag there is a photograph. I get it out and hold it above me, making sure Emmy can 'see' it too, even though her eyes remain closed. 'Do you remember taking this? I had to dig through a box under my bed this morning when I took the kids over to Mum's.' It's a picture of me and Jory before a night out nearly four years ago, hugging and making silly faces. I am wearing tight black trousers and a red shirt with tiny white hearts on it, alongside heels and a baseball cap I'd put on just to be goofy. It's a daft photo, one of hundreds I have of us messing around while getting ready, but I remember this night more than the others.

'Something happened, that night, Em. But I think you already knew that,' I say. 'You kept grilling me, the next day, when I came over to yours for a roast dinner. I brushed it off as a simple hang-over, but you knew. And I knew you knew. I was just trying to forget about it.' I watch the gentle rise and fall of my sister's chest, remembering her knowing smile the morning after. 'It was only half of a something, really. A kiss outside and then I went back to his, but we didn't, you know, not in the end. It was the weekend we had all that snow.'

The memory of that evening comes flooding back. The hours we spent inside the pub are blurry but my recollection gets sharper after we left. My shoes slipping on the icy decking outside the pub. A charge appearing between us that hadn't been there – or at least, one we'd never allowed to be there – before. The bubbling anticipation of knowing that something was going to happen. His hands on my face as we kissed, snowflakes in our hair. Falling in the door, coats abandoned at our feet as he began unbuttoning my shirt, cursing his fingers for being frozen. Fumbling with each other's clothes with an urgency I'd never felt. God, I'd wanted him and I could feel he wanted me to, too. But when we stumbled, laughing as we fell on to the bottom of his stairs, our hands still exploring each other, Jory had pulled his face back and said, 'Beth, stop. It's the drink, this isn't a good idea.' And despite me trying to tell him it wasn't the drink and that it was a great idea, the moment had gone, as though we'd been slow dancing and the lights had come up. We had untangled ourselves and sat there on the bottom step, catching our breaths and exchanging 'what were we thinking' sheepish glances. Jory made us both a coffee and we drank them there on the stairs, talking it through, vowing to never let a moment of madness ruin our friendship. Because that was what it was, we both agreed. A moment of madness. We would lock it away, covering the awkward feelings in the weeks that followed with 'What *was* in our drink that night?' jokes. The Winter of 2015.

Emmy's arms are outside her bedsheets and I place my hand on top of her hand. 'Nothing has ever come close to it, Em. All those waste-of-time dates I've sat through, pretending there were

212

butterflies. Yesterday's hug reminded me of the night we don't talk about. That's why I dug out the picture.'

There is a sudden pressure beneath my hand, as though something is gently lifting. I sit up straight but keep my hand on top of Emmy's, my eyes fixed on her. *There!* A knock, so small you might not see it, but unmistakable to the touch. I sit very still for a long while, willing her to move again, but she doesn't. I know what I felt, though. It was a nudge. A nudge from my big sister. The nudge I was hoping she would give. *Life's too short, Beth. Tell him how you feel.*

'Thank you,' I tell her, kissing her on the forehead. 'Though if this all goes tits up, I'm blaming you. And Hugh Grant.'

Twice in the fifty-mile drive back to St Newth I almost talk myself out of it. What if I've got it wrong and the doorstep fizz of feelings wasn't mutual? What if Sadie really is the one for Jory? Who am I to come between them? Neither of them deserves that. But my sister's finger nudge, and thoughts of how Doug ran out of time, lead me to conclude that the greatest risk lies in *not* doing something so I turn left instead of right after the bus stop and now, here I am. Parked just down the road from Jory's, about to write on the back of a photograph.

Throwback Thursday (the print edition)
The best night I ever had, bar none. I still think about it all the time. I would do exactly the same, sober. (Maybe without the baseball cap.) I just wanted you to know that, on the off chance you fancied going for a drink to recreate it. Snow not guaranteed. If you're not on the same page, just ignore this awkward note and I promise I'll never mention it again. Beth x

There's no sign of his van and none of the lights are on but I still post it through his door and hurry back to my car as though the letterbox is on fire. I've done it now. It's out there. It would be tempting to hover out of view until he returns but there's something more important I need to do. I need to drive to Mum's and tell my family that Emmy moved her finger and that this time I saw it for myself. She heard what I was saying and she responded with a movement. Dr Hargreaves can't confirm that's what happened – the timing of Emmy's finger movement could have been coincidental, unrelated to what was being said – but *I* know. It was a sign.

SEPTEMBER

24

'Has the Richardson deal come back from Credit yet, Beth?'

Malcolm stops beside the printer on his way back from the toilet and hovers over me. One of his shirt buttons has popped open but he doesn't appear to have noticed, which cheers me up no end. I needed something to cheer me up. It's been nearly a week since I posted a photo in an envelope through Jory's door. A week of zero acknowledgement. For the first few days I held on to hope but the last of that hope evaporated this morning when he messaged to say, 'Just checking in to see how you're doing.' Someone who has received a declaration of feelings wouldn't casually *just check in* if they felt the same, would they?

'No. It's still in the queue.' My phone vibrates and he shoots me a look. 'It's my niece. I have to get this.' I check the time: 3:52. Mum is there doing after-school supervising so it's a surprise to hear from Polly. I immediately worry that something bad has happened and it takes me right back to the call from Dad on the day of the accident. 'Hey, everything OK? What's happened?'

'Nothing's happened.' Polly's voice is flat. 'I just can't find my swimming bag. Have you seen it?'

'Oh. Have you tried the back of the kitchen door? Why do you need it, anyway? This morning you said you couldn't be bothered.'

'I've changed my mind.' I can hear her rummaging around in

the background. 'Nope, not there.' I picture the house as it looked when I left this morning: somewhere between burglary and war zone. 'What about the cupboard under the stairs?' I put my hand over the phone and apologize to Malcolm: 'Sorry, won't be a sec.'

'I've got it,' she says, without sounding at all triumphant. 'Nan wants a word.'

'Actually, Polly, I'm working so I've not really got—'

'Hello, love!' Too late. Mum is shouting down the phone as she always does when using a mobile. 'Is work going OK? How's the big promotion?'

I wince, hoping Malcolm can't hear her. 'Yep, all fine, I'm pretty busy so—'

'I just wanted to say that we'll take Ted back to ours for his dinner tonight as it's just him, all right? You have a nice time.'

'Bye, Mum.' I hang up. I'm not sure I'm going to have that much of a *nice time* in the hour that separates now from going home, but I need to crack on regardless.

'Everything OK?' Malcolm's tone is softer than normal, which immediately makes me suspicious.

'Just a little issue at home but all sorted. My mum is looking after the kids.'

He clicks the end of his pen. *Click click click.* 'I wanted to run something past you.' There it is. 'I've got to leave early tonight for an appointment.' He pauses before *appointment.*

'Right,' I say, glancing at all the work I've still got to do.

'I'm scheduled to be dialling in to a regional sales meeting at five forty-five and, as I'm sure you'll appreciate, I can't dial in if I'm not here.'

He's not got something to run past me at all, he's after a favour. 'You want me to dial in for you.' I regret opening my mouth almost as soon as I do.

'Oh, would you? It's a lot to ask so that's very kind,' he says. 'I assumed you wouldn't be able to stay late but as you've said the kids are with your mum tonight . . .'

It feels like a trap. 'Can you not move your . . . appointment?'

His eye twitches. 'No,' he says, before scribbling numbers on a Post-it. 'That's all the information you need to dial in and I'll send you an email in a second with our stats for this month.'

'Great.' I fight the urge to do the sarcastic double thumbs up I usually give Mum.

A red message appears on our screens to tell us that the Richardson deal has been declined by Credit. Malcolm is inflating with rage. If he blows up any more he'll pop open another button on his shirt. I put my hand up and tell him I'll phone James from Credit to try to talk him round. I have saved something in my favourites that might help with our appeal.

'Fine. As I was saying, dial-in codes for the sales meeting are on one Post-it and the alarm code is on the other. You'll need to set it before you leave.'

'Got it.' I've found what I was looking for. I print it and decide to strike while the iron's hot, see if I can catch James from Credit now before the sales call.

'So, you're happy with what you're doing, as I've got to make a move now?'

'Yes.' Honestly, if Malcolm actually wants me to get any work done he's really going to have to stop talking to me. I tell him again that it's fine, he can go, before I pick up the phone and prepare to sweet-talk our underwriters.

It is *quarter to seven* by the time I put my coat on to leave. I turn the office lights off and head down the stairs and out to my car. The conference call was not a quick 'phone in your monthly stats' affair at all and I am really cross with Malcolm for sending me in unprepared. At one stage, the regional manager, Steve (because all regional managers are called either Steve or Chris), asked me about projections and pipeline. I didn't have a clue. At least the day ended on a semi-high when James from Credit approved the deal he had previously declined. Talking him round gave me a little buzz that I think might be something close to job satisfaction and, for the first time in my life, I'm not looking for a way out of my job.

I wonder how Polly's getting on at swimming. Before the conference call, I texted Mum to say I had to work a bit later as a favour for Malcolm and her reply made no sense whatsoever.

OK love, are you meeting him there?

Obviously, I wasn't meeting him there, I was going instead of him (and not actually *going* anywhere because it's all done over the phone). I really hope when I'm her age I can still send messages that aren't completely batty.

As I drive the long straight between Bude and the turning for St Newth, two figures in the distance catch my eye. They look young and this really isn't a good road to be walking along. The red backpack on the left is similar to Polly's, the one I was trying to help her find over the phone this afternoon. It's not her though, as she's at swimming. As I get closer, I feel my heart rate quicken. The flash of strawberry blonde hair on the right looks a lot like Rosie. I check my mirror to make sure there is nothing behind me before slowing down to get a better look. Unless they have doppelgängers, it is them. What the hell?

I beep the horn and they both jump. Rosie's face is a picture, pure guilt for having been found doing something she shouldn't be, or rather not doing something she should be. Polly's face, however, is blank, as though she doesn't care at all.

'Get in, both of you.' I've put my hazard lights on and, as they throw their bags in the back and climb in, a van shoots past my side at such speed the car shakes. *Definitely* not a safe road for them to be walking on.

'I'm really sorry,' Rosie starts, eyes wide with panic.

'I'm not going to tell you off,' I say, and she relaxes until I add, 'That's up to your mum to do.' I rejoin the road, sneaking a glance back at Polly, who is staring vacantly out of the window. 'Well?'

'Well what?'

'Really? You're going with *Well what?* when I've just found you crawling the streets.' Perhaps *crawling the streets* is a bit of a stretch when they're bunking off swimming club at seven p.m. on a Tuesday but they've got form and Polly knows it.

'I don't know what you expect me to say.'

'Start with where you were going.'

'Nowhere really.'

'Nowhere?'

'Just hanging around. Nan dropped us at the pool and we were walking back. I told her Rosie's mum was giving us a lift back.'

'For god's sake.' I nearly say her nan should have known better than to trust any Polly-and-Rosie tales, then I remember that her nan doesn't know about the sleepover misdemeanours, or Polly's bad parents'-evening report or her intercepting school communications, so would have no reason to doubt it. 'More lies, Polly, that's the issue. And if I hadn't been working late I would never have seen you, and you'd have lied again, and then again. I don't know how I'm supposed to react to it. I honestly don't know what I'm supposed to do with you.'

Polly shrugs. 'I thought you were going out for dinner tonight anyway?'

'What are you talking—' Realization hits me in a wave of horror. *Oh my god.* 'Oh my god, Polly. *Albert!*'

'Wait, so you are going out for dinner?'

'Yes! I forgot. *Fuck.* I just forgot. I need to – I have to tell him, he'll have been waiting. I can't believe I've done this.' I check the clock on the car. It's just after seven p.m. and we were supposed to be meeting at six p.m. He'll have been and gone, surely? Or will he still be there? I don't know whether to turn around and head to the restaurant or continue home to see if he's back. I chuck Polly my phone. 'Can you call him please?'

'I'm not calling him.'

'*Call him*,' I growl and she must sense the urgency in my voice because she does. Rosie is completely silent, probably relieved that a new drama has taken over from theirs.

'No answer,' Polly says. 'It's the old lady from next door on his voicemail message I think, saying "Albert can't come to the phone at the moment" and then she says, "Do I have to press something to save it?"'

'Mavis,' I say. 'She set his phone up before she died.' Instead of going straight over the roundabout, I swing all the way back round it on to the road we've just been on. Polly tries his mobile three more times before we give up. I don't know his home number. We drive the few miles to the seafront in silence.

'Stay here,' I say, slamming the door and running up the grassy bank that leads to the restaurant. Ocean View, it's called, two of its four walls perched over the Atlantic. I look through the vast window as I run past, searching desperately for Albert, to no avail. At the door, a young girl with a clipboard and plaits smiles at me.

'Have you got a reservation?'

'Yes, no – *yes*, I had one for six p.m. but missed it and I know I've missed the table so I'm not after any fish – really sorry about that – but I'm looking for my friend.' I am talking at her so quickly and with such panic that she puts a hand on my arm and gently steers me inside, away from the door and towards the bar. I launch into a description of Albert and she asks me my name before nipping off to get another waitress who was doing front of house on the early teatime shift. We chose an early teatime because Albert said he wasn't very good with eating late and he could come straight from Tuesday Group at Age Concern. He won't have had his car here because they send a minibus out for Tuesday Group and I was going to give him a lift back. *What have I done?*

The waitress with plaits returns with another waitress, who is pointing to a table at the far end of the restaurant. 'Are you looking for the elderly gentleman?'

'Yes!' I say, following her gaze, hopeful I might find him yet.

'I'm afraid he left about ten minutes ago. I felt ever so sorry for him, he was very sweet. Said his date didn't turn up.' She shakes her head crossly until she catches my expression and realizes I was the date. 'I did say I'm sure whoever he was meeting must have got held up.'

'I tried to call,' I say, even though it's feeble because I didn't call until I was already an hour late.

'Did you try calling here?' the waitress with the plaits asks.

'No. I called his mobile but there was no answer.'

The other one is looking a bit more sympathetic now. 'I'm pretty sure he didn't have his mobile because he asked to borrow our phone.'

'To phone me? But he wouldn't have known my number.'

'No, to phone a taxi. We phoned one for him in the end and gave him a calamari starter on the house while he was waiting. I couldn't bear to see him sitting there all dressed up in his bow-tie. He tried to leave us a tip, just for the free starter and tap water. We didn't let him,' she says.

I feel terrible. The worst I have felt about anything in a very, very long time. The bow-tie information is enough to tip me over the edge. If this had been Mum or Emmy or Jory it would have been bad enough but with Albert, and with me knowing this was to be his first meal out in over two years, it is nothing but unforgivable. 'Thank you for being so kind to him,' I say, my voice catching in my throat. 'I just completely forgot about tonight. I've had a lot on.'

The waitress with plaits nods then goes back to the front door where more customers are waiting to come in. The other waitress is just about to go back to the kitchen when she calls after me. 'He left something actually. I forgot. Hang on.' She reaches behind the bar and pulls something out before handing it to me. It's his copy of *Little Women*, with a folded sheet of book-club questions tucked inside the cover. On top of the book is a yellow rose. Last week when we were chatting over the fence I told him I didn't much care for flowers but that the yellow roses in his front garden were 'decent', which made him laugh. It takes me a moment to realize that this was a gift for me, for our date.

'Did he know he left them?' I think I already know the answer.

She nods. 'Yeah, sorry. He told me he didn't need them any more.'

I thank her again before slaloming around tables on my way to the door. Outside, I look down at the beach, quiet for this time of year. It would have been packed earlier when the sun was out, but now there are big clouds covering everything. I am tempted to walk down, to find a rock or a gap in the dunes where I can sit and cry until hopefully the tide comes all the way in and takes me back out with it. But I can't do that because Polly and Rosie are in the car and I need to get home to see Albert. I need to explain.

When he opens the door, there is no sign of a bow-tie, just his usual dark brown cardigan and cords.

'Albert, I am so sorry,' I say, knowing it's not enough but unsure how to make it enough.

'These things happen,' he says. He is upset, I can tell. He sounds different.

'But I am *so* sorry,' I repeat. 'I feel terrible. I had to work late, unexpectedly, and then there was this deal that got declined and this conference call I had to—'

'It doesn't matter, dear.' He smiles to show me it doesn't matter but the smile is a small one.

'Let me make it up to you,' I say. 'Please.'

'I don't think so, no.'

'But . . .' I don't know what to say. 'Can we do it another day?'

'I really would rather just get back to normal, if you don't mind.'

Back to normal. 'To our book-club sessions at mine?' I say hopefully, that hope fading when he shakes his head.

'Back to my normal, here at home. I'm a little tired now, Beth.' He wants me to leave.

'I'm really sorry again.'

He nods and then gently closes the door, leaving me standing on his doorstep with my mouth open.

Back inside Emmy's, I collapse on the sofa. Mum must have tidied up because the coffee table smells of furniture polish and I can see the floor. 'Did Ted go down all right?'

'Yes, no problems, love.' Mum exchanges a look with Dad, who has made us all a cup of tea.

'What?'

'It's nothing to worry about,' Mum says. Nobody has ever, in the history of all words ever spoken, said 'It's nothing to worry about' then followed it with something there was nothing to worry about.

'OK, so just tell me what it is.'

Mum looks at Dad, his cue to jump in and tell me what's occurring. 'He had a bit of an episode at nursery.' He puts my mug of tea in front of me and pushes the biscuit tin alongside it.

'What do you mean, an episode?'

'He got very upset. They were talking about families and painting pictures and all the other kids were talking about their mummies and daddies.' Dad looks at his feet.

Oh, Ted. My heart breaks for him and I am also angry. 'Was it not a bit fucking insensitive of Happy Chicks to choose family-tree painting as an activity? Of course he was going to be upset.'

'It wasn't like that, love,' Dad says. 'Natalie says they had a discussion about how families and households come in all shapes and sizes – you know, that little lad with the glasses, he has two mums, doesn't he? And another girl lives with her nan.'

'Terrible business, that was.' Mum shakes her head. 'Mother overdosed on prescription painkillers. Anyway, I don't think we can blame nursery for Ted getting upset. I think it was more that the other kids painting their mummies and daddies made him think about his mummy and daddy. He was absolutely fine by the time we picked him up, wasn't he, Jim?'

Dad nods through a mouthful of biscuit.

I can't bear to think of him being upset when none of us are there. 'Poor Ted. I forget that he must still be having a really hard time making sense of things. The impact is less obvious than it is with Polly.'

Mum frowns. 'They're both coping remarkably well, I'd say.'

I reach for a custard cream so I don't have to respond. Polly came in the house before me and flew straight upstairs. By the time I'd finished grovelling at Albert's door she was back downstairs, with wet hair, telling her grandad about the tumble turn she'd been practising at swimming club to try to shave vital seconds off her time. I should have told them then and there that she was lying. But she is still hiding something from all of us and if she thinks the adults looking after her are ganging up on her, she's surely even *less* likely to open up about what's really been going on. That's the reasoning I keep coming back to, to justify keeping it to myself. But she isn't opening up and I am getting further and further out of my depth.

'Is something troubling you, love? Other than Albert.' Dad is studying me intently. 'I'm sure he understands now you've explained. Beth? Is something the matter?'

It's not like me to hide my troubles from my dad. He has always been the king of making things better, reminding me that to err is human, even when I have been err-ing more than the average person errs. I think about what it would feel like to speak my fears out loud over this cup of tea.

And then I think of my sister. Of her conviction, in spite of everyone else's doubts, that I was the right person for the job. If I let everything spill into this room I am conceding defeat and, if I concede defeat, I let Emmy and Doug down. I shake my head. 'Everything's fine, Dad. I'm just tired.'

25

We all wake up later than normal. I didn't close the curtains properly and the first thing I think about when I open my eyes is how dusty the light in the living room is. Then I remember Albert, in his bow-tie with his yellow rose, waiting nearly an hour for his date who never arrived. I reach for one of the sofa cushions I've chucked on the floor and put it over my head. Ted is stirring upstairs. I think that must be what's woken me. He sometimes chats to himself in his bed for a bit. I yell up to him. 'You all right, Ted?'

'Is it morning? Can I have Weetos?'

It's Wednesday. Mum says Emmy only lets Ted have chocolatey cereals, or chocolate spread on toast, at weekends. But neither Mum nor Emmy are here, are they? I am.

'Yep and yep,' I say. 'I'll do it now.' I grab one of my many jumpers hanging on a clothes horse in front of the radiator and pull it over my pyjama top before padding out to the kitchen. There's no sign of Polly. 'Time to get up, Pol!' I shout.

'I'm not going,' comes a muffled reply.

'You've got twenty minutes until the bus comes. Do you want toast?'

'I'm not going,' she repeats. *Excellent.* I have Ted on Wednesdays and usually we spend the day here, with the occasional trip to the village shop or the park thrown in when we've run out of everything in the cupboard or Ted says he wants to go on the swings. After his nursery episode yesterday, I was thinking of doing something a bit different with him today.

He appears with a bed head and Mr Trunky. I give him a big cuddle, which is my way of telling him I'm very sorry to hear he was upset when the other boys and girls were painting their parents at nursery yesterday. Polly is close behind him and sits down at the dining table in her dressing gown.

'I'm not going in today, Aunty Beth,' she says. Her eyes are red.

'Do you want to talk about it?' I say.

'No. I'm just not going.'

I'm about to press her further when I have an idea. I put Ted's breakfast on the table. 'OK,' I say.

'OK?' Polly stares at me.

'That's what I said.' I gesture at the kettle. 'Do you want one?'

'Uh, sure.'

'You can stay at home today, and I'll phone the school to tell them you're ill or not up to it or whatever you prefer, but there's one condition.'

Polly narrows her eyes. 'What is it?'

'You have to join in with something me and Ted are going to be doing.'

Ted looks up from his Weetos. 'Is it Play-Doh?'

'No, but it is fun. Well, sort of. Hopefully. It's something I think the three of us should do together, anyway.'

'Will it take long?' Polly asks.

'I shouldn't think so.' The honest answer is that I have no idea. It might be a total disaster, but I've got the upper hand now I'm letting her stay off school so we're at least starting the day more positively than yesterday finished. There is a pang in my chest whenever I think of Albert. I can't shift the thought of him telling me he wants his life to go back to how it was before. He must have been so upset last night.

When we've finished breakfast, I head up to get myself changed and get some clothes for Ted. I hover outside Emmy and Doug's room. I have been avoiding going in wherever possible but I hid a bag in Emmy's wardrobe a couple of weeks ago that I now need. I am in and out in seconds, keeping my eyes focused on the wardrobe so I don't look at their bed as it was left on the morning of Friday 15 March, or the photos on Doug's bedside table, or the little trinkets lined up neatly on my sister's dressing table beside her bottle of CK One, the perfume she has been wearing for two decades. I close the door behind me and carry the bag downstairs, carefully emptying its contents on the dining table. Polly stares at the two large glass jars and pack of coloured card now in front of her.

'Oh god, it's not a *crafty* thing, is it?'

'No,' I say. 'Though we will need scissors and pens.'

I grab Emmy's craft basket from the sideboard. She has used her label maker to write 'glue' on a pot with glue sticks in and 'scissors' on the scissors pot. It's just about the only basket that remains as organized as it was when she was last here and that's because I haven't attempted to do any of this stuff with Ted. I figured that was what nursery was for.

Polly picks up one of the jars. 'Are these for putting hot chocolates in? Lottochocco in town does hot chocolates in jars and they're amazing. They put loads of whipped cream and a unicorn horn on top.'

'No, it's nothing to do with hot chocolates.'

'Right, so what is it to do with?'

'Your dad,' I say, and her face darkens as though a cloud has passed over our heads.

'My dad is in Devon,' Ted says.

'It's *heaven*, Ted,' Polly says, 'if you believe in it, which I don't.'

'Nanny said he's in Devon,' Ted says, looking at me for reassurance.

I give Polly a warning look. *Don't you dare upset your brother.*

'*Heaven* is in the sky, Ted. That's right. We wave to Daddy sometimes, don't we?'

He smiles and waves enthusiastically at the ceiling. 'Yes! Like this!'

I only wave when Ted's with me but sometimes when I'm on my own, I look up at the sky and give Doug a little nod.

'What has Dad got to do with glass jars?' Polly says.

I sit down and pull out some coloured card. 'They're memory jars.'

'No. No way,' Polly says, before I've even told her what we're going to do.

'All right. Well then, get yourself changed and I'll drop you at school. You'll only have missed the first lesson.'

She sits down reluctantly, just as my phone rings. Malcolm Work. I reject the call because it is my day off and I worked late last night. I know it's not directly Malcolm's fault but I'd probably have remembered my book-club date if I'd got home at a normal time rather than staying to take his place on a call because he was tied up with an 'appointment'.

Ted is taking lids off all the pens. 'I'm going to draw a train.'

'OK, well, I've got something else that we can do first.'

He sticks out his bottom lip. 'I want to draw a train.'

'OK, fine, you can start doing some drawing on here –' I hand over a piece of card – 'and Aunty Beth and Polly are going to start doing some writing on these bits once we've cut them a bit smaller. You can help us with what to write as it's going to be all about your daddy.'

'Do I have to do this?' Polly says.

'No,' I admit. 'But Ted was feeling a bit fragile at nursery yesterday and I thought this would be a good way to show him that we're still thinking about your dad. It's been six months now, Pol, and I'm worried if we don't record his memories now, then . . .' I look at the black squiggles Ted's drawing on his paper.

'You think he's going to forget,' Polly says, her voice quiet.

'I don't know, I just know that I can't remember anything from before I was his age. Can you?'

'No.'

'But he still has memories of his dad *now*, and I think your mum would maybe do this sort of thing, if she was able to, but she can't, so I'm going to give it a go. I had planned for me and Ted to do it anyway, but a lot of his memories I won't know, will I? But you will.'

Polly reaches for a pen. 'Do you want to talk about Daddy, Ted?' He doesn't look up from his picture. I'm about to step in when Polly surprises me. 'Do you remember when he used to give you horsey rides around the living room?'

'Yee-hah!' Ted says, which I think means yes. He makes a claw with his hand. 'And he was a monster, raaaah!'

Polly writes *horsey rides* and *monsters* on purple rectangles of card. I think I remember Doug chasing them around the house as the monster. There was always a lot of shrieking before Emmy told them all, Doug included, to calm down.

For the next twenty minutes or so, Polly and Ted fill up their jars. Some of Polly's memories she shares but most she doesn't and I don't ask her to. It's only when she starts crying and I put my arm around her that I can see she has written her memories as though Doug will be reading them. The green one in her hand says, *I miss you dancing in the kitchen*.

'Oh, Pol.' I squeeze her shoulder. 'He was so proud of you.'

'No he wasn't.' She fights me on this point every single time. She is looking down at her hands. 'You don't know anything.'

I hold my hands up. 'Do you know what, you're right. I don't know anything. But I am trying to know. I am trying to help.'

'I know you are,' she says. She fiddles with a piece of card then opens her mouth to say something before closing it again.

Come on, Polly, you can do it. Talk to me. I don't say anything for a while, freeing up the space for her to say more if she wants to. She begins doodling, a flower and a bee followed by a rainbow.

Several times I get the feeling she is about to say something but she never does and eventually the silence is broken by Ted, who is now bored with drawing and has started taking memories of his dad back out of the jar.

'Shall we go to the beach?' I say. I don't know where the idea has come from, I just feel like we could all do with getting out of the house. Ted is immediately talking about sandcastles and paddling, pulling at his sister's sleeve to ask if she'll paddle with him.

'But you told school I'm not well,' Polly says. 'Can't I just stay here?'

'No. We'll go to the beach then this afternoon you can hide in your room or do whatever you want. Look how much Ted is enjoying your company. He hardly sees you at the moment. Just one morning together, it's all I'm asking. For him.' It's probably not fair of me to use Ted like this but I know it's my best chance of getting her to come.

'Fine,' she says.

Good. It's what we all need. As I'm putting Emmy's craft supplies back in their box, I spot a pack of notecards. I take one out and scribble a note to Albert, to put through his door before we leave. I hope this one has greater success than my last letterbox note, which Jory still hasn't mentioned.

Albert,

I just want to say sorry again for last night. I know it was a really big deal, going out for dinner for the first time since losing Mavis and I know I let you down. I've been reading Little Women and I only wish I was more like one of the March sisters. Jo is my favourite so far. (I was bitterly disappointed to find that my namesake is the sick one.) I understand why you are disappointed with me. I just want you to know that if we go back to the way things were before we became friends, I will miss you.

Love Beth x

26

'Pick a spot, Teddio.' I gesture at the wide expanse of golden sand.

'I can't see any spots,' he says and I laugh. He's not even looking, far too busy dragging his little bucket and spade along behind
him. Polly is carrying his brand-new net under her arm. She's
been quiet since we did the memory jars. Not her usual angry-at-
the-world quiet but a more contemplative quiet. There was a
moment when I thought she was about to talk to me – *really* talk
to me – in the car, but the words never came and I'm not going to
push it. Ted is humming a little tune, excited about our impromptu
trip to the beach. Before leaving, we searched everywhere for his
bucket, spade and net but couldn't find any of it so after we'd
parked up, we walked round to the souvenir shop on the corner,
the one with all the postcards outside, and I bought him one of
everything as though we were tourists.

Despite the warm weather, the beach isn't busy. It's midweek
and most kids are at school. We plonk ourselves about halfway
between the beach huts and the sea. I tell Ted that we'll need to
go and get some wet sand if we're going to make castles but he
ignores me and fills up a bucket of warm, dry sand before tipping
it over and giving it a tap with a spade. I watch as it collapses.

'I did a magic tap,' he says, peering closer at his spade as though
the magic might not be working.

'You *did*, but the sand needs to be wetter. Come on.' We run up and down the beach collecting buckets of wet sand for ages until we've built a circle of sandcastles. I am out of breath and collapse next to Polly, who is deep in thought, staring out to sea. It's the longest I've seen her without her head buried in her phone for a long while.

'Can we get sticks for flags?' Ted says.

'In a minute, your aunty Beth needs to recover. She's not done that many steps since she was made to do a beep test in PE.'

'We need sticks for flags,' he says again. I do what I always do when he doesn't listen the first time and give him a snack.

'Do you want anything to eat, Pol?'

She shakes her head. We sit listening to Ted crunch on his crisps. When he's finished, he hands me the packet and trundles off to survey his sandcastle empire. He seems to have forgotten about the urgent need for flags so I close my eyes for a moment, enjoying the sun on my face. The sound of gently crashing waves and seagulls and other people's laughter is creating a feeling close to relaxation.

For a few minutes, neither Polly nor I say anything. When I open my eyes, she is staring at Ted, who is busying himself with more digging.

'I think the beach is a hit,' I say, laughing as he starts jumping over the sandcastles. 'Your mum used to bring him here all the time, didn't she? Maybe he's missed it.'

'Yeah.' Polly's voice is cracked and though she has turned her face away from me, I can see from the shake of her shoulders that she is crying. I rummage in the bag for a tissue and hand it over, edging myself closer until we are side by side, our knees up to our chests. I realize, as she dabs at her face, that today is one of only a few times since the accident that I have seen her get upset. She has been angry more than anything and though that anger has at times led to confrontational tears, I haven't really seen her *sad*. Not like this.

'Do you want to talk about it?'

She shakes her head and sniffs at the same time.

'Was it doing the memory jars? I'm sorry if it upset you.' She is crying harder now and I stretch my arm around her. 'Oh, Pol. *Is that what this is about?*'

'No. Maybe.' She shrugs. 'I don't know.'

'We don't have to do that again, if it's too hard.' I avert my eyes from the man to the side of us who is attempting, unsuccessfully, to preserve his modesty with a towel as he swaps pants for a pair of trunks.

'No – it was nice,' she says. 'I'm glad Ted now has those things written down. I just—' She stops herself and, after months of not having a clue how she is feeling, the urge to shout *You just what?* is so fierce I force myself to count slowly in my head. I get to thirty-five before she speaks again. 'I just feel so guilty.'

'Why?' That doesn't make any sense at all. When she doesn't immediately answer, I recommence the counting. *Forty-one, forty-two, forty-three . . .*

'There was this picture. One I'd taken. Of me.'

Despite not giving any information about the picture, from the way Polly says it, looking down at her hands, I suspect I know the sort of picture she might be talking about. I am shocked but also not shocked. Shocked because she is my niece and it doesn't seem two minutes ago that she was into Barbies and colouring books. Not shocked because she is fourteen and if I'd had a smartphone at fourteen it would have been lethal. I don't understand how this relates to her being upset about the memory jars but I don't question it, keeping my eyes on Ted as he moves behind us to collect some stones in his bucket.

'OK,' I say. I mirror her gaze out to sea.

'That's what Kate was talking about, at Ted's party,' she says.

Now I'm even more confused. 'Kate knew about the picture?'

'No, but that was the phone drama she said Mum was upset about.'

'I don't follow.'

Polly exhales a long, shaky breath. 'When I was trying to sell my old phone, this woman messaged, who wanted to buy it. I replied to tell her it had gone but somehow I managed to attach that picture. It was never meant for her.'

I nod to show I am listening. I am a bit uncomfortable with the information that there was someone the picture was 'meant for' but I work hard to keep my face neutral.

'And then she blackmailed me.'

My neutral face combusts. 'She did *what*?'

'She had a screenshot of everyone in my friends list, said she was going to send them all the picture.' Polly's voice is now a whisper. 'I really thought she would and that everyone at school would see it. It was awful.'

'Oh, Pol.' I can just imagine the panic, how scared she must have been.

'She asked for a hundred pounds. Dad found out after I said I needed money for a new swimming-club tracksuit. He emailed Coach Draper to complain about the cost and discovered the new tracksuit payment wasn't due. When I wouldn't tell Dad the real reason I was asking for money, he took my phone away and found the messages. And the picture.'

'Oh god.' I'm not sure if I feel worse for Polly or Doug in that situation.

'He was so good about it. He made me tell Mum and we had this big chat about everything. Mum got really upset – about the photo – but they told me everything was going to be OK.'

The agony on her face as she talks about her mum and dad has brought a lump to my throat. She is clearly anguished about sending that photo in error. 'Polly, we *all* do stupid things when we're teenagers. You don't need to feel guilty about that.'

She is shaking her head. 'I'm not guilty about the photo.' She turns her face to me then, her eyes wide and cheeks wet with tears. 'I'm guilty about the accident. It's my fault, Aunty Beth.'

'No it's not. How can it be?'

'Dad was really worried about the photo being shared. He kept saying, once it's out there, it's out there for good. And he wasn't happy about the idea of handing over any money but him and Mum thought it was the best thing to do, to make the problem go away. I should have just let her send it to all my friends. Now I wouldn't care if the whole world saw me naked.' I think back to the changing rooms after Polly's first gala, when she was behaving erratically. She fiddles with the laces on her trainers. 'That's where they were going, that Friday. To see her. That's why it's my fault.'

My head is trying to catch up with my ears. I twist round to check on Ted, who is hovering in front of a woman eating a sandwich. I think I understand, at least partly, what Polly is saying but it seems so unlikely that Emmy and Doug would go and confront this random woman face to face to hand over a hundred quid. 'Did they actually tell you that was where they were going?'

'No, they told me they were going for a mortgage meeting, the same as they told you, but . . .' She reaches for her phone and scrolls through to find something before handing it over to me. It's a message from Emmy.

> Don't worry about the photo, darling. We're sorting it so don't give it another thought. We'll pick up sweets and popcorn for later. Love you, Mum xx

I check the time stamp on the message. Half an hour before the accident. I think of my sister and Doug, setting off on a mission to protect Polly. 'It's still just a terrible accident, Pol.'

'But Dad wouldn't have died if it hadn't been for me! I wondered at first if I had got it wrong. I wanted to be wrong. But then I found that letter, with the other mortgage appointment date on.'

'So you hid it . . .'

'I panicked. Nan was nagging Grandad to put all the paperwork in a folder and I quickly shoved it in a drawer that nobody ever uses. I was going to take it out again but the drawer got stuck. Until you got right in there wiggling that bloody knife.'

'Why didn't you just tell me all of this at the time?'

'I couldn't. As soon as I found out they'd lied about where they were going to cover for me, I couldn't breathe. It has been on my mind constantly, but I didn't want to say it out loud because then it would be true. Even though I know it's true. I just wanted it to go away.'

The Polly I've been living with and worrying about for the last six months suddenly makes more sense. Her anger, the acting up at school and her disgust whenever someone tried to tell her that her dad was proud of her. She has been so caught up torturing herself for the role she played in her mum and dad's fate that day, even though this is *not* her fault, that she hasn't been grieving. Until today, when she was faced with a jarful of memories.

'You need to listen to me, Pol.' I put my hand on her leg. 'The accident, regardless of where your mum and dad were going, is *not* your fault.'

'I wish they hadn't gone. I would do anything. I miss them so much.'

'I know. There's nothing I can say to make losing your dad feel any easier. But your mum is still here. She has so far defied all the odds stacked against her and we need to keep the faith that she will defy some more. We're kind of a team now, even if you've drawn the short straw by being assigned your hopeless aunty as your teammate.'

Polly smiles and it's like sunshine. 'You're not *hopeless*.'

I raise my eyebrow. 'I am a bit hopeless. But I promise to work on my development areas, like shopping and washing, if you promise not to worry about all this stuff on your own.'

She nods. 'I'm really sorry, you know. For being such a nightmare.' She looks over her shoulder. 'Aunty Beth, where's Ted?'

I swing myself around in the direction of where Ted is playing. 'He's bothering the lady with a sandwich.' Only I realize, as my eyes search for his red T-shirt, that there is nobody in the spot where he was. 'Oh my god, he was right there. Just a minute ago.' Has it really been just a minute since I saw him? I have been distracted by this chat with Polly. Has more time passed than I've realized? It is now lunchtime and there are significantly more people on the beach than when we first arrived. All around us are locals who have ventured away from their shops or their desks, making it much harder to spot a blond head of curls. He can't have got far. There is an uncontrollable panic rising in my chest. It's the sort of panic no amount of *in for 4 and out for 8* can ease.

Polly begins calling out for her brother, weaving between the lunch-break goers in the direction we last saw him. I stay rooted to the spot, scanning as far as I can in every direction, praying he's close by and just hidden from view, even though I don't truly believe it's anywhere near crowded enough for him to be obscured. What if he's been taken? You hear of horror stories. How it only takes seconds. How soon do I need to raise the alarm for kidnapping? Or drowning? I am almost certain he hasn't gone down towards the sea because he was behind us, further up the beach, and I would have seen him go past. Wouldn't I? What if I missed him? What if he took himself for a paddle? Would there have been time? Barely. But it's not impossible.

Polly is asking people if they've seen a blond boy in a red T-shirt. His fishing net is by my feet but there is no sign of his bucket and spade. He must have wandered off with those still in hand. The sound of gently crashing waves and seagulls and other people's laughter is no longer relaxing. *Where is he?*

Polly is running back towards me, waving to get my attention. 'Someone said they saw him,' she pants, her hands on her knees. 'He was with a woman in a blue shirt, going back up the beach.'

'What? When? How long ago?' Had the woman eating a

sandwich been wearing a blue shirt? She might have done. I wasn't looking closely enough.

Polly is close to tears. 'I can't see them anywhere. What if the lady in the blue shirt has taken him and put him in her car?'

'More people are good than bad, Pol,' I remind her, trying hard to believe it. We keep running, as fast as is possible on sand, the pair of us frantic. I should call the police. I have tapped 999 into my phone but as we run alongside the lifeguard lookout, a lifeguard in his late teens shouts down, asking if we are all right.

'No, I've lost my nephew, Ted. He's four. Red T-shirt and navy shorts, curly blond hair.' I point towards where we had been sitting, our cluster of sandcastles now being jumped on by other small children. 'He was there approximately five minutes ago. I turned my back for a second and then—'

He cuts me off. 'Did you say a red T-shirt?'

'Yes! Have you found him? Please god say you've found him.'

'I'm not sure, just give me a second.' He steps back and talks quietly into his radio before gesturing with his palm for us to stay where we are. 'Someone's coming to talk to you.'

'Who's coming? Where's Ted? Has he been hurt?' I feel like I am going to be sick. 'Please tell me, is he all right?'

'He's there!' Polly points diagonally up the beach. I follow the line of her finger and, though he's quite far away, it is unmistakably Ted. He is holding hands with a female police officer.

'Oh thank god!' I drop to my knees, relief flooding through me. Everything is trembling and I fix my eyes on Ted and the on-foot police escort he now has. There's another woman beside them, with a blue shirt. I peer closer. It's the woman who was eating a sandwich. What is going on?

Ted has pulled his hand away from the police officer's and is running towards us. The officer is talking into her radio now and as they approach she says something to the blue shirt lady, who nods as though a question has been answered.

'Look, Aunty Beth, it's the police!' Ted seems excited to see us and clearly has not been as traumatized as we have by the short time apart.

The police officer crouches down to Ted's level and speaks gently. 'Hey, Ted, who are these guys then?'

'Aunty Beth and Polly.' He sticks out his chest proudly.

'I'm his sister.' Polly has picked him up and has her face in his hair.

'And did Ted come to the beach with you guys today?' She is smiling but is still behaving slightly cautiously.

I reach for Ted's hand. 'He came with me. They both did. He was playing right behind us. The last thing I remember is turning to see him watching this poor lady who was trying to eat her lunch in peace. He's not good with respecting personal space, not when there's food involved anyway. When we looked around again, he had gone.'

Sandwich lady in the blue shirt looks absolutely mortified. 'God, I'm so sorry. He started speaking to me and seemed to be on his own. I did look around the beach, but I think you must have had your backs to us at that point, so I didn't think you were with him. I asked him' – she lowers her voice – 'I asked him where his mummy or daddy was and he started crying, saying, "I don't know where Daddy is" and then "Mummy's tired." I thought he was lost. It didn't even occur to me that he was here with somebody who wasn't his mum or dad.'

My heart is still beating faster than it ought to be. I feel dreadful. 'Polly, why don't you help Ted build a couple more sandcastles before we have to go home?' She nods and carries Ted back towards the net and towel we abandoned a few moments ago. 'I can't believe I let him out of my sight like that.'

The police officer smiles kindly. 'It happens *a lot* at the beach, believe me. I think in this instance it wasn't aided by there being a misunderstanding over who Ted was here with.'

242

'I know but I didn't even see him walk off with a stranger. She could have been anyone – no offence.' I smile at Sandwich lady. 'The reason he cried when you asked him where his mum and dad are is that they were in a serious car accident. His dad died and his mum – my sister – is still in hospital.'

The police officer nods. 'Something clicked when you said Ted and Polly. Obviously as a force we've been devastated by what happened to your family.'

' "Where's your mum or dad?" is a tricky question for Ted. He probably thought you meant where are they in general as opposed to where on the beach. I'm just glad there are good people looking out for him when I fail miserably.' I thank them both again before rejoining Polly and Ted, who are deep in concentration, writing in the sand with sticks. I sit down next to them, fighting very hard not to cry.

'Polly did my name, Aunty Beth!' Ted points at the letters. 'It says Ted!'

I return the biggest smile I can muster, which isn't very big at all, the reality of how much worse it could have been still on my mind. Mum is going to go crazy when she finds out Ted was lost. Usually, I can rely on Dad to talk her round, but I'm not sure he'll even try to this time. This isn't like messing up the washing or being rubbish at cooking dinner, it's serious. For six months, I've been trying to prove that I'm up to it and all I have managed to prove is that I'm not.

Polly says more to me in the car on the way home than she has in weeks. I can sense that a weight has been lifted since our chat and, despite the Ted drama, I am glad. I, on the other hand, feel heavier than I did before we left this morning, but that isn't Polly's fault.

As I turn in at the bus stop, I spot Mum and Dad's car outside Emmy's. *Oh joy.* This means I'm going to have to face the music about the beach drama straight away. It crosses my mind to ask Polly to keep a secret and say nothing about us losing Ted (in return for me not mentioning the photo, which understandably she doesn't want to explain to her nan and grandad), but I know I can't do that. Not because it's the wrong thing to do – even though it is – but because there is zero chance Ted won't mention the excitement with the policewoman and the walkie-talkie (and I'm not prepared to stoop to the low of asking a four-year-old to keep a secret in order to make me look better).

Mum is waiting on the doorstep. Ted has nodded off so I lift him gently out of his seat and carry him to her. There is sand on his face and in his hood.

'There you are,' she says, furrowing her brow when she spots Polly, before calling through to the kitchen. 'She's back.'

I can hear voices. Who is she talking to? Surely it's only her and Dad here? Maybe the Family Liaison Officer is here. But how would Mum and Dad have known that?

'I didn't know you were coming round—' I start, but she cuts me off as she takes Ted from me.

'Your boss is here,' she hisses.

'What? Why?' Could this day get any worse?

'I'll see to Ted. And, Polly, you can tell me why you're not at school.'

I walk slowly through to the kitchen, struggling to understand why Malcolm is in my house, which isn't even my house, on my day off. I find him sitting at the table having a cup of tea with Dad. He is overstepping the line, that's what he's doing. Taking the piss.

'Beth, where have you been?' Dad looks at the clock. 'Malcolm here has been trying to reach you for hours. He came to ours, as that's the address on your file, so we brought him over here as we thought you would be home.' He catches sight of Polly. 'Why is – never mind, doesn't matter.'

'We went to the beach,' I say. If I sound defensive it's because I am. Defensive and confused as to why this whole set-up looks and feels like a telling-off when I haven't yet shared the thing I'm expecting a telling-off for. For one irrational moment, I convince myself that someone – the police, perhaps – must have beaten me to it and told them all about Ted getting lost at the beach. Then I remember my family dramas would have nothing whatsoever to do with Hexworthy Finance. 'What's going on?'

Malcolm looks hassled. I can't imagine any of the deals in the pipeline causing worry at a level to match the concern on his face.

'Beth, did you set the alarm last night, before you left?' His voice sounds different to normal. I can't work out if he's worried or furious. I think perhaps he is both.

'No?'

He lets out a groan, as though he has a really bad stomach ache, and I find myself staring at him with my mouth open.

When he speaks again his voice is clipped, the words coming through his teeth. 'I asked you to set it, when you left.'

'When? I don't even know how to.'

'When I was telling you about the meeting. I gave you two Post-it notes, which I left in your tray. I told you one had the conference call dial-in code on it and the other had the alarm code. You said, *Got it*. I then sent you an email with our sales figures for the meeting and added a PS reminder about the alarm.' He gets out his phone to show me the email he sent, waving the screen under my dad's nose at the same time. Dad nods and I want to shout at him for nodding.

The rising panic that had only just subsided since leaving the beach is back. It will be a miracle if I don't have a heart attack before my next birthday. I peer at Malcolm's phone, scrolling down to read it. I remember him talking about the conference call code but not the alarm. I think back to our chat, how focused I'd been on my computer screen and the deal that had just been declined by Credit.

'I didn't hear you say anything about the alarm. The PS on the email is *tiny*. Even the email title is "Conference call". Why wasn't it "Conference call and alarm"? I've never set an alarm. I didn't hear you ask me about it. I don't think you did.' I'm stuttering. It's unfair of him to put me on the spot like this, outside the office, in front of my dad.

'I put the alarm code on a Post-it. I reminded you in the email,' he says, his voice a little louder now. 'Someone broke in.'

I gasp. 'What?' I say, even though I heard him perfectly well.

'They got in and nobody was alerted because there was no alarm.'

'Did they take—'

He shakes his head. 'Not a lot but it's not about what they took, Beth. It's about the fact they were able to get in and potter around inside the office without triggering the alarm. I know we have a clear-desk policy for data protection but still . . .' He puts his head in his hands.

I think about how my desk was left, files in every tray, a notepad with customer names and telephone numbers scribbled on it beside my keyboard. I vaguely remember watching a clear-desk training video where a woman in a suit walked around a fake office talking very seriously about the risks of leaving personal information on show. I'd lost the will midway through and started sending Jory memes. He'd sent back a David Brent one that had made me laugh out loud after I'd told him that Malcolm had a touch of the Brent about him. It doesn't seem at all funny now.

'There's clearly been a misunderstanding.' Dad leaves the table to boil the kettle again. 'If Beth says she didn't know you'd asked her to do the alarm, she didn't know you'd asked her to do the alarm. Another tea?'

Malcolm waves his hand to decline the tea. 'But I did ask her, she just wasn't listening. And now we're potentially in a lot of bother.' He gets to his feet.

'I'm sorry,' I say, 'I didn't hear you telling me about the alarm because I was focusing on the response from Credit on that deal.'

He narrows his eyes. 'Did you not wonder about the alarm? Did it not occur to you as *you*, the last person in the office, the only late worker, left? Did you not wonder whether there might be some responsibility attached to you leaving the building?'

I shake my head. 'We've all got passes to get in and out, so I know the doors lock automatically. An alarm didn't cross my mind. What's going to happen now, about the break-in?'

He picks up his suit jacket and drapes it over one arm. 'The police are going to review the limited CCTV footage and in the meantime we just have to pray that they didn't stay to snoop around during the break-in. It looks like the most snoopable desk was yours.'

I wince. There's not a lot I can say to that. 'Is there anything I can do?'

'Not really. I came to find you because I was hoping you *had* set the alarm and that the reason it didn't go off was more a technical one. I wouldn't have bothered you, on your day off, had it not been urgent.' He looks at Dad. 'Apologies for the inconvenience, Mr Pascoe.'

My neck feels prickly and hot, the same way it did after Doug's funeral when I thought I was on the verge of a panic attack. The pressure of competing responsibilities has been spiralling for a long time but today is proof that I can't be trusted to keep all the balls in the air. I'm not up to it. What if next time it's worse than not setting an alarm? Worse than losing Ted? I have been ploughing on, kidding myself I'm doing OK, but it's not OK, is it? None of this is OK.

I follow Malcolm out, my palms clammy.

'I will see you in the office tomorrow, Beth.'

'No.' There is a rush of blood in my ears. I have messed everything up.

He meets my eye. 'No?'

'I can't.' I'm shaking.

'You can't come in tomorrow or . . .' An uncomfortable silence fills the space between us.

'I don't know.'

'I see. Well, I can't run a business on *I don't knows*. Let me know, by Monday at the latest, one way or another. If I don't hear from you, I will be forced to advertise your job. I can't work for very long without an assistant, as you know.'

'I know. I'm sorry.' As I close the door, Mum appears. She has obviously been listening.

'You've never quit?' she says. 'Oh, Beth. *Why?*'

'Because I'm a quitter,' I tell her. '*When the going gets tough, the Beth gets scarpering.* That's what you said, wasn't it? You were right.'

'I didn't . . .' Mum seems flummoxed to have had her own words quoted back at her. 'But you've been doing so well with this job.'

'No,' I say. 'No, I haven't. I haven't been managing to keep on top of things and now there has been a break-in, because of me.'

'But there is no need for you to quit. With any luck, the police can sort it.'

'Nanny, I saw the police!' Ted runs over to us.

'That's nice, love.' Mum ruffles his hair and gives him a wide smile. 'Shall I make you some lunch?'

'It was a lady police when Aunty Beth and Polly weren't there.'

Mum's smile dissolves and she looks first at Polly and then at me. 'What does he mean, when you weren't there?'

I feel a headache coming on and I pinch the bridge of my nose, my hands still shaking. 'There was a bit of an incident at the beach. I was about to tell you but then Malcolm—'

'It wasn't Aunty Beth's fault,' Polly says. 'One minute he was there and then—'

248

'Can I have cheesy sauce soldiers?' Ted is jumping up and down. Mum picks him up, kisses his head and takes him into the kitchen, shooting a look I can't see but can just imagine at Dad.

'Mum?' I call after her.

'Please can we talk about this later, Beth? It's nearly two and Ted hasn't had any lunch.'

'But—'

'Later. He needs to eat.'

27

It's Friday night and I am watching rubbish telly in a house that's not mine, without the people I'm supposed to be looking after even being here. I have been craving space for a long while but I didn't mean like this. This doesn't feel like a self-care and relaxation kind of space nor the letting-my-hair-down space I had in mind when I dreamed of a night off. It feels lonely.

I fiddle with the little yellow paws of Ted's Spot the Dog cuddly toy that was wedged between the sofa cushions. Mum took the kids back to hers 'for a few days' on Wednesday evening. There wasn't a discussion about it and I didn't argue. They are both better off there. I have no idea when 'a few days' ends and I didn't want to ask. Polly was reluctant to leave but I backed Mum and Dad up and said she ought to go. Ted was excited for a sleepover at Nanny's but thought I was going, too. 'You can sleep next to me, Aunty Beth!' he'd said, as Mum led him out to the car. 'We can stay up until seventy o'clock.'

'I would love to but I've got to stay here and do a few jobs. I'll see you *really* soon though,' I told him, waving him and Mr Trunky off before closing the door and crying for an hour on the hallway floor. I have done very little in the two days since they left except sit here on the sofa, not-watching telly and mindlessly refreshing my phone. I can't even throw myself into work because I think I might have left my job, though I still haven't sent an email confirming this either way. Even my book is punishing me, reminding me every time I see it propped next to the fridge that I let Albert down. His telly is blaring through the wall and I picture him sitting on the brown sofa with his brown slippers on. I don't think it's a Western this evening as the sudden bursts of noise sound more like canned laughter than they do gunshots.

Mum has phoned on both days to check in on me, and Dad has messaged to tell me I should join Polly and Ted back at theirs. I've replied to say I'm OK here, even though I'm not OK, because I can't face the sight of their disappointed faces. Mum hasn't said very much at all about Ted getting lost and in some ways her silence is worse than when she just gives it to me straight.

I keep replaying events from this week in my head. Leaving the office late on Tuesday and not setting the alarm. Albert in his bow-tie, waiting for me in the restaurant for a whole hour and then telling me he wanted things to go back to how they were before. Ted going missing and being returned by the police. The fact that it could have been so, so much worse. I have also remembered, after seeing Polly tagged in one of Rosie's photos on Facebook, that I haven't told Rosie's mum about finding her and Polly walking on the main road when they should have been at swimming. I meant to tell her straight away, when I dropped Rosie back, but I was in such a hurry to get to Albert's to explain myself that I put it off and now . . . well, now I don't know if I have the energy to tell her, to admit that I've handled that wrong on top of everything else.

Food being the last thing on my mind, I haven't eaten all day and my tummy is protesting. I put two pieces of bread in the toaster before digging out a jar of chocolate spread. I think about Friday nights before the accident, almost always spent with Jory in the pub. I wonder if he's there with Sadie now.

I listen to the clock tick as I eat my toast. There are roughly two ticks between every drip of the kitchen tap. *Tick, tick, drip.*

On the counter is a pile of post I was meant to hand over to Dad so he could make sure all Emmy and Doug's paperwork and house admin is up to date. I glance at the clock. *Tick, tick, drip.* It's still early evening, I could take it round to Dad now. I have been really missing the kids and it would be a good excuse to drop in and give Ted a cuddle. I think back to the look Mum gave me when she heard about Ted getting lost. How her features re-arranged to spell 'I knew this would happen.' Maybe I could just see what the letters are before deciding what to do. They might all be junk.

I open the letter at the top of the pile. It's for Emmy, informing her she has prequalified for a credit card with a £5,000 limit. I start a 'junk' pile. *Five grand* though. I don't think I've ever been sent one of these, certainly not since I had a little hiccup paying my phone contract last year.

I brush the toast crumbs from the table and open the second letter. This one is an appointment reminder for Doug, from his dentist. I smile sadly at the photo of Ted and his dad stuck to the fridge, the two of them squinting at whoever took their photo. 'You had great teeth, Doug,' I say. I add it to Dad's pile.

The third letter comes in a fancy envelope from a posh hotel and spa. I unfold it, expecting it to be generic marketing about a special offer. It's a surprise to find a typed letter addressed to Emmy and Doug personally.

Dear Mr and Mrs Lander,

Despite several attempts over the last few months, both via email and on the mobile number provided, we have not been able to reach you so are trying one final time to make contact. If you have changed your mind and are no longer wishing to explore what Eagle Park has to offer, please do let us know and we will take you off our list. If you would still like an appointment with Sandrine, we currently have

Strange. I wonder if Emmy won a competition for an afternoon tea or something and wasn't able to let them know she could no longer attend. It does say 'appointment' though. Appointment doesn't make it sound like she's a prize-winner.

I'm about to put the letter in the Dad pile when I stop myself. It's not the sort of admin that requires executor-of-will paperwork – an email or quick phone call will do the job – and it's not like I've got a lot else to be doing. I dial the number and I'm just gearing up to leave a message when a woman answers.

'Eagle Park Hotel and Spa, Elena speaking, how can I help you?'

I check the bottom of the letter again. 'Oh, hello, Elena – uh, yes. You recently wrote to my sister and her husband about arranging an appointment. Emmy and Doug Lander?'

'Are you looking to rebook the appointment?'

'No. Actually' – my eyes find their way back to the photo of Doug and Ted on the fridge – 'my brother-in-law died earlier this year.'

'My god, I am *so* sorry. That's awful. I apologize if the letter caused any upset. I will of course update our records.'

'I just wanted to let you know why they didn't contact you, to tell you they couldn't make their appointment.'

'Thank you. I know Sandrine gets busy this time of year – everyone wants to see the grounds to get an idea for photos for the big day – so she probably just wanted to make sure they wouldn't be disappointed if everything became booked.'

Photos for the big day. I breathe out slowly. Emmy and Doug were looking at Eagle Park with their wedding party in mind. The big celebration they always wanted. I look at the sketch at the top of the letter, a sweeping drive and fountain surrounded by pea-cocks. It's not unlike my sister to order brochures and start planning for things years in advance, I'm just surprised she never mentioned it. Then again, it's not the only thing she didn't mention.

'That's odd,' Elena says, as though she is thinking out loud.

'What is?' I carry my plate over to the sink.

'It says here that Sandrine spoke to your sister the day before the appointment and they were definitely still coming. I think that's why she's kept trying to make contact.'

'Really? But Emmy hasn't spoken a word to anyone – quite literally – since March.'

'March, that's it. Friday the fifteenth of March. I'm so sorry again, I've updated the wedding list and . . .'

I'm not listening to the rest of what Elena says, instead going over and over the date in my head. *Friday 15 March.* I hang up and before I've had a chance to process the updated information, my phone rings again. *Mum and Dad Home.*

'Hey,' I say.

'Hello, love.' It's Mum. 'Are you busy?'

'No, but I've just started going through some of Emmy and Doug's letters and there was one—'

'But you're not going out or anything?'

'Where would I go, Mum?' *And who with?*

'Right. Good. That's good.' She sounds weird. 'Are you able to come over? In a minute?' I can hear crying.

'Is everything all right there?'

Mum sighs. 'It's Ted,' she says. 'He's got himself in a bit of a state and he's not really settling. The thing is –' she sighs again – 'he says he wants you.'

28

'Tell him I'm on my way. Has he got plenty of teddies?'

'He's got Mr Trunky,' Mum says. 'He didn't ask for any others.'

'Mr Trunky is the one for cuddling but he likes lots of teddies near his head,' I say.

'Since when?'

'I don't know, he just does. I should have given you the photo too. I didn't think.'

'What photo?' Mum is sounding increasingly frustrated. She moves away from the receiver and I hear her saying, 'Aunty Beth is on her way.' Ted's crying has subsided into more of a whinge.

'Of Emmy and Doug. Actually it doesn't even need to be the one we normally use, it can be any photo of them. He likes to say night-night to them both. And the Colosseum actually, but that's less important. Maybe try a photo.'

'He's watching *Toy Story* with Polly at the moment. I might just wait, as you're on your way.' She lowers her voice. 'He kicked off pretty badly just now, Beth. Your dad and I, we struggled to calm him down. I've never seen him like that before.'

I have, I think, but I don't say it. In any other circumstance, I would love to tell Mum that I told her so, that I've had to deal with the same, but I would rather Ted wasn't upset at all. 'I won't be long.'

*

When I pull up at Mum and Dad's, Ted is looking out of the window. I wave and he grins back at me.

'Has he calmed down?' I throw my coat on the bench inside the door. Ted runs out of the living room and clings on to my leg.

'He's fine now.' Mum won't meet my eye.

'Oh, well, that's good then.' I kick my trainers off and lift him up for a cuddle. 'Shall I take you up and tuck you in? You're not sleeping in Aunty Beth's room again, are you?' I give him my best pretend angry face and he giggles.

'I am! I'm sleeping in your bed,' he says.

'What? Sleeping in *my* bed? You little rascal. We'll see about that,' I say, tickling him under his arms until he's laughing and squirming so much it's hard to hold on to him. I half expect Mum to launch into her usual words of caution about winding him up before bedtime but she doesn't say anything. It's past his bedtime already. Dad comes out of the kitchen to see what all the giggling is about.

He kisses Ted on the head. 'Night, champ.'

'Grandad, I'm having a sleepover with Aunty Beth,' he says. That wasn't exactly what I meant. Dad looks at me quizzically.

'I wasn't – I hadn't intended on staying,' I say.

'But you might as well stay, now you're here,' Mum says. 'It's not like it matters that you haven't packed a bag. All your stuff is here. It's still your room . . .'

It doesn't feel like my room. It doesn't really feel like my home any more, which is weird because I'm not sure Emmy and Doug's feels like home either. It definitely doesn't without Polly and Ted in it.

'You have Mr Socks and I'll have Mr Trunky,' Ted says. Mr Socks is the only bear I have kept from childhood that still sits beside my bed.

'Well, I can't say no to a sleepover with Mr Socks, can I?' I look between Mum and Dad. 'I'll be down in a bit. I need to talk to you both about something anyway.'

'OK, love,' Dad says. 'Shall I put the kettle on? Or is this a "glass of red for you two and a whiskey for me" affair?'

I'm about to tell him I wouldn't say no to the latter when Mum beats me to it. She looks frazzled. 'Wine, Jim. I'll get the glasses.'

Ted is asleep within minutes. I was poised to go and get one of the photos hanging in the hallway for our night-night ritual but after tucking him in with Mr Trunky and Mr Socks, he finds his thumb and begins snoring. After carefully removing my arm from underneath him, I sneak out to find Polly waiting for me on the landing. She drags me into the room that used to be Emmy's bedroom but has been a spare room/office/gym (with an exercise bike that I think might be older than me) for the last fifteen years.

'Whoa, Pol. Where's the fire?'

'Mum and Dad didn't go to see that woman,' she says. 'About the phone.'

'No – I know.' I frown as she shuts the door behind us. 'Wait, how do you know that?'

'What do you mean, how do I know? How do *you* know that?' She shakes her head. 'Doesn't matter. I know for certain they didn't go to see the lady who asked me for money. I messaged her.'

'Well, that was silly.'

Polly is talking very quietly but very fast. 'After our chat on the beach, I decided I needed to know for certain whether that was where Mum and Dad were going. I unblocked the woman who caused all the hassle and messaged her. She said she was never going to send that picture to all my friends but when I said I could get her the money, she didn't tell me to stop because she really needed it. I think she was desperate.'

'She sounds charming.'

'But then she heard about the accident on the news. Recognized the name. She actually tried to message me to tell me she meant no harm with the photo but couldn't because I'd blocked her, just like Mum had told me to. Mum and Dad never made any plans to visit her in person.'

'So when your mum texted to say it was sorted?'

'Well, they did give her the money. Dad sent a Paypal transfer. A hundred quid so she would delete and never share the photo.'

'What a piece of work she—'

'She sent it back! She returned it.'

'But you don't trust her now, surely? She could have saved and made copies of that photo. She might still share it.'

Polly shakes her head. 'I don't care! Don't you see, I don't care about that any more. The photo is nothing, it's not what's been making me feel sick for months.'

'I know.' I can see the relief on Polly's face. The knowledge that wasn't where they were going when they had the accident. That it wasn't her fault despite thinking, all this time, that it was. She frowns. 'There's something I still don't get, though, Aunty Beth. I hid that mortgage letter because I saw that the date wasn't the right one and I knew then, or I thought I knew, that they must have *said* they were going for that appointment to cover up their trip to sort out my problem. But if they never made plans to see the phone lady and they weren't going for their mortgage chat, then where *were* they going? You know, don't you?'

I nod. 'I do and that's what I need to talk to your nan and grandad about. They're expecting a chat downstairs. I've been avoiding a chat with your nan, to be honest. She's not best pleased with me at the moment.'

Polly grimaces. 'I think she was a bit cross about us losing Ted.'

'No, it's not "us", it's only me who's responsible for that. I'm meant to be responsible for both of you. And I've been thinking about coming clean to Mum and Dad about the rest of it.'

'The rest of what?'

'I know you don't want to mention the phone and photo business and maybe we don't need to, but when it comes to everything else, it's cards-on-the-table time, I think. I haven't been doing a good enough job of managing things with you, and Ted, and my job, and the house, and I can't pretend I'm coping with it all any more. I'm tired of kidding your nan and grandad that we're doing OK and there's no point trying now in any case. I've been rumbled.'

Polly steps forward and I think she's reaching for the door handle but she pulls me into a hug instead. 'I know Nan is mad at you and I know you're not very tidy, or good with hoovers, but I think you've done a really good job.'

'The hoover debacle was actually *not* my fault.' I give her a squeeze. 'Come on then, let's face the music.'

We head downstairs together, a united front. Mum hands me a glass of red and I take a seat at the dining table. Polly pulls up a chair beside me and briefly rests her head on my shoulder. Mum and Dad share a look. It's one I don't recognize, for a change.

The four of us sitting around the table like this, without any food, feels a bit like a meeting. I suppose it is a meeting, of sorts, and like any good meeting, someone has to kick off proceedings.

'I found out where Emmy and Doug were going on the fifteenth of March,' I say. 'They didn't have a mortgage appointment. They were visiting Eagle Park Hotel and Spa.' Three confused faces stare back at me. Dad mouths 'Eagle Park' several times, as though it might ring a bell if he keeps repeating it. 'They were looking at it as a wedding party venue.'

'Oh.' Polly bites her lip.

'They never were,' Dad says.

'A wedding party venue,' Mum whispers.

We sit with that thought for a while then I get my phone out to show them some pictures from the Eagle Park website. 'It's pretty fancy, isn't it?'

Dad looks closer at one of the wedding-package pictures. 'I hate those little canopies.'

'*Canapés*,' Mum corrects him.

'Same difference, love. There is nothing worse than eating standing up, juggling your drink at the same time. It's very stressful.' When Mum tuts he adds, 'Don't think I wouldn't have told Emmy and Doug that, because I would.' Polly and I nod in agreement. He would.

'I can't believe that was where they were going,' Mum says. 'It explains that letter with the funny date you found.' Polly shuffles in her seat beside me. 'I must say, I'm a bit sad they didn't tell me they were going to look around a potential wedding venue. I would have had *loads* of good ideas to offer. I'd have been very helpful.'

Dad avoids meeting my gaze and I take a large sip of wine, understanding at once why Emmy and Doug might have wanted to keep at least the first venue visit to themselves. 'Do you know, Mum, I'm sure the girl on the phone mentioned that only two people are allowed on a tour. Maybe they wanted to surprise you when it was all booked?'

Mum nods sadly. 'I imagine that was it. That makes more sense, I suppose.'

'So . . .' I clear my throat. There is a confessional atmosphere to the evening and I'm more than ready to roll with it. 'Are we going to have a chat about everything else then? I've been doing a lot of thinking since – well, since Ted got lost and I possibly quit my job.'

Mum looks at me and then at Polly. 'Do you think this is a conversation just for us grown-ups?'

'No.' I shake my head. 'I think Polly should be here. If that's OK with you, that is? Polly understands far more than we give her credit for, anyway.'

'OK.' Mum looks at Dad. 'We've been doing a lot of thinking too. Your dad said something last night and I haven't been able to stop thinking about it.'

'Did I?' Dad looks just as surprised as anyone. 'What was that then?'

'You said that I don't always understand why Beth does things because she does them differently to how I would do things. And' – Mum fiddles with her wedding ring – 'differently to how Emmy does things, too. But that simply pointing out that we would do things differently isn't always helpful.'

'That's very insightful, Grandad,' Polly says. Dad winks at her.

Mum tops up my glass, and then hers. 'I find you baffling at times, love.' *Baffling*. 'And because I've been so busy worrying about how you have been coping with all the little things, like tidying and iron-ing, I haven't taken any notice of the big things. My mind always sees what needs doing and tries to fix it, that's all. I have been hard on you – without meaning to be. Your dad has made me realize that.'

Dad still looks surprised by his contribution. I think of all the recent times I have felt attacked by Mum's criticism of me. I've never stopped to consider that maintaining a certain standard of cleaning and cooking and organization has been her way of cop-ing with all that's been going on.

She is starting to look rosy in the cheeks. 'When Ted asked for you tonight and you started telling me all the things you do to settle him – I hadn't noticed all that, I didn't –' She looks at Dad. 'He relaxed as soon as I told him Aunty Beth was on her way, didn't he, Jim?'

Dad nods. 'He did.' It makes my heart sing, hearing that.

'And I should have helped you more,' Mum says. 'Not just with casseroles and swimming-club lifts. I mean with that big stuff, too. I'm sorry. You needed more support.'

Now I feel bad that she is feeling bad. 'Right, well, Polly and I have some things we want to tell you. Don't we, Pol?'

'No,' Polly says, but I raise my eyebrows and she holds her hands up. 'OK, OK. But I want you to know that none of this is Aunty Beth's fault.'

'None of what?' Mum has put her drink down and is looking at us both with concern.

'I lied about going to a sleepover at Rosie's and went to a house party instead. But I didn't do drugs or have sex with sixth-formers.' Polly glances at her grandad, who coughs mid-sip of whiskey. I nudge her to keep going. We might as well get it all out now. 'And I've been getting into trouble at school. All my grades have dropped and I hacked into Aunty Beth's emails to stop her getting messages from Mrs Sandford about it.'

Mum is shaking her head. 'But you both said parents' evening went well?'

Polly continues. 'I've been bunking off swimming. Aunty Beth picked me and Rosie up from the side of the road when she forgot she was supposed to be having a date with Albert. I've been an absolute nightmare to live with, Nan. But I'm not going to be like that any more. I know you won't believe me but it's true.'

Mum frowns. 'You've fallen behind at school?' Polly nods. 'And you've been lying about where you've been going?' Polly nods again. 'But, Beth – you didn't tell us any of this. Why on earth not?'

'Because I wanted to sort it out myself. And also, if I'm honest . . .' I pause. 'Because I knew if I told you everything that had been going on, it would prove you right. That I'm not up to the job of being Polly and Ted's guardian. That Emmy and Doug made a mistake, choosing me.'

'Oh, Beth,' Mum says, her eyes filling with tears. 'That's not what I think at all.'

'Isn't it?'

'No!'

'Because I've really been trying, you know?' I feel my own eyes getting teary. 'It just all got a bit much, all at once. But that doesn't mean I don't want to do it. I do. I know I have a history of quitting. But not this time. This time I'm not going anywhere.'

'Well, that is music to our ears, love.' Dad reaches across the table and squeezes my hand, and then Polly's. 'You two are actually very similar, do you know that?'

Polly grins. 'Yeah. Except Aunty Beth would *definitely* have had sex at the party.'

'Polly!' I am laughing though – we are all laughing – and it feels like medicine.

'Do you want a coffee, Dad?' I tie my dressing-gown belt around my waist as I walk into the kitchen.

'Yes please, love.' He is massaging his temples.

'And a paracetamol?' I slide the packet along the worktop towards him.

'Yes please. I think I'm coming down with something.' He pops two from the packet and we both laugh. It's a longstanding family joke.

I've gotten off lightly, considering the two bottles of red Mum and I got through. My eyes seem to be taking a little longer than usual to focus on the kettle and my mouth still tastes of Malbec despite this being my second coffee of the morning, but I don't feel dreadful. 'Is Mum up?' I ask.

Dad looks at the clock above the Aga. 'It's nearly nine, Beth. Is the Pope Catholic?'

'Good point.' I have never known my mother to have a lie-in. Even with a hangover (that she would never admit to having) she gets up and washed and ready to face the day.

'She's taken Ted for a walk to the shop,' he says. 'Needs some ingredients, apparently.'

'Oh good. How was she, this morning?' I carry our coffees over to the table.

'In what way?'

'Just, you know, after everything we chatted about last night.'

'I think she's relieved,' Dad says. 'We both are.'

'Me too.' I take a banana from the fruit bowl and peel it. 'Is Polly going with you this afternoon, to the hospital? I don't mind going instead, if you and Mum want to do something?'

Dad looks up from his sports supplement. 'I think your mum and I are both going today, and we'll take Ted with us. Your mum's got that Eagle Park wedding party business on her mind. Wants to see Emmy. And Ted said this morning he wanted to come. We'll see what Polly wants to do when she wakes up. Do you fancy coming too? Full house?'

'I won't, if that's OK.' The four of them already make two sets of two-at-a-time visitors and I'm going tomorrow.

Dad nods. 'Why don't you see what Jory's up to today then?'

'Hmmm,' I say through a mouthful of banana, and Dad laughs. 'What's funny?'

'I can't work you two out. For years you have been thick as thieves and now you're barely talking because he has a girlfriend, even though you don't want to be his girlfriend. Is that about the measure of it?'

'No. Yes. We're not thick as thieves any more, that's for sure. We're whatever the opposite of thick as thieves is. Thin as . . . nope, can't think of anything.'

'Well, that's a shame. I know I'm old and I don't understand the modern world and your reliance on WhatsIt messages—'

'WhatsApp.'

'WhateverApp. But *why* can't you still be friends, exactly?'

'It's complicated.'

'Is it though? If you can't be friends because you are more than friends then . . .'

'Jory is with Sadie now, Dad. He has made it clear he is happy with Sadie. And I am happy that he is happy. I just miss my friend.'

'So tell him that. See if he's free this afternoon.'

I crinkle my nose. 'I think I'll just catch up on the washing or something.'

Dad looks behind the curtain then peers under the table. 'No sign.'

'Of what?'

'I'm looking for my younger daughter, similar height and hair to you but would never voluntarily spend a day doing housework.'

I roll my eyes. There's something more important than washing that I ought to do today anyway and it doesn't involve the excruciating agony of messaging Jory who knows how I feel about him but evidently doesn't feel the same. I just need Mum and Ted to get back with some golden caster sugar.

I've kept one eye on the net curtains and not spotted any movement, so it takes me by surprise when I hear the chain rattling and the door opens. He usually has a peek before opening.

'Beth.' He looks equally surprised to see me.

'Hi.' There were lots of things I planned to say at this moment, but it now feels awkward.

'Would you like to come in?' He gestures at the hallway behind him.

'Yes please, but only if you don't mind.'

He shuffles back to let me in and we go through to the living room. I was starting to miss the fifty shades of brown. I put Mum's cake tin on the coffee table. 'These are for you, Albert.'

'For me?'

'A peace offering.'

He takes the lid off and a smile creeps into the corners of his mouth. A small one but unmistakably a smile. 'Bakewell tarts. How did you know?'

'You mentioned them when we were talking about Mavis. They probably won't match up to hers and, full disclosure, I had quite a lot of help making them.'

'You made them? That's very kind of you.'

'To be honest, Mum made them and I just hovered like a spare part, trying to stop Ted eating raw pastry. He was loving the little glacé cherries too.' I perch on the edge of the sofa while he makes the tea. When he's brought it over, and while he is busy choosing which Bakewell tart to eat, I take a deep breath. 'Albert, I'm so sorry about our book-club date.'

He places his tart down carefully beside his cup and saucer. 'You've already apologized.'

'I know. I just want you to know how bad I felt, and still feel, about it.'

Albert looks down at his tea. 'I hadn't been out to dinner in a very long time.'

'I know, I'm so sorry. I would still love to have dinner with you some time but I know that's not what you want and I understand why. I wouldn't want to reschedule a dinner with me either.'

He shakes his head. 'It was humiliating when you didn't turn up. The girls in the restaurant were so kind but I felt a silly old fool. As though it was stupid of me to ever think I could have an evening out of the house without my Mavis. I am much better off here with my frozen meals and my telly.'

'Please don't say that. If you had been having dinner with someone more reliable than me – which is literally anyone else – you would have seen that you can still have a lovely time doing these things. I let you down. I'm really, really sorry.'

'You've got a lot on your plate and I overreacted. I was just feeling sorry for myself. These are lovely. Mavis would approve of the generous icing-to-cake ratio.'

'Oh good. I'll tell Mum. They've gone to the hospital to see Emmy today.' I fill Albert in on the events, revelations and reconciliations of the last few days, minus the bit about Polly's picture falling into the wrong hands because I think the whole concept of sending nudes to other people you're not necessarily even in a relationship with would blow his mind. I tell him I have let everyone down in one way or another this week, not just him, so he definitely shouldn't take it personally.

'You should go to work on Monday,' he says. 'Get back on the horse, so to speak. You haven't let everyone down as you say you have, but you risk letting yourself down if you don't give yourself another chance.'

Deep down I know he is right. The chat with Mum and Dad last night has made me feel less fearful of the responsibilities I have taken on and now that I've admitted I haven't been managing to do it all, I know they will help. 'I'll email him,' I say. 'Do you know you are full of wisdom and fast becoming my favourite friend, Albert. Extra points have been awarded for always seeing the best in me, even when I've been an idiot.'

'That lovely Jonty with the van sees the best in you, too.'

'Jory,' I say, though I suspect he knows this now and is winding me up. 'What makes you say that?'

'It's obvious he cares very deeply for you.'

'Is it?'

'It's plain to see he's smitten, dear. Clear as day.'

'He's not smitten with me though, he's got a girlfriend.' *And I gave him the chance to choose me instead.* The photo-note rejection is too humiliating to share.

'So you keep saying.'

'What do you mean, so I keep saying? He has got a girlfriend. And anyway, I've been messaging someone else myself.' It's true, I have, but I know Albert will read more into this than is really there.

'Oh, I see. That's good. The swimming coach? Goodness me, I'm being nosy. Ted mentioned him, that's all. Do you send each other those little pictures?'

'Emojis? Erm, yeah. Sometimes.'

'Lovely. And you like him, do you?'

'Yeah, he's nice.'

'As nice as Jory?'

Cut to the chase why don't you, Albert. 'Different to Jory.'

'I see.' Albert stacks the saucers and picks up the tray. 'I was courting another young lady before I met Mavis.'

'Were you really?'

'I was. Lily. She was lovely.'

'What happened?' I have visions of a young and broken-hearted Albert mourning the death of his first love.

'Mavis happened. I was in love with Lily, or at least I thought I was, but with Mavis it was different. As though we had known each other for ever. It felt unkind, telling Lily I wouldn't be able to see her again, but it would have been even more unkind to continue courting her when my heart belonged elsewhere.'

'It's not like that with Jory though,' I say. 'We were best friends long before I started having boyfriends and he started having girlfriends. I'm not new on the scene. I've always been there.'

'I think that's why you are where you are, dear.'

'What do you mean?'

Albert stands up and makes his way back towards the kitchen. 'There's always been more to lose.'

29

I'm just pulling into the hospital car park when Polly phones. It must be lunchtime at school. I answer on hands-free. 'Hey, Pol. What's up?'

'Nothing's up. Have you got a pen handy?' I can hear teenage chat in the background.

'Not *right* this second as I'm just about to park the car.'

'Oh dear. RIP Mum's other bumper.'

'I do beg your pardon?'

'I genuinely think I could reverse better than you and I've never driven a car. Ted probably could, to be honest.'

'Slander, that is. I'll have you know this is quite a big car. And spaces in car parks are too small for modern cars. And the other day that hedge came out of nowhere.'

'Grandad says that wasn't even a parking space and you basically just reversed into a bush.'

I laugh. 'Does he now? Well, you don't need to worry today as I've found an easy space I can drive straight into.' I turn off the engine. 'Right, what do I need a pen for?' Polly is saying something to her friends. It sounds like she's telling them she'll catch them up.

'Sorry, yes. I thought of something else for Ted's jar. A Dad memory. And I didn't want us to forget it. Ted definitely still remembers it for now because we were talking about it the other day.'

Oh, Polly. 'Good thinking. But I don't need a pen. You just make a note of it and we'll write it together with Ted at the weekend. If you want to, that is.'

'I'd like that.' She lowers her voice. 'It was about Prod and Tickle.'

'Plod and Tickle?'

'Prod.' She laughs. 'Dad used to do this funny thing – actually, do you know what, I've got a video of it. I'll send it to you.'

'Yes, please do. You're OK though? Everything OK at school?'

'Everything's fine. I gotta go now though, Rosie's waiting for—'

'Cos I can check. I've got an app and I'm not afraid to use it.' I probably should be afraid to use it. I marked Polly as absent on the school app three days last week when she was there.

'You'll give Mum a kiss from me, won't you? Tell her I love her.'

'Of course I will. I'll see you later.'

When I go to get a ticket, the man waiting behind me at the machine seems to do a double take as I walk past him but I convince myself I'm imagining it. When I make it upstairs to Bracken ward and Keisha *immediately* starts laughing, I know I'm not imagining it. 'Why are you looking at me like that? Have I got something on my face?'

'You literally have.' She points at my forehead and peers closer. 'Some sort of pig, by the looks of it.'

'Oh for god's sake. I forgot all about that.' It's one of Ted's stickers. Sometimes when I'm tired we play a game of doctors where I'm the patient (no exceptions) and I let him wrap bandages around my legs and stick things to my face in exchange for the previously underappreciated luxury of lying down in the middle of the day. When I dropped him off at Mum and Dad's before coming here, Mum was waiting for us in the garden so I didn't get out of the car and I clearly haven't come into contact with a mirror since I cleaned my teeth this morning. I peel the sticker off and look at it.

'Peppa Pig?' Keisha asks.

'Chloe,' I say. 'Peppa's cousin.'

'Right.' She smiles. 'I think Dr Hargreaves is hoping to catch you today.'

'Is she? Why, what's happened?'

'Nothing bad, don't worry.'

'Something good then?'

'I don't know.' She looks as though she does know but isn't about to tell me. 'Wait to see what she says, eh?'

There are flowers next to Emmy and a card from Kate:

Enough of the long nap now, Em, I really need my Stay and Play buddy back. Reuben's mum keeps trying to talk to me about her new business ideas. She's torn between placenta paintings and placenta coasters. Save me.

'She's lovely, Kate is.' I kiss Emmy twice on the cheek. 'The second kiss was from Polly. Shall I get stuck straight in with today's news? The main good-news story on our bulletin is a toss-up between Ted having his second dry night in a row and me managing to get the bins out on time *and* do Albert's for him.'

Emmy looks as though she is in the middle of a vivid dream. Her brow is ever so slightly furrowed and her eyelids occasionally twitch. I give her hand a squeeze and carry on talking to her. 'Today's top bad news is probably that I had a sticker on my forehead for hours before noticing and, not only that, I was able to tell Keisha that it was Chloe and not Peppa Pig based on the colour of their dresses. That's what life has become. Oh, and I've been messaging Greg. There is a lot to like about Greg . . . honestly, Em, he's like one of those centrefold posters we used to get in *More* magazine *and* he's dead nice, and funny. But . . . well, you know. It's tricky. I can't shut down my Jory feelings.'

Polly has sent through a video and I press play, immediately transfixed when I hear Doug's voice. He is kneeling on the living-room floor with Ted in front of him.

'Say hello to my little friends,' Doug says, looking back at who-ever is filming. It's Emmy, I realize, when I hear her laugh. He holds up one index finger and moves it towards Ted. 'This is Prod. Say hello to Prod.'

'Hello, Prod,' Ted says, already beside himself with giggles.

'And this,' he holds up the other index finger, 'is Tickle. Say hello to Tickle. He'll be sad if you don't say hello.'

Ted is laughing so hard he can barely speak but I just about make out, 'Hello, Tickle.'

From behind the camera Emmy is in stitches and I smile through tears as I watch Doug poke Ted playfully with 'Prod' before reaching for his underarms with 'Tickle'. The video fin-ishes and I stare at my phone. It's the happiest and saddest thing I have seen in a very long time.

'Could you play that again?' Dr Hargreaves has appeared beside me and makes me jump. 'Sorry, Beth, I didn't mean to star-tle you.'

'No, it's OK. I didn't see you there.' I tap to replay it.

'Can you increase the volume at all?'

I nod, turning it up and angling the screen towards her. Dr Hargreaves isn't looking at my phone though, she's looking at my sister. 'What is it?'

'Have you seen her eyes or mouth move during your visit today?'

'Her eye twitched. And last week Mum said her mouth moved into a smile and then back again. But you said those movements are involuntary.'

'Play that video again.'

I do as I am told, an unmistakable flutter of excitement in my chest. 'What's going on?'

'We've observed more movements this week and, unlike before when their timing appeared random, Emmy does now seem to be responding to certain cues.'

'Oh my god, that's incredible. So she can hear us, is that what you're saying?' I search Dr Hargreaves' face, not wanting to get ahead of myself, but this time I don't think I am.

'As we have stressed from the beginning, it is impossible to predict with any accuracy how long a coma will last, whether a coma patient will recover and if they *do* recover, what that recovery will look like. But we have been continuing to monitor Emmy and there has been a definite upturn in where we would score her on that scale. She has gained a total of two points since this time last month.'

'Do you think she is going to wake up?' My voice has become a whisper.

'It's still not possible to say but where previously Emmy was in what we would call a vegetative state, I am satisfied that she is taking small steps towards what we call a *minimally conscious state.* I am always cautious with my good news, as you have learned, but I am deeply encouraged and I think playing videos such as that one and continuing to chat to her might help even further.'

'I don't know what to say.' I am fighting back tears.

'Keep doing what you are doing, Beth. Keep the faith. I'll leave you to it.'

When she has gone, I cry and cuddle my sister then I play the video one more time before heading back to the car and phoning Mum. I ask her to put Dad on speakerphone – which takes a frustratingly long time as she keeps putting me on mute instead – then I repeat, as best I can, everything Dr Hargreaves just said. *Improved score. A step away from vegetative to minimally conscious state. Deeply encouraged. Keep the faith.*

'I can't believe it.' Mum is shocked, I can tell.

'Absolutely brilliant news,' Dad says. 'Your mum and I will be visiting in the morning. We should do something tonight, all of us? I know it's small steps but it's important to celebrate—'

'*The small wins,*' Mum and I say in unison.

'Exactly. Are you going in to the office, Beth?' Dad says.

'No. Malcolm's giving me a call so I'll take it at Emmy's, where it's quiet. I'll come straight over after though. Can we have dinner at yours? I haven't got much food in . . .'

'That's not like you, love,' Mum says.

'Blah blah, love you both, see you soon.'

When Malcolm phones, he sounds weary, and though I try to engage in small talk about the rain we're expecting, he cuts straight to the chase.

'Beth, I really need you to come back to work.'

'Oh.'

'If you want to come back, that is?'

'Yes! God, I wasn't expecting . . .' I'm pacing around downstairs. 'I didn't know if, well, you know, after the alarm . . . I was defensive when you came here to the house but you were right, I should have set it. And now it's caused you all this stress.'

'No, it should have been me on that call. And yes, the alarm wasn't set but I was expecting far too much from you already. I can see how much work you were doing, now you're not here doing it. Come back, please. If I sound desperate, it's because I am. You're efficient at managing my workload, you're good with the customers *and* you can talk round Credit. I can't do that. It always ends in a row.'

I smile, savouring this rather unexpected grovelling. 'I will come back. But I need to manage your expectations a little better, before I do. I don't want to be working late or checking work emails on my days off. I will work hard when I am there but I am not going to do more than the hours we agree because I have another important job to do.' I look around the room at Ted's toys and Polly's clothes and my sister's pot plants sitting beside memories of Doug we're keeping safe in a jar. 'Here at home.'

NOVEMBER

30

'It can't be any worse than the last one,' I say, switching off the engine and angling my legs towards Polly.

She scrunches up her nose. 'I think your pep talks need a bit of work.'

'I'm right though, aren't I?'

'Yeah, I suppose.'

'Are you ready then?'

'No.'

'Come on. We'll be cheering extra loud. I know you hate this sort of chat but your dad would be so proud of you. And your mum will be too.'

She unbuckles her seatbelt. 'OK. Let's do this.'

'Two secs.' I grab my lipstick from the little cubby hole by the gearstick and pull down the visor to put some on.

I can see Ted eyeing me strangely from his seat. 'Can I have a crayon?'

'It's not a crayon, it's a lipstick. Lipsticks are for grown-ups.'

'You have to share.' He wags his finger at me. 'Take it in turns.'

'I would share if it was a crayon but it's not a crayon.' He pouts at me and I pull a silly face until he laughs.

I've made the error of positioning our bags near the vending machine, which Ted now has his face pressed against. I steer Ted over to Mum and Dad, passing Greg on our way over. He looks tense. It's a big evening for the team.

'Break a leg,' I say.

'Thank you.' He touches me lightly on the shoulder and out of the corner of my eye I can see Mum and Dad looking at each other. Despite pretending otherwise, they are clearly desperate for me to couple up with someone. 'How's Polly feeling?'

'She's fine,' I say. 'Nervous, of course, but it's completely different to last time. So you can stop worrying.'

'OK. I'd better get poolside.'

'Brill.' *Brill?*

'Aunty Beth put crayons on her face.' Ted points at my lips. 'In the car. But she wouldn't share.'

Greg laughs. 'Did she? Well, it looks great.'

I push Ted towards his nan and grandad. 'Cheers, buddy,' I say.

Mum and Dad are concentrating hard on not looking at me, their eyes fixed on the pool, which is perfectly still as nobody has got in yet.

'Oh hello, love, I didn't see you there.' Mum gives me a kiss on the cheek. Dad joins her in mock surprise at our arrival and I roll my eyes.

'You are terrible liars, you know that. Has she come out yet?'

'She's over there.' Dad points to the benches at the deep end of the pool. The swimmers all look the same with swimming caps and goggles on their heads but I recognize Polly's navy costume with a flash of neon green down its side from the time I spent staring at it while she was pacing naked in the changing room. I study her face as best I can from this far away. She looks anxious but she is chatting with her swim mates, a far cry from her detached demeanour last time.

As we wait for the first race, I check my phone and find I've had a message.

I HOPE THE GALAL GOES WELL I DONT KNOW HOW
TO DELETE SO SPELT GALA WRONG LOVE ALBERT

I have grown rather fond of Albert's shouty telegrams. I can only imagine how long it takes him to type each one. I'm in the middle of replying to say thank you and tell him that we should have another catch-up in the garden soon when a friend request pops up on Facebook. Sadie Grace.

I stare at it. *Sadie Grace*. She doesn't put her surname because she doesn't want her students to be able to find her. Jory does the same, though his is simply Jory C as he knows people (me) would take the piss out of Jory Colin. I already knew she was on here as Sadie Grace because I've looked her up but I have no idea why she would be adding me as a friend. I have a creeping dread that I've somehow left evidence of my digital snooping. I hover over the Accept and Decline buttons. I don't want to be her friend but I don't want her to know that I don't want to be her friend either. Why *wouldn't* I accept it? I hit Accept and put it back in my pocket, refocusing on the mounting buzz around the pool.

Polly's first race is the individual medley and she does well, coming second. We cheer and clap and stamp our feet and I have to stop myself from crying again, which seems to be happening a lot at the moment. After that there are a few races she's not in, which is just as well because I have to take Ted to the toilet. When we get back, nerves are building for the 200-metre mixed medley relay, the one where it went so wrong last time. The lad who is usually the finisher in their team, whose dad Ted called a *stick-head*, is having a serious conversation with Greg.

'He's pointing at his leg,' Mum says. She looks over at his dad. 'Is it his leg?'

He nods solemnly. 'I told him to lay off the breaststroke. It always causes him problems. Classic swimmer's knee. He's not going to be able to do it. After all that training.' Greg is talking to Polly now. Her head is down. There is a lot of gesturing at the starting blocks and nodding from both of them. 'He's going to put your girl last. I hope she's not going to have one of her funny turns.'

I feel Dad tense beside me and I squeeze his arm. 'She was quite unwell last time, actually,' I say. 'But she's on top form now.'

Polly's brow is furrowed and I worry for a moment that she is becoming overwhelmed again. Relief floods through me when she looks over and gives us all a thumbs up. It's time.

The team's first reserve, who wasn't expecting to be in this race at all, is first up. Backstroke first. Swimmer's Knee Dad is mumbling about the reserve being slow and it being best to get his leg of the race out of the way, the others can catch up. Polly's backstroke is strong but if she's going last, she'll be doing crawl. It's a lot of pressure.

'Go on, lad,' Dad says as the starting pistol fires. Our stand-in has less power than the other three swimmers on push-off but isn't far behind them on the return lap and our breaststroker is only a couple of seconds behind the others diving in. She does well and it's neck and neck by the end of the second breaststroke length. But our third swimmer's butterfly is weaker than his competitors and we are falling further behind by the time Polly is poised on the block waiting to go. The other swimmers are already a few metres ahead when she dives in over the top of Mr Butterfly but Polly is fast. She appears to be splashing less than the others, each stroke less frenzied and somehow larger than theirs. The gap starts to close. My heart is beating so fast and I begin screaming. 'Come on, Polly!'

Even Mum, who is fiercely against 'making a spectacle' of herself, is jumping up and down. Ted has his hands over his ears and is frowning at all the shouting. By the time Polly tumble-turns at the shallow end, she has passed two of her competitors but still has a way to go to catch up with the girl in the lead.

'There's not enough distance to make up the time, she can't do it.' Dad is leaning so far forward I think for a moment he's going to topple over.

She edges closer . . . and closer still . . . until there's just one arm's length in it. They've gone under the flags now, less than 5 metres to go. *Come on, Pol.*

It's so close for the final few strokes that I can't work out what's going on. Around me, there is confusion. We stare at the four figures in swimming caps as they grip the edge of the pool, eyes appearing from underneath goggles as they look up at the faces on the side, waiting for confirmation one way or another. All at once there is a deafening roar and I know the result as soon as I see Greg and the other swimmers from Polly's team running towards her, arms in the air.

'She's only bloody done it!' The dad who was worried about a repeat of her funny turn just moments ago pats Dad on the shoulder. 'Absolutely outstanding that final leg was. Fair play.'

As she lifts herself out of the pool, she turns to look at us. My heart is absolutely bursting with pride. She's only bloody done it indeed.

I avoid the Facebook message I've had from Sadie until Ted is in bed and Polly is having a bath. It's been a good evening, a high in what has felt like a run of lows, and I'm not ready for something to mess that up. Perhaps I ought not to read it at all. I hold my phone in my lap and put the telly on, kidding myself for ten minutes that I'm watching whatever drama is on ITV. It's no use. I open the message.

Hi Beth,
I hope you're OK. Sorry for messaging out of the blue but I wondered whether we might be able to have a chat?
Sadie

Oh god, what does that even mean? A chat about what? Why has she messaged to say she wants a chat and not just put what she wants to chat about *in* the message? I carefully compose a reply, deleting and changing each word at least three times.

Hey Sadie,
Of course. Happy to have a chat. How can I help?
B x

I fetch a drink and by the time I return to the sofa I can see that she is typing. A whoosh tells me she has replied.

Would it be OK to talk in person? x

An in-person chat with Sadie is the stuff of nightmares. I want to reply 'No thanks' but I also want to hear what she has to say.

Sure. You're welcome to come here? I'm home now or we can arrange a time to meet over the weekend?

New message: Sadie

I'll be there in half an hour.

I have a funny feeling in my tummy, as though Sadie has found something out and is coming over to tell me off. I give myself a mental shake. She can't be coming over to tell me off. I haven't done anything. It takes me ten minutes to get myself up from the sofa and then all at once I am in a panic, flying around downstairs, shoving toys back into baskets and plumping the cushions. I have never in my life plumped cushions but, for some reason, this feels like a cushion-plumping occasion. It takes me another ten minutes to decide whether to get changed out of my pyjamas and in the end

I decide not to – because I don't want to look like I am trying to impress her – but I do throw a jumper over the top, brush my hair and pinch my cheeks so I look a little less tired (because I am trying to impress her). When I hear Polly getting out of the bath I call up to tell her that Sadie is popping over and she leans over the banisters in her towel and says, 'Miss Greenaway's coming *here*? God, that's awkward. Don't worry, I'll stay up here.' After thirty minutes, I am biting my thumb nail anxiously and when there is a gentle knock at the door, I force myself to count to ten so Sadie doesn't know I have been like a coiled spring, waiting for her arrival.

'Hey, come in.' I open the door and step backwards. 'Shall I take your coat?'

'Oh, thanks.' She takes off her camel-coloured trench and hands it to me. Reiss, size 8. It's definitely a grown-up coat. I bet it's dry clean only.

I hang her coat on a peg that's already piled high with Ted and Polly's stuff. 'Can I get you a drink? Tea? Coffee? Or wine? I've got a nice bottle of white in the fridge. Or a red somewhere. Though you might not want wine if you're driving. I expect you're driving. Are you driving?' *Stop talking, Beth.*

She follows me through to the living room. 'A glass of wine would be great, thanks. Whatever's open though, don't go to any trouble. I'm not driving – I'll walk over to Jory's in a bit.'

'Are you staying at his then?' *Why have I asked her that?* 'Sorry, stupid question, of course you are, that's why you can have wine. Does he know? That you're here, I mean?'

'No.'

'Ah. OK. Well, make yourself at home.' I gesture to the sofa and she takes a seat, her back bolstered by two very plump cushions.

When I return with the bottle of white and two glasses, she is looking up at a photo of Emmy, Doug, Polly and Ted. 'That's a beautiful picture. How is Emmy doing? Jory said she's shown some promising signs recently.'

Weird. I haven't really given Jory any recent Emmy updates but perhaps he's been speaking to Mum. 'Yeah. She's doing OK, thanks.' I hand Sadie her glass then sit myself cross-legged at the opposite end of the sofa. 'Well, not *OK*, that's probably the wrong word. But she's shown a few significant signs of development lately. All of them small but to us they feel massive.'

'I bet. You've had such a tough year, I don't know how you've coped.' She pauses. 'I'm sorry for interrupting your evening, Beth, I just' – I keep my eyes fixed on her as I sip my wine – 'wanted to ask you something. And you don't owe me an answer, I know that, but I would be really grateful if you might give me one.'

'OK. Ask away.'

'It's about Jory. Well, more specifically, about you and Jory.' *Oh god.* 'And why you're not speaking to each other any more?'

'We are!' I say. It comes out fast and squeaky.

'Right. You see that's what he says, too.'

'Well, there you are then.' My throat is suddenly very dry.

'But I know how close you were, how much you used to see each other, talking and messaging every day. And all those famous nights out you used to go on.' Am I imagining it, or did she look away when she said 'famous nights out'? *Surely* Jory wouldn't have shown her that photo? Oh god, the note. No, he wouldn't have done. 'And now you don't see each other, or phone each other, yet he still talks about you all the time. Literally, *all* the time. So it makes no sense to me that you're not hanging out together any more. I know you met up for that walk with Ted in the forest – which Jory loved – but when I suggested us all going for a drink, or even just you two going for a drink to catch up, he said you wouldn't want to. Which is a bit strange, don't you think? Why wouldn't you want to?'

'I've got a lot on,' I say. 'I don't really have time for drinks at the moment. I've always got Polly and Ted to think of.'

'But surely he could come here, like I am now? Or you could

chat more often on FaceTime, like you used to. The thing is, Beth, it's not just the not seeing each other that has confused me. Something else has been bugging me, too.' She looks down at her lap. 'He is a bit cagey when he talks about you.'

'What do you mean, cagey?'

'There was one Saturday night when we were out for dinner and his phone kept going off every five minutes.' The evening after Ted's birthday party. The texts. Has she read them? I can feel myself going red. 'Other people have said stuff to me, too. About you two. Nothing major, just the odd comment here and there about there being more to you guys than just friends. And that night, fuelled by a bit of Dutch courage, I asked Jory outright if there was. He was very defensive about it – and he's never defensive, about anything – but he was certainly defensive about that. Told me I was obsessed with you, and then we had a row in the restaurant because his whole mood had changed, he was honestly so *weird* after reading your messages.'

'Sadie, I—'

'I don't want to make you uncomfortable and I also don't want to meddle in a friendship that was there long before I was on the scene. I just know I can't invest any more of my feelings in a relationship with someone whose own feelings might be invested elsewhere.'

My heart is beating so fast I'm surprised she can't hear it. 'We have been best friends for twenty years, that's all. It's a whole lot of history.'

'I know, which is why it makes even less sense that you've as good as stopped seeing each other.' She is studying my face. 'Don't you want to re-create some of those trips to the pub?'

'There's nothing going on between us, not like that,' I say, because it's true. 'I shouldn't have bombarded him with messages that evening. It was during a low point here. I'm really sorry it caused a row.'

Sadie nods slowly, as if trying to take it all in. 'So I've put two and two together and made eleven?'

I mirror her nodding. 'Yes, and actually I've started seeing someone, too.' *What have I told her that for?* 'It's very early days.'

'Oh.' She looks surprised. Good surprised. 'That's great. I didn't realize – I feel like a bit of a plank now.'

'You're not a plank. It's been a crazy year and I am sad Jory and I haven't found quite so much time for each other but it's not what you think it is.'

We chat until Sadie has finished her glass of wine and it's a bit awkward but not entirely unpleasant. She doesn't want another glass, when I offer it, because Jory is expecting her at his. She's not going to tell him she popped in here, she says. There's no need when I have simply confirmed what he's already told her: she has nothing to worry about.

'I'm glad we had this chat.' She picks up her expensive coat. 'Jory told me I was seeing things that weren't there, and I don't want him to think I've gone behind his back looking for more of those things. That's OK, isn't it? Or do you think I should tell him? Are you going to tell him?'

I shake my head. 'I'm not going to say anything.'

'OK. That's good. Thanks, Beth. I hope things work out with you and Greg, too.'

'Thanks. Wait – how did you . . . ?' I don't remember mentioning who it was that I've been seeing. If you can call it 'seeing'.

Sadie puts her hand to her lips. 'Me and my big mouth. Jory mentioned it.' She looks at me sheepishly. 'It was during our dinner-table row. When I went off on one about all your messages, he told me you were going out with Greg. I thought he was making it up to throw me off the scent. Now I realize I sound like a crazy person. I'm not usually quite so crazy, I promise. Night, Beth.'

'Night.'

When she's gone, I return to the sofa and stare at the telly. After half watching the weather, I switch it off altogether and take our glasses out to the kitchen. I picture Sadie arriving on Jory's doorstep, satisfied that there is nothing more to his best-friendship than she already knew. I should be relieved, too, safe in the knowledge that I won't need to duck out of sight if I see her in future, but I can't steer my mind away from Jory telling her I had a boyfriend. Based on *what* exactly? He didn't come face to face with Greg on the doorstep here until the morning after Ted's birthday – the morning after their meal – so how could he have mentioned Greg before then? It doesn't make sense. And twice Sadie mentioned Beth-and-Jory pub trips of yesteryear *and* asked if I was sure I didn't want to re-create one. Was that wording purely coincidental?

Maybe it doesn't matter who said what. After all, Jory has made it clear who he wants. That's why she is there, with him, and I am here, in my sister's kitchen, running wine glasses under the tap, wondering how years of avoiding saying something that might risk me losing my best friend has ended up with me losing him anyway.

31

The wind is behind us and my hair is blowing across my face and in my mouth. I search my pockets for a hairband to no avail and when I glance back at Greg's BMW, I assess the chance of a hairband being in his glovebox as low.

He points to a spot a little further along the pebble beach. 'The wind's really picked up, hasn't it? If we tuck in over there it's a little more sheltered. Sorry, I didn't think it would be quite so blowy.'

I smile. 'It's fine. Over there looks great.'

After dumping our stuff down Greg pulls out a Thermos and a packet of tiny marshmallows. 'Hot chocolate?'

'Why not.' I'm not a huge fan of marshmallows but it doesn't feel like the right time to say so when he's gone to all this trouble. He looks at me as he pours us both a cup.

'You look amazing, by the way. Is that more crayon on your face?'

'It is. I always like to colour in my face before coming to the beach on a day when the winds are hurricane force.'

Greg winces. 'Are you cold? I've packed a blanket.'

'No, I'm fine. Sorry, I promise I'm not one of those women who can only be outside in the sunshine.' I reach out my hands to take the hot chocolate, my fingers brushing his as he passes it over.

'I know you're not. When I asked you out for a drink I was kind of hoping for a proper drink.'

'Sorry, it's just tricky, with the kids and everything.'

'Stop saying sorry.' He is rooting around in his bag. 'For fuck's sake. I've forgotten spoons. For the marshmallows.'

'Nightmare,' I say. 'Well, that's the date ruined.'

He laughs. 'Don't take the piss, Pascoe. Do you know, I used to find your piss-taking really intimidating?' Our eyes meet for a moment. Windswept, hot-chocolate-holding Greg is quite the picture.

'Did you? When?'

'During the swimming-club years. You gave as good as you got on the banter front and, well, I dunno. The other girls didn't.'

'I might have overdone the teasing back then. Sorry, if so. It was probably just my way of flirting with you. Treat 'em mean, and all that.'

'Well, 2002 Greg was definitely keen. I was gutted when you quit.'

'Of course you were. My backstroke was legendary. I must admit, seeing Polly in the pool, it has made me regret throwing the towel in. I've always been quick to quit stuff, as soon as things got tough or a bit serious. It's not a personality trait I'm proud of, actually.'

'Nonsense. You're being too hard on yourself.'

'That's what Jory says.' *Why* have I said that? Greg's mouth moves when I mention Jory. It's a small movement, barely a twitch, but the mood undeniably shifts. *You idiot, Beth.*

'Ahhh. It really is like 2002.'

I grimace. 'Sorry.'

'Why are you sorry?'

'I don't know.' Because I mentioned Jory and now it's weird.

Greg looks at me quizzically. 'I always thought you'd be married by now. You and old Clarke.'

'Pah! Hardly likely.' My *pah!* is way over the top and Greg raises his eyebrows.

'Really? You know he hates me solely because I like you.'

'He doesn't *hate* you.' I put my hot chocolate down. 'He doesn't know you.'

'Well, he's always been pretty standoffish with me, that's all I'm saying.'

'Right.' It's not like Jory to be standoffish with anyone but I can't argue that the way he was looking at Greg on the doorstep wasn't exactly friendly. 'Well, we're not here to talk about Jory.'

There is an awkward silence, then Greg tips the rest of his marshmallowy hot chocolate out over the stones. 'Do you fancy a little walk?'

We gather up our things and head down towards the sea. The wind has died down but the water is grey and choppy, the same as it was when Jory and I went for our spontaneous dip. I look sideways at Greg, who is zipping up his rucksack after putting the flask of hot chocolate back in. Greg is a good guy. He deserves to go on dates with someone who will stand beside him on a beautiful beach and not be thinking about someone else.

'Listen, Greg – about today . . .'

He puts his hand up. 'You don't need to go there, honestly. We're on our first date, and a daytime one at that. I really like you, but you don't owe me an It's-not-you-it's-me speech.'

'No, I know. But for the record, it really isn't you. I like you, too. You're funny and you've got pretty buff since school it has to be said. Like, *really* buff. There's a lot to like.'

'Thanks. I'm thrilled by the buff review, obviously. But, alas, the buff isn't going to be enough, is it?'

I shake my head. 'You're right about this only being our first date but even so, we've been messaging quite a lot, haven't we? I'm *so* sorry if I've led you on. I've been enjoying getting to know you better. It's just . . .' I sigh. 'It's complicated.'

'Is it? I'm not sure it's as complicated as you think it is.' He studies my face. 'Oh, *come on*, Beth. Clarke's mad about you.

Always has been. And he's a very lucky man, because you're mad about him, too, aren't you?'

I stare out towards the horizon. My feelings for Jory – my true feelings – have been creeping in and making themselves known for a long time and now they are crystal clear, as though a blurry camera has been sharpened into focus. But it's too late, because despite my hinting in a pretty major fashion that I wanted to be more than friends, he is with Sadie.

Greg picks up a stone and launches it into the waves. As he bends down and reaches for another I do the same, until we are in a rhythm of throwing and splashing.

'Any woman would be lucky to have you, you should know that.'

'Just not you.'

'Not me. I'm sorry.'

'It's OK. I'm a big boy now. I won't cry like when you left the swimming team.'

'You did not cry.' I stroke a pebble between my fingers. 'Tell me you did not cry.'

'Er, OK . . . I did not cry. And if I did have a tear in my eye, it was only because I knew you'd fucked our 200-metre mixed medley time by leaving. What a bitch.'

I laugh and it's hard not to feel a bit sad. I genuinely really liked the idea of me and Greg becoming a something. The problem is, there's another idea I like more.

DECEMBER

32

Just two of Malcolm's deals left to check over then I'm done for the week. Unfortunately, he has made an error on the first one. I check my watch.

'Malcolm, if I eat my lunch at my desk to get these two through, is it OK for me to leave a bit earlier today?' I hold up the chart and point my pen at the extra zero he's added. 'There's a mistake on this one.'

'Oh bollocks. Sorry, Beth. And yes, fine to leave a bit earlier if you need to. Exciting plans?'

'The birth of baby Jesus.' I type the correct value into my computer. 'As told by three- and four-year-olds.'

'Right. Shall I make us a coffee?'

I put my thumb up. 'That would be lovely.'

When I've finished the penultimate deal, and my coffee, I check my phone. Three new messages: Kate, Albert and Polly. I open them in order.

New message: Kate

Leila's got a tinsel halo Ted can have for tonight if you still need it? I bloody love a nativity. And yes, absolutely fine re visiting Emmy this eve xx

New message: Albert

HELLO BETH ITS ALBERT A BIG PARCEL HAS COME FOR YOU THE DELIVERY DRIVER TOOK A PHOTO OF MY SLIPPERS I DONT KNOW WHAT THATS ALL ABOUT NO RUSH TO COLLECT

New message: Polly

Hey, Rosie's nan said that a dinner lady told her that another dinner lady told her that Mr Clarke and Miss Greenaway have split up . . . just FYI, even though you 'don't care'. See you later, P xx

I stare at Polly's message. *Mr Clarke and Miss Greenaway have split up.* What does that mean? Could it . . . ? No. Because if their break-up was influenced in any way by me, I wouldn't have heard about it via second-hand dinner-lady gossip. Jory would have told me. And he didn't.

The church hall is rammed and for once I'm grateful for Mum's insistence on turning up obscenely early to get the best seats. Polly and I slide into the chairs Mum has saved us in the second row.

Dad reaches across, holding a folded piece of paper with *Happy Chicks Nativity* on it, a grin on his face. 'Your mum was in the front row until she got moved back by a lady who told her that the front row is for the actors. *The actors!* All of them under five.'

'Shhhhh, Jim.' Mum shakes her head but she is laughing, too. I smile but it must not be very convincing because Mum tilts her head to one side. 'Are you OK, love?'

'Yeah.' I look around at the sea of parents, Mum's eyes still on me. 'It's just, well, you know. It's sad that Emmy and Doug aren't here.'

She nods. 'Doug loved all of this, didn't he? Always got the afternoon off work.' She gives my arm a squeeze. '*We're* here for Ted today though, that's what matters.'

Mum's right. More than anything, Emmy and Doug would be worried about the kids being OK and, between us, we're not doing so bad on that front.

'Is that on silent?' Polly gestures at my phone. 'Be good to avoid a repeat of parents' evening . . .'

'Oh god, it isn't.' I switch it to silent then glance up at the stage. No sign of toddlers in costumes yet, so I might just have time to send the message I've spent the last two hours constructing in my head. I lean closer to Polly. 'What you heard about Jory and Sadie. How reliable is your intel?'

Polly shrugs. 'Dinner lady intel is pretty solid. And Jory's been looking glum whenever I see him in the corridor. Like this.' Polly does her best serious-face impression. 'Are you going to hit on him now then?'

I swipe her on the leg. 'No, I am not going to *hit* on him. I'm just going to message him, to see if he's OK.'

'Who are you hitting on, love?' Mum's face is suddenly very close to mine, with Dad's poking out at an angle behind her.

'*No one.* Bloody hell.'

'Jory and Sadie have split up,' Polly says. 'Aunty Beth's in there like swimwear. On it like a car bonnet.'

'On it like a what?' Dad says.

'For god's sake.' I shake my head at all of them and finish drafting my message.

I heard about you and S. Hope you're OK? Just wanted to say I'm always here, if you want to talk. I get that things might be a bit strange after what I wrote in that note but my hurt pride aside, I still hoped we'd be friends. Would love to see you soon. B xx

A sudden quiet tells me the play is about to start and I hit send. One by one, the nursery children take their places on stage. I crane my neck trying to find Ted and, when I do, I feel a smile spread across my face. He is wearing what looks like a pillowcase with tinsel around the edges and the halo borrowed from Kate. I peer closer. It *is* a pillowcase with tinsel around the edges. When he spots us he jumps up and down and shouts, 'I'm an angel!' We wave back, beaming, and out of the corner of my eye I see Dad passing Mum a hanky.

As the ensemble begins singing 'Away In A Manger', a naked doll is retrieved from underneath the manger and wrapped in muslin. Joseph misses the birth as he needed a wee. There is a hurried exchanging of gifts from the Wise Men – 'I bring you Frankenstein' being a highlight – then it's time for a final hymn and a group bow. It's the most chaotic and most brilliant ten minutes of anything I've ever witnessed, and when the angels step forward we stand and cheer, with a collective something in our eye. When I see Emmy tomorrow, I'm going to tell her all about how Ted did her and Doug proud. And his nan, and grandad, and sister, and especially his aunty Beth. All of us, impossibly proud.

Ted, still wearing a pillowcase and halo, goes home in his nan and grandad's car so I can nip to Albert's and get the parcel, without little eyes prying. A big parcel means the Christmas toy shop delivery has arrived.

Traffic is backing up behind a tractor on the road into St Newth and as I inch the car forward, a reply comes through from Jory. My phone is synced to the car's audio system and the notification is read aloud, a robotic voice asking me a question.

'You have one new message from Jory. Would you like to read it?'

I tap my fingers on the edge of the steering wheel, not sure I'm ready to hear his reply. Fuck it. 'Yes.'

There is a pause. 'What note?'

What does he mean, what note? The note, Jory. *The note.*

The robotic voice hasn't finished. 'Do you want to listen to the message again?'

'Yes.'

Another pause. 'What note?'

I tap the voice command button. 'Phone Jory.'

'Calling Jory.'

He answers after two rings. 'Hey.'

'What do you mean, what note? You know what note. Unless you're saying *What note* because you want us both to pretend there never was a note, in which case I sort of get it but at the—'

He cuts me off. 'Beth, I have no idea what you're talking about.'

'The note I wrote on the back of that photo.' The tractor pulls into a layby to let the queue of cars get past and we are on the move once more.

'What photo?'

Surely now he's just having me on. 'The photo of us, where I put that stupid cap on. The one that was taken *that* night . . .'

'I know the photo, Beth. I haven't seen it for years.'

'But I put it through your door. I wrote a note on the back of it.'

'When?'

'I don't know. Ages ago. Actually I do know, it was just after you'd brought Ted's present over.'

'Shit. What did it say, this note?'

'Just stuff. About me and you.'

'Stuff?'

'Yes, *stuff*. You really didn't see it?'

'No.' He exhales slowly. 'But I have a feeling Sadie did. I *knew* she'd seen or heard something.'

'Oh dear. I have a feeling she did too.'

'What do you mean?'

'She came to see me. Grilled me about us. She didn't want you to know we'd spoken so I told her I wouldn't tell you.' I had been feeling sorry for Sadie but this must mean she found the note before Jory did and made sure he didn't get it.

'So, what did it say?'

I groan. 'Please don't make me spell it out.'

'Can I at least have a clue?' I can hear him smiling.

'It said I think about that night all the time.'

He coughs. 'Interesting. I do too.'

'Do you really?' I've parked up in front of Albert's and my legs are trembling.

'Absolutely. Worst snowstorm for years.'

We are both laughing then and though I don't yet know what all of this is going to mean, I think I might have got my best friend back.

Albert has been re-enacting the moment the delivery driver took a photograph of his slippers. 'And then he said, "Stand back please." Just like that! Did you see it?' He peers at me over the top of his glasses.

'See what?' I'm still trying to digest Jory never getting my note. He hasn't been ignoring what I wrote. He simply didn't know.

'The photo of my slippers?' Albert points again at his feet.

'Oh. No. But it's probably online somewhere if I wanted to track the parcel.'

'Fascinating.' He slides the box towards me. 'It's quite a heavy one.'

'Christmas presents,' I say. 'For Ted.'

'Lovely. How was his play?'

'Hmm?' Sadie must have hidden the photo. Or thrown it away. I picture her setting fire to it.

'Ted's play. Is everything OK, Beth?'

'Sorry, it's been an overwhelming afternoon.'

'Sounds to me like a cup of tea is in order. Shall I put the kettle on?'

'Go on then. Only if you're sure I'm not intruding.' He opens the door and I shimmy past Ted's box of toys. 'I can't stay long though as I've promised Ted I'll watch *Arthur Christmas*.'

'OK, dear.' He shuffles through to the kitchen and I follow, pulling up today's emails on my phone to find the one to say my parcel had been delivered. When I find it, I click through to the picture. Sure enough, it's a close-up of Albert's socks and slippers. I put my phone under his nose and stifle a giggle at his wide-eyed wonder. 'My slippers on the interweb, Beth. Who would have thought it?'

After he's poured the tea, I give him a summary of my conversation with Jory. He listens carefully then is silent for a moment before leaning forward on his brown sofa. 'I wish you had told me about this note sooner. I could have told you he hadn't seen it.'

I laugh. 'I mean this with the greatest respect, Albert, but a couple of conversations about not churning up your lawn with his van wheels probably doesn't make you his greatest confidant.'

'No, of course. But I have seen him a little more than that.'

'In the village?' I know he's bumped into Jory a couple of times in the shop.

He shakes his head. 'He's been coming here.'

'*Here?* Why? When?'

'After school, on days he knew you'd still be at work. I am sorry, it feels a bit cloak and dagger now I've said it like that.'

'But why would he come here?'

'To check how you were doing. I never really understood why you'd fallen out – you both insisted you *hadn't* fallen out – but there he was, popping in, asking me not to tell you he was popping in.' Albert grimaces. 'Truth be told, I'm not sure if I put my foot in it, Beth. There was one day I told him I didn't understand why you couldn't be friends when you were both courting other people.'

'But I wasn't—'

'No, I realize that now. But Ted said you were messaging Polly's swimming coach and, in my day, that would have counted as courting. I'm very sorry if I said the wrong thing. I rather hoped things might work out between you two. That's why I told you about Mavis, and Lily before her. When Jory spoke about Sadie it was clear to me she was his Lily and you were his Mavis.'

My brain is working hard to catch up. I think back to Sadie telling me Jory had told *her* that I was seeing Greg, despite him not coming face to face with Greg on the doorstep until the following day. And of how she remarked on Emmy's progress, as reported by Jory, when I knew I hadn't spoken to him about Emmy that week. It was as though he was getting up-to-date information elsewhere. And he was. I just would never have guessed he was coming here, taking time out after a busy day of teaching to drink tea with Albert and check in on me.

'This is a lot to take in. I rather hoped things might work out between us, too. That's why I wrote him that note.'

'But he didn't see it?'

'No. I think Sadie did though.'

'Ah. And what has young Jory said, now you've told him what was in the note?' Albert smiles, a mischievous smile, and I smile back because I know what he's doing.

'I haven't told him. Well, I *have* but only sort of.'

'Well, he's a clever chap but he's not a mind-reader, dear. Maybe it's time you did.' He puts his cup down on its saucer. 'Now, show me that photo of my slippers on the interweb again.'

33

There are two tubs of chocolates open at the nurses' station and 'I Wish It Could Be Christmas Every Day' playing on a radio further along the ward. We were told last week, after another positive-progress chat with Dr Hargreaves, that we would all be allowed to visit Emmy at the same time today. It's only a small difference but it has lifted our spirits. It's still weird, spending this morning on Bracken ward rather than following our usual Christmas morning traditions at home, but even if we had stayed at home, nothing could have gone ahead as normal today without Emmy and Doug there.

'Well, don't you all look festive?' Keisha smiles warmly at us as we pass her on our way to Emmy's cubicle. 'Great jumper, Jim.'

Dad smiles proudly at his Fair Isle jumper, which isn't strictly a Christmas jumper but the red and gold on it coupled with the Christmas hat from the cracker Ted's insisted we all wear does make him look the part. Polly is wearing new make-up she got in a set from Rosie that makes her look about nineteen. She is carrying her cracker hat, promising Ted she'll put it on 'in a bit'.

'Father Christmas came to my house,' Ted says. 'When I was asleep.'

'He never did!' Keisha says, her mouth to her hand in surprise. 'Well, you must have been a very good boy this year, then.'

Mum's hat keeps falling down over her eyes and she adjusts it with one hand, the other carrying a bag full of presents for Emmy. 'Happy Christmas, Keisha love,' she says. 'Will you get home for your dinner, after your shift?'

Keisha shakes her head. 'Not today, no. We're pushing it back a day in our house. It'll be a proper Christmas Day, presents, dinner, charades, the works. Just a day later than everyone else.' She gives us a wave then continues on with her round, humming as she goes.

It's momentarily a bit stilted when the five of us crowd around Emmy's bed. We're used to seeing her in shifts, each of us with our own way of spending the time we sit by her bedside. It suddenly feels daft to have turned up in smart clothes and hats from crackers, bearing gifts as though we're on the doorstep of a relative who is cooking us lunch and not someone who has been asleep for three-quarters of a year. Luckily, Ted doesn't feel awkward about wearing his snowman jumper and Christmas tree badge that lights up and plays 'Jingle Bells' whenever he presses it. He climbs on the edge of his mum's bed and begins singing along to its tinny tune. 'Uncle Billy lost his willy on the motorway, *hey!*'

Dad looks from Ted to Polly and back at Ted again. Polly coughs and points at me.

'Oh, Beth.' Mum shakes her head. 'Why does everything have to be so vulgar?'

'Willy is hardly vulgar, mother. Besides, judging by the music Polly listens to, it won't be long before he's exposed to a lot worse.'

'You're not listening to that "R and B", are you, love?' Dad nudges Polly gently. 'Your aunty Beth used to listen to some terrible music. Your mum had much more sensible taste in music at your age.'

'Actually, I think you'll find Emmy's taste was deeply uncool.' I edge towards the bed and touch Emmy's hand. 'And I would say that if you were awake, as you know. Am I proud that I had the Mis-Teeq album and still know all of Alesha Dixon's raps off by heart? No. But it's significantly less tragic than your love of Steps and the fact you genuinely thought you might marry Lee.' I google-image Lee from Steps to show Polly.

She makes a face. 'Gross.'

'*Tragedy*.' I rotate my hands around my ears and Polly is so horrified by my dance moves that it makes me laugh. And feel old. Not as old as Lee from Steps though. He's forty-five next month.

'Shall we do the presents?' Mum gestures at the bag then lowers her voice. 'How are we going to do this then?'

I reach over for the first present. 'I guess we just take it in turns to open them for her. That's if you don't mind, Em? Feel free to wriggle your fingers or toes in protest so we can leave them for you to open.' I am joking but all of us look at her fingers and toes. There are no signs of movement but her sleep looks lighter today, as though she is napping and might yawn and stretch at any moment. I wish she would.

We take it in turns to unwrap her gifts and read her cards. Polly unwraps one of Ted's nursery paintings that has been framed. Dad unwraps the latest issue of her favourite magazine and tells her that they've bought a year's subscription so they can read it aloud when they're here. Ted (with a little help from Polly) unwraps Polly's gift, a dainty stained-glass lantern with a little door that opens to reveal a tea-light holder. Her mum had pointed it out on one of their last mooches through Bude before the accident, Polly says. We all miss our mooches with Emmy. I am holding it together well until I unwrap a soft, light blue dressing gown with white clouds on, a gift from Mum. The gift tag says: *Something cosy to help you settle back in at home when you're better, love Mum*. I don't know what it is about this present in particular, maybe it's the thought of Mum writing a message for a daughter who can't read it, or maybe it's holding a physical present on my lap that I can picture my sister in so clearly, but I feel broken as I read it. By the time we say our Christmas goodbyes and kiss Emmy on the cheek to go, we are all – with the exception of Ted – in tears. Ted doesn't notice the crying because Keisha catches him on the way out and lets him choose three Heroes and three Quality Streets.

I watch the way my mum and dad hold on to each other as we walk out towards the car park, how they are a unit, a team. I think of Emmy and Doug, how they should have had the chance to grow old together until they were grandparents in their sixties and seventies and beyond. And I think of me, in thirty years' time – or more, maybe when I'm the same age as Albert – and wonder whether I'll have someone to lean on, or even someone to miss leaning on. It had seemed hard to imagine for a while, but recent developments, alongside the warm fuzzy glow that Christmas brings, are making it easier to picture. I reach into my pocket for my phone and smile at the message on the screen.

'What are you smirking at?' Dad is on my shoulder.

'I'm not smirking,' I tell him. But I am.

Emmy and Doug's kitchen is like a steam room with heat from the oven and all the pans on the hob misting up the inside of the windows. I open the back door to let in a blast of fresh air and pick up the bottle of Prosecco Mum has put out on the patio to chill. We teased her for storing the booze and cans of fizzy drink out here to free up space in the fridge but the Prosecco feels just as cold as it usually does. Mum is running her usual tight ship, the rest of us only getting in the way of her preparations with our offers of help. Dad was washing and drying the dishes in an attempt to get ahead but every now and again she yells, 'I'm still using that, Jim!' and crossly flicks the tea towel at him, so he's given up and started to build one of Ted's new Duplo sets instead.

Mum is shouting at me from the kitchen. 'Is your guest still coming, Beth?'

'*Yes.* As I have told you already, three times.'

Dad looks up from the Duplo ice-cream stall he's constructing. Building is taking longer than it ought to because Ted keeps taking the blocks off before it's finished. 'She's being very mysterious about this date of hers, isn't she?' He winks at Polly.

Polly nods. 'My money's on Coach Draper, which is going to be *all* of the cringe.'

'I was rather hoping it might be Jory,' Dad says, searching my face for a clue.

'Jory's away for Christmas,' I say, unable to hide my disappointment. He'd said yes to accompanying his mum on a festive break to his aunty's when he was keen to get away from St Newth. Now he's not quite so keen to be away but couldn't let his mum down.

'So who is it? If it's Coach Draper . . .' Polly reaches for another piece of Chocolate Orange.

'*Greg.* You can call him Greg outside of swimming.'

'Whatever. If it's him, I'm not sitting next to him because he'll probably start talking about backstroke.'

'Well, it's not Greg so you don't need to worry about swim chat.' I messaged Greg to wish him a happy Christmas and he replied with the same. We're going to see each other through Polly's swimming and I want us to be friends.

There is huffing and puffing coming from the kitchen as Mum starts to flap. Her flapping usually means the last few bits are in the oven and she's thinking about plating up. Apparently, the plating up is the most stressful part. I wouldn't know as I've never cooked a roast dinner or any dinner that involves timings written on a notepad, but I'll take her word for it. Sure enough, our instructions arrive via an urgent bellow from the other side of the dining table.

'Jim, can you carve the turkey please? And, Beth, you can set the table. *Nicely.* Don't just chuck the cutlery in the middle like you normally do. Use the nice glasses.'

'Yes, chef,' we say in unison, laughing when she swears back at us, a sure sign that she's in the thick of cooking stress.

'And he's definitely coming, this mystery guest of yours? Because I shall be annoyed if I've warmed too many plates.'

'Yes, that must be a great fear, the spare warm plate.'

I have just finished laying the table when there is a knock at the door.

'I'll get it!' Polly barges past me to get there first.

'You little sod,' I tell her and she turns around and sticks her tongue out.

'Is he here?' Dad stands up, placing the Duplo ice-cream stall up on the side before Ted can sit or tread on it. 'Or she, of course.'

I can faintly hear Polly at the door. 'Oh. Hi.'

I smooth down my dress. 'Sounds like it.'

Mum and Dad hover behind me, their eyes on the living-room door. Our guest, when he enters, has made even more of an effort than the rest of us put together, a smart shirt underneath a knitted tank top with reindeer and a sleigh on it. It's the most ridiculous yet brilliant Christmas jumper I've ever seen.

'I'm not late, am I? I hope I haven't missed your famous roast potatoes, Moira.'

Mum struggles to hide her surprise and, despite her smile, I can tell she is slightly crestfallen when she realizes my hot date for Christmas dinner is eighty-three. 'It's good to see you, Albert. There are plenty of roasties, don't you worry. Make yourself at home.'

Dinner is lovely and I am grateful for Albert's presence. We all are. He brings a different dynamic to proceedings and in many ways that makes it easier than it would have been if it had been our usual arrangement but with Emmy and Doug missing. Before tucking in, we raise a glass to them both and, while we're eating, Polly tells us about the year Emmy bought Doug a posh face moisturizer, not realizing it was a gradual tanner. He'd used it liberally and by New Year's Eve was as orange as an Oompa-Loompa. It's funny and sad at the same time.

When I walk Albert to his door (I insist as I'm worried that his unsteady legs will be even more wobbly after his fourth glass of fizz), he puts his hand on my shoulder. 'Thank you. Today has been lovely, really it has.'

I surprise him by going in for a hug. 'Pleasure. I hated the thought of you on your own while we tucked into our feast next door. And you're great company, so never think it's a charity mission. It was easier with you here today than it would have been if you weren't, so really you were doing us a favour.'

He nods. 'I usually dread Christmas. Last year, I watched Westerns all day and went to bed early so it would be over sooner. Your sister invites me every year, did you know that?'

'No,' I say. 'I had no idea. Then why haven't you ever—'

'I didn't want to admit that I was lonely. And isolated. And all those other things you see on the adverts where volunteers phone old people with no family. I never wanted to become one of those people. I just wanted it to never be Christmas. It's not as lonely on all the other days.'

'Well, I am going to have to tell Emmy that my Christmas dinner invite was more persuasive than hers, just so you know. There aren't many times where I have any edge over my sister, so I have to make the most of these rare occasions when they do happen.'

Albert laughs. 'You're not so different to your sister, you know. Louder, a little more –' he selects his next word carefully – 'chaotic. But your heart is a good one, just like hers. And you have spirit. You don't think it's a coincidence that the books I chose for our book club were about strong women, do you?'

I shake my head. 'I thought they reminded you of Mavis.' It dawns on me that he was trying to give me a little boost. 'Can I tell you something?' I step back from the porch to check that Mum hasn't followed us out.

'As long as it's not another apology for the book-club evening all those weeks ago.'

'No, it's not that. I am still mortified though, sorry. No, it's about Emmy.' I falter, wondering if I should be speaking this out loud. Albert's nod encourages me to keep going. 'I've spent a lot of time worrying that she will never come round. That there will be no recovery. I know Mum and Dad have felt the same, and Polly. It's been our biggest fear for so long. But recently there have been signs that she could turn a corner after all, and now sometimes, before I go to sleep, I lie there worrying about what she will think if she *does* come round. Whether I'll have done a good enough job holding the fort. And even though I know I've screwed up many times this year, I also know she'd be really touched that we've made friends. So, whatever happens, I hope you'll come to Christmas dinner next year. And I insist you come to Mum's for New Year's Eve.'

'I might be washing my hair,' he says, a glint in his eye. 'But I'll see what I can do.'

'Good. Now put a Western on and get yourself tucked up, Old-timer.'

'Roger that.' He steps inside his biscuit-coloured hallway and turns back to look at me. 'I think your sister would be impressed by how far you have come, Beth. I know it's been a remarkably difficult year, but – and I do hope it's not inappropriate of me to say so – I also think it might just have been the making of you.'

I don't quite know what to say to that, so I nod goodbye then retrace my steps home. Ted is in the window, illuminated by the twinkling Christmas-tree lights, and when he spots me, he waves and gestures excitedly at his brand-new helicopter that his grandad has found batteries for, keen to show it off. I mouth *Wow!* and he beams, the sight of his smile warming me up from the inside out. It's rare, accepting a compliment or praise, but I think Albert might be right. I *have* come a long way since the day of the accident. The Beth from that morning would be proud of this Beth. And I think my sister and Doug would be proud, too. I really hope so, anyway.

34

It's quite hard to know what to wear for a New Year's Eve party that isn't really a party, more of a gathering. I run my eyes over the choices. We're at Mum's and I have been afforded the luxury of an hour to get ready on my own, courtesy of Dad watching *Paddington* with Ted, but so far I've been standing for ten minutes in front of my open wardrobe.

It has been a strange week. The limbo between Christmas and New Year is an odd one at the best of times and I had something close to a panic attack on Boxing Day. Such a silly thing but it suddenly struck me as terrifying that we are leaving behind one year and starting a fresh one without Doug, and with Emmy still in hospital. I don't know if I'm ready to leave behind the year that Doug was alive in. From tomorrow, it will be the accident that happened last year. It puts a greater distance between now and before. I don't know if I am ready for more distance. I don't know what that's going to mean. At the same time, I have always loved the promise of a new year, and this year there is a lot to be hopeful for.

I have ruled out my sparkliest dresses and skirts on the grounds of them being too fancy for an evening where I won't be leaving my mum and dad's garden. I settle on a black leather mini skirt and emerald off-the-shoulder top that I team with tights and gold hoop earrings. I go to town on the make-up because I have the time to and because it feels good to sweep some bronzer across my cheekbones and even out the lines that have undoubtedly multiplied around my eyes since this time last year.

Ted is going to be sleeping in with me tonight and I pull his pyjamas out of the bag. Polly is in the spare room, her mum's old room, and I knock on the door before going downstairs. 'You OK, Polster?'

'Yeah, I'm fine. Rosie's on her way over. Can we have some wine tonight?'

I place my hand on my hip. '*Wine*? At fourteen? Absolutely not.'

She narrows her eyes. 'But you said that maybe . . .'

I put my finger up. 'You are not having wine but I *did* buy you some alcopops. I am going to phone Suzy in a second and see if she is happy for Rosie to have one or two. *If* – and only if – she is, then yes, you can.'

'Do you really have to phone her though?' Polly gives me her best puppy-dog eyes.

'Yes. It's called being responsible. It's new to me, I'll admit, but I best start the new year off the right way. Lest we forget what happened that time you told me to text rather than phone. Besides, I like Suzy. And your mum would definitely phone to check.'

Polly smiles. 'No, she wouldn't. She would let us have a weak vodka and lemonade made with 99 per cent lemonade, as a treat. Even though it's basically the same strength as those shandy tins you can buy without ID.'

'God you're right, she would.'

Polly is looking at my outfit. 'You look nice. Is Albert coming round again?'

'He is actually.'

'Oh goodie. Seriously though, you're wearing earrings *and* perfume so you must be expecting somebody else? Who's coming?'

'I'm not sure yet.'

'Interesting.'

'We'll see, eh?'

When Mum isn't looking, I change the playlist from 80s Classics to Party Starters because 'Total Eclipse Of The Heart' isn't really getting the party going.

'Another drink, Mary?' Mum has invited most of the WI and they certainly know how to knock back a drink or two.

'Ooooh, just a little one for me, dear.' I fill up a big one and she doesn't complain.

Polly and Rosie are in the living room drinking Smirnoff Ices and listening to Drake on Rosie's phone. Suzy appreciated the call and said a little alcopop was fine. Mum has already taken me to one side and expressed concern that alcopops are a gateway drug, but I have explained that I think the pair of them having a little drink tonight, safe at one of their nan's houses, doesn't mean we are kick-starting a drug dependency. I also told her that at Polly's age, Emmy and I were off our faces snogging boys in the football-club stands, at which point she put her hands over her ears and went to check on the M&S canapés. Dad is still not comfortable with the idea of canapés so is going to eat his on a plate with a knife and fork, he says.

Albert arrived at half past eight in a bow-tie. I wonder if it's the same one he wore on our date that never was. I was worried that it would be too much of an ask for him to come here, away from the comfort of knowing his house is next door to escape to, but Mary and co seem to have gladly taken him under their wing and at last check he was playing a card game in the dining room.

The evening is going well. Ted is roaming around getting lots of fuss, currently bothering Kate and Leila. Mum and Dad seem relaxed. It is only when I go to rinse some glasses that I feel suddenly overwhelmed and a little guilty that Emmy is in hospital on her own. That we are not there with her. That Doug died and we are toasting the new year as though it is a celebration. It feels wrong. I am wiping tears from my cheeks with a tea towel when I sense that I am no longer alone.

'I know that Kylie song is bad but it's not *that* bad.'

'Jory,' I say, though it's more of a sob.

He pecks me on the cheek. 'Are you OK?'

'I can't believe this.' I am half laughing, half crying now. 'I had highlighter on my cheeks and everything.'

He takes a bottle opener from the side and flips the cap off a bottle of beer. 'Nope, you've lost me.'

'I got dressed up,' I say. Gesturing at my face that is now puffy and probably black with mascara. 'I wanted to look exquisite, for a change.'

Jory laughs. 'Exquisite, eh?'

'And then you turn up and I look like a dog's dinner that's been rained on.'

'My favourite sort of dog's dinner,' he says.

'Beth, is there any more of that rosé?' Mary crashes into the kitchen. 'Oh, hello, Jory love, I didn't know you were here.'

I pass over the whole bottle of rosé. 'It's all yours. Is Albert OK in there?'

'He's having a wonderful time. They're playing Rummy now and Beryl has put some money in. It's all to play for at the moment. I'll leave you two to it.' She winks, then crashes into the door frame on her way out.

Neither of us says anything for a moment. We have been speaking on the phone and messaging every day that he's been away, but this is the first time we've seen each other since I told him about the note. The suspense has been unbearable. 'Listen, Jor—'

'Ted wants a drink.' Dad bustles in and fills up a glass. 'I think he's had too many Haribo as he's doing a lot of breakdancing. Is it the Haribo, do you think? Do I need to give him something else?'

'He's overtired,' I say. 'I didn't think he'd be staying up until midnight but there's no hope of him going to sleep now, not when he's seen all the excitement down here. He definitely shouldn't have any more sweets though, and maybe he could have some warm milk, to calm him down a bit? Do you need me to have him?'

'No, you leave him with me. He can come and help me with the music outside. It's nice to see you, son.' He squeezes Jory on the shoulder.

'You too, you're looking fresh in that shirt, Jim.' Jory waits until he's out of earshot. 'How the tables have turned, eh?'

'What do you mean?'

'Your dad, asking you for advice about what to do with Ted.'

'Oh right, yeah, I suppose.' I haven't really thought about it like that but he's right. 'They still don't trust me to get the bins right, though. Or cook anything other than my three-meal repertoire.'

'You're up to *three* meals now? Go on then, what are we talking?'

'Well, pesto pasta obviously. Plus chilli, made with a jar of sauce but Mum doesn't know that, and fajitas.'

'Blimey. Never thought I would see the day.'

'Yeah, well, neither did I.' We smile at each other. 'I'm really glad you came back today.'

'Me too.' Jory picks at the label on his bottle of beer. 'I saw Albert on my way in. I asked him if he thought You Know Who was going to be here.'

'Voldemort?'

'Very funny. Mr Muscle.'

I laugh. 'Oh right, I see. No, there's no Greg. And you knew he wouldn't be here so don't be a plonker.'

'I think Albert might have overestimated what was going on between you two.'

'Well, that was always the danger in adopting someone in his eighties as your informant. Have you ever had a text message from him?'

316

Jory laughs and gets out his phone, opening an unmistakably Albert conversation written entirely in capitals. 'Legend,' he says.

'Legend,' I repeat. I look out of the window. 'Do you want to go into the garden for a bit? Dad's got a fire going.'

He frowns. 'I didn't bring a coat. Shall I nip back across the road and get one?'

'No, don't worry, my big coat's still at Emmy and Doug's so I'm going to have to borrow one of Dad's. He has loads. I'll get you one, too.'

'Since when did you have a "big coat"?' He follows me out to the utility room.

'I have lots to say about coats now. Yesterday I told Polly to take her coat off in the car or she "wouldn't feel the benefit".' I hold up two of Dad's fleeces. 'Do you want the green one that will make you look like a *Countryfile* presenter or the brown one that will make you look like a birdwatcher?'

He reaches for the brown one. Jory is taller than Dad so the arms are a little bit short. I put on the green one, which is long in the body and reaches the bottom of my skirt, making it appear as though I am wearing a walking fleece and tights as my New Year's Eve outfit. I strike a pose. 'I imagine this finishes off my outfit rather nicely.'

'It's actually not bad.' Jory does up his zip. 'I'm excited to see what shoes you go for.' He points at Mum's gardening clogs which are next to the back door. 'If it's those Crocs, I'm afraid I'm going to have to leave.'

I lean across him for some wellies. I feel my skirt riding up underneath the elastic of the fleece, but I bend down further to get the boots anyway.

'Jesus, Beth.'

'What?'

'You know what. It feels all kinds of wrong to be looking at you like that when I'm stood here wearing your dad's fleece.'

I raise my eyebrows but don't say anything. We've had almost two decades of friendly banter that sometimes veers into flirting, but other than that one night, that's as far as it has gone. Tonight, after the revelations of the last couple of weeks and now finally being alone together in a very small room, it feels different. Like maybe our usual line has already been crossed.

I pull the wellies on and we head out into the garden. Polly and I did a pretty good job out here earlier. It didn't look like much during the daytime, but the fairy lights we draped over the fences and wrapped around the bare branches of Mum's apple tree have made the garden glow. Dad has got a fire going in the metal bin he uses to burn garden waste. On the patio, he has pulled out an extension lead from his shed and plugged in a speaker. He doesn't know how to get the music to play, so Polly and Rosie are sitting cross-legged on a blanket putting together a playlist on Polly's phone, with Ted's help. Unfortunately for them, Ted has a long list of music requests, so they are having to do alternate kids' songs and teenage choices. It's quite the juxtaposition when a Billie Eilish song fades into the *Hey Duggee* theme tune. I don't tell Polly that I prefer the latter.

Ted runs over, his hands around my legs. 'Aunty Beth do the funny dance!'

'No way.' When Ted pouts I say, 'But I definitely will *later*.' I just have to pray that he forgets.

Jory nudges my shoulder gently with his. 'Fajitas, big coats, funny dances . . . I'm starting to think I don't know you at all.'

'Oh I don't know. I'd say you know me pretty well.' I call over to Polly. 'Pol, can I leave Ted with you for a second?' He goes to sit on his sister's lap, reeling off more nursery rhymes that he wants on the party playlist. She gives me a thumbs up and as I steer Jory away from the makeshift dancefloor I can hear her telling Ted that he can have 'The Hokey Cokey' straight after Drake. I lead Jory past the apple tree and we tuck in along the side of the house where the music is quieter.

'Dammit. I should have brought us some wine.'

'Do you want me to get us some?' He points back at the house.

'No,' I say and the fierceness of it takes us both by surprise. 'Sorry, it's just if you go back over there you'll get stopped by Mary, or Albert, or Mum, or next door's dog, and then Polly will tell me that Ted needs a poo. Something will stop us actually having a moment to talk. Let's just forget the wine. We can get some in a minute.'

'All right, so let's talk.' He sits on the wall of the raised bed Dad has built out of sleepers and I sit down next to him.

'I'm not really sure where to begin,' I say.

Jory looks down at his trainers. Converse, the same as always. 'I read your note. Sadie put it in a bag with some other bits she dropped back even though I never asked her if she'd taken it.'

'Oh man. I feel bad that she saw it. And that it contributed to the break-up.'

'I wouldn't feel too bad. We would have broken up anyway.'

'Would you?'

'Oh, Beth. *Beth, Beth, Beth, Beth, Beth.*' He hits his palm against his head with every 'Beth' before angling his knees towards me and placing his hand next to mine, our little fingers touching. 'It was doomed from the moment she realized I fancied someone else.'

I laugh. 'Sorry, I know this is a serious chat but your use of the word "fancied" reminds me of the days we used to talk about our crushes on the bus while listening to your Walkman.'

'*You* used to talk about your crushes.' Jory is looking back towards the house. 'I hated it when you told me who you fancied on the bus.'

'What? No, you didn't. You used to tell me who you fancied too. That Kimberley Williams for starters.'

Jory shakes his head. 'I never fancied Kimberley Williams, not really. I mean she was all right, but I wasn't that fussed one way

319

or the other. I just told you I liked her because otherwise it was a one-way traffic of crush chat. You had quite the list.'

'I was like thirteen or something. Of course I had quite the list.'

'Well, I didn't. I just liked you.'

I am suddenly hyper aware of my little finger against his, as though there is an invisible charge between them. 'You never said you did.'

'I tried. I tried several times back then. But you'd put me so clearly in the Friend Zone, it seemed pointless. I always backed out of telling you how I felt, usually after you told someone that you thought of me like a brother. As we got older I thought a few times that maybe you were starting to feel the same, but let's be honest that was mostly when you'd had a few glasses of wine or were on the rebound. I know we joke about the Winter of 2015 but we were both so clear after what happened – or nearly happened, half happened – that it shouldn't have happened that I was terrified of ever being honest. I didn't want to lose you as a friend. That was more important than anything.'

'I didn't want to lose you, either.' We are now sitting as close as we possibly can be, but still aren't looking at each other. I stare at the moon instead.

'I've never known how you felt.' Jory's voice is quiet. It's a statement, rather than a question, but I think it warrants an answer.

'Then ask me now. Ask me now how I feel.'

He shakes his head. 'I can't.'

I rest my head on his shoulder. 'Well then, I'll give you some clues. What would you say if I told you that I stalked your social media pages every day and that it felt like self-harm, seeing a picture of Sadie in your coat?'

He puts his head down to rest on mine. 'I'd say you were unhinged.'

'And what would you say if I told you that after I thought you'd ignored my note and chosen Sadie over me, I tried to feel something for Greg, but when he handed over a hot chocolate and his fingers touched my fingers, I didn't feel anything.'

'I'd say I hate the thought of his fingers touching you at all.'

I laugh. 'Before the accident, I would go out for dates, Jor. I'd dress up, I'd smile and sometimes the guy would be really charming. Not always, lest we forget the guy who said he was twenty-nine when he was clearly nearer to fifty.'

'Or the one who sent you a picture of his penis while you were still eating dinner.'

'Or him. But even when they ticked all the boxes, they still fell short. And I'm not talking about the penises.'

Jory lifts his head. 'Did you hear something?'

There is a cough and Mum appears, her face peering around the corner. 'Oh, thank goodness. I didn't know you two were here, I thought someone had gate-crashed. Sorry to, erm' – she looks between the two of us – 'interrupt.'

'Why would somebody gate-crash our New Year's Eve garden gathering?'

'Well, you know what the youths are like.'

Ted runs round the corner and pulls himself up on to my lap. 'Found you!'

'I wasn't hiding.'

'Grandad said you were.'

'Right,' I say weakly.

'It's nearly midnight!' Ted says.

'Way past your bedtime then,' I say.

'We can count to ten. Polly has a song called Old Man's Wine.'

'"Auld Lang Syne".' Mum strokes Ted's hair. 'He's struggling to grasp the concept of a countdown because the numbers are in the wrong order and he seems to think three, two, one is only for the rocket thing you do, something about a swing? Anyway, I think we're going to have to do a count-up instead. Are you two coming?'

'Is it really that time already?' I take my phone out of my pocket. Ten minutes to go. I get to my feet and follow Ted, mouthing 'Sorry' to Jory.

'It's fine,' he says as he gets up and follows us back to the patio. Everyone has come outside, and I put my arm around Polly. 'Are we really counting up from zero to ten?'

'Mum says we have to, for Ted. And then I have to play "Auld Lang Syne". The pressure.'

'I'm sure it's nothing you can't handle. You've been a star this year. Your mum and dad would be so proud of you and I won't hear otherwise. I am proud of you, too.' I don't wait for a reply as I move closer to Albert, who also appears to have borrowed one of Dad's coats.

'I thought you might have been kidnapped by Mary. Happy New Year, Albert.'

'Happy New Year, Beth. I hope next year brings some happiness for your lovely family. You deserve it.'

'Thank you. And thank you for being such a good friend to me this year.'

He nods. Dad dings his glass with a spoon and all eyes turn to him. He isn't going to make a speech, he says, he just wanted us all to take a moment to toast the ones we are missing. There is not a dry eye in the garden as we raise our glasses and say, 'To Emmy and Doug.'

I look around at our family and friends. Mum and Dad have started slow-dancing in the middle of the patio, the pair of them emotional and a bit merry from the wine. Polly and Rosie are practising dance moves from a viral online video, Ted at their heels trying to copy. Albert is standing in the middle of three ladies from the WI and winks at me when I catch his eye.

There is so much good here. We have a huge Doug-shaped hole in our lives and, for now, we're still navigating an Emmy-shaped hole, too. But there is a richness of life and friendship and hope being built around the edges of all that grief and worry. Without a shadow of a doubt it has been the worst year of my life but it has also changed my life and not all of it has been bleak.

I feel a hand on the small of my back and smile as I come face to face with the brown fleece. 'You wanted me to be honest,' I tell him, 'so here it is. I don't think of you as a brother. I think at one stage maybe I did, or I told myself I did, but the thoughts I've had about you recently would be illegal if you were my brother.'

Jory laughs. 'Is that so?'

'I think you're hot – really hot. However, I regret to inform you that you've lost a few sexy points by dressing as my dad.'

He keeps his hand on the small of my back, moving his other hand around to join it. I can feel Mum and Dad looking at us, but I don't care. Jory leans his face in closer. 'I promise not to dress as a rambler again. And actually there is something I would like to say to you, too. Not that I think you look hot – though strangely that fleece and tights combo has turned me on a bit – but that's not my main announcement. The main one is that you are the best person I have ever known, bar none, and I love you. I always have.'

A smile unfolds from the corners of my mouth and spreads all the way to my ears. 'Sorry, I don't think I caught that last bit?'

Polly gives Dad the nod and he shouts that it's almost time for the countdown, reminding us that this year we will need to count up instead of down. He picks Ted up and puts his hand in the air.

Zero.

Jory puts his mouth against my ear and every hair on my body stands on end.

One.

'I *said* I love you.'

Two.

'That's good to know, thank you.'

Three.

'And I thought maybe I could take you out.'

Four.

'As your best friend . . . ?'

Five.

He shakes his head. 'On a date. Throwing out the rules. Winter of 2015 style.'

Six.

I press myself closer against him. 'Definitely not like a brother then.'

Seven.

'Definitely not.'

Eight.

I put my hands on his face and there is nothing I can do to stop myself from giggling. It feels forbidden, crossing a line I've always said we wouldn't cross and it's nothing short of absurd to be doing this, in my mum and dad's garden, after all this time. I kiss his bottom lip. 'I love you, too.'

Nine.

There is a surge through my entire body when Jory kisses me back.

Ten.

'Happy New Year, Beth.'

There is cheering to the side of us. I don't know if the cheering is for the new year or for us. Perhaps it is both. I put my arms around his neck as a bagpipe version of 'Auld Lang Syne' kicks in on the speaker. Ted is shouting because he wanted everyone to count to forty-seven and doesn't like the sound of 'Old Man's Wine'. His grandad spins him around and around on the spot until his whingeing is replaced by shrieks of laughter. The stars above us shine like glitter and I tilt my face upwards and nod. I hope Doug knows, somehow and somewhere, how much we are missing him.

I can no longer quash the hope that is singing inside my heart every time I think of my sister. Next year, when we're standing under a starry sky, Emmy is going to be here, too. I cannot *know* that she will – not for certain – but hope is giving way to belief and that belief is getting stronger by the day. She is going to be insufferable on the I-told-you-so front when she finds out about me and Jory and I am more than ready for it.

I look at Polly, who is smiling in our direction. When she catches me looking, she puts her fingers in her mouth and mimes retching.

I rest my head on Jory's chest. 'Happy New Year.'

Acknowledgements

First and foremost, I would like to thank my stupendous editors, Frankie Gray and Imogen Nelson. Receiving your feedback at every stage has been an immense privilege and I am *so* grateful for all your help and hard work. Thank you to my agent, Hannah Ferguson, for helping me to make the leap across to fiction in the first place. I might have underestimated the size of the leap but I'm so very glad we went for it. I would also like to thank every member of the Transworld team who has been involved with designing, marketing and cheerleading my book (Carlsberg don't do publishers, but if they did . . .) and my copyeditor, Mari Roberts, for making the manuscript sparkle.

To my lovely dad, I am incredibly thankful for all your encouragement and advice. You have always been the biggest champion of my writing and I won't forget the day I talked you through the entire plot, nor the day a letter came through with your handwritten second-draft feedback notes. I knew you being retired would come in handy. Tina, Ena and Andrew – thank you, too, for your ongoing support, love, and the greatest gift of all: childcare!

To friends old and new, from school-mum friends to fellow-author friends, thank you for all your boosts along the way. Special mentions go to Jayde, Beth (the original Beth), Emma and my MOB (you know who you are). Katie Marsh, thank you for sending KEEP GOING messages at just the right time and reassuring me that everything was going to be fine, even when I messaged to tell you I'd written unpublishable tripe that needed burning.

To my Generator co-working-office pals – too many of you to list (but Tom, Jon and Martin, you deserve a mention because you've endured the worst of my moaning) – thank you for the mickey-taking and the chicken wings. You have lived this book adventure with me and brightened up every work day.

My darling boys – Henry, Jude and Wilf – thank you for sticking with me, even when my laptop appeared surgically attached to my face. It is nothing short of a miracle that some of this book was written at the same time as home-schooling you during a pandemic. Let's repress that memory and never speak of it again.

Thank you to my husband, James, for your unwavering belief and for allowing me to steal Prod and Tickle *and* your love of 'Rock 'n' Roll Star'. I love you.

And last but by no means least, thank you to *you*, the reader. It means an awful lot that you decided to give this book a chance. Without you, my dream job would still be a dream.